THE PAX CHRONICLES

BOOK 1

PEACE SEEKER

A NOVEL BY

JUDITH HAND

Questpath Publishing
San Diego, CA

Published by
Questpath Publishing
San Diego, California 92128

Text and cover layout by Robbie Adkins, Adkins Consulting, Murrieta, California, www.adkinsconsult.com

ISBN: 9978-1-7329488-3-9

Printed in the United States of America

This book is dedicated to
women, now and into the future,
women who will help to shape human history.
And to my husband, who shared with me
my life's greatest joys.

So it will come to pass that when
women participate fully and
equally in the affairs of the world,
when they enter confidently and
capably the great arena of law
and politics, war will cease; for
women will be the obstacle and
hindrance to it.

  'Abdu'l-Bahá
  the son of the founder of Bahai,
  May 1012

Metanoia – a Greek word meaning "change of mind." Its full meaning implies repentance, making a decision to turn around, to face a new direction, to experience a transformative change of heart.

Shoot At Their Feet

August of 2023, Bangladesh

In sultry heat a small convoy of limousines, vans, and motorcycles—sharing the road with belching diesel trucks, buses, taxis and man-powered rickshaws—ascended low hills through the Chittagong District of Bangladesh, cutting its way through the teeming city of over six million people. The Bangladeshi Minister of Education had warned of local opposition and for safety he rode in the middle limo. He'd suggested that a "controversial celebrity" such as Claire Alden should ride directly behind him, yet Claire, as a gesture of good will, chose to ride in the first car.

Seated now in air-conditioned comfort, she turned away from the window and gripped the hand of Aminah Roy, the headmistress of the Chittagong Academy for Nonviolent Conflict resolution. Such a capable hand, Claire thought. Warm. Sturdy. An army of well-funded Aminahs could educate every child on the planet.

"It's because of you, Aminah, that the Academy is getting this national recognition. This day is a triumph. I'm so grateful. AFWW is too."

Aminah squeezed back.

Ramin Ali, Aminah's assistant, smiled. "They should be." Distressingly thin, yet handsome, he seemed to Claire to be in his late twenties.

At forty-four, Aminah was two years younger than Claire, but while Claire's blonde hair had not yet begun to turn, Aminah's many steely gray streaks in ink black hair implied a life of hardship. The Chittagong school was the first of thirty-seven primary schools that Claire's eleven-year-old international charity, A Future Without War, had opened in the poorest of poor countries. Twenty-five of them had not survived the 2020 pandemic. Because of Aminah and Ali, the Chittagong Academy had.

Today her camera team would capture stunning footage to take home to use for promoting AFWW's efforts. Exotic buildings and foliage. Thrilling colors, including her red sari worn over a short-sleeved orange blouse and Aminah's blue one over rose. Their saris were a striking contrast to Ramin's white pants and tunic.

Shops lining the busy road to the Academy sold curries, *dal,* and *chapatti* stacked like tortillas. Even inside the limo Claire smelled the savory aroma of saffron and fried *parata* bread. Tables and racks offered colorful baskets, sunglasses, shoes, and cell phones. People they passed stopped, pointed, stared or waved at the passing motorcade. A few yelled or heckled.

The caravan's Ansar motorcycle escort, armed state paramilitary guards dressed in black helmets and Kevlar vests, had positioned themselves three in front, three behind. Following the lead motorcycles, Claire's limousine turned a sharp left into a wider, tree-lined street to face at least a hundred angry bearded men in white turbans and robes. Fists raised, they rushed forward, blocking the entourage. A shiver rippled up Claire's spine. Beyond them an even larger crowd hovered around the Academy's entrance.

Ramin squared his shoulders. "Oh, no, not again. Not today of all days."

The quaver in his voice, which only moments before had been full of good spirits, alarmed Claire even more. She searched the protestors' banners bearing snaky green letters for something in English, some clue.

The bearer of a sign yelled in accented English, "The academy is a school of whores!" He charged past the three lead Ansars to the front of her limo. Sweat streaked the young man's bearded face. Eyes wild with rage stared at her as he yelled at her window and spit. Claire raised her purse in a shielding reflex.

"Zealot!" their turbaned driver yelled back at the young man.

"That boy is the son of Imam Kamal Islami." Aminah sounded worried.

Their driver cranked the wheel hard to the right, entered a side street, spoke urgently into his cell phone and then clicked it off. "You are having nothing for to worry." He steered the caravan away from the angry throng. "We enter the Academy from another way."

Claire had seen three or four oxblood-colored turbans of the Village Defense among the protesters. These local constables usually avoided helping the Academy against Islamic extremists, partly out of fear and partly because some didn't approve of the school's high enrollment of teen-aged girls. She watched as one of the three Ansar guards dropped behind and disappeared. Had he done so to help manage the protestors at the front gate? Shouldn't he stay with the caravan?

The Minister of Education had assured her during their planning that half a dozen Ansars would send a strong message without appearing heavy-handed or provocative. Claire had not been entirely reassured. Lately her appearances incited increasingly hostile protests in predominantly Islamic countries. Looking to head off any need to use force, something about which she felt great concern, she had insisted on hiring extra guards and expected to see at least some of them at the gate.

She asked, "Where are our Blue Tigers?"

Aminah, frowning, peered out the window for a better view. "Maybe they keep the mob from the main entrance. I see another one of our Ansars has also stayed behind."

The limos zigzagged past rust-streaked whitewashed buildings, then along a muddy canal that smelled of fish, moss and rot. It finally slowed alongside mud-brick walls. Bright green weeds sprouted everywhere, even from the pavement cracks.

A small sign read in Bangla and English, "Academy of Nonviolent Conflict Resolution, North Gate." Several dozen waiting protesters began yelling.

"Oh good…" Ramin said, his tone ironic. "Only a handful."

A shadow fell over the scene. During monsoon season dark clouds often blocked the intense sunshine, but everyone here would be used to rain, so if anything spoiled the day's award ceremony, it wouldn't be the weather.

Ramin pointed toward a grove on the right. "The young mulberry trees."

Claire knew the trees were significant beyond feeding the silk worms of this self-sustaining silk farm, but couldn't remember why.

"Do you not recall the *salish* against us six years ago?" he said. "Fools like those behind us burned three hundred trees because some of our young women were using them to become independent."

Aminah added, "I keep thinking things will settle down, but the more we succeed, the more hostile the fundamentalists become. Change is very frightening to so many. I think they must be especially angry today that a government minister is recognizing our achievements."

Claire looked back at the pale green leaves on the small mulberry trees. "Should we hire guards for your tender little grove?"

"If only we could afford to," Aminah said. "I do not yet trust the locals, and outside guards like the Blue Tigers are expensive." She and Ramin exchanged looks. "And easily bribed."

These were brave people. They defied the comforts of tradition every day and could never feel secure. And AFWW required this sacrifice of them. Claire looked directly into Aminah's soulful brown eyes. "I won't let anyone defeat us. Your school will thrive. I promise you. We'll survive and succeed."

The limo stopped. A second limo pulled in and then the third, out of which stepped the Minister and other dignitaries. The minivans disgorged assistants, including two of Claire's staff, one of whom, the videographer, was five months pregnant. Claire gathered the hem of her sari and stepped from the limo into tropical heat. Aminah wrapped her rose and gold silk scarf around her head. The group trekked toward the school's amphitheater.

Claire inhaled lush afternoon air. Birds trilled, reminding her of the songs of meadowlarks on the ranch of her childhood. Then a call like the "go-away" birds she'd loved in the African bush. Distant yammering from the horde at the main campus gate blended with the buzz of flies and cicadas. Ahead, several blue-helmeted, blue-shirted "Tigers" stood smoking by an Olympic-sized, green aquaculture pond. Two of the young men, sullen-faced, armed, and not looking a day over fifteen to Claire, flicked cigarette butts into the pond. Casually slinging rifles over their shoulders, they sauntered off toward the campus perimeter.

Thunder rumbled somewhere in the east, a storm rolling in from the Ganges delta. Finally at the outdoor amphitheater, the group ascended to the stage. A seated overflow crowd of perhaps a thousand parents and children cheered. The Academy's band struck up the theme song from Claire's old TV show, "Cooking for Lovers," a song everyone still delighted in playing for her. "Hey good lookin', Whatcha got cookin'?"

She chuckled and waved. She was never going to escape from that wacky song—not even in Bangladesh, not even though that part of her life seemed to belong to someone else in some other lifetime.

Flowers garlanded the dais and side pillars of the stage, perfuming the air with Jasmine. A girl in her early teens took Claire's hand and led her to one of the seats of honor. On her green-cushioned chair lay a single pink rose in full bloom, a bit wilted with the heat.

Claire's breath caught, but she picked the rose up along with the card beside it. She could feel eyes watching her. The Minister of Education sat down beside her. Of all things…could the rose be from the mysterious person who'd started sending them to her every so often? Here? Now?

The carefully handwritten note said, "We most gratefully do honor of your presence here today as you do honor of us. Please accept this *Bashra* rose. It is descending from the roses which the Mughal Emperor Babar brought for us in 1500 C.E." The president of the Student Society of Future Leaders of Bangladesh had signed it with her name.

Other women picked up roses too, so her secret *friend* hadn't sent it. Feeling a bit silly over her mistake, Claire smiled. The idea of the anonymous rose sender being here in Chittgong was ridiculous.

From the audience screams erupted. Claire looked up to see an onrushing mass of white clad bearded men charging toward the stage. The band stopped. Everything spun into turmoil. Students, parents, and guests roared.

Chaos! Her pulse raced; her heart seemed jammed into her throat.

Two Ansar guards charged into the crowd. Toting rifles and yelling in Bangla, each fired a warning shot into the air. The third, protecting the Education Minister, also fired a warning shot. Where were her hired Blue Tigers?

Four men grabbed Aminah. Ramin tried to free her, and others grabbed him as well.

"Stop!" Claire screamed. The attackers paid no attention. It was as though the thugs knew they wouldn't actually be fired on, especially here in this place dedicated to nonviolence. Did they think, maybe even know, that the warning shots were merely for show?

One man yelled at Aminah. "Whore!" He stepped forward and pulled something from the bag slung across his shoulder. "A holy *fatwah* denounces you. One hundred and one stones!"

The imam from the crowd at the front gate. But *fatwahs* were illegal now. They couldn't possibly think they could get away with this. Stones the size of potatoes began flying. A jagged one hit Ramin on the cheek. Blood flowed. Others on the stage, including the education minister, ducked their heads under chairs.

A stone hit Claire above her right breast, a white-hot bolt. She fell, then scrambled behind the podium. "Get back! Take cover!" she yelled at her assistants, fear flashing like scalding water through her. The pregnant young woman was kneeling, only partially protected by her chair, her camera aimed at the stoners. "Get down for God's sake!" The camera crashed to the floor and then to the ground as another assistant pulled the woman back.

The lone guard on stage seemed frozen. Claire screamed at him. "Shoot at their feet!" The air stank of gunsmoke and dust.

Aminah lay on the ground, red wounds on her face, neck, and arms, struggling to creep to the of the stage, coughing. Claire fought a wave of nausea.

The warning shots had had no effect. A barrage of stones hit the guard's shoulder, knocking his rifle from his hands. With a clunk audible over the crowd's roar, it landed at the feet of the crouching Minister of Education. Another barrage of stones caused the guard to duck, then he froze. He simply stared down at his rifle,

What the hell is wrong with him!? A handful of men from the rabble charged toward Aminah. The leader, the *imam*, carried a fist-sized stone.

On hands and knees, Claire lunged, scrambled to the rifle, landed on her belly, and grabbed it. The rifle weighed more than those she'd used at the ranch in her old life. Instinctively she rolled into a firing position. She aimed at the imam's feet.

Even as she pulled the trigger three times, she had the thought, Violence! *Why, dear God, can't it be otherwise? Will we never change?* The sound deafened her, the recoils walloped her shoulder. The imam braked to a halt, almost comical with a look of astonishment, mouth slack and eyes wide. The men behind him stopped as well. Clearly they had not expected anyone to fire on them. The guards had all been bribed, she was sure of it.

"Take another step and I'll blow off your kneecaps!" she screamed at him in English, knowing that he probably wouldn't understand the words but would, without doubt, understand her intention.

Aminah lay still, a dark red pool widening around her head.

Aminah!

People huddled and many appeared to be screaming or wailing but Claire heard only a ringing in her ears.

Aminah!

Rocks had stopped flying. A gust of wind brought a sudden downpour of rain—and at long long last, the Blue Tigers. Under the onslaught of rain and the guards, the churning crowd scattered. Within fifteen minutes Claire sat in frozen shock in the seat of a medivac helicopter. Earmuffs dimmed the beating sound of the blades above her head but the vibration rattled her bones as the craft lifted and headed toward Dhaka. One medic adjusted Aminah's oxygen. The other probed her vein with an IV needle as Claire held onto Aminah's other hand.

How Wrongs Are Righted

Claire stared in shock at Aminah. The dear woman's skin was so alarmingly cold. *Aminah must not die.* Rage morphed into panic. Aminah would be impossible to replace as headmistress, but as a trusted friend… her passing would blow a crater in Claire's world. She stared out of a Plexiglas pane at the late afternoon sky which was reddening as the storm clouds receded.

To save Aminah, she'd picked up a gun and shot at people.

The motor whump-whumped with such roaring force it threatened to overpower the timing of her racing heartbeat. She could not stop the images of blood spurting onto the white clothing of the rioting man as she'd fired at his legs. To erase the chaotic mental movie she leaned closer to the pane and peered down at rain rivers running through the city below, the green hills of Chittagong speckled with shanties—teeming with rabid fanatics.

She turned back to Aminah and fresh anger sent hot blood to her cheeks—God, she shouldn't think of them in that way, and with such hatred. But they'd forced her to use the very thing she was publicly and very visibly dedicated to stopping. Violence.

She had studied and prepared to practice the power of standing outside her anger before it turned to hate, but sometimes that was just inhumanly hard to do. Their stupid *fatwahs*, their overwhelming fear of change, of loosing control of their women or of empowering them in any way. Allah forbid that they should be able to accept women as equals. Still, she should have been strong enough to stay calm inside. She felt like a fraud.

How could she ask her supporters to go on taking brave stands in the face of such blind hostility? At the beginning she'd felt in her soul that she'd chosen the right path, but maybe she'd gone too far.

When leukemia killed David her world shattered. Her husband, her best friend, her love. Seventeen years of happiness gone in three months. Then in a very real sense, she'd lost John, too. Because David wanted it, she and David had deceived their beloved son. Because of the illness, John had discovered the deception.

Her fifteen year old had renounced her. All because of what her mother had called "Claire's need to control the truth." John had moved in with his grandmother, and Claire had felt as abandoned as a castaway on the moon. What was the point of anything?

Then Rachel's e-mail had arrived. "Come stay with me. I'm living in the highlands of Sumatra below blue volcanic mountains that poke up into the clouds. Palm trees and pines. My little bungalow overlooks black rooftops that point up at the ends like water buffalo horns. I'm studying their women-centered culture. The Minangkabau." Rachel Wexler, her dearest friend from college and still her closest companion was an anthropologist. "A family here has sort of adopted me. It's a small village. A thousand souls. You will be so welcome. Come. It'll be just like our time at Brandeis. We'll be roommates again."

Claire had already walked away from the TV cooking show and stepped down at EClaire, one of the most profitable business conglomerates in the world. Leaving was easy. She packed one bag and left within the hour. For several months in the Minang village she simply went through the motions of being alive.

But one evening a teenaged boy who should have been on watch went off gambling—with a cousin's money. This allowed his clan's water buffalo to stray into a neighbor's patch of rice seedlings, seedlings that would have been painstakingly dug up and used to plant an entire paddy, a clan's lifeline. The buffalo had devoured the entire patch.

Word spread like flooding water, a crowd gathered, and everyone argued. Gambling some said, was a huge temptation to young people who were drawn to the cities. This was destroying their way of life. Clan loyalties tore one way and demands to set things right tore another. Tempers were raging. Clearly a fight was imminent.

Suddenly, with the unmistakable bearing of a leader, a proud fat woman named Teejop stepped forward. She'd irritated Claire, strutting around and bossing people. Now she and the chief solemnly announced a meeting. People nodded and dispersed, heading to the village center.

Surprised, Claire had turned to Rachel. "What's going on?"

"You're going to see a demonstration of how wrongs are righted here. There will be no violence. It's simply not acceptable."

Claire sat in on a long public session. Rachel explained that the young man had been on the verge of leaving his people for city life. His mother's clan barely had enough rice. They would be unable to make amends. Some called out that the boy should be strongly punished by shunning. Claire watched the youth's face harden. A shunning would surely make him more determined to leave.

Others still cared for him, and his family. They argued for a different solution: a small apportionment of rice from several of the clans if he agreed to personally re-cultivate new seedlings. For some time there was arguing mediated by Teejop. Finally the boy's father promised a water buffalo calf to the cousin. And if the young man worked hard to make restitution, a certain betrothal awaited him. The boy brightened. The male chief had the final word, but the women of the clans owned the land and controlled the rice, and their input had been vital to finding a solution that delivered an acceptable sense of fairness.

A reconciliation ceremony followed. Cakes and drink, proverbs and song. Rachel translated the rites, and Claire especially loved the Minang concept of the union of complimentary male and female forces. The Minang had a saying. The hard and unfeeling nail protects the soft but sensate fingertip; and logs that lean against each other build the best fire.

Claire had felt a warmth, a hope, a vision growing deep inside. Humanity was not hopelessly aggressive. All present laid hands on top of hands and then touched hearts. Claire joined in, returning their shy smiles again and again, touching hands, touching hearts, and she fell in love with nonviolence as a way of life.

These people were neither more nor less fully human than anyone else, but they had found a nonviolent way to manage the folly and darker impulses of individual members. According to Rachel, this remarkable culture had lasted for centuries, and four million Minang still followed this peaceful way. Claire had never heard or seen anything like it.

"When the Muslim religion swept through" Rachel said, "the Minang simply adopted aspects of Islam that are in harmony with their own reverence for nature, their male and female balance, and peaceful ways. They essentially overlook those aspects that do not fit."

The more Claire thought about this, the more extraordinary and reasonable it seemed.

"You have time on your hands," Rachel added. "The world has more than eighty nonviolent cultures. Why not visit a few?"

Claire had set off on her travels. Her journals written in those peaceful places became the basis of her book, *Creating the Future*, and the inspiration for AFWW. Work became her solace. Building the academies had led her to Bangladesh. And now Aminah was paying the price for change.

Dear friend. I am so sorry you've been hurt. Again Claire became aware of the dreadful coldness of Aminah's hand. Was the price too high?

Dusk settled in. Claire studied her own reflection in the window. She looked much the same as before David died. Inside, though, she was so different from the light-hearted yet determined career woman she'd been. She'd rejected when she was twenty the career in diplomacy her ambassador father envisioned for her, believing the world such a chaotic mess that her contribution couldn't possibly make a difference.

After Sumatra, she knew better. She had changed. People could change. The difference between a village and the globe was vision, will, and power. If she could make a TV cooking show into a global enterprise, she decided, she could do the same with an idea for positive change that mattered profoundly. She had money and influence and she would make them count.

Today's rioters weren't the first to test her resolve. She warmed to the thought of Sumidar, the fighting and then the treaty. Four years ago she'd been with an AFWW team in the small Indonesian country when violence erupted. The U.S. Ambassador, a friend of her father's, asked her to help negotiate a settlement. She'd worked harder than she ever had and helped achieve an accord. Two years ago, for her schools, the book, and the Sumidar Accord, the committee for the Nobel Peace Prize had seen fit to make the former TV cooking maven a Nobel Laureate.

During Rachel's last field study before returning to Brandeis she'd written to Claire, "Seems like everywhere I go in the world, I see your picture on walls, from apartments to grass huts. My favorite was you alongside JFK, John Lenon, and Princess Kate, each in a hand-carved frame in a tiny hut in Peru."

Yes, there had been great progress, but now Aminah was suffering. What if Aminah didn't make it? God forbid!

A medic suddenly moved Claire aside as the other one cut through Aminah's bright blue silk shell and bra. He bared her chest and slapped on some kind of clear goo. The other applied paddles in a frantic effort to jumpstart Aminah's heart.

Mortals With the Power of Gods

The Last Saturday in August

Savik Kodaly, along with a dozen other suits, descended from the CET corporate jet onto the landing pad at the vast Coherent Energy Technologies complex outside Stamford, Connecticut. As a former cowhand, juvenile delinquent, Green Beret, and still addicted adventurer, he couldn't help but marvel at the vital part he'd played in steering his friend's laser company toward this day, one CET had worked toward for over seven years. Today was an existential test for PeaceMaker. If the weapon didn't work, CET investors would start bailing and support in Congress for the entire weapon system would evaporate.

Originally focused on global communications, the CET wonks had developed, in their "spare time," some daring theories concerning the superiority of free-electron lasers—FELs—over gas-dynamic and solid state lasers. They applied their theories to space-based laser weapons for satellite anti-missile defense and had developed an impressively successful prototype. Greased by insider connections, government grants soon swelled CET coffers. Savik, as chief legal counsel, had helped structure the defense proposal to attract additional investors and designed what everyone proclaimed a brilliant corporate legal structure. CET soon tripled in size.

Winston Hughes strode beside Savik toward two waiting shuttles. "Nothing like the fear of attack to get taxpayers to fund the most brilliant discoveries in the history of human-kind," he said. Winn was not only Savik's best friend since their days at Harvard Law School. Winn was CEO of CET, *and* the source for the company's very very inside connections. His daddy was Ronald Bramfeld Hughes, the Secretary of Defense.

"Mortals with the power of gods," Savik said. "No matter what the Lana Boswells and Claire Aldens of the world think, war will eventually reach into space and we absolutely must control the high ground."

"And any patriot would want to be prepared." Winn slapped him on the back. "Right?"

Two covered shuttles whisked the dozen execs and silent partners from the mini-airport toward the admin building, passing an eight-hole putting green and an artificial lake complete with a pair of honest-to-god white swans. Beyond the greens lay the three-story accelerator that stretched two city blocks in length and hummed in a steady drone.

The other men, as Savik himself had done, were probably imagining how they'd spend the fortunes they'd eventually make if today's test went well. The CET contribution to the total PeaceMaker system was the "IBIS" laser cannon. It looked like a bird's long bill with wings and was the gravy lode in the entire project. If the test succeeded, and if Congress then passed the needed appropriation, CET would be awarded a two-and-a-half billion-dollar contract.

Savik's personal cut through his founder stocks in CET and his firm's signing bonus would be 3.75 million up front. The investors would get advances too, and they'd all cash in on megabucks when the first ten satellites in the PeaceMaker constellation were launched. The eventual Defense scenario called for two hundred satellites, which could mean continuing contracts throughout the rest of Savik's life.

And it all pretty much depended on today's test—that and silencing the peaceniks. Savik would have a hand in that too. Later that evening in fact.

The shuttles reached the sparkling water fountains of the admin building, which cast rainbows over an ultra-modern, white boomerang-shaped structure with walls of blue-green glass.

One of the men said to Savik as they stepped off the shuttle, "My guts are in knots."

In minutes, the group had reached the tower room where thirty or so specialists and project managers were watching three seventy-six inch TVs. The middle screen received a private CET satellite transmission from a site at Pt. Mugu, California. At the moment it was monitoring the satellite's platform, launched hours earlier. The talking head said, "The PeaceMaker platform is now in stable orbit fifty miles up."

Great! Stage One, no sweat.

On the two other screens, CNN ran a digitally produced animation. With blackness behind it and the blue planet curving below, PeaceMaker seemed to be hovering, protecting, beautiful. Savik thrilled to the images.

One of the men placed a Bloody Mary in his hand, but Savik set it aside. "If this test screws up, I'll most likely want to go puke in one of Winn's fancy johns."

On CNN, Tawana Thompson said in her distinctive, husky voice, "We are only moments away from this crucial test of all the system's components. In all earlier tests, PeaceMaker failed to detect or destroy missiles quickly after their launch. Ability to do so would make PeaceMaker an enormous advance in our country's defenses. A CET spokesman here at Pt. Mugu can tell us more...." She addressed a man in a white jumpsuit. "FELs, free-electron lasers, represent quite a departure from the original Department of Defense space lasers approach. Why the switch to the CET IBIS laser?"

Winn's CET man said, "FELs obsoletes other lasers. The Earth's atmosphere is generally a barrier to lasers, but FELs allow tunability, a phased array which—"

"Tunability?...In simple language, please."

The spokesman answered cheerfully. "It's like a soldier being able to quickly change his weapon, from a pistol to an automatic to a shoulder-launched Stinger. PeaceMaker can select the best wavelength, say, an infrared beam to penetrate atmospheric interference. We can, for example, deploy both continuous infrared rays and a single, devastating megawatt blast of X-rays. These blasts can be delivered anywhere in space or on the earth's surface using the infrared rays as the carrier. Like riding piggyback."

"Also anywhere on the earth's surface?"

"That's correct."

The camera moved in for a close-up on the lady reporter. "This ability to penetrate the atmosphere and reach the earth's surface is the feature of PeaceMaker that especially alarms its opponents." The screen cut back to the animation as she continued to speak. "And now some eight hundred miles out in the Pacific, the simulated 'enemy' is launching a missile. Stage two."

Savik felt his heartbeat speed up.

A male voice on the Point Mugu monitor said, "ATP registers nuclear target acquisition."

"Yes!" Winn yelled, along with the rest of CET project managers and specialists. He explained for the suits. "The system has correctly figured out that the warhead is nuclear. It has nuclear materials. It's not space junk or a telecommunications satellite run wild."

On CNN, an incessant beeping began. "Ground monitors have picked up the rapid beeping of the missile's signal. As long as it beeps, a mock bomb is headed toward the USA."

The animation then showed a missile that split into decoy missiles.

A tech at Pt. Mugu faced the camera. "Stage three. PeaceMaker systems are scanning decoys to decide which is carrying the 'nuclear' payload."

The Pt. Mugu control center appeared on the middle TV monitor. Dozens of analysts were listening to the missile's incessant, nerve-wracking beeping. Sudden sweat cooled Savik's temples. Seven years of development…it could all go to hell in an instant.

On the screen showing the simulation, the male voiceover said, "The hope is that by being able to blast a nuclear warhead closer to an enemy's territory early during the launch phase, instead of closer to the U.S., PeaceMaker will deter even the contemplation of such attacks."

Beep-beep-beep-beep-beep—

Savik wanted to yell at someone to lower the volume. Clearly the 'armed' missile was alive and healthy, aimed at Northern California. If PeaceMaker failed it would be remotely blown to bits by explosives.

The talking head at Pt. Mugu said, "Ninety more seconds."

Beep-beep-beep-beep-beep—

One minute, fifty-nine, fifty-eight, fifty-seven, seconds. Hemorrhaging droplets of time.

Savik reached for the Bloody Mary and gulped it. Thirty-three seconds, thirty-two….

Silence.

Was it…?

Techies on the Pt. Mugu TV were bent over their radar screens. Their hands shot up. Voices blasted out a cheer. By the time the successful hit was announced on CNN at 11:19 EST, no one at CET was watching TV. Grown men in expensive suits were jumping up and down, hugging each other, and hooting.

When mania finally yielded to mere slap-happiness, Winn stood on a coffee table. "Hear, hear!" he said, "I want to remind you of what Keith Spy-in-the-Sky Hall once said as Director of NRO. 'With regard to space dominance, we have it, we like it, and…'" Winn yelled out the last, "'we're going to keep it'!!!!"

The mania returned. The doors to a dining section were thrown open. Champaign corks popped. Cigars were lit. Buffet tables offered caviar, lobster and spitted meats. PeaceMaker would be the heart of America's Space Corps. America would be safe. The CET men were heroes.

And they would soon be rich heroes.

You Sure Don't Look Like Her

Manhattan – The Last Saturday in August

John Alden Trask adjusted the showerhead to "jet pulse." Hot water needles relaxed knotted muscles, the aftermath of torture. *But freely chosen torture.* He smiled.

He did get a kick out of pushing limits every now and then, especially when he needed a little cash. So he'd spent seven straight hours on the tennis court under the intense regimen of his angry coach, who always wanted more from him. Lots of people wanted more from him.

Much to Coach's disgust, John never sought the big prize, the million bucks. But today in practice he'd given his best, pushing his endurance to learn his potential power—should he ever decided he truly gave a shit.

He was up thirty K from the L.A. and Indianapolis tournaments and had squeaked into qualifying for the U.S. Open in Flushing Meadows. The competition itself launched day after tomorrow. Maybe a million bucks was out, but thirty K more for placing would do fine. Fifty would be sweet.

He stepped from the shower into pine-scented bathroom steam and toweled off. A massage and rub-down would go great if he had time. He didn't. Not if he wanted to make a media-catching entrance at the pre-tournament press reception with Fance Showalter. Shock and awe.

He imagined tomorrow's tabloid or sports or even society page:

"John Alden Trask, son of Claire Alden, escorted exotic dancer, Fance Show, to the renowned Flushing Meadows event. Miss Show's act can be seen four nights a week at Whispers, a night club near La Guardia."

Topless pole dance not to be missed.

John grinned, picturing the stunned look on his mother's face when her secretary or some other underling showed her the hot little item and, with luck, a scandalous photo accompanying it. Dear Mom was far too busy to bother with reading the sports pages for the occasional one-liners about her unimpressive son, but someone paid to manage his mother's image would insist that she check out the news byte.

He settled for a quick shoulder stretch, pushing his right elbow as far around toward his left shoulder as possible, burning the knot out further.

Fance would do a massage later tonight….or in the morning if tonight she wore him out in bed.

He listened next to the bathroom door. She was awfully quiet. She'd turned on some TV show. He spiked his porcupine black-with-bleached-ends hair with gel, slipped on black slacks and a short-sleeved gray linen shirt that didn't hide his barbed-wire armband tattoo, and opened the door a crack. He wanted to watch her a moment, the stripper behind the scenes looking a lot like other women.

Make that only a little. Fance was special. Even without her make-up the prettiness of her features stood out. She sat in his bed naked, the sheet under her breasts, smoking and twisting a strand of her hair. "Impressionist" hair, waist length, pale blonde with pastel wisps of peach, lavender and aqua. From a distance her hair shimmered, fairy-like. You had to be up close to see the actual colors, a pleasure he was lucky enough to frequently indulge.

She guffawed—the earthy stripper again.

He stepped into the room. "What's so funny?"

"This was a great one. Your mom's in a black wig, 're-inventing' her-self into a 'senorita' and talking about how cinnamon along with chil-ies is an aphrodisiac." Fance blew smoke, grinning with pleasure. "Then your mom says, 'You know what really lights my fire? A truly great food processor.'" Fance laughed again. Her green eyes sparkled. "Her shows were so fantastic."

"You're watching old reruns on the *cooking* channel?"

"Classic Recipes." Her face hardened. "Strippers cook too, you know."

He punched the power off on the TV, walked to the side of the bed, snatched her cigarette away and stubbed it out.

Fance frowned. She studied him, then brightened, refusing to let him bring her down. "You sure don't look like her. Which means," she said, pouring honey into her voice and looking him over slowly, "that your dad was one handsome, dark-eyed devil."

Her clothing lay on the bed, ready for her turn in the bathroom. He grabbed up a black outfit, the kind his mother called "a little black dress." "What's this for?"

"Why so grouchy all of a sudden? It's to wear tonight."

"I want you to look hot. Not like you're going to a damn funeral." He heard the edge in his voice. He was pissed. Dammit. Her admiration for "Cooking For Lovers" had pushed the button that always triggered the same old, uncontrollable response. Why did everyone in the whole world worship at his mother's shrine? If they only knew....

Fance slid out of bed, stood, found her purse, and pulled out another smoke and the lighter. Her lips twisted into a taunting smile. "You want me to look like a stripper. Gotcha."

Instead of placing the cigarette between her lips, she held it between her teeth, lips parted while she lighted it, a gesture that somehow conveyed the fact that she'd do what he wanted, but she held a small part of herself away from his control. The cigarette was her dignity at the moment. Her defiance.

Hell.

Only a first-class loser would do anything to make Fance feel bad. Which pretty much everyone who knew him or knew of him thought he was. A loser. A fuck-up. A playboy. He especially hated that one. Everyone saw him that way except Fance. Well, and Grandmere. He ignored the cigarette, and headed for the kitchen.

"There's a phone message," she called from the bathroom before shutting the door.

In the kitchen of the elegant art deco pied-a-terre that he rented for a nominal fee from Grandmere he listened to the most recent message.

"John, darling, it's Mom...I'm not sure what's in the press, but I'm just returning from...a very rough trip to Bangladesh. Grandmere is going to be with me at the Tabor Towers tonight. We're hoping you'll join us there for brunch tomorrow morning. At ten o'clock. Please...I miss you....I'd love to see you....We're going to watch you in the tournament....I love you, son."

Oh, yeah. Love. Lots and lots. Right.

He hit *erase* and turned on the kitchen portable to watch ESPN. Tennis rankings. Talking heads predicting tournament winners while showing shots of favorites—which didn't include him. *I am such an asshole. God, I should have let Fance wear the black dress.*

She was a knock-out. No one would miss that no matter what she wore. He'd hurt her for the worst of reasons—he'd wanted to shock dear Mom.

Fance stepped into the room. He took one look at her and felt all the blood in his body race to one spot. *Jesus.*

A dropped-waist swatch of silver that hugged her hips would probably count as a micro-mini skirt. Legs...miles of them. Tan, smooth, flawless.

Bare. A dancer's thighs and calves. Slim ankles strapped in silver. Spiked silver heels.

"Is this what you had in mind?" she asked, voice playful. She'd forgiven him. As usual.

He was working his line of sight upward, and couldn't quite speak. A silver knit halter-top hung skimpily over her peachy breasts. Great cleavage. More breast exposed at the sides. His heart worked hard to support biological imperatives.

She turned, lifting the long hair to fully reveal her tanned bare back, its groove at the base of the spine being one of his favorite places to kiss and caress. She started to sway her hips the way she did in her act.

"Don't do that." His cheeks puffed out as he exhaled. "I need some ice water."

He moved toward the kitchen. She stopped him. "I'll get it."

She left, hips still swaying, taunting. He thought about his tennis rating. That ought to calm him down. She returned with chilled water, which he gulped.

He drew a breath, set the glass down, and put his arms around her. She smelled faintly of lilacs. A multi-string choker of what looked like tiny ice cubes glimmered at her neck. He parted the sparkles, kissed the cleft between her collarbones and worked his way up to her ear.

"It's not like I want to be a jerk," he whispered.

She kissed him on the nose.

"Stay close to me tonight," he said.

Fance smiled her showgirl smile. "Let's go give them something to talk about."

A Deep Red Rose

Manhattan, Tabor Towers

August heat steamed New York city as it had Bangladesh but with ninety percent humidity instead of heavy rains. Claire's air-conditioned limo ride from JFK, however, caused no sweaty discomfort.

Her watch said 5:20. She could almost be on time if she didn't need to change. The TARA women might admire her, but if she showed up in a simple business suit, she might seem purer-than-thou, off saving the world while they shopped for gowns the society pages would coo over. Ostentatious largess and being ever upbeat was a basic fact of fundraising. She'd looked forward to this event for months. She enjoyed the TARA members. AFWW needed the money. Fundraising during the pandemic years had been nearly impossible. Claire must play to win or her schools might be the losers, so she would change clothes and cloak her sadness and fear for Aminah.

Cocktails were scheduled at six. She hated to be late, but the extra day in Dhaka to deal with the aftermath of the stoning put her arrival in New York smack up against the wall. Claire had called her executive assistant, Jocelyn Chao, from Dhaka, but had kept her account of the riot brief. Joss had still insisted—quite unnecessarily—on the bodyguard who now rode up front with the driver. Claire pulled her cell phone from her purse, called Joss, who was slightly hysterical that Claire hadn't yet arrived, and filled her in.

"My, God, Claire! What an ordeal! You should have told me sooner—"

"No time. I was lucky to make a flight back. At one point, I thought I'd be hauled off to prison for using the rifle. Fortunately none of the protesters want to face prosecution for stoning Aminah Roy, and filing a complaint against me would mean an admission of guilt. And my using a weapon wouldn't be ideal press. So the lawyers are dealing with it."

"How is Aminah?"

"When I left she was alive but in surgery. I'm hoping for an update any minute. Cover for me, Joss, and talk to my mother." Claire gauged the traffic. "I'll be there in about a half hour."

"I just can't believe you, of all people, shot at someone."

"I know." Claire breathed deeply. Memories of the amphitheater had haunted her all day. "I just refused to let them get Aminah. You know, I've never claimed to be a pacifist."

Claire ended the call. She thought of John again. She called the pied-a-terre, letting the phone ring and finally leaving another message. Her son never picked up if he saw her number on caller ID. She tried his cell phone. Same result. It crushed her a little every time it happened.

By 6:02, the limo reached the underground parking of the extravagant, skyscraping Tabor Towers. At that very moment, two floors up, five hundred ball attendees were probably schmoozing in the mezzanine outside the Grand Ballroom. The bodyguard opened her door and she stepped out.

Men in tuxedos held the arms of women in shimmering gowns. Valets parked limos. New York. From abject poverty to fabulous wealth inside one day. It felt surreal.

The driver sent her bags up with a bellhop. At the airport the bodyguard had delivered an envelope from Joss with Claire's room number and key—which made him not entirely superfluous. She would not have to endure a check-in. Unrecognized in a straw, roll brim hat and sunglasses, she raced with the guard through the Towers foyer past the four-story waterfall. Her cell phone chimed and the digital display showed a Bangladesh number. She hurried to a semi-secluded spot between potted ficus trees.

Ramin spoke slowly. "Aminah is now conscious." His voice lowered. "She has lost her right eye."

A hot rush of rage stiffened Claire's spine as she saw Aminah in her mind again, lying so horribly still. She pictured Aminah's beautiful brown eyes.

"Claire...?" Ramin said. "Aminah said, 'Tell Claire we will not let them defeat us. I promise you. We will succeed.'"

Claire's throat tightened, tears welled. Aminah would live, and despite everything, she had returned Claire's exact promise.

"You are there?" Ramin asked.

"Yes." She cleared her throat. "I love her and . . .admire her so much, Ramin. And you too. Will you tell her that for me?"

"Yes...I will. Thank you." A few more words and she ended the call.

She and the guard stepped into a mirrored elevator that whisked her upward almost to the top floor. Joss had arranged for her to share a suite with Maman. Leaving the guard outside, she entered the common living room and dropped her purse by a fragrant bouquet of gardenias in a French antique porcelain vase on the marble-topped entry table. The combined value of the vase and table alone would probably equip a school's computer lab.

The face of a gilt clock said 6:15. Fifteen minutes late for cocktails.

Shadowy movement and a fluttering of wings brought a flash of red tail feathers and a simultaneous squawk near her face. She flinched. "Aw, Alex, you startled me."

Her African Grey parrot had landed on her shoulder, bobbing his head with delight to see her. Obviously Joss or Maman had let him loose to have the run of the place. Something shiny flashed in his beak. "What did you bring me, huh?" She cupped her palm.

He dropped a gold earring into it. "You bandido!" he announced.

She chuckled. "Pilfering my jewelry box again, you shameless thing."

He flew off into one of the two bedrooms.

"Oh, Claire." In a peach silk kimono, her mother, Nicole deNevers Alden, swept into the common living room from the bedroom opposite. It had been two months since their last visit. Her mother paused dramatically. "You are late! But, thank God, safe! Risking yourself like your father did while off saving the world! They've been calling, my sweet! Adam, the TARA women, the hotel people. Jocelyn is a bit hysterical."

A sapphire-blue, beaded silk gown lay over Maman's arm. "The cleaners did not deliver the dress you wanted. Jocelyn fetched this one and arrived with it only thirty minutes ago. Everything else, she has laid out for you. That young woman is obsessive."

Claire took the gown, hugged her mother with one arm and kissed her on both cheeks. "It's good to see you, Maman. I've missed you. I thought you'd already be downstairs."

Alex landed on her shoulder again, something beige and lacy in his beak.

"Oh, you silly thing!" Her mother lifted skin-tone bikini panties from the bird. "Well, now. What is this?" Her eyes widened. She smiled at Claire. "You've met someone, *cherie*?"

Claire snatched the panties. "Hmmf!" A bit uncomfortable to explain to her mom that she'd lately wanted to remember she was still a woman. Since David's death she'd rarely given a man even a flirtatious look and only twice had thought she might have found a "possible." "Doing the girl thing again, I guess."

"I am impressed. But now hurry. *Vite!* I will tell them you're on your way."

"*Vite! Vite!*" Alex cried. "*Vite! Vite!*"

Claire sped into her bedroom. Joss had stocked the closet with a few outfits for the long weekend, lingerie in the drawers. Her bags had been delivered. She freshened up and changed quickly. The dress really was too slinky for the occasion, and she had to daub makeup at the décolletage to hide the bruise from the stone. Her quick transformation took less than ten minutes.

At twenty to seven she hurried into the shared living room. Maman sat near the window, gazing at the summer evening sky. Maman's simple black dress, slit at the side, revealed sheer black hosiery over legs still shapely at seventy-four. Smooth white hair framed a noble face, fluffed in back, stylish and a bit naughty. Diamonds cascaded at the ears, her only jewelry.

"My god, Maman, you are beautiful. And that Parisian cut alone was worth your trip."

Her mother blushed. "*Merci, merci.*" She deflected further praise. "That bird has . . . decorated the floor over by the window. No towels there. The hotel maids will not thank you."

"Alex likes to look out the window." Claire stepped into her shoes. Alex had been with her since the beginning of 'Cooking for Lovers'. Fans adored him for blurting zany lines from his hundred-word vocabulary. "He's more famous than I am." She smiled. "And I always clean up after him."

Her mother snatched up her shimmering little rhinestone bag, and stood. "You did call John, I hope. He will join us for breakfast tomorrow?"

Claire sighed. "I left a message." Which her son would probably ignore. "I asked him to please join *Grandmere* and me." John definitely wouldn't come if the occasion was only with Claire, and her mother knew it.

An awkward moment hung between them, her mother obviously wanting to say something that might offer a way to heal her grandson's resentment, and knowing there was no point, and that they were in too much of a hurry anyway.

It was her mother's turn to sigh. "Well, then, let's GO. Oh!" She turned toward the table by the window. "Perhaps it's important. This came while you were changing."

She pointed at the lone deep red rose in a crystal vase. As if the bloom exuded some spell, Claire ignored the time, approached the vase and breathed in the rose's heavy perfume. Like the others before, it wasn't a typical florist's rosebud. It had opened a bit, and its red seemed drenched in wine. She plucked up the accompanying card, typewritten.

Her mother said. "I knew you had an admirer."

"I have no idea who sends them. They aren't signed. But the quotes come from a book called *The Language of Roses*."

"What does it say?"

"'I offer a language that says what I can't.' Then a quote from the rose book. 'The deep infusion of burgundy tones proffers the sensual, arousing a response from the very earth itself.'"

Claire's pulse sped up a bit.

"Oh, my," her mother said, frowning and her tone suddenly wary. "Such . . . intimate phrasing. How many have you received?"

"Four, over the last few months." Claire again inhaled the earthy scent of the bloom.

Her mother frowned. "You remember my friend Georgette's daughter Elaine?"

Nearly twenty years ago, a man who sent Elaine rough poetry scrawled onto graphic pages torn out of *Hustler* magazine had stalked and killed the young woman.

"I'd hardly put hybrid roses in the same category as what that pervert sent to Elaine."

"You think your admirer is simply shy? No, Claire. There is something wrong here. He does not identify himself."

Claire sighed, returned the rose to the vase, and headed toward the door. "It's just a rose. And we're late." She opened the door and felt a gentle touch on her arm.

"It's not just a rose. A mother knows things." Her mother's eyes showed deep concern.

"I love you, Maman. But you don't need to worry about me."

PeaceMaker

Tabor Towers

Claire insisted the bodyguard wait at the VIP entry as they paused outside the Tabor Towers grand ballroom. Maman was at her side. Claire was wondering if her father's old friend, Ambassador Adam Forsythe, would have cleared his calendar to join them. She peered in at the magnificent decorations for the TARA Ball, the highlight of the annual weekend affair that Women in the Arts for Peace sponsored.

Maman asked. "What is Tara? Somehow related to *Gone With the Wind*?"

Claire smiled. "Tara is an Indian goddess of peace."

Of all the women sitting at the head table, none wore anything as revealing as Claire's own dress. Nervous little butterflies took wing in her stomach. Beryl Steinmetz, a program director at NBC, waved and gave Claire's gown the once-over. *Maman* nodded toward a woman in amber satin. "Isn't that the actress who champions land mine protests?"

It was, and beside her, HBO's Lily Waterman…so many people in a position to help. *Let me inspire them to open their hearts and wallets wide.*

Speech! Notes! With the call from Bangladesh and all the fuss over Alex and the rose, she'd forgotten to send her notes down so that Joss could put them on the lectern.

A woman in sheer lavender silk floated toward them—the TARA event coordinator. She gushed her welcome. Following her, Claire stepped into the large ballroom with its chandeliers the size of Volkswagens, one of which would launch a small Academy in Kenya. The massive floral arrangements alone would pay for…She stopped herself.

Her mother took her arm. "I know what you are thinking. So much opulence when so many are destitute. But I'm thrilled to be here, love. This is also part of life's tapestry"

Claire squeezed back. "I'm pleased too."

Most guests were, of course, already seated at their tables. As the coordinator led them through the hall, many turned Claire's way, pointing or waving.

"Claire!"

"There she is!"

The small orchestra stopped and a lone pianist began playing *Claire De Lune*. The room burst into an ovation as attendees interrupted their dinners to stand. Claire waved as she reached the speaker's table, wishing timeliness had permitted a more discreet entrance.

Claire spotted her assistant, Jocelyn Chao. And there was Adam, her father's old friend. Adam Forsythe, the current U.S. Ambassador to the U.N., escorted Claire and her mother on occasion. Claire held her arm toward Adam and applause swelled to even higher decibels. Adam waved, then held the chairs as Claire and her mother were seated. Claire signed to Joss, who took up a position behind Claire. The crowd settled again.

"Inexcusably late!" Adam whispered, taking his seat.

Claire started to explain. He leaned closer and silenced her with a kiss to her cheek, his gaze lingering a second at her cleavage. "Such beauty purchases a thousand extenuations, and you two are the most beautiful women here."

Her mother beamed. "Silver-haired and silver-tongued. Ever the diplomat."

He rubbed his hand over his hair. "After four years of cajoling bullies, hotheads, and demagogues, a teenager would go gray ...."

"You must be speaking about the press," Claire said in mock seriousness.

Adam grinned. "Them too."

Claire leaned behind her mother to Joss. "I've left my notes in the room. In the black leather attaché." She passed Joss the room key. "Save my life, please, and fetch them."

Joss whispered, "Do you know we've been frantic over the Dhaka mess? Pryce was close to dispatching a platoon of personal bodyguards."

"Pryce should stick to PR." People at the table were silent, as if straining to hear their urgent whisperings. "Right now, everything depends on my speech. So please..."

Still frowning, Joss hurried off. The salad course was on the table, but Claire couldn't eat. She tried mentally to run through the speech.

Joss finally returned, learned close and spoke softly. "I have torn everything apart. I couldn't find them. Can you give me better specifics where to look?"

People kept glancing at them. Dessert and coffee had just been cleared.

Claire sighed. "You'd never make it back in time. I'll have to wing it."

"PeaceMaker was in the news today," Joss whispered. "You could mention that. Its laser system is working. Looks like they're going to go ahead with that abomination. Some European leaders are already upset."

Claire stared. The PeaceMaker system had gobbled up staggering sums of money and would continue to do so, robbing assets that could be used to help people and foster so many needed social changes. A PeaceMaker talk might not charm her audience—and she simply must charm them—but Joss was right. The satellite weapon was an abomination that could never establish nonviolence and could ultimately counteract the freedom, equality, and just future that AFWW stood for.

The evening's emcee, Rhoda Carr, approached the microphone.

"You'll wow 'em," Joss whispered. "I have a gut feel about tonight." She left Claire for a seat in the audience.

Bringing Boswell Down

Explorers' Club – Upper East Side, New York

Across town from the TARA gala's crystal chandeliers, tuxedos, and ball gowns, Savik Kodaly and Adrienne Grantham entered the Explorers' Club, a place where members left civilized life-as-usual at the door and stepped into a world of possibility, faraway places, adventure, and kindred spirits. Savik loved this old place, a perfect way to celebrate the PeaceMaker success.

His arm on her waist, he glanced at Adrienne's expression as they strolled through the six-story building's foyer, crammed with over a hundred years' worth of trophies, flags, maps, weapons, masks, bones— fascinating junk from every nook and cranny on the planet. He was hoping she'd say something like, I could spend days looking at this collection and learning the stories behind each piece.

"Nice crowd," she said rather flatly as they stood among clusters of people on the second floor. "I'm sure your talk on…mapping the inner Mongolian terrain is a huge draw."

Her lukewarm response disappointed him, but she was clearly trying to be a good sport. He took her hand and let a kiss linger alongside a sapphire dinner ring that matched the color of her eyes. Adrienne was sharp as a cut jewel, and ambitious as well, attributes he and his friends were counting on.

She was an important key in their battle to secure the PeaceMaker contract, but Savik wasn't ready to talk business or politics yet. He intended to bask in the glory of his latest adventure, Adrienne at his side completing the picture. With Winn and others, Savik had completed a horseback trek through one of Mongolia's most remote high plateaus. The EC had extended the honor of carrying the club flag. Tonight he would return the banner with a helluva story. He felt a rush of satisfaction as every male in the vicinity checked out her curves in a satiny cobalt dress and the glossy black hair that brushed her shoulders in soft waves.

As a lawyer, he rarely dated other lawyers, but Adrienne was worth making an exception, a standout, an up-and-comer assistant attorney in the Justice Department's New York District office, prosecuting tax fraud and evasion. Tonight's objective with Adrienne wasn't to bed her but to do something that needed doing. It would also fast-track her career—a win-win bedfellows situation if ever there was one. Still, Savik felt a pinch of guilt.

"I need a drink," Adrienne said.

Need. Was she bored already? He steered her toward the bar. The stares continued. Comments buzzed. Savik suppressed a chuckle. When it came to lookers like Adrienne, the world's adventurers—thrill-seekers and scientists alike—simply became "guys."

Age thirty-three, Adrienne seemed ideal marriage material. His own years totaling forty-four, he'd probably have to start considering women up to age thirty-five. Beyond that, experience had proven they were just too picked over, the bloom fading, the attitude growing desperate, or worse, contemptuous of men. Still, Adrienne had at least heard of the Explorer's Club, unlike his last, even younger date.

He placed his hand at her waist again, and then let his fingers inch upward so that he could feel the weight of her breast with the tip of his thumb.

She turned and smiled, a look that said, what took you so long?

Tonight was the third in a series of expensive evenings with her, begun just after he'd first sent her the incriminating information on U.S. Senator Lana Boswell, arch enemy of the PeaceMaker. Boswell's husband, and likely Boswell herself, was dirty. Bringing Boswell down was essential for U.S. security, and armed with what Savik had given her, Adrienne Grantham was just the soldier to do it.

What he'd offered Adrienne—anonymously—was politically lethal stuff. From the few discreetly probing questions he'd already asked, however, she seemed leery of using it. Doubtless not sure of the source. It was critical that he make sure she never knew the actual source. Tonight he needed to ferret out the reasons for her hesitation and put her at ease—if he hadn't already tipped his hand. Encourage her to follow up on her own. Later, if they worked out as a couple, there would be a time to tell her the truth. Savik was an honest man, but the timing could be damn sticky if things worked out romantically.

Winn had met her at a party and lost no time suggesting that Savik wine and dine Adrienne to enlist her help in getting rid of Boswell. Savik had been eager to share time with Adrienne, and his well-toned male sixth sense told him that Adrienne was eager to date him too.

Truth was, he didn't yet really know her all that well and over the years he'd grown certain of at least one thing: he wanted a woman who understood another itch as basic to him as sex, his drive toward high adventure.

Savik had never felt more satisfied than when he was pitting himself against the elements, or as a Green Beret, clearing villages hit by guerilla raids, or back in Montana riding horseback through the mountains in winter. Women couldn't understand one of his best memories: a night in a Thai lockup for crossing a crooked cop. He'd debated everything from politics to the merits of AK-47s with an inmate who turned out to be from the Royal Geographical Society of London. Would he ever find a woman who could understand that instead of going to Aspen or Monte Carlo he'd rather visit old Roman battle sites in Turkey and North Africa?

They were almost to the bar when Winn called out, "Savik. Over here."

Winn and Savik shook hands, but Adrienne stepped back and merely nodded to Winn. This was both odd and uncomfortable, since Winn had introduced them. The PeaceMaker's success today was all over the news, and, of course she'd know of Lana Boswell's opposition. Surely she didn't connect Winn's company to PeaceMaker. But she probably did know that Winn's dad, the SecDef, strongly supported PeaceMaker. Time for a distraction from any hint of politics.

"What would you like to drink?" he asked her.

She let go of his arm. "No. Let me. What would you like?"

Something had made her nervous. "J & B, neat," Savik said.

She squeezed his hand and moved off for the bar.

Winn said, "Who'd'a thought an up-tight justice lawyer would be such a babe? And her circuits definitely light up around you."

Savik wondered if she was avoiding being seen with Winn.

"So will she go after the Boswell bitch?" Winn asked.

"I think I can coax her intentions out of her tonight. If I press her too hard, though, she'll start wondering. But let's talk about this later."

"Hey, you can do it," Winn said. "You persuaded me that freezing my ass off in Mongolia would be fun." Winn looked in the direction of the bar and elbowed Savik. "Just make sure you slip her every inch of your charm tonight."

"Let it rest, Winn!" Sometimes his friend just didn't know when to quit, but for Savik, Winn was the closest thing he had to a brother.

Adrienne returned. Savik tried to generate some enthusiasm for his talk on Mongolia as Adrienne swirled the olives in her martini, staring at Winn. In a serious tone she asked, "Your company, Coherent

Energy Technologies. That's lasers, of course. So—what kind of lasers does CET specialize in?"

Oh, god, her wheels were turning, connecting some carefully unpublicized dots, dots Winn spent good PR money to camouflage from any prying interest. No need to stir up a frenzy about nepotism concerning the Secretary of Defense and his son's business interests.

Winn gave his standard answer. "Mostly in lasers for communication and image tracking, and some research in free-electron lasers and their applications."

Yeah, like PeaceMaker satellite laser systems. The whole world would know soon enough, but again, timing was everything.

"Hey," Savik said, "It's our night to relive adventure, remember?"

The crowd was moving into the auditorium. Winn leaned close enough to whisper, "Whatever else happens tonight, buddy, you find out if Adrienne Grantham is on board. Lana Boswell has got to go down."

White Rose Petals

Tabor Towers

Rhoda Carr, a comedienne who'd emceed the Academy Awards, stood at the microphone. The tall redhead with spiky hair spoke in her classic deadpan. "This guy named Aristotle said that women are only half a man and don't have the ability to manage worldly business."

The TARA audience groaned or laughed. Claire rolled her eyes.

"I got news, oh wise guy." Rhoda made a face. "Tonight's speaker, the maven of television cooking, founder of the EClaire publishing, retail, and financial empire, global champion of women's rights, author of *Creating the Future*, and Nobel Peace Prize winner…ain't a man."

The audience clapped and laughed. Claire felt the scary weight on her shoulders of having to follow Rhoda Carr without notes. *Senator Lana Boswell!* The senator's name bubbled up from Claire's subconscious. She knew just the perfect place in her speech to ask people to support the senator's stand against the PeaceMaker plan.

"And if that wasn't enough…" Rhoda's expression turned wicked. "…everyone in this room owes at least one hot night to Claire's amorous recipes. Now…"

Rhoda stopped to allow the laughs to die down. Claire felt a blush spread as she grinned.

"Now she wants to share with us a recipe for saving the whole world." Rhoda smiled warmly. "So old and new fans of EClaire, supporters of A Future Without War, and Women in the Arts for Peace, I give you Claire Alden."

To loud applause, Claire stood. Adam also stood beside her and beckoned the busboy who brought out a huge bouquet of red roses.

Adam placed them in her arms and kissed her on the cheek. She pulled away, smiling, thanked him, and beamed at the wildly applauding crowd.

The pianist reprised "Hey Good Lookin', Whatcha Got Cookin'." At the lectern she sat the roses aside. "I'm so glad that Rhoda made us all laugh," she began, "because laughter lets me know I'm with my human family, no matter where I go in the world."

She told them about kids in Bangladesh so eager to get to a school on the other side of a filthy river that they made pontoons out of plastic liter pop bottles from a dump. "They emerged wet but laughing. Why? Partly because they are children, but also because they have a human spirit with a sense of perspective. They were laughing because of the load on the pontoons: shoes. Their school's headmistress wouldn't allow dirty shoes. The children laughed because shoes got a ride while they did not."

Claire felt the audience—they were strongly with her. "I laughed with them because they were such brave little troopers. Such places where shoes have more importance and dignity than the children make me determined to build yet another school, yet another health and family planning clinic, another community center, another place for women to gather to plan ways to make their community's life better. And with your help, we are making these changes happen."

Rapt faces. Enthusiastic applause. She had to bite back the urge to add, "Just the kinds of outreach programs our apparently heartless President has axed."

She touched on the cornerstones of A Future Without War and then plunged. "You all know I try to avoid politics, but today's news about 'PeaceMaker' is alarming. This space-based laser weapon system, the undying spawn of Reagan's Star Wars program from Cold War days, must not be tolerated. It can never bring peace. It's a falsely named, senseless, bottomless money pit. The mega-billion dollar cost of implementing it could be used instead to provide clean water and sewage systems the world over, educate every child here and globally, and establish healthcare systems worldwide—instead of hanging a worldwide threat over our heads.

"Think of it! U.S. weapons sailing through the space covering our entire globe. When I imagine it, I shudder. You are all women dedicated to peaceful solutions, and so I urge you to please contact your Congressperson to support Senator Lana Boswell's efforts to halt the so-called 'PeaceMaker' program."

The expressions on the faces in the audience had grown serious. They wanted more stories, and humor. They wanted to feel good. She lauded successful programs TARA had funded. By the time she began her closing remarks, all seemed to have gone smoothly. "I hope to see you all again in Washington at the upcoming AFWW Unity concert. In unity we have power."

A woman at the back of the room wrapped in a brown silky shawl entered from one side and moved swiftly forward along the perimeter of the tables.

"We love our country, its democracy, freedom and opportunity," Claire continued. "The USA could once more be that shining beacon—"

"Liar!" the woman shrieked, her gaze aimed directly at Claire. "Daughter of SATAN!!! You shame women! You bring tears to Allah!"

The audience gasped in collective alarm.

Two men in gray suits and wearing earphones materialized and put themselves between Claire and the women. Another man in a gray suit grabbed the woman by the arms. As he escorted her firmly toward a rear door she continued to scream. "Allah will be avenged!" She struggled, kicked, broke free and threw white rose petals toward Claire.

Claire knew immediately the symbolism. Probably most of the people present did. White rose petals were the mark of the TOA terrorist group, Tears of Allah, so named because white roses were believed to grow out of Allah's tears.

Two men from hotel security caught the women again as other guards converged. One last time the woman screamed. "Allah will destroy you! *Allahu akbar!*"

A Cowboy From Montana

Explorers Club – Upper Westwide, New York

The master of ceremonies lumbered to a podium beside a twenty-by-thirty foot screen. "Tonight our honored speaker is a man I'm told the ladies think bears a resemblance to a certain tall, dark handsome actor . . ." He gestured toward Savik with mock disgruntlement, as if he had no idea why anyone would think such a thought. ". . . but who also possesses the determination, smarts, and organizational ability to bring off this kind of extraordinary expedition."

Savik squirmed a bit, grinned, always a bit chagrinned by comparison to the actor, George Clooney. His looks might impress Adrienne, but for the Club's members—still mostly men—only performance counted.

Adrienne rested her warm palm on his leg "You'll knock 'em dead," she whispered.

The emcee outlined Savik's adventures with no mention of his day job. Few people here would be the least impressed that he was a full partner in Smithson, Crandall, Kodaly, and Klein, the largest corporate law firm in New York. They reserved their awe for those like themselves bold enough to search out the planet's remaining secrets.

Savik shook his host's hand, and then at the lectern brought up the first photo of a magnificent Mongolian vista with the guys, their guide, a Hun dog, five mounts and remounts, and pack horses all silhouetted against rolling landscape and a vast sky like that of his childhood. "For a cowboy from Montana," he said, "going to Mongolia is not unlike going home."

He led his listeners across grassy vistas and snow-capped peaks, bedded them down beside shaggy camels and blue lakes, invited them into the round, white felt tents called *gers,* the traditional dwellings, and placed them among a running herd of stocky Mongolian horses— "probably the ugliest and toughest horses on the planet," he said. "These horses love to run. The word for giddyup is *tchoo.* If the man riding next to you says *tchoo* without warning you, your horse will be off at a gallop. And in Mongolian there is no word for whoa."

The laughs put him at ease. When he finished forty minutes later, applause and cheers gave him a rush. Not bad for a barn-mucking scraper from the Montana sticks.

"That was amazing," Adrienne said as they left the club. "Exotic, hard-to-believe thrills. You packed it all in." The look in her eyes said that tonight bed was a sure thing.

A passing cab honked as it hurried down the boulevard. The humid afternoon had cooled into a balmy night. He spotted a curbside cart selling flowers, took her hand, and drew her toward the roses. He picked out, sniffed, and paid for a perfect red bud and offered it to her.

"You're a constant surprise, Savik. It's lovely."

She seemed genuinely intrigued by his lifestyle, but he'd discovered that many women faked interest, at first. He waved down a cab. "The Piedmont Building on West 60th," he said to the cabbie.

Inside, Adrienne slid close and pressed against his side. He felt a familiar male stirring, but restraint was required here. He needed more, much more, from this night than sex.

Adrienne asked, "How many street lights are on the block in front of the Explorers' Club?"

He grinned. They'd played this game twice before with the number and makes of cars in a lot and number of tables in the restaurant—minutes after they'd left the premises.

"Too easy. Eight lights. Two with cars illegally parked in front. Two at the alleys. And one with a loiterer standing beside it."

"How do you do it? Tell me! Tonight I insist that you tell me! It's uncanny. Even scary."

"Nothing magical. Just training. Learning to be observant was mandatory in the Green Berets and I still find it useful…" He caught her eye and smiled. "…to entertain dates."

"You don't need to entertain me," she said, placing a hand on his crotch and smiling. A perfumed heat rose up from her cleavage. He lifted her hand and kissed the palm, keeping his gaze riveted to hers in a promise of more to come.

She moved away a little, studying him, then shifted focus. "So, tell me, cowboy, how do you know blue-blooded Winston Hughes?"

"Harvard Law roommates. A scholarship for me, but obviously Winn got there the insider's way." He kissed the tips of her fingers.

"Winn is a determined bachelor if there ever was one. Are you?"

That pesky female question. He traced her palm's lifeline. "Such a serious turn to the conversation. Let's just say that I'm going to owe him some serious cognac for connecting me with a brilliant and beautiful woman I'd never tire of looking at."

It was true. He'd be interested even if Adrienne wasn't the key to eliminating Boswell. When they reached the apartment, the doorman admitted them into The Piedmont's white and gray marbled entry, famous for its Tiffany four-tiered chandelier.

He said, "My whole condo has a great view. Especially the bedroom."

Her voice came back low and husky. "I always enjoy a great view."

If She Is Dirty...

The Piedmont Building

Savik stepped into his condo behind Adrienne and waited in the darkness a moment to allow the view from his wall of windows—a stunning wedge of light-spangled Manhattan—to work its magic on her. The soft glow of city lights worked another kind of magic on Adrienne's skin and deepened the shadows that moved across those breathtaking contours of her cheekbones, neck, and between the tops of her breasts.

"Wow," she whispered.

"I was thinking that same thing." He pressed her against him and kissed her neck.

She gasped, turned to face him, and drew her leg up around him, clamping him to her. Her short satiny dress slid up to reveal a bare thigh. *Whoa.* Adrienne was always five moves ahead of him.

And he didn't particularly like it. Nothing was his idea.

He stepped backward with one foot so that her body weight fell against his slightly as he held her in a classic tango pose. "Shall we dance?" He spun her, letting her know that he controlled the moves. He stopped and held her close. "I bought an album I thought you'd like."

He had to slow things down or he'd never be able to casually steer the conversation onto Lana Boswell. He released her, and the sharp, smoldery gaze she sent him as she tossed her bag onto the slate-gray leather couch unsettled him. Was she upset over his failure to respond to her advances?

He dropped his sport coat and tie on the couch and loosened his shirt collar. He switched on the CD player in the entertainment center. "You said you like Norah Jones. We can listen while I make us a drink."

She smiled and handed him the rose. Behind the wet bar, he stuck it in a glass of water, thinking of the ways to win a woman's heart. Listen to her. Share her secrets. "It's why so many goddamn women throw themselves at you," Lynda had raged in the middle of their divorce, positive he'd betrayed her. He hadn't. He just liked women. But on the first two dates with Adrienne, she'd revealed she was originally more interested in designing clothes than in law, so it would take some effort to fake a lot of interest there.

He blended their drinks and poured them into clear cut-crystal glasses purchased in Venice when he and Lynda had still been married and reasonably happy. Pretty much.

Adrienne lighted candles in the entertainment center, examined photos and artifacts. Then drink in hand, she moved toward the coffee table and ran a finger along the wooden sword displayed in its ebony stand. "Why a wooden sword?"

"It's a Roman *rudus*. Rather valuable and rare. Not intended for fighting." He moved closer. "The Emperor presented a *rudus* to gladiators who survived long enough to retire. If that thing could talk, the stories it would tell."

"Mmmm."

She resumed her exploration. She disappeared into the den and he steeled himself and followed her. She was contemplating his battlefield table, peering intently at the miniature, authentically painted wooden warriors that represented Caesar's forces laying siege to a city in Gaul. Tents. Horses. Catapults.

She gave him a puzzled look as if she thought he were nuts. "What's all this?"

No "Wow! How impressive!" from her. He felt a twinge of disappointment. "It's a hobby. Rome and things Roman. Particularly battles or sieges. I recreate events while reading about them. I'm reading Caesar's *Commentaries*."

"Why the interest in Rome?"

"Power. Romans wielded it in a way the world had never seen. Not long after Caesar conquered Gaul, he changed history. Republic would become empire. The Republic was moribund, wracked by civil war, so Caesar returned in force to put the Roman house in order. But no Roman army was ever supposed to march on Rome."

"I gather Caesar's did." Her interest now seemed genuine.

He nodded. "The return from Gaul was the famous crossing of the Rubicon River that separated Gaul from Italy." Savik downed his drink. "Hundreds of years of republican government—poof!—gone. The fall of a republic can, at the end, be quite sudden, before the people even register it."

She did that woman thing of tossing her hair back. "I've seldom been seduced by intellect...." Somehow a hook at the bust of her wrap-around dress had come undone, and she leaned forward, inviting him to finish the job. "I think it's working. . ."

He kissed the tops of her breasts lightly but pulled quickly away. "I'm glad you don't find ancient history totally dull." He led her by the hand out of the den and toward the coffee table. "But I do have more contemporary interests as well."

"Oh? Current warfare? Politics? Do you care, for example, if Hass is reelected?"

He shrugged. "It's not Hass I care about. It's the security of this country, but that's not the contemporary issue I had in mind," he said, and gestured toward the coffee table.

Now for the tricky part. At the sofa, she stepped out of her heels. He sat and pulled her next to him, right in front of the magazines—*National Geographic*, *Outdoors*, *Forbes*, and on top of all of them, *Harper's Bazaar* with a photo of Senator Lana Boswell on the cover. It had taken Savik's secretary days to find the right magazine having articles on both women.

Adrienne said, "Savik, surely you don't read *Harper's*."

"I do for something special. I had my secretary do a search on you. Typical lawyer snooping. I'm really impressed, Adrienne. One of America's fifty most up-and-coming lawyers." He picked up the *Harper's* and handed it to her with Boswell's face as conspicuous as possible. "Page 57."

She took the last sip of her drink, watching him, either puzzled or suspicious. "I'd forgotten that Lana Boswell is on the cover of this issue. What do you think of her?"

And so to the heart of the matter. "You can probably guess what I think of Boswell. She detests Hass. Obstructs him at every turn. She and I probably disagree politically on just about everything."

"I hadn't given her much thought until recently." Adrienne took another sip.

"Oh?" Yes? And…? He shifted around so that she could lean her back against his chest.

She put the magazine back and curled her legs onto the sofa. "I've been given some information on Boswell. Mostly on her husband. I can't mention any specifics, but it looks like she may not be all that admirable a person."

"She's dirty?"

"I can't mention anything else. It just troubles me."

"Are you going to…pursue it?"

"I probably shouldn't have said anything."

"Fine. I understand. But for what it's worth, I consider Lana Boswell a dangerous woman, and if she *is* dirty, it's your patriotic duty to expose her."

"Strong talk."

Savik pretended to mull things over. "Do you realize that if what you have turns out to be true, Adrienne, your career would go ballistic?"

"Very strong talk."

"You could just ignore me." He kissed the back of her neck.

"Not possible."

She turned to face him, and he kissed her, hands sliding over the satin.

He said, "Let me show you the view from the bedroom."

She took his hand. In the bedroom, he caught her in his arms and planted a slow deep kiss. She eased away and unbuttoned his shirt while he palmed her breasts. He unfastened the dress, letting it fall, and she stood there in her oh-so-feminine lavender bra and matching panties. Her scent was of musky readiness as he unhooked straps and fingered the lace until nothing more covered her.

"God, you're gorgeous," he said.

They didn't use words again until she whispered, "And I'd thought your night moves were a bit slow…."

He moved over her. "Only when they need to be."

. . . . .

Savik lay still with his eyes closed. Another first time. It wasn't that he kept running tallies. Quantity wasn't the issue. He marked the moment, though, because somewhere in his psyche a deep past pleasure had left a high water mark and he was thinking, was tonight as good as it gets? Anything above this wasn't a memory was it? Just fantasy, something he had come to imagine through the years as something special. What the hell else could he ask for? He watched her breathe with the slow pace of one sleeping. A tiny disappointment presented itself. Damned, if he hadn't been hoping she'd say she had to leave so he could sleep alone.

Never satisfied…Jesus God, he was hopeless. Restless as a smoker out of smokes, he left his bedroom and turned to his work, finalizing notes for tomorrow's emergency corporate meeting, on a Sunday no less. Around two thirty he hit the pillows and curled up to Adrienne, mind still running the treadmill of concern for details of the meeting…and of the woman he intended to see beforehand.

If Someone Means To Kill,
They Will Find A Way

The morning after the ball, Claire sat across from Maman at Terrace at the Top, silently staring down at Central Park eighty stories below. In the distance, August haze blurred the silhouettes, making buildings appear to rise out of golden mist.

Claire only briefly took notice, seeing instead images from last night's dreams. Beautiful roses turning brown and then black. Her son John told her he didn't want his children to know her. Of course, he didn't have children, but this was the logic of nightmares. Maman lay in a boat moving toward black sea. And the TOA woman whispered, "Allah will destroy you."

"Are you ready to order?" a young waitress asked.

Claire looked at her mother. "Evidently John's not coming. We might as well."

Maman patted Claire's hand and ordered almond crepes with apple-smoked sausage.

"My stomach is still in a knot." Claire said. "I'll have a muffin and a melon wedge."

After the waitress left, Maman said, "There will never be a perfect time to tell John what he needs to know, *cherie*. And the longer...."

"I've been thinking of it so much lately." This was the destination their conversations often reached. "I'd always thought if I let him go, he'd come back to me on his own..."

"My darling daughter, *bien cherie*. Have you really let him go?"

"What do you mean? I never see him. He doesn't return my calls."

"He tells me you send him self-improvement books, motivational CDs, brochures, applications for this...this...SALT."

"LSAT. Of course. That was the agreement. He could major in athletics if he agreed to go to law school. The tennis thing is something to help him find himself. But it's time he grew up."

"And you see this as letting him go so that he will come back to the plan you have for his life? This is your plan, *cherie*. not his. This need to control—"

Claire threw up her hands, bumping the table so that china and silver clattered. Heads turned toward her, cups and forks suspended in midair.

She waved and gave a little reassuring smile to the suddenly quiet diners, then lowered her voice.

"John is behaving like a privileged playboy. If any number of young men in my schools had his advantages, they'd be running for office by now. David would have persuaded him…"

Her throat ached in an effort to choke back sadness that overtook her when she thought of all the ways in which she—and John—needed and missed David. Eight long years now.

Maman set her cup down, her expression earnest. "If John knew, it might be just what he needs to turn his life around."

"Or I could lose him entirely. Don't you see that?" She took a deep breath. "I can't risk it. I won't. I couldn't endure if I lost both of them."

Mercifully the food arrived. Maman eagerly switched topics. "How I love crepes," she said of the perfectly folded golden crepes, sprinkled with shaved almonds.

Guilt stabbed at Claire. Maman tried unfailingly to keep Claire's relationship with John open to the possibility of re-connection. Such cheer and loving determination deserved Claire's gratitude, not edginess.

The smell of the freshly baked muffin restored Claire's appetite a little, and she forked a slice from the fan of honeydew melon wedges. "Your outfit is the color of my melon!" Claire said. "And that pretty shawl must have come with the dress."

Her mother relaxed into the level of girl talk until Joss bounded their way.

"We still have ten minutes," Claire said looking up to her assistant. "And this time I have my notes."

Joss ignored her. She plopped down next to Claire. "Morning, Nicole. You look gorgeous in that color."

"*Merci.* You also look very nice."

Joss never wore make-up. Maman tried to be gracious, but when it came to Joss there was always a certain hesitance in her words. Today Joss's expensive lavender silk shirt and black slacks did not flatter her Asian complexion and extreme thinness.

Joss smiled at the weak compliment and grabbed a muffin from the basket.

Claire passed the butter and jelly tray. "Is this about that TOA woman last night?"

"No." Joss thrust a newspaper at Claire and then pressed three pats of butter onto the muffin followed by two scoops of plum preserves. "Snide article by your 'best fan,' Phyllis Colson." Joss was hyper, a hummingbird fated to consume several times her weight daily or die.

Claire unfolded the paper. There on a sports page was John and a leggy blonde in a metallic bathing suit…no, that was supposed to be a skirt and perhaps a halter-top. She studied John's face. His smile, aimed directly at the camera, seemed to gloat. Hey, look at me, Ma. I'm a playboy and there's nothing you can do about it. Have I ruined your day yet?

Claire tossed the paper onto the table. Her mother picked it up.

Joss said, "You probably ought to skip reading it, Nicole. The woman hates Claire."

Maman said, "Well, this is a pretty young woman in his company, not a young man. At least…." She'd almost said, 'at least people won't think John's gay.' Her gaze darted to Joss. "Oh, dear. I just mean Claire shouldn't be angry. I mean, don't you think she's pretty, Joss?"

"Sure. She's hot."

Maman blushed to the roots of that silvery-white hair. Claire knew she hadn't meant any negative implication that Joss was a special connoisseur of women, but that's how it sounded.

Maman lifted her napkin to her lips. "You know, I'm just going to shut up now."

"Claire," Joss said, brushing it off, as usual, "you've gotta get that kid into therapy or something. This looks bad to contributors."

"You mean something like, 'Claire Alden is a cook who raised a brat. What gives her the right to interfere in others' lives all over the world? Who does she think she is?'"

"Oh, no, no. *Non*," Maman said. "No one thinks this."

Maybe I do. Claire laid a fifty on the table. To Joss she said, "Is that all?" Joss checked the time. "Let's walk and talk."

As they all headed for the elevator, Joss said, "I have news on the AFWW concert. Good news first. Travel expenses for the delegations from Cameroons and Zambia are all funded now. Second, Carly Simon will sing 'Let the River Run,' in person this year."

"Oh, that *is* wonderful, Joss."

Joss held the elevator door for Maman. "Now some news you're going to hate. Pryce called me this morning. The security people were already pestering him about an increased level of security. Pryce says that because of last night's lunatic, they'll likely double everything. That's another three hundred guards and several thousand bucks."

"I hate having guards hovering all over the concert. The money could be better spent—"

"Pryce says the insurance company won't cover us otherwise, and if they don't, we can't hold the concert at all." Joss touched her arm. "It's a price that has to be paid, love."

Claire slumped against the elevator walls and sighed. "Go ahead."

The door opened onto an explosion of voices. A thousand people were pouring into the ballroom. Flashing again briefly on her nightmare image of the TOA woman, Claire stepped out into the crowd.

Maman said, "Your father always said that if someone means to kill, they will find a way. Extra security only makes them more devious."

Sphere 9

Washington, D.C.

Still humming the morning's recessional hymn, Secretary of Defense, Ronald Bramfeld Hughes, stepped from the brightness of the August Sunday morning into the shade of a canopied entry to the Cork and Bull Restaurant. Two of his Secret Service men entered before him to ensure security. Another stayed with him while the fourth stayed with the limo.

Hughes nodded at a man in a gray suit in front who was smoking, sitting on a wrought-iron bench, one knee trotting in place. The man stubbed out his butt, rose, and approached Hughes.

"Good morning, sir," he said and extended his hand, thumb down.

Hughes shook his hand, feeling the expected small narrow case which he palmed and then pocketed. "And a glorious morning it is."

The man, code named "Hyjinx," moved on down the street. Inside, Hughes spotted retired Air Force Chief of Staff, General Clifford Stanhope, waiting. Not a churchgoer, Cliff was dressed informally in a sport coat, golf shirt, and slacks, unlike Hughes who'd worn a Saville Row suit to attend St. John's 8:00 A.M. service along with his wife Millie and the President and his family. Cliff had asked to meet, panicked over a problem with the PeaceMaker campaign.

Hughes, as usual, attempted to outgrip the general's bionic-vise-like handshake. With innuendos and wisecracks, Cliff often managed to convey a mild contempt for a Secretary of Defense who'd never served in the military, so the show of strength was necessary. What really annoyed Hughes was that at only five feet nine, he had to look up to Cliff's six-two. With his bumpy nose crooked to the side, Cliff had the kind of face that would be an advantage in the military or maybe the Russian mafia. Still ramrod in his mid-sixties, Cliff would turn your bowels to jelly if he followed you on a dark night.

The headwaiter hurried over. "Your table is ready, sir," he said, bowing slightly to Hughes. He led them to a secluded booth in the rear. Hughes slid in. With mousy brown hair, pale round cheeks, and too many liver spots, Hughes accepted that he would always be a behind-the-scenes man, a chess master using other men as his knights and pawns. Strategy and brains had made him one of the most powerful men on Earth.

Their waiter hustled right over. "Your usual?" he asked. Hughes gave a minimal nod.

"I'll have coffee, steak and eggs," Cliff said, "Black. Rare. Scrambled. Nothing else."

His look suggested he could throw the waiter in lock-up if the man got it wrong. The waiter left but quickly returned with Hughes's weekly Bloody Mary, the only alcohol Hughes allowed himself—on Sundays. "Thank God that damn Shakespearian play season is over," Cliff added, apparently stalling. Their wives were promoters of the National Endowment for the Arts events at the Lincoln Center. This reminded Hughes of Claire Alden, whose seat at the last several events had actually been close to his and Cliff's.

Hughes asked, "You hear about the Tears of Allah woman who threatened Claire Alden's shindig last night?"

"Yeah. On late night news. Good thing that TOA bitch is in custody. They should all rot in prison"

Last night Hughes had had an absurd dream about the TOA woman and Claire. Both were in prison. Claire wore that blue gown that revealed her shoulders and the tops of her tits.

Cliff was talking, face gone deadly serious. "…so the whole deal could go south." Cliff booted up his laptop and inserted a flash drive. Only a handful of Sphere 9's board members would ever know what Cliff was about to reveal. A sheen of sweat glazed the forehead of the man whose harsh military strategies earned him the nickname *Icepick*. Cliff clicked open a file marked "PeaceMaker: Component Industries." The screen revealed a prototype/test model of the graceful, white bird-like image of the PeaceMaker satellite, sometimes called IBIS because its solar panels spread like wings, and its laser canon extended like the long bill of a fishing bird. Hughes leaned closer, making certain his words could not be overheard. "This baby isn't an ibis, it's a goose that's gonna lay golden eggs."

Cliff blotted his brow with his napkin. "We're facing a potential disaster, Ron."

As president of the offshore Geiga Bank, Cliff managed the finance end of the private equity firm, Sphere 9, modeled after the phenomenal Carlyle Group that had rocketed to prosperity after 9/11. Sphere 9 made no attempt to hide the fact that it earned millions off the defense industry. Hughes, from deep background at the Pentagon, regularly expedited contracts favorable to the shareholders. Retired Generals and Admirals served as board members and officers—men like Cliff.

Hughes sipped his Bloody Mary, unrattled. The hefty millions Sphere 9 currently raked in could explode into several billion when the PeaceMaker program was implemented. And there was absolutely nothing wrong with that. Keeping America safe and preserving the status quo deserved compensation. Exactly one year after Hughes left office—one year to meet the letter of the law—Hughes would publicly replace the current puppet as Sphere 9 Chairman of the Board with Cliff its CEO. Nice and legal. And then they'd reap the amazing return on the PeaceMaker venture. Hughes would never reveal to anyone, not even his son Winn, that he and Cliff, in secret deals from behind closed doors, had arranged the financing of Winn's company.

Hughes said, "Winn is thrilled with the test. We're taking care of Congress." *Savik Kodaly better come through.* "I make sure the Pentagon rubber stamps. So why are you sweating?"

"It's not that simple." Cliff scrolled through files. "We have a competitor for the free-electron laser canon. And three of our component companies are in trouble. Geiga Bank has seized their assets, but we can't restructure in time. We can't win the bid without them."

"What? Jesus! Tell me right now that you came here with options."

"At this late stage, we'd have to simply buy replacement companies. I worked damn hard to find three good ones, but the buyouts would require capital that would plunder Sphere 9's other assets and bankrupt Geiga Bank if our companies don't win the bidding."

Hughes's chest tightened as if his heart had slammed to a stop. "Son of a bitch." He carefully took a deep breath so that Cliff wouldn't notice. "Let's see them."

Cliff's steak and eggs arrived without so much as a sprig of parsley. The waiter set their food down nervously. Hughes smiled and ordered that the busboys stay clear.

Cliff pulled up info on a French firm in Canada that built parts for state-of-the-art solar panels. He scrolled further showing a Brazilian niobium mine. He clicked another screen. "We're in position for a hostile takeover of this cool-plasma lab in Tennessee."

Hughes tried for nonchalance. "They make their own sauerkraut and rye bread here." He was trying to recover his appetite. Sauerkraut dangled over the edges of his rye crust.

Cliff eyed the sandwich with disdain. He sopped his eggs in beef blood before forking them into his mouth. Finally he said, "This package could go as high as four hundred-fifty mil. We're talking pretty much all-or-nothing here, Ron."

"Do it! And buy out the electron laser guy, easy or hard."

Cliff dabbed at the sweat on his upper lip. Clearly, as far as Hughes was concerned, their breakfast meeting was over.

Cliff pulled the flash drive and turned off the notebook that was never connected to anything but a thumb drive and charger. "We'll make it happen. The world is a goddamn scary place, Ron. We're never going to kill all the goat-humping terrorists with any war. But with PeaceMaker, we can reach the motherfuckers anywhere, and they'll know it. That'll stop the bastards."

Hughes, who rarely swore, stood, thinking how profane military men were. "Well, with these local Tears of Allah maniacs, it might not be politically correct to zap *them*, but we could sure zap their overseas cousins in retaliation. That'd make 'em think twice."

He left three twenties on the table. SS men in tow, he walked out with Cliff, shook his hand quickly at the door, and parted. In the back of the limo as he headed home to Millie, Hughes pulled a cell phone from his breast pocket and speed dialed Savik Kodaly's number.

After five rings, a groggy voice announced, "Savik."

"This is Ron. You still in bed?"

A pause and rustling noise on the other end. "Sorry. Wait a sec. Uh…'scuse me." Finally Savik said, "Adreinne's still here."

"So did she take the bait?"

"I can't talk now. I'm late. I have a meeting at Tabor Towers. I'll have to call later."

"Make it soon." Hughes hit "end," hating it when world-changing events depended on the sensibilities of women.

He opened his own laptop, booted it and inserted the flash drive Hyjinx had delivered, then scrolled to the report he'd requested: on the Tears of Allah woman who'd disrupted the banquet of Claire's group. First name, Naheed. She'd been arrested and had made the mistake of bragging that Allah's vengeance would happen very soon. The FBI was called in. Homeland Security took over. "Imminent threat" was invoked; she was further sequestered from the protections of law. The classified report listed enhanced interrogation techniques they'd employed. The President had reinstated their use "for imminent national security reasons."

Hughes selected the video attachment and turned the sound down so he could hear but his driver couldn't. An interrogator held a naked, young Middle-eastern woman by her long, wavy hair. With a quick swipe, he cut the hair off with a knife.

A second man duct taped her mouth, covered her head with a black hood, and tied her handcuffed hands behind her to a chest-level hook on the wall, forcing her head down. Her round tits hung below the hood.

Hughes fast-forwarded during the subsequent four-minute pit-bull attack. Odd to see the accelerated, darting actions of the attack dog, tearing at her legs. The woman at first fought back, kicking at the beast. Finally her interrogator pulled the dog off, lifted the hood off, asking again. She nodded. It was depressing looking at her there all bloody.

The second man unhooked her and she dropped into a chair shoved under her. Hughes slowed the speed to normal. The woman was shaking. His own breathing quickened and he swallowed hard.

One ripped the tape off her mouth. Another gave her an injection. She calmed down and finally spewed names of members of "Tears of Allah."

Hughes figured most were already known, some names so common they were the equivalent of John Jones and Jane Smith. When asked certain names, she readily agreed. She was saying anything she could think of to avoid the dog. Finally she admitted that an attack on a celebrity would take place soon.

Her interrogator spoke kindly to her. "When and where, Naheed?"

The pitch of her voice rose as high as a child's, soft and tentative, holding back tears. "On the infidel Claire? It could be...her? I swear by Allah, they do not tell us the planning."

Claire. The thought alarmed Hughes. Why did he find Claire Alden so fascinating? He loathed her ideas but was drawn to her nevertheless. He looked out the window of the limo, and, seeing the Bethesda Naval Hospital, shut his computer down. He was nearly home.

These terrorists were rabid beasts, sending their women to do their dirty work, forcing good men to torture women. Tabor Towers security for the upcoming Claire Alden speech in New York would be plenty adequate. Still, he envisioned for a moment the upside of what would happen if suicide bombers did get through to her. Hurting Claire could ignite a national rage that would make taxpayers wake up. They wouldn't just approve PeaceMaker, they'd demand it.

He smiled, then drew a deep breath. It was staggering, and humbling, to think of the power God had allowed to flow into his hands. Hass always deferred to him, and usually without much question. So in truth it was actually Hughes who was the most powerful man in the world. And he intended to keep it that way.

He felt a stirring in his groin. He'd always prided himself on the moral fiber required to remain faithful to his wife, no matter that his fantasies might sometimes stray. How fascinating the connection of sex and power. And sex would once again play a useful role in his fate and that of the nation if Savik were successful with Adrienne, and she then went after the Boswell woman.

The thought was in some ways blasphemous, but God did work in mysterious ways. The refrain from the recessional hymn came back to him—Praise God from whom all blessings flow. He hummed it as the limo pulled into his driveway.

Women In Kaftans

New York

Savik checked his watch. Despite the pressures of the day, he still intended to see Claire Alden. The dark-skinned cabbie caught Savik's eye in the rearview mirror.

"Traffic is a beetch this morning," he said with an Indian accent. "You George Clooney?"

"No. But I get that sometimes."

Savik punched his cellphone speed dial for the tenth floor Tabor Tower legal offices of March and Jankowski. The massive Tower housed restaurants, shops, and offices on floors ten through fifteen in addition to its hotel rooms. The secretary answered. "Good morning. March Jankowski."

"Janell, this is Savik Kodaly. You're a peach to come in on a Sunday. I'll drop off the Whitmere files as soon as I arrive, but Claire—you know, Claire Alden—is giving an address downstairs at eleven. I'd like to catch at least ten minutes of it. Can you delay my meeting with Jankowski thirty minutes?"

"Sure. Everyone knows she's speaking. Big crowd already. Police cordons. Armed guards all over. I'm impressed that you want to see her. I'm a big fan. I'll let Mr. Jankowski know about the delay. It won't be a problem. He's got another crisis."

"Thanks, Janell."

The cabby caught Savik's gaze again. "You going to listen to the Claire? She very nice. I am from Sumidar, and she bring my people peace. I love the Claire."

"A lot of people do."

A brown van with darkened windows pulled in front of the cab and stopped at the curb. A lone woman in a blue kaftan and turban jumped out and headed for Tabor Towers.

"Good place to stop," the cabbie said.

Savik paid his fare and, brief-case in hand, exited the taxi quite a distance from Tabor Towers. The entrance was overflowing with people. A great many were women, and many wore ethnic garb like you'd see in some soft drink ad showing everybody in the world happily drinking the product.

He noted at once a significantly beefed up security. Janelle had been right about that. Two guards were patrolling with dogs. Dogs were good, but even they couldn't guarantee safety. He could name ten explosives that dogs couldn't detect at all.

The woman in the blue kaftan was well ahead of him. Speedy gal for someone so heavy. She and another woman, similarly dressed but in a green kaftan converged on the steps without greeting.

He gripped his briefcase and, flanked by gold ropes cordoning off the streams of human traffic, moved in the direction of the two dark-skinned women in kaftans and turbans. At least they seemed to be women. Something about their walk—a stiff, heavy gait—struck him as peculiar.

He followed them through security check stations looking in bags and briefcases for weapons. His briefcase passed.

People around him jabbered away, wildly excited about getting in to see Claire. But not the two women. A pushy group of mannish women in slacks, the kind Willie called "feminazis," cut off his view of the women in kaftans.

Annoyed and feeling disturbingly curious, he dodged several clusters to follow them. Mobs milled around in front of the elevators, reminding him of sheep being loaded into cattle cars. To avoid the hoard, he decided to take escalators. Savik hurried toward an *up* escalator, still trailing the kaftanned women. In passing, he noticed a sign:

Nobel Prize Winner, Claire Alden

"The challenge of our generation: To end war."

Second Floor Ballroom, 11:00 a.m.

End war. Yeah. Right.

At the Mezzanine level he stepped off and turned to take the escalator up another floor to the ballroom. The place was a security nightmare. Watching the women, he felt an uncomfortable itch at the back of his brain. It was the kind of itch that, from his Green Beret training, called for immediate attention.

The women, still in front of him, separated. No smiles. No hugs. No "see you laters." One took the up escalator. The other headed toward the elevators. Her stride was stiff. Her back abnormally straight.

He stepped onto the escalator a bit behind the woman in blue. She pulled a cell-phone out of a bag and gripped it like the remote control of a TV, not like she planned to make a call.

He was already rushing up behind her before he was fully aware of his thought.

Bomb!

They stepped off the escalator. With one hand he grabbed her arm and with the other grabbed the "cell phone" that his gut instinct registered as a detonator. He shoved her against the nearby wall, pinned her to it, swept his free hand over the front of the kaftan—and felt unmistakable bulges that couldn't be anything a woman would wear.

She flailed. Kicked him, screeching something he couldn't understand, and strained to snatch the cell phone he held just beyond her reach.

A security guard, from fifty feet away, launched himself in their direction.

"Bomb!" Savik yelled again.

The woman raked fingernails down his cheek leaving a trail of fire on his skin. Her body still pinned against the wall with his body, he held up the cell phone device for the guard to see. "Suicide bombers. There's another. Dressed the same, in green."

Savik flung the detonator into a huge ficus pot, then, struggling to keep her from escaping, pinned her arms to her sides. The guard braked in front of them. He and the guard thrust her onto the floor. The guard pulled out handcuffs. "Clear the building!" Savik commanded. I'm going after the other one!"

The second women, apparently having used the elevator, was near the entry to the grand ballroom where Claire would probably have started speaking.

Claire. His Claire!

Pushing surprised and complaining people aside, he sprinted toward her. "There's a bomber in this building," he yelled. "Clear out. Clear out!"

The turbaned woman passed through the entry into the ballroom. Pulse pounding his ears, Savik ran toward the security guard positioned by the door. The man, who had been talking into his communicator, whirled toward the ballroom entry and dashed inside.

White Programs Splattered Red

"What a beautiful sea of faces, women's and men's," Claire said, sweeping her arm to embrace her several hundred listeners. There was Maman, sitting at the far end of the head table just below the podium, looking up at Claire and beaming maternal pride. She waved discreetly at Claire, and Claire winked back.

AFWW logos hung all over the hall, emblazoned on long emerald green banners draped from the twenty foot high main ceiling. The introductions were over, the thank-yous said. The audience was ready for a satisfying main course.

"Empowering the world's women is critical to any hope for creating a future where war fits in the same relics-of-the-past category as witch-burning, gladiatorial games, and slavery. All of you know how I feel about balance. Women and men are partners in living, partners in creating. We know what government by men alone produces, for better but also sadly for worse. We see it all around us. The global community needs to experience metanoia. A change of heart that will change cultures. For starters, our U.S. congress needs to fully mature into a near fifty-fifty ratio of women and men...."

A movement at the door to her left caught her eye, a woman coming in late, dressed in a green kaftan and turban. The woman hurried along the colonnade of green marble pillars that circled the low-ceilinged perimeter of the room, staring fixedly at Claire.

A guard ran in behind the woman, pointed a gun and yelled at her. "Freeze!"

"*Ensha'Allah!*" the woman screamed.

A blast of sound, a fireball of red and black. A massive wall slammed against Claire's body, flattened her on her back, slammed her head against the floor.

She lay stunned, deaf, blind. No thoughts.

Then came shrieks, screams, wails, the sounds of falling debris. Glass trickled like water drops from a sprinkler. Slowly her mind registered the tiled ceiling of the ballroom.

She sucked in a breath. Now her lungs burned as though she'd inhaled fire. Panic choked her. The need to flee jerked her upright. And then the thought, *Maman.*

Claire pushed to her feet. Swaying. Her head swam. She put her hands to it as if to keep it from flying off her shoulders. Maman.

The hall resembled a battlefield, its deadly center to her left. Bodies on the floor. Shattered tables. White programs splattered red. Many people were standing, but dazed. A tossed salad of everything smaller than a table was all mixed in chaos.

And in the space, now utterly ravaged, from where the woman had entered, from where the blast had erupted, stood…Savik Kodaly.

She put her hand to her forehead. *Not possible. Am I dying? Going insane? Savik Kodaly?*

"Maman!" she cried out loud, like a lost child.

This Wasn't Battle

Savik had seen battle. This wasn't battle, it was butchery of innocents. The results looked, smelled, and sounded like his worst day in Syria. Blood. Urine. Choking dust and ash. Acrid explosive residue. Moans and screams of the wounded and dying. A severed arm, this one a young woman's with rings on three fingers and a small tattoo on the forearm.

Along the ceiling, water cascaded from broken pipes that should have set off overhead sprinklers. Fires burned here and there, but people were grabbing extinguishers along the walls.

He scanned the front of the room. *Where was Claire?* The bomb had detonated nearer the front, but he did not see her. He scanned to the back of the ballroom. Barely touched. People clogged the doorways, trying to escape. Some were helping the wounded.

Above him a chandelier made a tearing sound, and lost its hold on the ceiling. He flung himself at a youngish woman in its path, tackling and pinning her to the floor only inches from shattering glass, crystal shrapnel shooting out and ripping his sleeve. The woman seemed okay. He scrambled to his feet and helped her up.

"Sherice…" she croaked. She moved toward a body hidden under the heap that had been the chandelier.

He lied. "I'll help her. You go on. Help others to get out." If the woman under the chandelier hadn't been dead from the blast before the chandelier hit her, she was now. His help, her friend's help, they were both too late. "Sherice," she cried out again, and fell to her knees, staring at the massive pile of shattered glass.

He felt a slight tug from behind on his pant leg. A desperate gray-haired woman stretched her arm toward him from under an overturned table. He grabbed the edge of the table and heaved it upright and away from her.

"Please," she said, her voice cracking.

He knelt and reached for her. She clutched at his jacket and pulled herself toward him. Another woman lay beside her, one of her arms bleeding dark blood. He pulled the second woman around so he could place the first woman's hands just above the bleeding wound. "Press hard," he commanded. "It's not an artery, but you have to keep pressure on until help arrives."

The woman nodded. A third victim under the table, a nattily dressed gray-haired man who might have been a professor, was dead. His left leg lay in a still expanding pool of red. "This is a big hotel," Savik said to the two women. "Just hang in there. There's probably an on-site health center. Emergency services will show up quickly."

Security personnel had forced their way past the panicked droves and were now seeking more wounded needing help. He stood, searching for Claire. Over the anguished cries and desperate calls for help, he heard her voice. "Maman," she called out. Her voice wasn't all that loud, it was just that he knew it. He could still pick Claire's voice out of a crowd.

Bent and straining, she was pushing against a pillar. Savik thrust aside a bloodied, empty chair blocking his path and headed for her.

Trust John!

A pillar of green marble, a foot in diameter, blown out of the colonnade, had become a projectile that hit the head table, trapping the three women seated there under a flattened mess. Claire stared, horrified. The weight of the pillar was crushing them. The head table, cracked and its legs having broken in opposite directions, now, maddeningly, cradled the massive fragment in place. To free the women the pillar needed to slide back toward the wall, like a log down a chute.

"Move, goddamn it!" Claire screamed as she strained against the column. "Oh, god, Maman! Hold on!"

Weren't mothers of trapped children able to lift automobiles? Her arms ached. Her back burned. She sucked in a breath and imagined the column moving at her command as she pushed so hard she thought her guts would rupture.

"I'll help," said a male voice from the other end.

"Oh, yes, please. Hurry!"

The man kicked at something to clear away whatever was blocking the pillar.

She looked, and this time she knew she wasn't hallucinating. Savik Kodaly, hunched down, nudged her aside, and heaved the end of pillar upward. The hairs raised on her arms. The pillar moved. Claire shoved, felt the muscles in her neck and arms bulging. The pillar budged.

"Again on three," Savik said. "One, two, three!"

Hot blood rushed to her head. The pillar slid three feet, enough for Savik to use the broken table as a wedge to lift the column's weight off the trapped women. Two other men appeared and helped finish the lift.

As Claire dropped beside her mother the question flashed at the back of her mind, what about Joss? Had Joss been somewhere in the room?

God, Maman lay so still. For a moment Claire feared to touch her. The fear fled and she grabbed her mother's hand and touched her cheek. She sensed rather than saw that Savik moved toward the body of the TARA event coordinator and to Donna Devlin, president of Women in the Arts for Peace.

"Maman, I'm here."

A livid streak of red appeared at the corner of her mother's mouth and ran down onto her chin. Chills rippled over Claire's body. She could see nothing else wrong, nothing else amiss. No hurt limbs, no bloody spots on the lovely soft green dress. But, that horrid red streak. She felt tears burning down her cheeks.

Her mother frowned, groaned, and then her eyes fluttered open.

"Maman, my god." Her mother was going to be all right. Yes, she was.

"Something hurts so bad inside, *cherie.* I can't move."

"Someone will be here to help soon."

Savik knelt on the other side of her mother, looked toward the other women and then looked at Claire in silence. He shook his head.

"Both?" Her voice was a croak.

His grim expression told her what she couldn't bear to know—Donna and the coordinator were dead. *Not Maman, though. Please, god. I cannot lose anyone else.*

She felt her mother squeeze her hand. "This . . .not at all how I thought . . .it would be."

"Don't talk." Over her shoulder to Savak she said in desperation, "Why isn't help coming? Where are they? Why don't they hurry?"

"Trust John," her mother murmured. "Let him make own decisions."

"John loves you more than his life. Maman. You must hang on for him."

"Do this for me, Claire. . . ."

Claire felt a loosening of her mother's grip. "Stay, Maman. Don't leave!"

Her chest heaved and another, ominous blood streak coursed along the track of the first. Her eyes closed. She frowned again.

Claire kissed her mother's hand. "I'm here. I love you so much. Help is coming."

"Let him go," her mother whispered. She took a small breath, and then . . . utter stillness.

"Maman?" Claire stroked the uncannily limp hand. "Maman," she said, louder.

She felt Savik's palm on her shoulder.

She gasped, tasted the salty tears. She knew. *No. No. No.*

A man wearing whites knelt beside them. He reached toward her mother.

"Don't touch her!" Claire commanded. She drew a shaky breath. After a moment her voice softened, gentled. "We'll let her rest a while." She paused, a sudden weight of lonely future years pressing on her shoulders. "There's no need to hurry now."

I Don't Hate Her

Dressed only in sweat-pants, John opened the front door of his apartment, stepped out, picked up the Sunday paper and brought it into the kitchen. Fance was humming while frying bacon and watching a mute CNN on the portable. One of his old mesh T-shirts did nothing to hide the smooth curves of her butt. She'd gathered her hair into a loose ponytail of pastel and blonde waves, and from behind, he kissed the back of her neck.

She purred. "I hope you think this morning is as great as I think it is?"

"Mmmmmmmm." His exhausted manhood produced a minimal but still appreciative response. The coffee maker gave out its last gurgle. "Caffeine fix. Finally."

He poured them both a cup and then searched the sports pages for photos of them at the tennis tournament's opening party. Nothing in the sports section. Damn. Something had to be there. There'd been lots of camera flashes. He flipped to the society section.

"HA!"

Fance squealed. "Us?"

"Yeeeeaaaaaahhhh."

She sat on his lap and they looked at the picture, giggling and sharing memories of oglers. The smell of bacon about to burn made her dash to the stove. He fixed scrambled eggs with onions and chilies while Fance toasted English muffins. He read the article out loud as they ate.

When he finished, Fance said, "That Colson woman sounds mean. She digs at you—us—but in a way that cuts at your mom."

"Colson's a bitch. But I wouldn't be surprised if my mom did something to tick her off."

Fance frowned. "I read somewhere a girl should never fall for someone with a bad credit rating or who hates his mother. You don't really hate your mom, do you, John?" Her teaser of a smile returned. "Not that I'm falling for you…."

"Sure you are." He kissed her palm, making a loud smooching noise. She deserved an answer, especially after the way he'd gone off last night when she praised his mother's show. "I resent it like hell that my mother not only tries to run my life, but that she, who is not the perfect angel everyone thinks she is, believes she has the *right* to run it. But I don't hate her."

Fance wasn't looking at him. She was staring over his shoulder.

"Will that answer keep me on your list of good—"

"John!" She pointed at the TV. "Turn on the sound!"

As he reached for the remote, scenes of the interior of a devastated large building appeared on the screen. Then an outside shot of the Tabor Towers Building, roped off and surrounded by emergency vehicles. Tabor Towers....

Oh my God.... He stood and raised the volume.

"...update on the body count. Nineteen people were killed with many others wounded, some critically. About a hundred fifty people are being treated or rushed to emergency care. Ironically, the event was a convention supporting women as leaders in making war obsolete. Claire Alden, the guest speaker, is believed to be—" The reporter paused only a moment, then, "We're able to air footage from the scene released to CNN by the event coordinators."

The camera was on his mother. She was speaking. An instant, then a fiery cloud turned red and black. The image went dead.

The announcer spoke again. "The photographer escaped injury and began filming the devastation. We should have that footage for you momentarily. New York attorney Savik Kodaly, a former Green Beret, prevented another woman from detonating more explosives concealed on her body. So the only good news in this grim situation is that it could have been much worse. We go now to the inside view of the immediate aftermath of the blast."

There appeared a vast room, air thick with dust, people running. A crashing sound produced screams. A shot of a chandelier in a heap on the floor, dust rising and people scattering. The picture went black, as if a hand covered the lens. And then . . . .

John's insides knotted. A man was kneeling beside a woman who was, unmistakably, his mother, and cradled in his mother's arms was a woman with white hair. He swallowed hard. *Grandmere....*

It was only a split second on the screen, then back to a woman's face.

"What you just glimpsed," the newscaster said, "was Claire Alden, who is believed to have sustained only minor injuries, saying farewell to her mother, Nicole DeNevers Alden."

Fance was saying something. The reporter's voice blurred. John stood stock still a moment and then slowly walked toward the door.

He was halfway across the room when Fance tried to stop him. He pushed her away, grabbed his wallet, sweatsuit jacket, and keys from the hutch, opened the door, stepped into the hallway and started running toward the stairwell.

"John," he heard her yell. "Don't run away from me!"

He blundered downward, through the lobby and into the street.

Grandmere.

He ran until it hurt too much to run any longer. And then he just walked and kept on walking. When he finally stopped, he realized he had no idea how he'd arrived at Grant's Tomb in Riverside Park or where he thought he was going, and he was barefoot.

Would You Settle For
An Eye-for-an-Eye?

Alone in the house a week after the bombing, Claire stood in her closet staring. Was there anything she could stand to wear to Maman's memorial service? For days she'd worn the same sweats indoors and outside in the mild weather. Now she had two hours to pull herself together.

If John had come to see her, she would have rallied. If he had come and grieved with her, she could have honored Maman's last wishes and told him….Her mind fogged over with an image of Maman dying yet thinking only of reconciliation between her daughter and grandson. Claire's face grew wet again from tears that continued to seep without warning.

If only John would come. She brushed the tears away.

John was hurting as much as Claire was and probably dealing with it the way he had when David died. Fifteen at the time, he'd slipped off into the woods around the ranch in Washington for a week. She'd told this to John's girlfriend Fance when Fance called on the horrible day of the bombing. "But he has disappeared in New York City," Fance said. "He's totally alone."

Alone. Like John, Claire had isolated herself. Her dearest friends were tying to comfort her. That Sunday night her close friend Serena had cancelled sessions at her compound near Tuxedo Lake to be with Claire for a few days. Serena would be back in an hour or so to accompany Claire to the service. Yet even the friend the media called her "guru" had not been able to penetrate or lessen this crushing pain.

Her dear Rachel would be arriving soon too, but Rachel had such enormous problems of her own that Claire didn't want to burden her. Rachel's CMT had worsened, and she usually required a wheelchair. Des, Claire's groundsman, was always around, and wise enough to keep his distance. Florence, her housekeeper, did the same. Alex seldom left her shoulder or hovered nearby, preening her hair or nibbling her skin in what seemed like avian sympathy.

Something to wear. *Decide.*

Alex flew to the top of her bed poster and began preening as she rifled through hanging garments. Every possible outfit looked depressing, ugly. Clothing that would mark the last farewell. All because Maman had insisted on supporting Claire's crusade.

If only Maman had stayed in Paris a little longer, she would be alive. But she came to the speech and they killed her. And nineteen others.

I fight for women's rights all over the world, and it had to be a woman who did this!

She blindly grabbed a handful of dresses on hangers and threw them to the floor.

Evil, blind, fanatic bitches! Stupid, stupid, stupid! I hope their families' houses and their hatred-fostering mosques burn to the ground, and they all die of plague!

An exquisite hand-loomed Muslim prayer shawl caught her eye. The one she'd bought in Bangladesh for Maman. She snatched it off its hanger, opened a drawer, grabbed scissors and began cutting the material to shreds. Destroying felt good. Tatters joined the dresses on the floor at her feet.

"Messy, messy, messy!" Alex said, perfectly mimicking the housekeeper.

Claire stopped cutting. She stared at the pile on the floor. *Crazy woman.*

She started laughing, at first a high giggle and then belly laughs. She couldn't stop. She wrapped her arms around herself and bent over until the fit subsided. She straightened. The remaining bits of savaged cloth hung in her hands. "I loved this shawl, Maman."

She scooped up and hugged what was left of the shawl, backed up to the bed and sat, rocking back and forth as sobs shook her body. Alex flew onto the top of her head and resumed preening.

"Hello, sunshine," he said. Sometimes Alex got things so wrong.

She stood. Alex flew. The pale woman in her mirror had bloodshot eyes. "I need to get out of this damn house."

Spending time at the animal shelter was one of the few things able to take her mind off the horror. She had named her home "The Retreat" partly because its six woodland acres backed up against the State Wildlife Preserve outside Poughkeepsie. She found peace here, listening to the chatterings in the passerine aviary, feeding the Animal Shelter menagerie, watching Desi's dark form muck about in his boots and khakis.

Desmond Pruett was a divorced male nurse, an ex-navy corpsman burnt-out from his job in a hospital who only found comfort in caring for animals and so had become a licensed wildlife rehabilitator. Claire had hired him as groundskeeper but encouraged his rescue center for wildlife. Together they renovated the old barn, which now included a small apartment for him. Des became the official "doc" for the wounded or abandoned animals people began bringing to "The Retreat."

Leaving Alex inside—outdoors he'd be exposed to hawks—Claire crossed the narrow bridge that spanned the creek separating the "Wildlife Refuge" from the house and gazebo. She sought out Braveheart, a red fox that had won her over. Serena would know to find her here.

Braveheart slipped out from a wooden doghouse big enough for a Great Dane. Limping badly, he zigzagged to a boulder and then a birch stump, orange-brown eyes matching his coat color always watching her.

Des' approach took her by surprise. He carried a small bag of raw chicken. "Glad to see you out of the house," he said. He gave a chunk to Claire. She squeezed a leg and a thigh through the wires of the pen's eight-foot high grid fencing and then backed away to stand beside Des.

The squeaky-pump-handle call of a rescued bluejay with a broken wing accompanied Braveheart's dash toward the chicken. He snatched a piece in his jaws and ran back to sit in front of the doghouse, his tail a thick red paintbrush dipped in white at the tip.

"You've done wonders with Braveheart and his mate," Claire said.

"You really shouldn't—"

"I know. We don't name them. But with Braveheart, I can't help it."

If you name them, Des always told volunteers, you bond with them, and perhaps they with you, making the release back into the wild difficult for both human and animal. Rehabilitate and release—that was their motto.

Hearing footsteps on the bridge, she and Des turned. Serena Hestin joined them, dressed for the memorial service in her signature white embroidered with peace symbols and gold jewelry that symbolized various religions. Tall, part Hindi, dark wavy hair falling to her waist. Though her hair was streaked with far more salt than pepper, she looked much younger than her sixty years. Serena hugged Claire and then Des.

Des said, "I'm sorry I can't get away. Sick deer." He squeezed Claire's hand. "I am so very sorry, Claire. Your mother was a beautiful and special lady. And don't you worry. Your boy will turn up." He smiled at Serena and left.

"Worrying about John on top of all this, I'm going crazy," Claire said. "John loved Maman so much. How can he have just disappeared? Is he drinking? Is he hurt? God."

"Have you heard anything from Pryce or Joss?"

"Joss called an hour ago. Francine Showalter—Fance—still hasn't heard from John. They've all dogged the police but there's been nothing. I desperately need to talk to him."

"He may come to the service."

Something spooked Braveheart. He stood and crouched for a moment, then sped into the dog house.

"That fascinating face…" Serena whispered.

"Braveheart is special. He was found guarding his vixen," Claire said. "She was caught in a trap, poor thing, barely alive. She was also pregnant, and he was chewed up from fighting off who knows what predators, probably dogs….But he wouldn't leave her….Never left…."

Claire's voice cracked. Tears brimmed and a few spilled down her face. She swiped them away. Two people in her life had loved her enough to stand by her like this fox, fiercely to the death if necessary, and both were gone. David first and now, so cruelly, Maman.

Serena put her arm around Claire.

"I'm okay. So, anyway, Des saved them both." Claire nodded toward the fox's den. "The mother's paw is healed, and it's almost time to release her and the kits."

"Yours is a brave heart, Claire," Serena said.

Claire stopped. "NO! No, what I am is a total fraud." She shook her head. "I've started fantasizing ways of getting *revenge* on the Tears of Allah people."

"Mm-hmm."

"I have no solace. I can't summon the forgiveness and understanding my Quaker faith taught me. Line up a hundred of them, give me a gun, and I'd shoot them right this minute. With Jesus watching. Bullets right to the head."

She'd spoken as coldly and calmly as she possibly could, and still the words came out broken with emotion. Claire felt instant guilt and regret, shamed by the rage that burned her cheeks.

Serena drew a deep breath. "Ah…." She checked her watch. "Let's sit in the gazebo."

"I'm an emotional mess. How can I possibly face people?" She followed Serena into the structure, which overlooked the creek. Claire had expanded it into a meditation porch. For the last few days, any such attempt had miserably failed. Her prayers and thoughts simply melted into vague pools of shadow and light. Or a replay of unbearable images.

They sat on a bench, side by side. "What you need, if you're going to function," Serena said, "is to get the rage out of your system."

"I most definitely need something. I just destroyed an absolutely beautiful shawl."

Serena smiled. "I'm not going to ask for the details. But try this. Instead of killing a hundred of your enemies, would you settle for an eye for an eye? Tooth for a tooth? Imagine killing an equal number, twenty, and merely maiming a hundred more."

Claire forced herself to consider again a fantasy execution. Images of faces of the two captured Tears of Allah women popped into her brain. Faces ugly with defiance. Other faces came to her from the stoning in Bangladesh, yet already the fantasy of shooting or even stoning them was losing its appeal.

"It's a funny thing about rage," Serena said. "It knows no sense of proportion. It demands great drama. And rage can be used. A personal grievance can fuel a holocaust, or it can, instead, be channeled into positive action..."

"That's what you want from me, right? To channel the rage."

"It's what you'll want for yourself."

This was no doubt true, but Claire couldn't imagine fast-forwarding to such a time.

Serena added, "You and I both know that when the wounds heal a little more, you'll work even more tirelessly for your causes. And you'll find a way to forgive. For your own sake."

"You're right about getting the venom out. But forgiving...." She shook her head.

Serena gave Claire's shoulders a little squeeze. "It's time, dear girl, to get dressed."

Claire looked into Serena's brown eyes, then turned for one last look at the fox pen, the creek with morning light sparkling on stones and ripples, birch leaves dappling reflections in the calm pools, a blue jay that matched the blue of the sky.

A prayer formed. Please, make my heart brave. Guide John. Help me restore my... equanimity. Help us through this nightmare.

This Was Completely
The Wrong Time

Claire stepped into Manhattan's famous St. Patrick's Cathedral through a side entrance. The crowd of over two thousand mourners had entered and settled to the strains of Maman's favorite music from Faure, Debussy, Chopin, and Saint Sans played by concert musicians. Grateful for the privacy her mourning hat's wide brim provided, Claire searched the crowd for John, for a glimpse of his face, but none of the young men was her boy.

Disappointment threatened to crumple her into a boneless heap. Fighting back, she straighted and focused on the support she did have, the friends with her in the front row. Adam Forsythe would be speaking today. Maman had danced with him at the TARA Ball, her last dance.

Pryce Pierce sat on the end next to Adam. Always dapper in his closely trimmed mustache and goatee, Pryce was Claire's PR man, tall, lean, brown-haired with a receding hairline and strands of white at the temples. His cool gray eyes seldom betrayed personal emotions, but if anyone else in her inner circle was having thoughts of revenge against the terrorists, it was Pryce. She found this oddly comforting. He'd been with her from the very beginning, through thin gruel and thick gravy—from "Cooking For Lovers," through EClaire, and the joy of the Nobel Prize.

Joss sat next to Adam, equally indispensable to Claire, and as treasured as a niece. Rachel sat beside Joss, her wheelchair standing empty in the outer aisle. Serena sat to Claire's right.

To Serena she whispered, "He has to come." John would be there. He would. She scarcely registered anything, not even the magnificent music. She was desperate to talk to him, to help alleviate the guilt she knew was torturing him.

Joss took Claire's hand in a gentle squeeze of sympathy. Blue-gray rings under Joss's eyes revealed her fatigue and grief. Joss had done a terrific job organizing the service, including all the votive candles, hundreds of them, maybe a thousand. The votive candles were what Claire loved best about cathedrals. They cast the high walls and arched beams in a mystical, gentle light.

Maman had allowed Claire's grandmother, Rebecca Alden, to raise Claire as a Quaker, and like most Quakers, Claire usually preferred simplicity. All this elegance seemed a bit false to her in terms of the soul. Her very French Maman, however, would have wanted everything just as it was, the grand music, the candles, the pomp and stateliness of the priest and his entourage, all in churchly robes.

The soloist, a soprano from the Metropolitan Opera who'd attended the TARA Ball, began "Ave Maria." Claire pinched shut her burning eyes.

Near the song's end, a rustling on her left caught her attention. On the aisle, on the other side of Pryce, sat her son, his hair still ridiculously bleached at the tips, head bowed, his shoulders slumped. *Thank God.*

She wanted him sitting beside her so much that she almost called out. Instead, she extended her arm toward him. He didn't look at her. She withdrew her hand. At least he was there. He was her handsome, beloved boy, as always. He'd even worn a dark sport coat—she felt amazed that he had one—but he looked terribly ragged.

Adam rose and spoke of his memories of Maman as a diplomat's wife. Serena's talk stressed the need to make the most of every moment allotted on this Earth to loved ones. "Remember, as Nicole so often did, that love sustains us, not anger," Serena said.

John will probably think I put Serena up to that, Claire thought. *Instead of hearing the message, he's probably fuming at me for trying to chasten him for his anger issues through Serena.* Claire scribbled a note to Pryce asking him to help her keep John from slipping away at the end.

Her eyes stayed dry until the magnificent organ and twelve-piece orchestra filled the entire space with Bach's "Jesu, Joy of Man's Desiring." Tears rolled down her cheeks. *Oh, Maman, isn't it beautiful….*

The bishop gave a loving benediction, and the recessional began softly with the orchestra playing Pachelbel's "Canon in D." The Grand Gallery's massive organ with its nearly 1500 pipes joined in, the music filled the cathedral—and surely the hearts of those now leaving—with profound majesty. The music proclaimed boldly and unmistakably that the life of Nicole DeNevers Alden had been beautiful.

Pryce was shaking John's hand in both of his, performing his task of detaining her son while sounding as if all he had on his mind was sympathy. With Pryce and Adam joining her in friendly persuasion, they coaxed John to a small chapel off an aisle.

She couldn't stop herself. She removed her hat and hugged him. He allowed it briefly, but when he pulled away, he still wouldn't look at her. Pryce and Adam discreetly disappeared, on their way to the reception.

She touched John's jaw and lifted it gently so that he looked directly at her. His red-rimmed eyes held tears. "I know," she said, "that you are telling yourself that you are terrible for not coming to see Grandmere at brunch last Sunday. . ."

He squeezed his eyes shut and pulled away.

Oh, no. Did he think she was digging at him? "I just meant—"

"Well, whatever you meant, there's pretty much no getting around that one."

The unspoken part of this sentence was that he chose to believe he was a bad boy, rotten to the core, so what the hell, why fight it? Maman and his deep concern not to disappoint her was the only reason he'd graduated from college. Yet this wonderful young man wasn't rotten. He was just angry, and this was not the time or place to confront these issues.

"I've been aching to tell you that Grandmere wouldn't want you to blame yourself. Her very last words, John, were about you. Her very last words. And never never doubt that she knew you loved her."

He paced.

"And I love you."

He remained silent.

It hurt. "I looked everywhere for you. I've been desperate. Even Fance didn't—"

"Fance's ticked with me. She walked out."

"I'm sorry."

"Look," he said, "I have to go…."

"Where?" He'd obviously dropped out of the tennis tournament. "Why don't you come up to The Retreat for a few days?"

He shoved his hands in his pockets. "No thanks."

Someone tapped on the door. "Claire, the limo's ready." It was Pryce. "If you come now, the press won't find us."

"Just a minute." She touched John's shoulder. "We have to meet with the lawyers next week for the reading of Maman's will. She left you the apartment. Perhaps much more."

He covered his face with his hands a second and then wiped his eyes. "Mom, I need…time."

She felt Maman's presence, a whisper of conscience. *Trust him.*

She should tell him what he needed to know. Right then. Whether it meant she would lose him forever or not. Insist that he listen. Telling him was the right thing. Still, every muscle in her body tightened. Dread squeezed her throat shut. Grief. They were both grieving. This was, in fact, completely the wrong time. And, people were waiting for her.

"Perhaps I need time too," she whispered.

John nodded. He walked out the door.

She felt her heart racing. *Please don't let it be that I have done the wrong thing again.*

A Single White Rose

With Joss to refresh Claire's memory when she forgot a name, Claire had endured a reception line of over three hundred people. *So good to see you, thank you for coming. Yes, Maman would have loved the service.* She'd spoken to everyone, and most of the guests were fortifying themselves with food and drink. Her head throbbed.

She checked her watch. Twenty to three. She said to Joss, "Can I get away with leaving now? I want to round up Rachel and Serena and head home."

"Yes. Go. You look exhausted. I'll stay and do all the thanks-for-comings."

Claire glanced across the room, looking for the two women. And there, chatting with her lawyer . . . a man who made Claire's breath catch in her throat. "Joss, that's Savik Kodaly. Did you invite him?"

"At the service. He approached and asked if he could come by and speak to you. I thought that since he'd…helped at the…after the…" Joss teared up, clearly avoiding the word *bomb*. "Well, that it would be—"

"Yes, it's fine. Thank you."

Claire didn't want to say one more platitudinous word to anyone. She especially didn't want Savik to see her puffy face, her exhaustion. He looked tan and fit. She'd seen a picture of him a couple of years back at some social event with a young woman, probably early twenties, on his arm. Time had touched him gently, leaving only a few gray hairs at the temples, a few laugh lines. And on him they looked great. But what was he doing here? Not a word in over twenty years.

Again the strangeness of his timing puzzled her. Why had he appeared last Sunday? Could it have been only coincidence? And now today….a thought struck her like the bong of a great clock…could he have been trying to approach her…by sending the roses? An intense blush heated her cheeks.

He glanced her way, caught her watching him. She nodded, and he spoke a last time to her lawyer. She had to sit down or she just might faint. A brocade sofa near a potted palm offered support. She walked over and all but dropped onto it as he approached.

"May I join you a moment?" he asked.

She patted the sofa cushion and realized she'd never thanked him. Gratitude flooded her. *Thank you for trying to save her, for being there when I most needed you.* These words seemed strangely, inappropriately intimate. "I need to thank you—"

"No, no. No need at all. Please. I came to tell you how sorry, so…terribly sorry, I am that I didn't get there fast enough—"

"No…" She shook her head. "Don't say that." Words were needed. She searched and came up with a question she could answer all too accurately. "So, how long has it been?"

"Too long. But I've been following you."

Following?

He smiled. "All the way to the Nobel Peace Prize. I always knew you were smart and beautiful, but it seems the world has decided you're also profound."

"It's more true that I've been surrounded by profound people. My people are my strength. Always have been."

Savik's smile broadened, deepening crow's feet at the corners of his eyes in a manner she found attractive—apparently an effect it also had on many other women.

He crossed his arms. "Still charmingly humble."

There suddenly wasn't much else to say. Under other circumstances, they might talk about what they'd done over the years, but not now. Joss waved and pointed to her watch. Claire nodded. Joss left. To Savik Claire said, "I need a small favor."

"Name it."

"My PR man has hustled my friends to the limo. Would you mind walking out with me? In case my knees buckle."

They slipped away, walked to the elevator and rode down. The elevator doors opened onto the lobby where a crowd of reporters, having discovered the location of the reception, were lying in wait.

"Oh, no. I'm sorry, Savik…"

"No, it's good I'm here."

"Claire!"

"Just a few questions, Claire!"

"Not today," Savik called to them.

Claire indicated a hallway to the rear of the building that led to an alley and the waiting limo. "This way."

Savik grabbed her elbow, shielding her from the pursuing swarm. They raced to where the limo was parked as arranged. The driver loaded Rachel's power-chair as Pryce and Serena helped Rachel inside.

In the seconds before Claire could also jump in, the frenzied reporters circled her, Savik barring them with extended arms. Phyllis Colson, the columnist who had, for some unfathomable reason, relentlessly hounded Claire for years, led the pack. Questions hit in a barrage.

"Why was your son late to the service?"

"Where is your son?"

"Could you share with us your mother's last words, Claire?"

"Is this Savik Kodaly? What is your relationship to him?"

"Is your big unity concert cancelled?"

"Will you change your position on the PeaceMaker tests now that someone close to you has been killed by terrorists?"

Savik shouted, "Please respect her privacy, today of all days."

Claire gestured to Pryce, who shut the door on the other side of the limo and ran around to help. She forced a smile and called out, "Pryce has a statement for you."

Savik blocked the still baying reporters as Claire scrambled into the limo's back seat.

She couldn't get inside, however, before Phyllis Colson wedged a briefcase above the door's hinge, thrust her bony face above it and yelled, "Since Tears of Allah terrorists killed your mother and nineteen of your supporters, will you change your stand on nonviolence? Is it different when your own people are killed?"

Savik dislodged the briefcase. "Get away from her! This is not the time!" He slammed the limo door.

Claire waved and mouthed, *thank you,* to Savik, and the driver sped them away, leaving Pryce to deal with the mob. "Dear god," she breathed. In only moments the ebb of adrenaline left her weakened and shaking.

Serena and Rachel both made soothing comments. She listened to her friends, dazed, realizing she was staring at a single white rose, fully opened, in a bud vase which was attached to the inside of the limo's interior, beside the rear seat. A folded note was tucked behind it.

"Did either of you put this here?"

They claimed they hadn't. The driver admitted he'd left the limo unlocked—"less than a minute"—when he stepped out to buy a newspaper right after he parked it. Claire explained the rose situation to Serena and Rachel, including what her mother had said, and that they came from someone anonymous but omitting her recent notion that the sender could be Savik.

"Are you going to read the card?" Rachel asked.

She swallowed a long gulp of bottled water, then reached for the card and opened it.

"There's always a quote from a book called *The Language of Roses*. This one says, 'Since medieval times of secret *sub rosa* meetings, a white rose has stood for mystery. And in the mystery of endings and beginnings, a white rose marks both.'"

"Interesting," Serena said. "Isn't there anything more personal?"

Claire nodded. "It says, 'Sympathy for an ending, and hope for a beginning.' So, my friends, what do you think? Should I be interested or nervous?"

After a moment, Rachel said, "Anonymity is generally used for two reasons. Fear of taking responsibility, and fear of rejection."

"It's rejection," Serena said. "This person knows you…and couldn't stand rejection."

"Maybe there are other reasons," Claire said. "But you know, I'm bone-deep tired. I really don't want to try to figure out what they could be—good or bad."

Serena patted Claire's hand. "I have a feeling you're going to be receiving more of these roses until the sender thinks you are approachable."

"I'm with your mother on this one," Rachel said. "Be very careful."

The "Posse"

Damn tacky, Savik thought, as he watched Ronald Bramfeld Hughes, U.S. Secretary of Defense, return to the aft deck of the *Bimini Blue Marlin* after taking a leak off the starboard bow. There was a woman on board, for god's sake. Tilting left and right with the gentle swells, Ronnie returned to his seat and plunked down across from Savik in brooding silence.

Beside them, at a consistent fifty yards, ran an escort boat for Ronnie's Secret Service agents. The ocean's surface in the Bahamas on this tenth day of September was bright, smooth, and deep-water blue. Seated in a white leather deck chair, Savik leaned well back and stretched his legs. He inhaled tangy, sea-salt air. Normally an exhilarating trip, today the old fishing magic was missing.

"The Posse," they called themselves. Excepting the two pandemic years, Savik had made this trip with Winn and his dad on the second weekend in September regularly for many years, along with retired General Clifford Stanhope, of GeigaBank and Sphere 9, and publisher Quentin Frobisher. Cliff was their most avid fisherman. They were after tuna and shark, but there was the exciting possibility of a sailfish or the real trophy, a marlin. And there were other agendas, as always.

Ronnie attempted to skewer Savik with those hooded, coal-dark eyes that pretty much terrorized Ronnie's staff. "She should be thrilled to go after a tax fraud like this. But last weekend she cancelled on you, and you're pissed. You *have* been seeing her, right?"

"Who's pissed?" Savik countered. "I often camp alone."

Ronnie fired back. "Hey, Kodaly. Don't try to con me. You're pissed. All this gear slinging and short sentences says so. You fucking her or not?"

"I see Adrienne. As for sleeping with her—mine to know…." He gave Ronnie a look he hoped said, 'back off.' "…and yours to have wet dreams about."

Winn yelled, "Christ, Dad, this one's huge." Winn was fighting a mako shark. "Whoooooeeeeeeeee!!"

Savik killed the last of his beer. God, he thought, Adrienne was hot in bed. Gorgeous. Smart. But Friday at the cabin packing camping stuff, he'd expected her any minute when she called and cancelled. Her excuse sounded legit: "working hard on something special. I just have to keep at it." Yes, he was pissed. Damned, though, if he'd let these guys know it.

By one-fifteen, Winn had been duking it out with the mako for two hours and close to success. He looked, however, like he'd gone a few rounds with Godzilla.

The *Marlin's* captain, Skip Johnson, one buff guy, appeared from the main cabin and offered another round of cold beer. Savik wet his salty lips with a cooling swig.

Quentin's bald head was turning pink where he'd pushed back a billed cap with the logo of the Frobisher publishing mega-corporation. A stuffy, tame man, Quentin preferred hunting trips, probably an attempt to capture the feeling that he was a tiger, not a white-collar paper pusher. The ex-general was more interesting, but neither Savik nor Winn particularly liked Ronnie's friends. Friendship was a luxury among essential allies, and as major stockholders in Winn's company, CET, Quentin and Cliff qualified as allies of sorts. But nobody had any jokes today. Everyone but Winn looked at Savik with a scowl, despite the perfect Bimini day.

Ronnie had staked out the fighting chair next to his son's. Cliff sat in the third with military stiffness, still in great physical shape. Savik and Quentin had to content themselves with deck chairs. They wouldn't get a fighting chair unless they got a strike.

The sudden scree of a half-dozen gulls swooping and hovering on the breeze as Skip dumped bait irritated Savik—as did the whiz of Winn's line, usually an exciting sound. It was bad enough that Adrienne had bailed on the camping trip, but he hadn't been able to find out yet if she'd taken the Boswell bait, and these men would not get off his back about it. He knew too well how critical it was for PeaceMaker to secure funding in Congress, and that Senator Boswell as the steam behind the opposition truly deserved the legal ax from the Feds—courtesy of Adrienne. I get it, gentlemen, so kindly shut the fuck up, he wanted to say.

Skip headed up top to make sure the lines stayed aft and to back the boat when necessary.

Winn yelled, "It's close!"

They all jumped to their feet and hovered around Winn. The motor settled into neutral, and Skip slid down the ladder from the flying bridge. The mako's dark body drew closer.

"Jeez, it's huge," Winn crowed, never modest. His let-the-good-times-roll personality had won Savik's friendship in college, and it still cheered him. "This could be a record."

The dark shape thrashed back and forth in the water close beside the rear of the boat.

Skip grabbed the tagging pole. Wherever this shark finally ended up, today's tag would be reported to the Department of Fish and Game and the U.S. Fisheries Science Center. Savik had been the one to suggest that they switch to tag fishing because the numbers of the world's big game fish were plunging rapidly. After the requisite questioning of his manhood, the group had finally agreed to make the change, which was clearly for the better, when Savik had pointed out the PR value.

At last the mako surfaced and rolled to the side, revealing the absence of tube-shaped claspers. A female. Skip pronounced it a 440 pounder, jabbed the tag dart into the massive dorsal fin, and began the labor of getting the hook out with leather gloves, rope and pliers.

They had angled her around to the rear diving platform. Winn crouched there, grinning while Ronnie snapped a bunch of photos. Even though exhausted, she thrashed and rolled before Skip wrestled the hook out and cut the line. The mako took off and quickly disappeared.

Savik washed up and brought out more beer.

Winn grabbed a can and downed half in one big swig. His cheeks were growing more freckled under the intensity of the sun's rays, despite sunscreen. "Man, my back is killing me." He grinned, nodding toward where the mako had been. "You're not going to top that one."

Skip got the boat up to trolling speed again while his pretty wife Lily served chilled lobster, liver pate and black caviar.

"So, Savik…." Quentin wiped butter off his chin, "Adrienne avoids the wilderness?"

Yep. Back again to Adrienne. Savik gritted his teeth. "Look, I'm doing my best to hype her passion for career advancement. I've mentioned the possibility of a Boswell investigation twice within the week. More is going to stink to high heaven. Let's get OFF the subject."

"Okay," Winn said, agreeing for the others. "What's with Claire Alden?"

"Yeah," Cliff jumped in. "You're her hero. Saved her life."

"Didn't save her mother's life."

"Saved lots of lives," Winn added. "My good buddy."

Ronnie said, "You attended a memorial service for her mother. What's your connection?"

Savik took a slow pull of beer, thinking of the past and how best to explain it. "I knew Claire a long time ago. I was nineteen. She was twenty-one. Naturally I've followed her career. Who hasn't? Sunday was damn strange. She was at the Towers speaking. I had a meeting and decided to drop by briefly and hear her, and then I spotted those two women."

"Tears of Allah," Quentin said in disgust. "God, what a vile plague on the planet."

"It's one thing to fight the fuckers abroad," Cliff said. He looked gloomy. "But having them breeding right here at home, and bringing women into the fight, is God-damn terrifying."

Quentin snorted. "Claire Alden thinks they could all have a nice little chat and agree not to be bad anymore." He stroked a bushy eyebrow. "My wife thinks Claire Alden walks on water. A second coming of Gandhi or something. Thinks Alden's incredibly charismatic."

"Shit," Cliff muttered. "We should never have let Oprah get a toehold." They all laughed.

Cliff added, "I've heard Alden speak, though, and she is good. Ernest could take some pointers." Cliff loved to remind everyone that, he, like Ronnie, also had frequent personal contact with President Hass. "Our fearless leader's veterans speech was pretty embarrasing."

"It's true. The Ernest could use a big dose of Claire's brilliance," Ronnie said.

Savik was surprised by the facial expression and genuine tone of admiration in Ronnie's voice for anything about Claire.

Cliff scoffed. "My Sylvie considers Alden as toxic as Elizabeth Warren or that Senator bitch from California. And my wife is a terrific judge of character."

Savik laughed. They all looked at him. "Claire is nothing to worry about. She's nice and damn attractive, and she moonshined the Nobel Prize people. But she's no castrator. What harm does all her warm fuzzy talk do? She actually does some good without giving handouts."

"She crossed a line. Women like her, always going on about making changes," he practically growled the word change, "absolutely must not be given a forum." Ronnie picked up an empty beer can, placed it dramatically in front of him, his dark eyes now turned hard. "She publicly opposed the PeaceMaker tests and the use of lasers as weapons in space. Calls them the 'spawn of Reagan's Star Wars, a bottomless money-pit.' We can't have that kind of talk." He stomped the can with a loud crunch, picked it up, disked it overboard, and stared at Savik, as if he thought Savik might disagree. And no one was going to be allowed to disagree.

The scream of running line stopped their conversation dead. It was from Savik's pole on one of the outriggers above. He leapt up, as did Winn, to change seats. From the fly bridge, Skip handed the pole to Savik, who quickly strapped himself into Winn's fighting chair. Lily cut their speed. The Secret Service boat moved forward to stay clear of the line.

At that moment Savik's catch launched itself from the water into the sky. His mouth dropped open at the vision of deep blue and silver that disappeared with a fantastic splash.

"Good, God," Quentin exploded.

Cliff announced the obvious. "It's a fucking blue marlin."

Skip had taken over handling the boat and called out, "It's past peak season, but we've tagged some big ones in September. Looks over a thousand pounds, Savik, maybe a Grander."

"Blue's are the best, the very best." Cliff was almost crooning. "They've got the agility of the stripers, the strength of the blacks, and the speed of the whites."

Savik settled in for the battle. "This will be so much more fun than talking about women."

Four hours into what would probably be an all-night struggle, and just as the sun was setting rose and crimson red in the west, his cell phone buzzed.

Winn took the call and made the announcement. "There's going to be an article in tomorrow's New York Times. The Justice Department is looking into the taxes and business dealings of Andrew Boswell, husband and business partner of New York Senator Lana Boswell. That bitch is going DOWN!"

The Posse slapped Savik on the back and passed cigars around.

Life could sometimes be so damn good. Savik would bring the marlin in. He was sure of it.

They laughed and hooted, drank champagne, drank the rest of the beer, told fishermen's lies and bawdy stories, lit lanterns, and occasionally puked. They roared the night away. The only sounds Savik heard from the world outside their own voices was the motor, the irregular rattle of the rigging, and the slapping of the moonlit Caribbean against the hull as his battle with the great fish continued.

You Should Run For President

Claire had returned home from the memorial service and retreated again into grief, anger, frustration and guilt. She forced herself to take care of urgent business though, mostly working from her home office. Despite the warm days and mild nights of early fall, she felt cold most of the time, chilled now in her jeans and warm red flannel shirt. On this last Saturday in September, almost a month after the bombing, she sat curled up before warm red and yellow flames in the stone fireplace that had first lured her to this little converted hunting lodge, her Retreat. When she'd remodeled the place, she'd kept its wood floors and stairway, its open rafters, and shined the old oak to a rich toffee luster. She'd widened windows and added skylights.

The headlines that morning had intruded here and shocked her. Senator Boswell, the principle voice in Congress against the PeaceMaker, had resigned under a cloud. Disaster upon disaster. The changes Claire had made in the world now seemed insignificant. What should she do? She was back at a crossroads similar to the one that had taken her to the Minangkabau.

Rachel, visiting for the weekend, was on a campaign to cheer her, and Claire was resolved to go along. Preparations for the meal seemed as exhausting, though, as an expedition into the Himalaya, and the AFWW Unity Concert was next weekend. Working out finalities for the event felt like planning to *move* those great mountains.

Only a month ago, if anyone had asked, "What's the most exciting thing in your life?" Claire would have said the annual concert. A multitude would gather from nearly seventy nations and bond through exciting live music to launch another year of labor in the vineyards of nonviolence. Now, she just wished they'd do it without her.

"Peanut," Alex said, bobbing his head as he perched beside her on the back of the sofa, twitching his red tail feathers, and looking her squarely in the eyes.

"All gone."

Rachel rolled into the room in her new power chair, a marvel that could raise and lower her from bottom drawer level to cooking counter up to eye-level. "Let's get cookin'!"

She offered that beautiful smile—full lips and the tiniest gap between her front teeth. Rachel's hair, long, wavy, and chocolate-colored in college, was now shot with a steely gray she refused to color, and shorn to a fluffy bob that suited a professor of Anthropology. She sat looking energized in her electric blue sweats.

Claire asked, "Remember the wise old Minang women in their white headdresses? Singing that song of uncertainty? About fate being like a tree that falls after a storm, and no one knows in which direction, and you can only choose how to respond after the fall?"

"I know that song well." Rachel held up a hand that she couldn't straighten completely or use for gripping. She cocked her head with a honey-if-I-can-do-it-you-can-too look. "CMT wasn't something I ever planned on getting."

Instant guilt smacked Claire. "Oh, god, Rachel. Do I sound like a terrible whiner?"

Charcot-Marie-Tooth disease, CMT, had weakened Rachel's muscles to the point where her foot bones cramped into a perpetual arch and her toes curled upward. With shoe prostheses and braces, she could walk short distances, but a wheelchair had become necessary, and standing for long periods was out of the question. Without a faith, Rachel persevered on her own willpower and spirit. She inspired Claire. Claire with the strong, healthy body.

"You're just still grieving." Rachel turned the chair alongside the sofa to be beside Claire. "I can't offer the consolation of Serena's belief in reincarnation, or the Minang's belief that your mother still lives on another plane and that she can make her presence known. I certainly don't believe in your Quaker faith's eternal heaven." Rachel rubbed slow circles along Claire's back. "Nicole lived generously and with fun in her heart. And it's the way of things that her time is over. You'll honor her by moving on with the same generosity and sense of fun."

"I can't shake the feeling that it was my fault."

"Well, it wasn't. And honoring Nicole is how you defend yourself, and nothing would honor her more than for you to do what you can to end wars. You are needed. Especially now that Senator Boswell had to resign. There is no one prominent still crusading to oppose the PeaceMaker program."

"It's too much, Rache." Claire snuggled deeper into the sofa. "I'm a damn turnip, the kind they can't get any more blood out of."

Rachel scowled. "You *will* get over this enervation, you know. It's just a question of time. " She spoke in the husky voice created by years of smoking, an addiction only mastered two years ago. "Let's go cook up a storm." Rachel set her chair in motion.

Alex landed on the arm of Rachel's wheelchair. Machines fascinated him. The three of them entered the juniper green and tan kitchen with its shiny copper pans hanging on the wall. Alex flew to the central counter, found a pencil, and dropped it into Rachel's lap. "Peanut!"

Claire explained. "I'm out of peanuts. He'll probably drive us crazy all evening."

"I have something." From her sack, Rachel pulled out packages, veggies, and "Cashews!" She fed Alex one. With a screech of happiness he took it in his foot and flew off.

Good smells soon filled the room. Claire put a CD on that Alex loved—soft rainforest music with birdcalls in the background—and then brought wine bottles from the basement, an old Doloca Sarafin Merlot from Turkey and a dry white from the Gaia vineyards on Santorini.

The tap of the doorknocker sounded. Pryce soon appeared in the kitchen doorway and approached the bar counter. He never wore anything he thought common, like jeans, and looked sharp in slacks and a pale taupe sweater that set off his gray-streaked brown hair and goatee. Alex fluttered down to a bunch of red grapes, bit off a stem and single grape, flapped to Pryce's shoulder, and offered a greeting gift.

"Nice choice, Alex." Pryce popped the grape into his mouth, and Alex flew back to perch on Claire's shoulder. Pryce sat on one of the four barstools along one side of the central counter and downed a ripe olive.

"Your usual?" Claire asked. He nodded and she poured him a bourbon. "You're suspiciously early."

"Look Claire," Pryce said. "We need to talk before everyone else arrives."

"Shoot." Claire started chopping an onion.

"You need a staff of bodyguards. Someone should be with you at all times, not just for public occasions. This isn't negotiable. I'm sending over applicants in the morning."

Claire started to protest, but that required an emotional energy she didn't have.

"And I want you to keep an open mind about another issue. And trust me. I have for weeks been giving very serious thought to where your life—your career—should go. It's time…"

Claire shook her head, feeling her chest tighten. She started squeezing fresh lemon juice. Her life? Career? The farthest thing from her mind. She added the lemon juice and other ingredients into the blender.

"This next election is coming up," Pryce said. "And I believe you should run for President."

"President of what?"

"Don't be dense, my darling."

She chuckled. "Of the USA? Prycie, you do come up with some zingers." She began blending a lemon-honey-almond glaze to drizzle over fruit.

"I'm quite serious. Since Senator Boswell resigned, we've gotten many hundreds of letters and emails suggesting it. And since it's exactly what I was thinking, I knew the time was right."

Rachel stopped dicing carrots. "What an extraordinary proposition."

Claire sighed, and started chopping red peppers. "That's your craziest idea ever."

"Are you going to let me explain?"

"Let's make this very short. The answer is, No."

Rachel glared at Pryce as if she would love to be able to kick him.

"Next weekend is the concert," he continued. "We could announce your intention to run then. It would be spectacular. A mega news event."

"Pryce, I doubt that I can even make the concert, let alone—"

"Can't you just listen? Hasn't my vision always enlarged yours? When you thought a small cooking show in Seattle was enough, who said you could be bigger? Huge?"

"You did. You made 'Cooking for Lovers' happen, and I'm grateful. "

"We made it happen. And the same with EClaire, right?"

"I grant that you are a promotional genius. *Creating the Future* became a best-seller because of you. The AFWW concerts would never have grown to popularity and influence were it not for you. But—what you're asking for is different. It's simply not conceivable."

"It's not different. As always, I envision the maximum possible impact for what you believe in. You yourself say that the biggest hurdle to ending wars is the lack of a critical mass of leaders with vision, a workable plan, *and* perseverance. History needs a revolution for change led by a visionary leader. If you become president of this country, you can be the grain of gritty sand around which the pearl of a global peace can grow."

Claire scoffed. "You're a sucker for your own slogans. I'm a cook and a nonviolence activist, not a politician. The idea is . . . well, this time you're just wrong, Pryce."

He turned to Rachel, who had long since stopped chopping anything. "You tell her," he said. "I'm right aren't I? This is brilliant, isn't it?"

Rachel took off her glasses, set them on the countertop, and shook her head slowly. "Pryce, she barely made it for this dinner. This country is in dire trouble because of Hass. And I'd love to see Claire as President, but, you're pushing the bounds—"

"But you agree she'd be the leader the world needs?" He turned to Claire. "And powerful."

"Ooohhh," Claire said. "Why didn't you say so? I didn't realize that all I'd have to do to acquire more power is run for President. What a great idea, Pryce."

Pryce rolled his eyes. "It is. You have the magic touch. Virtually every enterprise you've launched since EClaire's beginning has done nothing but bloom and profit—"

"Pryce, this just isn't possible. Not on a personal level. Not on a political level. And certainly not at the national level. It's beyond silly. Before Hass no one without governmental experience or even a sterling military career has ever succeeded in a Presidential run. I doubt it will ever happen again. Americans have learned, I hope, that experience and track record counts."

"This from you!" he blurted. His tone shifted to one sharply accusing. "You say that it's a scandal for any women to still sit back and complain about how badly the world is run. That more and more women must step up to the plate." He paused for effect, his arms crossed. "I can get a great campaign manager, backing, and political connections."

Mouth open, Claire was about to slam Pryce. My mother and nineteen other people are dead. My son is off to god-knows-where again. Don't you dare talk to me about my responsibilities. But Rachel jumped in before Claire began screaming. "Look you two," Rachel said with that wonderfully sensible gravelly voice. "Other guests will be here soon. Let it go, Pryce. Claire just needs a relaxing evening with friends."

His face changed at once. He uncrossed his arms. "Oh, God, Claire. I was carried away. I'm sorry. I truly am."

Alex landed next to Pryce's bourbon and dropped Rachel's glasses into the drink. "Peanut," he said.

Rachel laughed and sipped her wine. Pryce smiled. Pryce pulled Rachel's glasses out of his drink and Claire cleaned them. The tension around them cooled.

The pilaf began to sizzle. She dipped a wooden spoon in, blew on it and tasted. The cranberries had plumped up. Cashews added just the right crunch. Claire felt hungry for the first time in a month.

"We need Claire to be able to do the concert," Rachel said.

Claire sipped the rich Turkish merlot, astonished that she noticed its flavor. She felt its gentle influence too, as if she'd been away in her mind and had just returned to the sensations of her body. It felt good. "I could get through the concert if you and Serena will be there with me."

"We'll all be there," Rachel said. "But you need to do more than just get through it, love. When Serena comes, she'll say vibes count in life. People read them, consciously and unconsciously, and you can't fake it. The energy people take away from the concert will be your own, multiplied twenty-five thousand times. So, I say, we still need to get you to a place where you can offer a positive spirit."

Claire hugged Rachel. She felt...better, no matter how crazy Pryce's talk. She laughed and shook her head at Pryce. "President of the United States. What a truly godawful idea." Pryce just smiled and raised his glass.

I Don't Like Killing People

Mateus Viliamu had to have this job. He followed the black guy, Desmond, up the wooden steps and onto the broad deck of the two-story home belonging to the famous Claire Alden. He checked his tie and pulled at the bottom of his suit jacket.

The worst part of being a bodyguard was wearing the damn dark suits. The best part was the pay. With an ex-wife and three kids and no real marketable skills except what he'd learned about fighting and defense in the military, he needed what this line of work brought in. The house surprised him. Most clients had homes around 30,000 square feet. This place was maybe 4000. Nice though, the way it fit in with the woods and stream and all. Desmond stepped inside, and Mateus followed.

"Make yourself comfortable," the guy said and left. Seemed friendly.

Lots of big windows let in plenty of light. Easy to bust through though. By the big picture window he spotted two chairs that would hold his six feet four inches and two hundred and sixty pounds. He liked this place. He started to sit down when he heard a loud shriek.

He tensed, hunkered, put his hand on his gun butt, and whirled toward the sound. A gray bird streaked toward him with a little silver dagger in its beak. It landed on his shaved head and dug its claws in a bit. He nearly jumped out of his skin. The Alden woman walked in.

"Alex!" she commanded. "Don't worry," she said, shaking her head. "He's harmless."

Mateus straightened, his heart crashing against his ribs. The woman held out her arm, and "Alex" flew onto it. Mateus palmed his head. No blood. He felt his pulse settle. Here he was, appearing to cringe at a little thing like a bird. Fuck all. "Never been real comfortable with birds." He sounded so lame.

She relieved the bird of the weapon. A letter opener. "When anyone arrives, Alex always brings a welcome gift. Sorry if he surprised you. I know some people don't care for birds."

"No ma'am. I like 'em okay. He just startled me. He's a nice lookin' bird."

"Well, if nothing else, you've just shown quick reflexes." She smiled.

Terrific smile and something else, a sort of glow of confidence. It was like that with lots of famous people. She took a chair opposite. He sat up, alert.

She laid a file folder on the table beside her chair. "Viliamu?" she said.

"It's Samoan. Father's side. My mom was Portuguese."

"Ah." She tapped the folder. "Your file says you were raised in Los Angeles, played football at Lincoln High School. Quite a good linebacker." She frowned, scanning the files. "Twenty eight…divorced…three children…served in the Army. Iraq and Syria. Infantry."

"Yes, ma'am."

"Mateus? Is that what your friends call you?"

"No, ma'am. Most people call me Humvee. Spelled just like the vehicle."

She laughed nice. Silky voice. Damn good lookin' for an older woman.

"Well, Humvee, what do you know about me?"

"I know you had the cookin' show. The business and all. I know about the bombing. And that you're pretty much opposed to war." He thought of the word. "You're a pacifist, right?"

"No. But that's a common misunderstanding. I'm committed to non-violence and ending war, but I hope I'm mostly a realist. Someone has to protect people from aggressors, so I admire our soldiers. We truly depend on them. But I'm dead set against launching wars, no matter the excuse. Launchng a war, if nothing else, is a sign of great failure of any great democratic leader." She put the folder aside and looked at him directly. "Why did you leave the Army, Humvee?"

With her, stick with the truth. "I found out first hand I don't like killing people."

She nodded. "So why did you become a body guard?"

"The pay. And I'm good at keeping people safe."

She smiled in a sad way. "You know, Humvee. I upset a lot of people. I'm an advocate for some serious changes, and change can feel scary for many people. There are people who do want to kill me. Protecting me could be very dangerous, starting with the concert next weekend."

Hearing that made him want to protect her. "You could count on me," he said.

Another smile. "You look uncomfortable in that suit. I'd want you to wear something else most of the time, something not so off-putting. You'd only need a suit for formal occasions."

He shook his head. "The suit is important to the job. It's like a sign that says, 'I have a guard, so don't fuck with me.' Uh-oh. Um. Sorry for the bad language." His grandmother, if she was alive, would've hit him up side the head. This lady might be a little prissy.

"Well, I can't have such a sign hanging around my neck. I need protection, but I don't want to frighten people away" She stood. "Let me see how you look with that jacket off."

Oh, shit. Bad to worse. He'd worn a short-sleeved shirt. He stood, shrugged out of the jacket. Her eyes widened at the sight of a solid wall of tattoos on his arms. A shame, actually. He liked this lady. It would have felt good to be protecting someone who thought about something other than making money and showing it off.

She said, "I'm impressed with that harpy eagle's head. In my opinion, the tattoos convey a powerful message." She didn't sit down again. "If I hired you, could you start tomorrow?"

"Yes, ma'am." He slid back into the jacket.

"What do you think of him, Alex?" she asked.

"Tough taters," the bird said, clear as a bell.

Humvee decided, as they walked toward the door, that he genuinely liked the bird.

They Share The Dream, Claire

Days of crisis. Twenty-five miles from the heart of Washington, Rock Creek Park bordered the five-hundred-acre Silver Wolf Farms Concert Center. The Center's massive semi-permanent tents could seat twenty thousand people and the surrounding greens extended seating capacity by five thousand. The AFWW staff had sold fifteen thousand tickets. All last night Claire had worried about an overflow crowd in sleeping bags that had spilled onto the grounds of Rock Creek Park itself, giving the three hundred security people, sanitation crews, park police, and park rangers fits. Yet somehow, the concert was underway.

"The bombing has fired people up," Pryce had said. "The concert is their stand, and somehow we've got to accommodate them. They're our growing army of peaceful warriors. They share the dream of a great peace revolution, Claire."

For many days he had seemed too chipper, as if he knew something special she did not. But she'd forgotten about Pryce's air of secrecy during the three frantic days with the staff working round-the-clock shifts to find accommodations in hotels, motels, and campgrounds.

At 2:15, Pryce signaled Claire to join him backstage. A new crisis loomed. The Tabor Towers bombing had also polarized people. Several hundred angry protesters marched outside behind police barriers. A sign that said, "Terrorists - SHOOT 'EM or NUKE 'EM! DON'T CHAT WITH 'EM!" stuck in Claire's mind. Claire, Humvee, and Pryce now stood in one of the suites for concert presenters and performers and watched CNN and MSNBC coverage from TV monitors.

A CNN talking head, Tawana Thompson, said, "Several families of those killed in the Towers blast are here and seem angrier with Claire Alden than with the terrorists, wouldn't you say, Jack?"

Pryce snorted. "They're a handful compared to our crowd, yet they get the media."

"It's not just their numbers," Claire said. "It's who they are."

Rhoda Carr, their emcee, swept in during a break after the opening act wearing a purple silk blazer and jeans. She joined them before the TV monitor. "My god," she gushed. "It's the gun-huggers. Gun-huggers at the gates!"

On the screen a huge poster read "EXPLAIN 'NON-VIOLENCE' TO TERRORISTS!"

"These protesters are different, Rhoda." Claire sank onto a folding chair. "Some have suffered my same loss. And I can't help feeling guilty. If it weren't for me and my speech-making, their loved ones would be alive." *Maman would still be alive.*

Pryce scoffed. "Let's keep the guilt thing very clear here. It's the Tears of Allah fuckers who deserve the world's contempt—fighting with their crack suicide squadrons."

Rhoda saluted him with her coffee mug. "That's good, Pryce. I'm going to steal it."

"Maybe not today," Joss called to Rhoda who was headed back toward the stage. Joss had brought in a tray of coffee mugs. "It wouldn't be tactful. Be tactful!"

Joss had read Claire's mind. Sometimes Rhoda crossed the line and offended people. No one could have anticipated when Rhoda was chosen as the emcee that this day would have a dark cloud over it.

Claire sipped gratefully. She loved Rhoda's sassy attitude, but today was different. Never at any of their previous concerts had angry protesters marched outside. Never had grief weighed so heavily on the mood inside. Rhoda needed to lift people's spirits without offending anyone.

Claire said, "If Rhoda is too tacky or frivolous or wacky or cheerful, or in any way doesn't strike the right tone—"

"The press," Pryce said, "will be all over us—and the entire AFWW movement."

Joss's cell phone rang. She listened a second and said, "Oh, thank god!"

"What?" Claire asked, brow wrinkled. "Are the protesters leaving?"

"No, but twenty-five more porta-potties are being delivered to the rear perimeter!"

"Praise the lord, indeed." Claire stood. "Time to feel the crowd." She donned her hat and sunglasses, linked arms with Joss, and they worked their way past techies and their dark caverns of equipment, their thickets of wires, and out to the concert area. Along with Humvee and another guard, she and Joss rejoined Serena in front of the stage right behind Rachel who sat in a front section Claire always reserved for wheelchairs.

From the stage Zabba brought the crowd to its feet with its old hits. No one drawing breath would sit still in their presence. A children's choir from the Kenya Academy of Nonviolent Conflict Resolution joined Zabba to close with John Lennon's "Imagine."

During breaks between music sets, half a hundred mega-sized television monitors broadcast a heart-felt homage to the lives of those killed at Tabor Towers. For each cameo, the audience fell relatively silent. Claire had already been through these tributes too many times and needed a break if she was going to achieve anything like positive energy to impart to their supporters.

To Serena she said, "I need to check the booths. And the crowd. Something feels strange."

Humvee and another bodyguard kept a discreet distance as they walked near her along the carnival-like perimeter. Over seventy Non-Governmental Organizations like Heifer Foundation International and Habitat for Humanity regularly attended the concerts. She stopped at the Forest Farms booth, one of her corporations, which specialized in reclaiming forests from slash-and-burn farming by planting money crops among the regrowth of trees. She checked out the kindling packs, coffees, teas, dried fruits, spices, and herbs, all packaged boutique-style for profitability.

Claire smiled at two husky guys, volunteers behind the stand, as she read the activist messages on their T-shirts. One said, "Condoms should be worn on every conceivable occasion," and the other announced, "Fighting for peace is like screwing for virginity."

She gave a thumbs-up. Suddenly recognizing her, the taller boy grinned.

Claire and the guards moved on to the "Ocean Art" booth where the sale of items created from plstics reclaimed from the Pacific Ocean helped fund an ocean plastic reclamation project. She was smiling as a flash went off.

A woman in a brown leather jacket held a camera pointed at Claire. Humvee and the other guard stepped between Claire and the woman whose expression wasn't that of an exuberant fan. It was more of a glare, eyes cold, and a twitch at the corners of the mouth. She flipped Claire off, and Humvee signaled for more security.

"Ambitious bitch!" the woman hissed. "Soon everyone's gonna know who you are." The words shocked Claire, but then she managed, "Sorry you feel that way." Two security matrons escorted the woman away. Claire was never quite able to steel herself against the crazies attracted to the glare of limelight.

Her jitters and a sense that something…unusual was going on still scratched at her mind. People in lines at the booths seemed excited, yet furtive. At 3:30 she hurried back to her seat as Bogey Stringfield began his biting anti-war songs. The crowd cheered as the camera zoomed in on Bogey's T-shirt message: *war is good for the economy like cannibalism is nutritious*. At 4:15, Barefoote and Skye, a Native American couple performed. Their gentle songs settled the audience for the keynote speaker, fellow Nobel Prize winner Safa Mufti. Her ideas could build a common ground for peace in the Middle East. This speech would be important. 4:45.

Serious make or break time for Rhoda now. This spot introducing Safa was the most likely place for Rhoda to blow it. The vivacious redhead bounded onto the stage, hair spiky, her toothy smile generous. Rhoda wore an AFWW T-shirt, as did all of Team Claire.

Rhoda applauded and hugged Barefoote and Skye. They exited, and Rhoda took the mic. "Is this a fabulous day or what?" The crowd responded with enthusiastic applause.

Dear god, Claire thought, don't let her mess up.

It Is Because I Denounce *Sharia*

Rhoda Carr gestured outward, beyond the thousands attending. "Have you bought stuff at all the booths?"

The audience applauded lightly, supportive. Claire held her breath.

"Yeah? Me too." Rhoda chortled. "I felt really good about eating five fair-trade certified, sustainably-farmed, organic donuts!" She waited for ripples of laughter to die down. "And energy-conscious person that I am, I bought a solar-powered vibrator."

Claire laughed. Thank heavens, so did the crowd. The kind of laughter that releases tension. Perfect!

Then Rhoda's expression, magnified on the huge monitors, grew serious. "You know, when tragedy hits, you feel like giving up. But you hang on, you decide to keep trying, and, well, that's the time to laugh again. Laughter heals. Right?"

The crowd murmured, heads nodded.

"So bear with me here." She paced. Stopped pacing. "Last night I learned a lesson I thought I should pass on. I been having some, how should I say, digestive difficulties for a couple of days. I was, you know, keyed up. Also haven't been able to sleep. Tense,…uh, holding too much inside, so to speak…."

Uh-oh, Claire thought, here it comes. She and Joss exchanged nervous looks.

"Never…" Rhoda stood still, face deadpan. "Never take a sleeping pill and a laxative on the same night. It really confuses your body."

Oh, good God, Claire thought. But the audience laughed again. So did Serena. Rachel turned around and squeezed Claire's hand. Humvee was grinning.

"Sorry," Rhoda said. "I know I should behave. I should be more proper. Actually, I want to introduce someone who got noticed precisely because she refused to behave. She spoke out. She got beaten up four times and jailed twice. A *fatwa*—a religious hit, a contract, rewarding her killer with money—has been called against her in six countries. Nevertheless, she has persisted. She is a civil rights lawyer from Huristan, dragging cases of the persecution of women before the courts and insisting that the Koran not only teaches against cruelty toward women, it proclaims them to be equally entitled to human rights. For this amazing work, she has earned the Nobel Peace Prize.

"My friends, I am proud to present to you a peaceful soul who scares the hell out of those who would abuse women and terrorize the world, Dr. Safa Mufti."

To massive applause, a petite creature approached center stage and bowed to Rhoda who bowed in return and then left the stage. Small, but like an exquisite butterfly, Safa drew all eyes. She wore a turquoise silken shawl over a red tunic with long pants. Gold jewelry gleamed in stage lighting that had come on with the lengthening shadows.

When the applause finally died, she thrust an open hand skyward. "My first words I say to the terrorists, you who dare to call yourselves avengers of the tears of Allah. The Prophet, peace be upon him, assured us that Allah glorifies peace and hates using righteousness as a pretext for violence and grasping power. The great jihad refers to the individual's improvement of self. Those killed in the Tabor Towers bombing are the *true* martyrs. You terrorists, YOU are the cause of many bitter tears of Allah."

She lowered her hand. "I am honored to be here with others who seek to rid this world of war. My friends, there is a *fatwa* against me because I denounce *shariah*. These contradictory and often extreme Islamic laws are based on ancient patriarchal traditions, and not, do you hear this word? *–not* on the words of the Prophet, peace be upon him. Let me say this the American way. 'Good! Old! Boys!' have put a self-serving spin on the Koran."

Ah, Safa, you so powerfully speak truth.

Claire looked at faces in the audience. Many heads were nodding.

"It is *shariah* that permits a man to be married for a half an hour," she continued. "*Shariah* allows a nine-year-old child to be married to a man of fifty years. *Shariah* allows so-called 'honor' killings, though the Koran urges compassion. It urges justice. Dignity. Even mercy."

She became a tiny thunderstorm, telling vivid and horrifying examples of "spinning" that prevented the Arab world from being the very pioneers of women's rights, the architects of peace agreements. "Change must come. Great enlightenment," she concluded, "not terrorism, should be what the world envisions when it thinks of us."

Chills of inspiration spread across Claire's shoulders and arms.

Safa bowed, waved, and bowed again as the audience jumped to its feet in a standing ovation. The curtain rose on the Indonesian rock-star-turned-philanthropist, Danny F, blasting out his hit song featuring the line, "if Allah is love, why is it about hate?"

At six, evening had already settled into a chilly night, but the crowd had become a single entity. Their energy, hope, their sense of justice, their commitment—anyone could feel the alchemy of such a fusion.

Escorted by her guards, Claire moved to the wings. Rhoda did an intro for her. Then, almost in a trance, Claire reached the lectern and gazed at an ocean of humanity. Their applause sounded as though it covered the entire state. Their momentum lifted her. This was her time to lift them.

"My friends," she said, "I'm knocked out flat on the ground with admiration for those who have appeared on this stage today! Through the sharing of their brilliance and magnificent visions, I'm elevated to new mountaintops! What about you?"

Cheers broke out and applause swelled again. Now if she could get them to grasp the idea so dear to her heart..."Our task, my fellow activists from all parts of this wonderful planet, is to unite. To join all others who are working to effect a worldwide metanoia. In unity there is real power."

A blank look of politeness clouded the faces nearest her. "Riiiiiight, you're thinking. What's a *metanoia*?" She paused a moment, then continued. "It literally means to change your mind, but it's more. It's a word signifying a deep change in heart and mind. A repentance for past mistakes. The kind of change I explored as I traveled and that I describe in *Creating the Future*. It's the kind of change people and organizations on all continents are searching for, working for. For AFWW, metanoia with respect to war means that Mars must shrug off his fondness for violence as a solution, and Venus must rise up in partnership to help govern."

She paused and moved to the meat of the speech. "How do you feel about the Pentagon's rush to put laser weapons in space without any meaningful public debate?" A great wave of hisses and boos swept through the crowd. She nodded in sympathy. Screams broke out. Figures—a dozen or more—rushed the stage from all points. They held up red arms and hands, the red color dripping over their clothing and a handful actually reached the outer edges of the stage floor.

"BLOOD IS ON YOUR HANDS...BLOOD IS ON YOUR HANDS," they all screamed at Claire. "BLOOD IS ON YOUR HANDS...."

Red Hand And Wild Blue Eyes

Claire saw it all as if in freeze-frame slow motion. The protesters closed in, their red hands waving, and then, when Humvee, her other body-guard, and security personnel tackled them from behind, they began dropping. One reached Claire. He grabbed her arm and ran his red hand down her body, smearing a streak of red on her white blazer and T-shirt. Murderous hatred glittered in his wild-looking blue eyes. Had she seen this man before?

"Bloody stinking bitch!" His spittle hit her before Humvee pinned him face-down.

Security personnel forced back fans who wanted to help rescue Claire. Someone handed her a towel. She shook all over, but refused requests for her to go back stage. "Why is it," she asked the audience when the protestors had been removed and the crowd noise died down, "that the idea of nonviolence and equality is so threatening to some people?"

This drew a universal cheer, which became another wild clapping ovation.

Claire finished her talk and then the curtain lifted behind her. All the day's entertainers joined together for the evening's final number, the song that had become the Unity Concert's anthem. For all of them, the phrase 'New Jerusalem' from this song was the perfect metaphor for their shared vision of a future in which humanity had united to demand an end to war, and won. Carly Simon herself walked onto the stage, took the microphone, and belted out the intro *a capella*, her voice electrifying.

"Let! the river run,
Let all the dreamers wake the nation.
Come, the New Jerusalem."

The beat began. The singers on the stage joined in. The second time through, words flashed on the television monitors for the audience and a camera panned their radiant faces as they added their passion to the swelling sound.

"We, the great and small, stand on a star
and blaze a trail of desire through the dark'ning dawn."

And then as the song's final words appeared on the screens, a caption popped up at the bottom: "Raise posters."

Rippling like distant thunder, thousands of white posters raised. Claire stared. Lit by the hundreds of lights, the signs simply said in red and blue letters, "Claire for President."

She glimpsed her profile on the television monitors, her face pale, mouth open. To her the image resembled the stricken way she'd looked on TV, kneeling beside Maman after the bombing.

Pryce. Damn it all. She gripped the lectern and sucked in air.

Posters waved, the audience whistled, cheered, and began chanting. "Metanoia! Metanoia! Metanoia! Everyone seemed joyful, super-charged. It should feel parasitic, all those people wanting more of her than she could possibly deliver. And yet, it didn't. Heart pounding, pulsing in her ears, she felt a surge of her own energy. Music started once more, and the crowd spontaneously sang again.

Ah, this was madness. Surreal and absurd. It was wrong to give people false hopes. She struggled to join in the singing.

I am going to kill Pryce.

Nonviolently, of course.

What should she say to them, how to tell them that what they were asking would not happen? Fortunately, the song's exuberant ending made evasion easy. She simply waved, managed to smile a little, bowed, and walked backstage. In the morning she'd give a statement saying, No.

Waiting in the wings, Pryce and Joss hurried after her. Claire couldn't look at them. She simply held her hand up in a "stop" gesture. They wisely complied. She stomped toward the tiny room she shared with Serena and Rachel.

Humvee followed, dismissed a security matron in the room and stayed outside the door. There would likely be some recriminations and rethinking about how so many people had been able to get close enough to Claire to have killed her—if they had wanted to. Sadly, even bigger restrictions would be put on her freedom.

In the little room, crowded with folding chairs and three roll-away beds, Claire removed her earrings, kicked off her boots, slipped off her paint-smeared blazer, jeans, and T-shirt. She donned sweats and sat on the edge of her bed, staring at nothing, her mind a mental salad of images. Finally she lay down to wait for her friends who would doubtless want to talk with her into the wee hours.

And then, time had passed and she jolted awake. A nightlight dimly revealed the sleeping forms of Rachel and Serena, the sound of their steady breathing a comfort. She lifted her cellphone from a small nightstand. The time was quarter to four.

Claire for President. Claire for President. Claire for President. President. President. Claire.

Okay, she'd write exactly what to say. Then she'd tell Joss…no, damn! Joss had to have been in on this ridiculous conspiracy. Claire wasn't ready to ask Joss for anything.

Serena, who would definitely have told Claire had she known, could tell Pryce to summon the press. Claire left the room, carrying her laptop. In the common area, she stepped around staff and technical crew in sleeping bags. She made tea in the kitchenette and worked at a small table for two hours on what ended up being a single paragraph that said "No thanks"—diplomatically.

At 6:06 the kitchenette door opened. Pryce stood there. Claire shut down her computer, rose, and headed for the door. Pryce didn't step aside.

"Talk to me," he said.

She glared at him.

"Do you want my resignation?"

"I want to drown you. You did it behind my back. You KNEW I didn't want this. You betrayed me! And you enlisted Joss. Running for President would be a hopelessly lost cause, so worst of all, you raised the expectations of the people in this movement. They're going to be disappointed. And constantly pressure me."

He opened his mouth. She leaned toward him and blasted ahead. "It's insane. But even if it weren't, I'm not up to it. My mother just died. That alone makes this idea egregiously inappropriate. You're an asshole. HOW could you DO this, Pryce? How COULD you!?"

He stared down at the black and white linoleum-tiled floor. "So you're firing me?"

That was exactly what she was thinking. "I need to have absolute trust in anyone as close to me as you are."

He raised his gaze and stared at her, eyes unblinking, resolute. "You want me to apologize? Well, I won't. I'm furious over what's happening to my country, to our world, and you have the vision, competence, and charisma to change it. I'm going to use every trick in my great big bag to get you to run. Claire…" He stepped closer. "Did you see their faces? Really see them?"

Phffft, she scoffed. "Don't try that mush with me. They were just pumped from the music"

"So you did see hope in their eyes."

"Okay, I saw it. But…." She sighed. "I don't know why I'm even talking to you."

"I do. We go way back, Claire, and deep down you still trust me because you know I've never steered you wrong."

"There's always a first time."

"That may be, but this is not that time." He grinned. "Pryce is right."

She leaned against the wall. "The answer is still NO. If you stay with me, are you capable of getting off this particular train?"

"No. But I'll never again do anything in this direction without your approval."

"It would be your last move working with me." She still felt like choking him.

. . . . .

At 11:00 A.M. Claire flew in a strained atmosphere to Newark with Joss. Rachel returned to Brandeis, Serena was off to Aspen to lead an inspirational retreat, and Pryce flew to La Guardia, which was closer to his Midtown condominium. Desi dropped Joss in Poughkeepsie and then in the late afternoon, he and Claire made their way, at last, to the Retreat. The moment she was inside the house she let Alex out of his cage.

He screeched and then said, "Look who's here." He flew around the room and returned with a piece of newsprint in his beak. "Peanut," he said.

"You've shredded my newspaper again."

Desi took good care of Alex, but neither he nor Florence let him out of his cage much in the house. Let loose, Alex tended to dismantle things. She brought a peanut from the kitchen, ignoring the enlarged pile of tasks in her in-box. She did check messages on the house landline. One from Adam, whom she hadn't seen since he delivered the eulogy for Maman, explained that something pressing had come up at the U.N. so he couldn't make the concert. "But you will be in my thoughts all day."

Alex flew to the top of one of her CD speakers, bobbing his head. He wanted Claire to play his favorite CD with rainforest sounds. Music on, Claire picked up USA Today. She opened it to the front page, its right edge completely frayed. There in big headlines with lurid color photos was the story of the concert's "bloody hands" protesters. And alongside a photo of the protesters stood Claire in another shot looking chipper, smiling.

The woman in brown leather had taken that shot.

CLAIRE ACCUSED at CONCERT the headline shouted.

A smaller photo showed people holding up signs declaring "Claire for President." Iron bands tightened around her chest as she read the copy under the photos. "Alden accused of having Tabor Towers' bombing victims' blood on her hands." And, "Benefit Becomes Political Rally." And, "Is Claire Alden a presidential candidate?"

The wordless message of the photos taken in sum—Claire was flippant about the protesters and happily exploiting the concert for political gain only a little over a month after her mother died. Could the image and message be any worse?

The doorbell rang. A young woman wearing green overalls with the trademark of Fleur D'Liv presented Claire with a rose in what appeared to be a silver bud vase. Claire signed for it and took it inside.

The opened blossom was beautiful, but a strange color, a sort of lavender, and the velvety petals looked silvery in the light. She read the card's message: "The 'British Sterling' tea rose is thought to heighten the elegance of sterling silver." —from *The Language of Roses*.

Alex landed on her shoulder and started gently nibbling her ear. She hesitated, staring at the folded personal note. This whole rose thing was starting to feel creepy. Who was this rose giver? Maybe Maman had been right to be alarmed.

She read the note. "This rose is elegant and reminded me of you. I am not far away. I admire your courage." The rose was beautiful, but the anonymity was maddening. And the "not far way" disturbing. She'd had more than enough of it. She flopped into a chair. So many weirdoes in this world....

She saw again the face of an angry man with red hands and wild blue eyes.

Like Being Stung By A Bee

Today Humvee and his new boss were finally out in the world again. It had been fifteen days since the Washington concert, and the two other guards in the rotation were bored as schoolboys in detention. She walked beside him as they approached the main library on the Vassar College campus. She'd dressed casual, jeans and a pretty blue silk blouse. He wore jeans, too, and a loose yellow shirt. He would have felt better carrying his Beretta but Claire Alden was one of a few clients he'd had who hired only non-armed body guards. His job was to anticipate a potential problem, avoid it, if unavoidable use superior muscle to take it out, or failing all of those, to cover her. He had accepted the potential risks of her terms.

She'd been quiet on the drive up, saying only that she was writing a book called *The New Jerusalem*. If she intended to fade from public life and just write, he'd soon need a new client. As they walked, he kept his gaze active, scanning the campus grounds.

She was talking. "We're here because letters Einstein wrote about the formation of Israel are kept in this library. They can't be checked out, so we'll have to come here for a few days."

"Fine, as long as we vary the schedule. Nothing predictable." He'd already noticed her obvious routines, something that showed a need to be in control, but it could get her killed.

A curved walk led toward a central tower between two wings. The building reminded him of some big fancy European church. He opened the door for her as two sexy chicks passed them walking out. This library stint might let him sample a lot of sweet eye candy.

He followed her inside past a reception desk of dark wood that looked old. They entered a two-story hall, and he scanned for ambush sites. Desks filled the room's center. Books crammed wall shelves and rows of bookcases made him nervous. Too many hiding places. The second floor—balconies on two sides of the big main room—held still more desks and book cases. More possible lines of fire. High arched-beam ceilings reinforced the feeling of being inside a church, and at the far end a window of stained glass just upped the sensation.

He stopped cold. "This is the first time I've been inside a library since grade school."

"A library is a church to me."

"That's the word I thought of."

This world of Claire Alden was going to be different from anything he had known. He felt excited in a strange way.

"I work in the special collections room," she added, all business, "a small room with nothing for you to do. Why don't you wait here? And I'll meet you at the entry desk at 11:30. We'll go into Poughkeepsie for pizza and then into the city for my EClaire board meeting."

He checked the collections room, left her there, and returned to the main hall. The first floor could hold maybe five hundred people, but he counted only thirty-two at the tables. All but three were young studious types. Two men, late fifties, looked and dressed like professors, all rumpled and into their work. A bearded man had come in behind a cluster of young people just after he and Claire had entered. In his forties probably. Neat. The guy had sat down and pulled a paperback out of a briefcase.

Humvee decided to case the entire room and upstairs before settling to wait. He found another fifteen people rummaging through bookshelves. Curious about the beautiful window, he asked the girl at the desk about it.

"It depicts the life of Lady Elena Lucretia, the first woman to earn a doctorate. From the University of Padua in 1678."

He was too embarrassed to ask where Padua was.

At 9:30 he settled where he could see anyone coming and going but wouldn't be noticeable and watched people while appearing to skim issues of Sports Illustrated.

The bearded guy with the paperback looked him over hard a couple of times. Not one other person had done that. Others glanced but quickly looked away. Humvee's warning system dinged. Paperback could just be some uptight guy who liked to hang out at libraries, but he had nervous eyes. And he held but as far as Hunvee could tell didn't really read his book.

The man's gaze settled on Humvee again. Humvee hid behind the magazine, aware that nothing about himself—not his size, his skin color, and most of all, not his tattoos—fit this scene. Maybe that was what Paperback found so interesting.

Eventually his watch said 11:25. He stood to go find Claire—he really did not like the vibes coming off the bearded man. Claire was coming from the collections room and entered the main hall. The bearded man stood and headed toward her.

Humvee ran. He threw himself in front of Claire at the very moment the bearded man jabbed at her with what looked like a ballpoint pen. Humvee felt the tip strike his right bicep as he shoved her away from the attacker.

He grabbed at Paperback Man's left wrist, but the wiry little guy was quick and sprinted through a crowd of co-eds entering the library. He'd dropped a small piece of paper. Humvee dashed after him and they raced across the vast lawn.

Humvee was closing in but the bastard hopped onto a motorcycle and roared off, heading for the nearby campus entrance. He zoomed past the information booth and disappeared into the street traffic. Mentally repeating the motorcycle license number several times, Humvee jogged back toward the library. His bicep felt warm. He found only a small, red spot. Like he'd been stung by a bee.

I don't like it," Claire said minutes later as she examined the spot. They were in her car. He was driving. "We're going to go right now and have a doctor look at it."

"What's on the piece of paper?"

"I don't want to talk about it now." She shook her head. "Later."

Someone Tried to Kill Your Mom

John awoke in a king-size bed to the sound of a woman singing in the hotel's bathroom. He reached toward the nightstand and hit the button that filled the room with the seductive music of John Mayer. His plans that morning didn't go beyond the next hour or two, but they were excellent plans. He sat up as the woman approached, fully dressed in what she'd worn last night when he'd met her in the Grand Wailea's Tsunami nightclub, a blood-red drop-waist top and black mini-skirt, showing a tan, taut midriff. She settled onto the bed's edge, smelling of the hotel's soap, scented with ginger and something tropical. Wild.

He took her hand and stroked the palm. "Are you sure you have to go, Kristin?"

She laughed. "It's Krystal."

"Right. With a K." He gave her an apologetic grin. "I'm bad with names. Sorry."

"I'd love to stay for…breakfast. But I have to be at work at 9:00."

"I forgot. You work where?"

She kissed his cheek. "The Jolly Roger. Will I see you at the Tsunami tonight?"

"Don't know. Not planning things." He touched the tip of her nose.

She pulled back and strode toward the living room. "I won't forget you, John Trask."

He grabbed a towel and wrapped it around his middle as she shouldered her tiny red purse and opened the door to the private patio, letting in the cry of a gull and the crashing surf.

He followed and watched her leave. Room service arrived promptly right behind her. Bacon…its smell revved his appetite—and reminded him of Fance and their mornings together. Since the bombing, Fance leaving, and his dropping out of the tournament, he felt like shit most of the time. He'd come to Maui thinking maybe something physical was the cure.

The plan was to stay for a week or so, and he had already generously tipped the concierge, room service, and maids. His suite offered the hotel's best ocean view. He'd insisted. "Cost isn't a factor." Wet-bar, TV, stereo, video, marble bath with Jacuzzi tub. Every day an Uber drove him all the way to Grand Wailea, Sprecklesville, or Ho'okipa beaches—and back.

He should be feeling great. Thing was, though, he didn't.

A twinge of guilt struck him over racing through the cash Grandmere had settled on him. He returned to the living room. Alone again. Too damn much time alone.

He swigged the coffee—fresh Kona roast. As he sipped fresh-squeezed orange juice, his cell phone chimed the theme from "Mission Impossible." The incoming number rooted him in place. He tapped to answer, throat tight, mouth suddenly dry. "Hi, Fance."

"Hi, John."

"I'm really surprised."

"Where are you?"

"Maui." He paced to the sliding door and looked out at green tree fronds, white sand, and stunning blue ocean. God how he wished she were here this very second. He put his palm to the glass and leaned on it, his head down, concentrating on her voice.

"Maui! I didn't know you even left New York. Where are you staying?"

He hesitated, guilt over his wild spending stabbing anew. "A…small place close to Sprecklesville Beach."

"You're windsurfing."

"Right. The weather's been perfect. I wish you were here, Fance. You'd love it." She didn't say anything. "You still mad?"

"I don't know. I didn't call about us. I can tell you haven't seen the news."

"Nope." This was probably not going to be good news. "It's only 8:30 local time. I just got up." He straightened and returned to the small breakfast table. "What's so hot?"

"Someone tried to kill your mother yesterday. She's okay, John, but her bodyguard, according to the New York Times, probably isn't going to make it."

He dropped onto a chair. "Bodyguard?"

"Apparently she's had several death threats. Isn't that sad?"

He snatched up the remote and clicked the TV on. "Do you have the newspaper story?" he asked, searching for the news channel.

"Yeah." She skimmed the when and where and then read, "The deadly agent ricin was injected into Mateus Viliamu who is in intensive care at Colombia Presbyterian Hospital. He is unconscious, fighting for his life. The mortality rate from ricin poisoning, which has no antidote, is as high as 90%. Doctors do not expect Mr. Viliamu to survive. A note dropped at the scene by the attacker read, 'A woman who doesn't serve man is an enemy unto the Lord. I must smite the enemies of heaven.' A note with the exact same wording was left after the fatal attack last year on Dr. Meredith Jaynes, author of *The Biology of Peace*."

John stood and started pacing. "Shit, Fance. My mom loved that book. Tried to get me to read it. She was really upset when Jaynes was killed."

"There's more. 'Mr. Viliamu was able to give the license number of the motorcycle his assailant used to flee. The man was captured twenty minutes later in a police chase. He's been identified as Alphonse Rendick, an out-of-work biochemistry lab technician.'"

"Well, at least they got him." The face of Phyllis Colson appeared on the TV screen with a panel of four talking-heads. "Wait a sec," he said as he clicked on the sound.

". . . expert on Claire Alden's career," the anchor said. "Who would want to kill her?"

The camera focused on the bitch columnist, Colson. She was always after his mom. The woman was sick. She wore an irritating I-am-oh-so-rational smile.

Colson said, "There are lots of people who'd want to kill a woman who has such destabilizing ideas." She shrugged in a way that said, 'what's so shocking about that?'

Into the phone John said, "Did you hear that?" He quickly punched up the volume.

Colson continued. "The police apparently have their man. We don't yet know much about him except that he's no fan of so-called liberated women."

"Sounds like that Phyllis Colson babe," Fance said.

"The problem is," Colson's tone sounded like a warning. "Claire Alden continues to grow more powerful."

Griswald, the anchor, jumped in. "She's admired by fans around the world..."

"Oh, puh-LEASE!" The camera moved in for a Colson close-up. "Claire Alden has the gall to think she knows what's good for everyone. And make no mistake, she's dangerous."

A man John didn't recognize chimed in. "You keep saying that, Phyllis. But what's so upsetting about calling for the world to commit to nonviolence? If anything, isn't it just silly?"

Colson flipped back her mass of long red hair. "If you believe that's all she's up to, I have a bridge to sell you in Brooklyn."

Griswald said, "Alden tends to stick to fundraising for worthy causes, building schools and microcredit. And amassing that fortune. Are you referring to political danger?"

"I am. You are aware of ABrightFuture.org. They mobilized 250,000 marchers on Washington to support the confirmation of that atheist Susanne Weinstein who now sits on our highest court. That same group is solidly behind Alden. That's power, and it's potentially political."

Fance interrupted his concentration. "John, Phyllis Colson bores the hell out of me. Secretly, I think she'd be happy if your mom was about to die and not her bodyguard."

He clicked off the TV.

"It's scary how many people might want to hurt her," Fance continued. "Right away, before they caught Rendick, everybody had a theory who the assassin was: someone from big oil, the Tears of Allah again, the KKK, the pro-lifers, those people who want wars in space. I just can't figure out why someone so good seems to make such drastic enemies."

So good. He wasn't going to get into an argument with Fance over his mother. Not ever again if he could help it. And as mad as his mother might make him, she sure as hell didn't deserve to be assassinated.

"You really should call your mom…but if you want, I'll call her and see how she is."

"I can't call her. Not yet. But I…I'd appreciate it if you called, Fance. Maybe call Joss."

"Okay. I miss you, you know."

"I miss you too. I love your voice, Fance. Where are you? What are you wearing?"

She laughed. "I'm in bed. I'm naked. And hot."

"I like it."

"I know."

His turn to laugh. "So where are you really?"

"I worked late last night. I'm at Starbuck's, wearing my grungiest jogging outfit."

"I wish you were here—"

"I wish you were here—"

They'd spoken at the same time.

"I'm going to do something about that," he said.

They said goodbye, and he punched in the number for the concierge to make a reservation for New York. "First available flight," he said. "First class or in the cargo hold. I don't care. Just get me there fast."

With Poisoning...Three to Five Days

The New York Presbyterian Hospital waiting room chair was hurting Claire's back. Joss sat beside her, all neat and professional in a jade green pantsuit. Still in her jeans, Claire had flipped through magazines, paced, and meditated, although since the Tabor Towers disaster, achieving any genuine state of inner peace had eluded her. Please live, she silently begged Humvee.

Surely they must know more about Humvee by now. She dared not pester the nurses again. At 3:30 someone changed the TV channel to CNN, and Claire read the crawler at the bottom.

"A DoD budget request tripled to include PeaceMaker development."

What a miserable waste. Few people had the slightest clue what this meant for America, financially or strategically. She closed her eyes, sick at the news. As if war on the planet's surface wasn't enough. No, it had to extend into space.

Joss's cellular chimed. She took the call. "Hi, Pryce." She listened, and then turned to Claire, "The police say Rendick is a loner. A religious fanatic of his very own religious sect. No big conspiracy, and they're also charging the creep for the murder of Meredith Jaynes."

Claire sighed, and Joss returned her attention to Pryce. "He is?" Joss looked directly back at Claire. "I'll see what I can do." She hung up.

Claire cut her off. "I'm not going to that fundraiser tonight. I don't care who Pryce wants me to see." Joss frowned. "Look, Joss, I've done my bit. Humvee may have given all he has to give. Some prices are too damn high."

Joss snorted. Her voice filled with contempt, she said, "I guess Humvee made his sacrifice so you can live out your days in safe, quiet, undisturbed, private comfort."

Claire gasped. She barely checked herself from slapping Joss. "How dare you say that to me!" In all their years together, Joss had never spoken like this. People stared at them.

Joss reddened and said, "I can't believe I blurted that out. But it's what I've been thinking. It's not fair, I know. I'm sorry. Really sorry, Claire."

Claire sucked in a long, deep breath. "Okay. Fine. Apology accepted."

Joss nodded, slumped in resignation, and returned to her cellphone. Claire forced herself to smile at people still watching, then pulled her cell from her handbag and checked incoming calls. One from Adam, who was extremely upset by the attack. The second number she didn't recognize and there was no message. She hit "return." After two rings, a voice said, "hello," and that was all it took for her to know it was Savik Kodaly.

One word. "Hello." She had wondered, after the concert, if maybe Savik had sent the lavender rose, but when he made no other contact, she ruled him out. But now, maybe not.

"Savik." She envisioned the dark hair and eyes. The teasing grin. She could hear the sound of distant voices, men laughing. "It's Claire Alden. Is this a bad time to return your call?"

"Not at all. Just coming in from a round of golf. Celebrating our… uh…the weekend a little early. Glad to hear your voice, Claire. Came pretty close to never hearing it again, didn't I?"

"The man who took the attack meant for me may not make it, so…yes."

"It seems you bring out the worst in some people."

She smiled, remembering Savik's sharp humor.

He said quickly, "Did I offend you? I just—"

"Not at all. It just brought back a memory of you." Oh, god, why had she said *that!*

"Look, I know your schedule must be packed, and things right now must be in chaos, but I've been wondering if we might get together for dinner. Even just coffee."

She suddenly couldn't imagine anything she would like more. But… oh, dear, no. That wouldn't work at all. No, no, no. In fact, never. "You're right. Now wouldn't work for me."

"Oh."

He sounded so dejected. And she loved it.

"Then let me just say it was good to see you, Claire, even under such tragic circumstances, and may I ask if it's okay if I try again later."

Trying later wouldn't change anything, but she felt too pleased to hear his voice to be rude. "Yes. Of course. Thanks for calling, Savik. I'm glad to be alive and I appreciate your concern."

When she hung up, Joss said, "I hope you don't mind. I gave him the number. His law firm is big time. You never know when they might come in handy."

"Right, Joss. You never know."

A nurse bustled up to them. "You have been so patient, Ms. Alden. The doctor said you could go in, but only for two minutes."

Claire followed the nurse into the intensive care section, and into a glassed-in room. Humvee lay on a bed with machines on all sides. The sight was a visceral blow. She recovered enough to ask, "What is all this?"

"He is fighting hard for his life. The poison is attacking virtually all of his organs. As you see, he's on a respirator. The other machine is handling kidney function, and of course he's on intravenous. That," she pointed to a blue box, "is a heart monitor. The doctors are impressed that he's still with us. With ricin poisoning, hanging on for three to five days means he has a chance at survival. He's tough, Ms. Alden."

"Thank you," Claire said. "It's Claire," she said. "Everyone calls me Claire."

The nurse smiled. "Two minutes," she said and left Claire alone with Humvee.

Claire worked her way around the kidney machine and laid her hand over his. He felt so hot. "I am forever in your debt. The rest of my life I owe to you."

The respirator wheezed. What an ugly sound.

"You're a bull of a man, Humvee. You can make it. You hang on." She stood quietly that way until she heard the nurse open the sliding door and together they left the ICU.

Joss met her, grinning like she'd won a shopping spree at I Magnin. "I've had a call from Fance. John is back in town, and he's back with Fance."

Claire felt a surge of pleasure. "Finally some good news. I like Fance."

"Fance said that John said to find out about you. How you're doing and all."

They headed toward the elevator, Claire's spirits rising in spite of everything. John was back. He had been concerned for her. Humvee would fight hard for his life.

And Joss was right. Claire still had contributions to make. Things worth living for, fighting for, and maybe even dying for. And she wasn't dead yet. "I need to apologize to you, Joss. I can't let the deaths of people who supported me mean nothing. Tell Pryce he won this skirmish. I don't know what he has in mind for tonight's EARTHCARE benefit, but book us rooms, and find me a gown."

Joss grinned. "Already did, boss. Just in case. You never know...."

A Politician, Which You Clearly Are Not

Claire sat surrounded by the faint scent of expensive perfume and the rustlings of a formally attired audience in the darkness of the Hayden Planetarium theater. The dynamic strains of the popular opening to "Thus Spake Zarathustra," the stunning theme used to powerful effect in *2001 A Space Odyssey*, started softly and swelled. Then, in voice overlay, Jodie Foster along with Tom Hanks narrated this premier showing of "Quest To Mars and Beyond."

"The universe lies before us," Foster said. "New places and new homes. But in our bones and being, we will always be 'of planet Earth.'"

The EARTHCARE benefit crowd murmured its awe at the spectacular visions spread across the massive dome. *Whoever dreamed up this site for tonight's event was inspired.* The panorama zoomed in on the Horsehead Nebula. Interstellar dust and gases formed a sharp black silhouette, as if a horsehead chess piece stood in the endless blackness of space.

The grandeur in the possibility of exploration of those distant realms excited Claire. Yet the presentation provoked troubling thoughts, about the fate of humankind. If her whole life had changed profoundly because of her travels, what kind of change would take place in the human community once Earthlings traveled to Mars and Beyond?

The possibility of moving out into the universe seemed like humanity's truest adventure, a noble destiny foreseen by ancients, implanted in our being, our marrow, our minds. But what if humans soured the glorious dream by extending violence and killing into that grand vastness? Putting weapons in space was profane, akin to tossing a grenade into a sanctuary.

She stopped herself. I must quit thinking about all the troubles in the universe. I'm no fun anymore. Pryce is crazy. I'll do all I can with AFWW and let the rest go. The scene changed to what Claire considered the ultimate symbol of human oneness—the famous picture of Earth taken by the Apollo 17 astronauts—a blue-and-white globe against the utter darkness of the void—as Tom Hanks concluded, "We must cherish what we have even as we dream of where we might go and of what we might become."

The music subsided. The theater brightened slowly, re-orienting senses still out in space. The audience of over four hundred gowned and black-tied *hoi polloi* clapped and bravo'd, Claire along with them. After two months of wearing black or just sweats, it felt good to be decked out in her deep merlot satin gown and garnet beads.

"This place knocks me out," Joss said, the hot pink of her silk bandeaux bright against a mannish black suit cut like a tux.

"Closest I've ever come to a religious experience," Pryce said, equally elegant in a black silk shirt and black tux.

Flanked by Joss and Pryce, Claire strolled out of the planetarium and down the spiral walk of the Heilbrunn Cosmic Pathway. Displays along the side illustrated thirteen billion years of cosmic evolution. Each of Claire's strides covered seventy-five million years as she and other guests moved downward toward the lobby. Several people greeted her with smiles and comments like, "I'm so relieved that you're still with us."

"You know," Claire said to Joss, shrugging, "maybe the best thing I could do for our cause would be to become a martyr. Boy does that ever get attention."

Joss grabbed her arm and squeezed hard. "Don't say that! Not even in kidding. You want attention? Walk around naked."

Claire laughed out loud.

Pryce chuckled. "Why didn't I think of that?"

As they were leaving the time passageway, they crossed that final, fascinating little line about the width of a human hair. Claire pointed at it. "Us," she said of the teeny span of the ages that had included humans.

"Ah, time," Joss exclaimed. "We're just a speck of spit in time's ocean." Her expression turned mischievous. "'I wasted time, now time doth waste me.' Top that, Pryce."

Pryce cockily adjusted his tie. "'Tomorrow and tomorrow and tomorrow creeps in this petty pace from day to day to the last syllable of recorded time.'" Right back to business, to Claire he said, "There's someone you should talk to. Let me see if I can find him." He excused himself.

Claire loved their eccentricities. One of these was sparring with Shakespearian quotations. Joss had majored in women's studies, and earned her masters specializing in archetypes in literature and mythology before her life went into a tailspin as she dealt with family and gender issues. Pryce had wandered far afield of his history major. Claire knew his opinion of every book he read, but felt sometimes that she didn't know the man himself as well. He occasionally made sarcastic reference to a wife he'd been married to for a year who apparently betrayed him. Claire had been to some of his family gatherings—stiff, formal events where no one hugged anyone. He seemed content to be married to his work.

The lobby of the Rose Center offered food and bar stations. "Look at those lines," Joss said. "The caviar always goes fast. Excuse me." She rushed ahead.

Claire stood alone a moment, marveling at the Rose Center. The inside was always lighted at night, and from the street or sidewalk, fifty-foot tall glass walls allowed passers-by a view of the massive eighty-seven-foot diameter sphere that housed the actual planetarium. Models of Sol's planets hung in orbit around the planetarium as thought it were the sun. Quite spectacular.

Claire caught a glimpse of a man's back and head. Savik!

The man turned to speak to the beautiful brunette on his arm. He wasn't Savik, yet in that split-second, she'd raced through emotional extremes: eagerness to see him, a mini-flash of jealousy of the brunette, and deflation that he was not who she'd wanted him to be. Not good. She was seeing Savik even when he wasn't there.

A classic "power couple" strolled toward her from the Hall of Planet Earth.

"Claire, love!" Beryl Steinmetz air-kissed both of Claire's cheeks. The CBS fifty-something program director in a black chiffon gown and wearing galaxies of diamonds was a regular at most of New York's A-class fund-raisers. Her wealthy husband, heading for a mini-bar, enabled Beryl's generosity. "You have been having a dreadful time." Without waiting for a response, Beryl continued. "I've been dying to introduce you to someone who may become the most powerful man in the world. If you can reach him, he could champion AFWW issues."

"Terrific. Who is it?"

"Senator Mason Crane."

Crane was likely to be the Democratic candidate for President, and thankfully likely to beat President Hass next year. A handsome man. "We've only met once and very briefly. I'm eager to see him again." *Very, very.*

With Beryl forging their path, they wove among the chattering social clusters and into the Hall of Planet Earth. Claire spotted Crane in a tight little group of four men in front of the Dynamic Earth Globe. Beryl, quite unintimidated, pulled right up to them.

"Senator," Beryl said, "super to see you again and looking so fit."

Crane and Beryl hugged. Claire was used to never being introduced since everyone recognized her. Instead Beryl introduced the three men Claire didn't know.

Crane said, "Both you ladies look stunning."

One man chimed in. "We were just discussing the very positive developments for the PeaceMaker."

A chill, like a cold knife blade, ran up Claire's spine. *Were you paying attention in the planetarium?* She bit back what she felt like saying as heat flushed her face.

Beryl said, "It's a damn shame, if you ask me, that the thing worked. It will be well nigh impossible for anyone in Congress to drag their feet to slow this juggernaut down now that all those systems do seem to work together."

The same man said, "With due respect, the PeaceMaker program is our best hope to win the war against terrorists. Speed in Congress is what we need. Not foot dragging."

Crane said to Beryl, "I gather you're not a fan."

"That expensive boondoggle is actually a crime against humanity," Claire blurted. "And gutting the Outer Space Treaty to allow its development will prove to be an astronomical disaster, if you'll pardon the pun!"

They all stared at her.

She smiled and pointed at the eight-foot sphere of the spinning earth on the nearby display, revealing through digital video deep, dark oceans and green continents, whorls of white. "It's so beautiful and what this program will do is spew weapons into the space above it. Is there to be no end to arms races, no line where we say, enough is enough?"

Crane, also smiling, said, "But this system can guarantee our security from missiles. I should think you'd be in favor of any system that helps ensure peace."

"Peace!?" She'd dropped her smile at "security." Honesty battled discretion for a millisecond before discretion lost. "The PeaceMaker program, as it is ridiculously named, is a techno-warrior's wet dream of domination. Any peace this weapon would bring would be the peace of totalitarianism. The current spin is that its function is to hit ICBMs carrying nuclear warheads, but this thing isn't limited to hitting targets in space. When fully implemented, PeaceMaker can incinerate targets on Earth. No house, no building, no government body, no group will be immune to blackmail by whoever's finger is on the trigger."

"Claire—," Crane had assumed what he doubtless considered a calming, rational tone.

"Senator—" She fixed his gaze with her own. "Are you saying if you could decide whether to cancel the program and shift resources elsewhere, you'd support it?"

People around them had stopped their own conversations to listen. She now wished that discretion had tempered her outburst, but it was too late. Crane, ever the politician, casually shifted and attempted to block Claire from the onlookers.

This further irritated her. "Do you think even our allies will sit still for this? So far this misguided money grinder has simply eaten up *our* taxes so no one—allies or enemies—cared if we pursued it. But if we might actually build and deploy, we'll drive the whole world into a unified alliance to stop us. This death ray on space platforms invites global war!"

The mesmerized crowd now numbered several dozen. Beryl had grown pale. Crane smiled, held his hands up in a calming gesture and said, "We just have to keep control—"

"And throw more billions down this sinkhole? To line defense contractor's pockets?"

Crane's face reddened and he squinted at her. "All right, Claire! Here is the reality. The PeaceMaker program does involve billions of dollars. Many billions of dollars. It supports whole industries and provides countless jobs and has for years. I'm a politician, which you, clearly, are not—and the political reality is that it can't be stopped. So what must be done is to manage its development wisely." His look and tone had been a bit threatening, but now he seemed pleased with himself and nodded at others as if he'd just won the debate.

She suddenly felt nauseated. This man would most likely be the Democratic nominee that she'd hoped would stop President Hass.

Beryl, apparently attempting to shift the conversation, put her hand on Crane's arm and spoke lightly. "Senator, we were hoping that you may have read Claire's book. That you'd champion a metanoia."

He frowned. "Metanoia?"

Claire spoke evenly. "It means to repent, to change one's mind and go in an opposite direction. If we don't change from an economy based on war to an economy based on ending war, our future will be endless war."

A resounding silence fell over the group and quickly spread to other groups, and only a murmur of peripheral conversation sussurated among the displays of plate tectonics, volcanoes, core ice, and meteorites.

Claire shook her head. "Excuse me." She lifted the hem of the gown, turned and walked away. At first she didn't know where to go or what to do. She'd very likely just made an enemy of the man who might be the next U.S. President.

I looked like a fool. A self-righteous fool at that. She wouldn't blame Beryl if Beryl was back there saying, "Claire does get a bit carried away. You know, I really don't know her all that well."

She fled outside, tonight's hulking guard right behind her. She sagged against a lamppost. This wasn't her way at all. Confrontational and belligerent. Her father would abhor her lack of diplomacy.

I must still be deranged by grief. That's the only rational explanation.

She was shaking and her knees felt wobbly.

Beside her a scuffling sound made her look up. Shutters clicked as cameras flashed.

An All-Out Fight To Win

Claire couldn't sleep. Wearing sweats, she took the elevator to the Broadway Marquis Hotel's top floor. When she stepped outside onto the roof terrace, the hum of New York in the streets below conveyed the movement of thousands of souls still awake and alive and pursuing happiness. Millions of people who did not care who was President of the United States.

They were making love, caring for a sick child, or in the middle of a night-shift job as a nurse or fishermen delivering fresh fish to the fish-market. They were unaware that the decision to put weapons in space was proceeding without their say-so, without any meaningful discussion as to the consequences. And when the PeaceMaker program drained the economy and drew these millions into yet another war, they'd be told it was to save us from the bad guys.

Utterly alone, with not even the moon's friendly face for company, she paced along the glass windbreak seething as she pictured Crane "talking reality" to her. *You damn fool.* "You're a short-sighted, blind leader of the willingly led."

As President, Mason Crane would not end the PeaceMaker madness, he'd support it.

The stream of sickening thoughts twisting through her mind resisted any "off" switch she tried. The success of the PeaceMaker test had raised the stakes; the damn thing had worked. This was the U.S. saying to the world, "We're in charge, and that's not going to change. Ever." Americans were looking at the ultimate in absolute power, and no one seemed concerned that it just might corrupt us absolutely.

She shivered. The October night had turned frosty. Her stomach was burning. All the rich party hors d'oeuvres were striking back. *Burns in the belly.* She stopped pacing. Her father's words came back to her. "When an injustice calls our name, it burns in the belly and sticks in the craw, and if we walk away from it, we cannot respect ourselves."

The night's blackness brightened and Claire looked up to see the moon appear from behind the clouds. *Dad. Maman. Help me. God, help me.*

I can't believe what I'm thinking I must do.

She returned to her room to attempt to sleep on her boiling fears. Maybe the drastic course of action she was envisioning would prove to be only grandiose histrionics of an overtired brain.

She stood at the bathroom mirror, thinking how China, Russia and third world countries, even America's allies would hate American satellites menacing their skies and every corner of their land. It would unleash an apocalyptic arms race. Former allies could boycott American products and embargo imports. Freeze the country's foreign assets.

And Claire's opponents thought *her* economic ideas were radical. "HA!" she said to her reflection. *PeaceMaker could start an economic tsunami the likes of which the world has never seen.*

Of course, laser deployment would happen gradually at first, she thought as she brushed her teeth. First they'd zap a terrorist stronghold and feel heroic, and everyone would cheer and condemn any opposition as traitorous. Then they'd zap suspected cells within the borders of former allies. And then anyone suspected of disloyalty, including dissidents inside the U.S. borders.

U.S. satellites armed with lasers in the wrong hands could turn tyrannical and ultimately mean the end of any government by and for the people. *Of course, any coalition or government really wanting to stop us might decide that their only remaining option was biological or chemical warfare. They'd convince themselves, as humans usually do when we're scared, that the end in this case more than justified the means.*

She slipped into a night shirt and climbed into bed. Her scenarios became a vivid nightmare where she smiled and handed out baskets of Forest Farms products as she stepped over incinerated bodies blasted by lasers. She found herself in a ball gown and dancing with Senator Crane who steered her into the middle of a dance floor and then left her there, staring up through a blasted ceiling as the crane-shaped PeaceMaker skimmed overhead, shining silver in a pitch black sky.

She awoke after a few hours of fitful sleep completely twisted in the bedding, but somehow feeling calmer. She rose, walked to the window, and drew the curtains back revealing a night-lit New York skyline.

That patronizing tone in Crane's voice came back to her. He thought she was naive. "I'm a politician, which you, clearly, are not," he'd said—as if being something other than a politician rendered her incapable of understanding economic complexities. Crane voted to allot vast sums of money that simply disappeared into the DoD at no personal cost to him, while Claire, as the head of EClaire, stood to *personally* lose millions and cause thousands of people to lose jobs, hundreds of economies to fail, all if she made wrong decisions. Where did he get the nerve to imply she didn't know what she was talking about?

She snatched a blanket, wrapped in it, and stepped onto the balcony. The moon had traveled across the sky and hung low in the west. She closed her eyes and meditated on the serenity prayer, repeating it, asking for the wisdom to know the difference between what she could change and what she couldn't.

She'd never sought power. Never. It had seemed to merely flow toward her, and she was good at mobilizing highly motivated people by example and by the power of her celebrity, and, of course, the persuasion of her money. This combination, plus her father's mantle of diplomacy and her lack of craving for personal power was what had enabled her to play such a central role in the Sumidar treaty. But President of the United States?

And there it was. She'd named it. President of the United States.

A shiver crossed her shoulders. *Before David died, all I ever wanted to be was a wife, mother, and great cook. Who the hell am I to shoulder such a vast responsibility?* Her body seemed appalled at the burden. Maybe the question should be: could she do a better job than Hass or Crane? Well, she knew the answer to that. Absolutely, she could.

And if she didn't stop this mad plunge into offensively weaponized space, would anyone?

She bowed her head. She also knew the answer to that question. Others had warned and protested for years against any changes to the Outer Space Treaty and its ban on offensive space weapons. But their voices were whispers on the public stage compared to hers. There was no guarantee, of course, that she could halt the PeaceMaker deployment, but she was probably the only one who had anything like a realistic chance.

And she did burn with a vision of how to defang the monster of war and a feeling for how to mobilize people to a cause. Vast numbers of people already believed in her vision. Many revolutionaries around the world, like Amina and Ramin, were already at work. She stepped back inside and sat by the window, thinking of the nurses and truck drivers, couples in bedrooms not thinking about their country, the executives, garbage collectors, and everyone in the middle. If she was to live in peace with herself, her course of action was clear.

She looked toward a pinking horizon in the east. The dark'ning dawn, as Carly Simon called it. She sat there until 5:00 A.M. then showered, dressed, made tea, fetched her cell phone and sat looking out at the gray Manhattan skyline.

Silver cities rise….

"Let the River Run." She thought of the impassioned, joyful faces lit with hope at the Unity Concert.

"We, the great and small, stand on a star and blaze a trail of desire through the dark'ning dawn."

She dialed Rachel's number. Rachel answered, sounding sleepy. "Are you busy?" Claire asked without a *hello*.

"Mmmf funny. Ha-ha." Rachel yawned.

"I've made a decision."

"Okay. 'm sitting up now. Blood starting to flow. I think."

"Senator Mason Crane is the Democratic frontrunner for the Presidential nomination, and he, like the current administration, wants to put offensive weapons into space. I can't stand it."

"Oh my god!" gasped the atheist. "OH MY god! You actually think you might…?"

"Yes."

"I have tears in my eyes. Are you really serious?"

"Yes. And I've never been one to make expensive token gestures. There are formidable obstacles, of course, but difficulties have to be considered opportunities." Claire took a deep breath. "And a run for President would be an all out fight to win."

My Son Is Dating A Topless Dancer

Soon after talking with Rachel, Claire ordered breakfast and then called Serena for a conversation like the one with Rachel. Afterward she called Adam Forsythe's secretary for an appointment. "The Ambassador has time this afternoon, Ms. Alden, or you can wait until he returns from Chile in five days."

She'd wanted at least one day to think before actually seeking Adam's advice but couldn't stand to wait five days and accepted the 4:00 P.M. time slot.

Now. What about Joss? Joss had known about the 'Claire for President' posters, and for a time afterward things had been rocky between them. Joss's betrayal had become a moot point and Claire's anger embarrassing. Indeed, if it hadn't been for the concert attendees' amazing response, Claire might never have considered running for President. If her often prickly assistant found out others knew about her decision to run before Claire told her—well, that would really set Joss off.

At times, Claire had felt that having Joss as her assistant was a bit like having a wife, the indispensable kind. They worked so well together that words were often unnecessary. But when there were issues between them, an emotional frost descended.

Claire had enthusiastically helped Joss resist the ties of a difficult past. Nine years ago, before she'd come to work for EClaire, Joss had considered herself a "high bottom drunk." She could keep her career alive, but her work was the only functional area of life. Her family had renounced her drinking and her lesbian lifestyle. Except for a cherished brother, due to be released from prison soon, and to whom she remained close, Joss was alone. The brother was a gang-banger mixed up with a violent crowd into all sorts of no-good. Through sheer will, Joss had been sober for nine years. In many ways, Claire and EClaire were her true family.

"Take two days off," Claire said to Joss over the phone.

"What? Really? You okay? I guess you've seen the picture of you slumping against the lamp post. I'm only two floors down. I can come right up."

"No, not necessary. I'm fine."

"Are you upset with me?"

"No, no. I just think we both need a little break. I know I do."

"You've met someone!" Joss gasped. "That Savik Kodaly called again, didn't he!"

"No." Claire sighed. "Don't obsess, dear girl."

"You're up to something."

"I need time to think.

"Okay, then, I'll visit my brother. Only thirty days and he's out. And think about what?

"About running to be President."

"Jesus, Claire!"

"I'm only thinking. We'll talk about it after I have time to think."

"Let me come up. Let's talk now."

"Not yet. I'm not ready. And you must not say anything to anyone until we do."

Joss insisted that Claire call her before making any final decision, then Claire ended the call.

At 10:00 the bodyguard filling in for Humvee arrived to take her to the hospital. Shaved head, strong jaw, five o'clock shadow. His name was Bobby. She liked him well enough but felt no special connection, as she had to Humvee.

Humvee was still unconscious, and his kidneys would never be what they were. The same nurse let her into his room for a brief chance to speak to him. But he would survive. She felt joyful as she held his hand.

"The nurse says you may be slowed down a bit, but if you want, you can still work for me. The next time I visit, we'll be able to talk. You may be out of here in two weeks and able to work in two months or maybe less." She squeezed his big fingers. "I want you back with me, Humvee. I'm going to really need you—if you're willing once you hear what I'm going to do."

. . . . .

Bobby delivered her at the EClaire building on Park Avenue. The staff was always effusive when she showed up. She ate sushi in the office suite that awaited her return at any hour day or night. She began arranging for others to assume more of her duties.

At 3:45 she left with Bobby. The mid-October air had felt nippy all day. Soon it would be Halloween and then Thanksgiving. Maybe she could persuade John to bring Fance to the Retreat for Thanksgiving. Claire didn't know Fance well, had only spoken to her twice on the phone, but each time she'd felt warmed by the girl's attitude. The news photo image of Fance in that tiny outfit poked itself into her stream of thought.

"My son is dating a topless dancer," she said to Bobby as much as to herself.

"Oh yeah?"

John dating a topless dancer! And Claire was contemplating the U.S. Presidency. Why had she never given a moment's thought about the implications of John's…issues. "Nothing is ever easy or straightforward is it?"

"Nothing but getting into trouble," he said. "I've found that's pretty easy."

She stared out the window. What would Adam say about John's lifestyle?

Late Tuesday afternoon traffic crawled down the street. They slowly approached the subtly curved U.N. General Assembly Building, its colorful flags of the nations waving in the breeze. Bobby maneuvered toward the U.S. Mission across the street where she would talk to the U.N. Ambassador about her candidacy for President of the most power-ful country in the world.

Your Running Mate Must Be A Man

Eager for Adam's advice, but also hesitant to speak because of the enormity of what she was proposing to do, Claire studied his back. He stood in front of a carved African mahogany sideboard, pouring her a cup of coffee. Fifty-nine last month, he was robust and still energetic despite the total silvering of once coal black hair.

Her father's partner and life-long friend had served as the U.S. Ambassador to the United Nations under the Hass administration for nearly three years now. A devout man of strong will and character, he was a moderate Republican. This made him a maverick in many ways. The problem, he'd told her six months earlier, was that he was growing increasingly opposed to his President's choices.

"Adam, how do you feel about the PeaceMaker test?" She was avoiding her main issue.

He handed her the coffee and smiled knowingly. "Your argument with Mason Crane grabbed a lot of attention." He sighed. "Let's just say I will be relieved to retire after the election, no matter who wins."

Not exactly a direct answer, but her father had taught her that a good diplomat chooses his or her own moment to reveal sensitive information. Adam might be wary that Claire was going to ask him to make a public stand through AFWW. Though she'd known him since childhood, three years ago they became close friends. In the midst of her two-year struggle to help Sumidar negotiate first an armistice and then the peace treaty, he'd unfailingly given her canny advice. His wife, Paula, had died shortly after the Sumidar treaty signing. Adam was devastated but carried on in a way that had impressed Claire, who understood firsthand his pain.

As he added milk to his coffee, she noticed how clean his desk was, unlike her own. What their offices did have in common was collections of photos and memorabilia gathered on trips around the globe. He took a seat opposite her. "Those unfortunate tabloid pictures of you slumping against a lamppost spoke volumes. I suspect you have something weighty on your mind, my dear."

Claire's palms felt suddenly sweaty. For the most part, the gossips hadn't been too unkind. Some had even helped the cause. CLAIRE STILL IN GRIEF NOW MOURNS PEACEMAKER BUDGET. But several suggested she was under too much pressure, meddling where she didn't belong—thank you Phyllis Colson—and heading for a breakdown.

"Adam, may God help me, I'm considering running for president of the United States."

He showed no astonishment, no ridicule, no amusement whatsoever, always the diplomat.

"Thank you for not laughing."

"I'm not even close to laughing. There's been a steady buzz ever since the concert."

He listened carefully to her story, her qualms about John, his ne're-do-well life, and Fance's job as an exotic dancer, and then asked, "Is that all of it?"

Her heart skipped a beat. He had asked and she couldn't lie to Adam, but some things were simply no one else's business. No one's. Maman was dead and Serena and Rachel didn't know the whole story and wouldn't tell if they did. "There is something deeply personal, Adam.... No one could possibly know about it."

He grunted. "You know as well as I do that everything comes out in a campaign. And a campaign against Hass *will* get down and dirty."

She shook her head. "Not about this. I will do everything in my power to see that it doesn't. But if it does, well, only family pride will be hurt, I should think. I would say what Bill Clinton should have said. It's absolutely irrelevant and no one else's business."

"No candidate ever has a perfect family or past, of course. Jimmy Carter had Billy. Hillary Clinton had her brother Hugh and husband Bill. Arnold groped women. George Bush had alcoholism and failure to show up for military duty. Hass has his three marriages and is frankly an outed misogynist and racist. You're a woman of sensible habits who was married to a man you loved. You've been, as far as I know, virtually celibate since. Am I correct?"

"There has never been anyone serious."

He appeared to be studying her, frowning.

"Adam, I'm going to fight this PeaceMaker program with my dying breath. Some risks are worth taking..." *...in the way that parents risk offering their children as soldiers in a war.*

Adam nodded gravely. "All the fighting I've seen...the lives I've bargained over. I originally thought this PeaceMaker program would be the ultimate deterrent, but now I see that it's a tragic, foolish, and dangerous blunder. My advice, Claire, is that you go for it."

She felt his words as a blow to her chest followed by a breath-stealing tightening. She'd obviously been unconsciously hoping that he'd tell her she was crazy and to forget it instantly.

"You have no political track record. That's your greatest liability. The choice of your running mate must compensate for that. Without the strongest possible running mate, you'll seem a quixotic idiot. If you'll pardon my bluntness."

"Bluntness. Honesty. If I do this, I'm going to desperately need both from my friends."

They sat in quiet a moment.

She asked, "What kind of person do you envision as a running mate?"

"Well, first of all, let's stop talking about 'person.' It must be a man."

She chuckled for the first time. "Yes."

"Then he must be someone who would bring sterling credibility. Someone profoundly respected, even across party lines. You can't hope to win without crossing party lines because the Religious Right is going to savage you. You can count firmly on losing that twenty-five to thirty percent of the vote right up front."

"A great many of my fans are what's called the Religious Right. Good people, patriots."

"Claire, the moment you announce that you're going into politics, people who have loved you because you're funny, a fabulous chef, and you have a good heart, they are going to ask your position on abortion, gun control, gays, big tobacco, trial lawyers, pharmaceutical companies, higher taxes—"

She laughed. "I get it. The free ride will be over. Still, I feel I know what they want deep down. Freedom. Freedom from fear. Fear of foreign enemies. Certainly freedom from fear of some weapon in the sky controlled by the government. And the kind of freedom of spirit that comes from knowing your kids have good health care and access to a good education. We can have those kinds of things or we can have the trillion-dollar PeaceMaker program. But clearly, there's not money enough for both. I believe I can convince them to trust me to guide the change that can get those freedoms for them as well as secure the nation.

He was silent a moment, then "How do you intend to proceed?"

"Well, I'll talk to Pryce first."

"I strongly suggest that before you even begin to approach backers and potential supporters, you have some idea of a short list for your VP nominee. You make clear that, of course, the decision would be made at a later time, but you must have your ducks in a very tidy row before you approach outsiders. And this VP issue is a big duck."

"Any ideas? Or could you think about it and get back to me with suggestions."

"Of course." His gaze drifted off.

Adam was evidently already turning over possibilities. She studied his face and the qualities that he had described about a perfect running mate took on a name. 'Nothing is ever easy or straightforward,' she'd said to Bobby less than an hour ago. But actually, sometimes things were. "Would you do it Adam? If I asked you, would you run as my VP?"

He smiled. "I've been looking forward to retirement from political life." He gazed at Claire intently. "I don't know if I could summon the necessary fire in the belly. Yet I do believe in this battle for the nation's future. In truth, for the world's future and the future of democracy. And you are very special to me. You know that I wouldn't give you my word on such a decision without a time of prayer and reflection. So I can't give a final answer today. But in your presence I'm feeling a strange sense of…history, Claire, a sense of destiny."

She felt a bit light-headed. "Good God. What *are* we thinking?" She stood and walked to a window overlooking the United Nations Plaza where the flags still waved jauntily.

"Frankly," he said," I'm amazed and somewhat sorry that it was Pryce, and not me, who made the suggestion that you run. You have passion, Claire. And equally important, vision. You've got it all. Your dad would not even be surprised. He always told me you'd do great things, but I'm quite certain he had no idea how great. And I'm not talking just about winning the Presidency."

There was a small part of her that wanted to shrink away from her decision and Adam's enthusiasm. Risks, she didn't mind. Fighting, she didn't mind. Hard work, fine. Grandiosity…? *No, no, no. Not me.*

The voice of his secretary spoke to them from the intercom on his desk. "Five minutes until your next appointment."

As he walked her toward the door he said, "You must know that I have admired you for years. Do you think we might have dinner when I return from Chile?"

She stopped. His expression seemed to reflect some message that she didn't understand.

Apparently sensing her puzzlement he hurried to add, "We could knock our heads together some more about this."

"Well, yes, I suppose dinner would be in order. I'll have Joss call your secretary."

"For dinner," he repeated.

"Yes. Dinner would be nice."

. . . . .

She returned to the Retreat alone, a quiet place to reflect despite Alex's screeching protest over her absence. Outside, the leaves of the trees surrounding her meditation pagoda burned with autumn fire.

She visited Braveheart, bringing him some chicken legs. She meditated almost an hour until dusk fell, then cooked her favorite dinner—fettuccini Alfredo—and ate with only Alex for company. The next morning she woke at peace.

Feeling calm, chipper, even playful, she called Pryce. "What could I say to you that would make you extremely happy?"

He stalled a moment, as if the question utterly baffled him. Then, "Why don't you tell me."

"You know I talked with Crane and what we bickered over...."

"I do read the tabloids, God help me. I find it necessary."

"So. Come on, Prycee."

"You argued over the PeaceMaker tests. This should make me happy?"

"Prycee, you usually think so fast."

He gasped. "Holy red, white and blue shit! Crane got to you! You're gonna run..! Claire!"

She belly-laughed, releasing a mountain of sturm, drang, slings, arrows, and general, all-purpose angst. "So...," she said after they'd both calmed down a bit.

"So...," he replied. "Okay. First step. Give me two weeks. Three at the most. We have to work fast, although I couldn't help giving the possibility serious thought already."

She couldn't suppress a smile. "Just in case."

He chuckled. "Just in case. I have a great campaign manager in mind. I'll set up meetings with the people we'd most need behind us. Backers. Party people. Getting any kind of party backing is going to be really tough. Crane is light-years ahead of us. But it's not impossible with Hass's poll numbers. It's wonderful. And you were right. You have made me very, very happy."

"Let's hope the fates arrange that we can all stay that way."

Tuna Kahunas

Claire tapped fingers on the arm of her chair beside an oak-scented fire in one of her friend Serena's Quest Circle VIP bungalows. Clutched in her other hand was her cell phone with files on the five key potential backers Claire would soon meet. Strains of Vivaldi's "Four Seasons," normally soothing, failed to lessen her sense of urgency.

Serena had graciously given each of these influential men and their families a bungalow for the day and access to the Quest Circle's many amenities. The men would be guests for lunch and could arrange private face time this afternoon with Claire.

Which of today's powerful men had the daughter who'd helped with the Unity Concert? She knew this cold. Why couldn't she recall it?

Claire rose and walked to the picture window, her mind racing, barely aware of the flaming reds and oranges of October on the trees across the lake. Red-orange bittersweet colors of low-growing flowers lined a meandering flagstone walkway through the expanse of a lawn that was losing its summer green. So much depended on today's meeting, the first of many to gain support. One point two billion dollars—what the Hass campaign, Hass PACs, and Republican Party had spent to get him elected again in 2020.

Claire was hoping to spend no more than thirty million of her own money. Much of her estate was already earmarked for AFWW. Today's potential backers were also experienced fundraisers who could help fill in the chasm between her millions and what was needed. Pryce had called today's five, "The Big Fish, the Tuna Kahunas."

They would have many objections to her challenge of a party stalwart like Mason Crane. They'd want a guarantee that a prominent, politically connected man would be her running mate. Adam Forsythe, during their dinner together had agreed to run with her if she asked. He was an out-of-the-box choice, being a long-time Republican, but one that would impress these men. But...Adam made her nervous. Over coffee he had made a subtle pass. "Claire, are you as lonely as I am? I am very fond of you, you know."

She treasured Adam's friendship, but she felt no sexual chemistry for him. When her answer was tactful but entirely non-committal, he'd actually blushed and deftly changed the subject. The dinner ended as it began, in good friendship. But what if his attraction to her didn't fade gracefully? With this attraction issue thrown into the mix, should she even mention today the possibility of a campaign alliance with Adam?

Ten minutes to go. She simply had to focus on the bios.

Pacing slowly, she studied Leo Lombardi's info. Leonides Lombardi was perhaps the biggest fish of them all, the Director of the vast Liu Foundation which was highly philanthropic, rarely political, and bigger now than even the Gates Foundation. Julia Claudia Castellioni, its founder, was the world's richest women and Lombardi's aunt. Pryce had said more than once, "Money is power."

This was a hard truth, something she found distressing, but understood. Until half of the world's twenty richest people were women the global patriarchy would continue to be firmly in control of humanity's fate. "Getting Lombardi on board may be a hard sell," Pryce had also said more than once, "You gotta wow Lombardi."

She knew his wife's name, his kids' names, his favorite pastime. He was thirty-nine, and, like his aunt, of Italian descent. Julia Claudia claimed ancestry back to Imperial Rome. This guy's ancestor probably inspired the term *patrician*.

Claire sat again. Three of the other four Tuna Kahunas were longtime Democrats. Although John Dwayne Gaylord, or J.D. as everyone called him, was married to a grandniece of Nelson Rockefeller. Source of his fortune: insurance.

She swiped left to Max Zell's file. Sixty-two. Money from waste disposal and now a crusader for responsible toxic and plastic waste disposal. Never graduated from high school. A patriot with strong party ties. He probably wouldn't want to put his money on a long shot and would be her toughest sell.

A log in the fireplace popped like a firecracker, and she jumped. Her heart had barely settled when a tap from the bungalow door's brass knocker jolted her again. Showtime. She called out, "Come on in."

Serena stepped inside, looking calm in white wool slacks and white tunic. "Well, they're all gathered," she said. "This is it, love."

"Yes. The first big test." Claire rose and quickly checked the mirror. She looked fine. A new feathered haircut shimmered with fresh streaks of paler blonde. The tobacco suede blazer with black leather hunting collar topped her black wool slacks, a confident look. "I haven't been this up-tight since my first 'Cooking For Lovers' show."

Serena drew her into a comforting hug. "You don't know just how persuasive you are."

The walk to the Stellar Conference Room wouldn't take more than a few minutes. Serena linked arms with her as they stepped outside. "I had a certain feeling about you," Serena said. "Almost from the moment we met. It just grew stronger when you left to go explore the world."

Claire had met Serena seven years ago at one of Serena's conferences in Sedona. Serena had been fifty-two, Claire thirty-nine. David had been dead for over a year. "Do you know" Serena asked, "how I've always looked at the results of your months of wandering? Instead of fusion cooking, you did fusion philosophy, all built on that Quaker foundation from your Alden grandmother. There is a reason for it all…."

"Let's not go there. It may be true, but nothing makes me more nervous than a politician who believes God called him or her to run for office."

Claire waved at two Quest Circle staff who passed them, smiling and nodding. She and Serena turned toward the conference room where her inquisitors awaited. "Oh!" Serena said, "Have you listened to the news this morning? I think there may be a crisis brewing with the mysterious Tears of Allah group."

Claire had started reading everything she could about the rabid sect, but very little was known. "I haven't read or heard today's news."

"Well, this could come up with your backers. The feds arrested eleven Muslim men. Just whisked them off to nobody knows where. They claim the men are linked to Tears of Allah. Others are saying the men's only offense is to protest the proposed ban on the *Adhan*."

"Now *there's* a potential political bomb in the making." Muslims across America were seeking permission to have the *Adhan*, or call-to-prayer, broadcast five times a day in their local neighborhoods. The *Adhan* Movement, as the media was calling it, had become the focal point of anti-Muslim sentiment. Recently, outraged Muslims had launched major protests against President Hass's proposal to ban the *Adhan* outright.

Serena shook her head. "It might be a long time, if ever, before we find out if these guys are linked to terrorism or not. Frankly, I don't want my tranquility poked by that sound five times a day, but to claim anyone who wants to hear it is a traitor isn't fair."

"It's not only unfair. Banning it totally—unless churches are treated the same—will inflame Muslims everywhere."

They reached the conference room. "No matter what happens," Serena said, "whether they say *yes* or *no* to you, you are providing a possibility for positive change that didn't exist before. Something powerful will result." Serena grinned. She knew full well that Claire didn't share Serena's strong sense of a purposeful cosmos.

But Claire did feel strongly the constancy and strength of Serena's love. "Thank you, dear friend for all your help." She took a deep breath and stepped inside.

Can You Deliver?

With Pryce doing introductions, Claire shook hands with each of their five guests. As she clasped Leo Lombardi's hand, she was reminded of someone. Very forceful, strong. Had they met before? She didn't think so.

Max Zell, downright ugly with his pock-marked face, nevertheless gave off gentle vibes. J. D. Gaylord wore an impeccably tailored suit and white shirt with garnet cufflinks. Lunyard, or "Lonnie," Ames was one of the world's biggest retailers, working hard to beat Wal-Mart, savvy but at the same time a philanthropist. Pryce said he might prove to be the most receptive.

They took leather seats in a semicircle in front of the spacious conference room's massive stone fireplace, aglow with logs that scented the air with pine and applewood. Pryce said, "You've all seen your proposal packets with the skeleton of our economic plan and probably have major questions. Who wants to grill Claire first?"

"Be glad to," Max Zell said in his booming voice. He spread his arms, palms upward. "Why yuh thinkin' a running?" His Bronx roots were a source of pride. "What is it yuh think needs doing that ain't gettin' done that you can do that no one else can?"

They all nodded, grinning. Had they not read the proposal?

Claire managed a chuckle. "Well, that does get right to the heart of it, doesn't it? Why back the dark horse?" She paused and established eye-contact with Zell. "America has problems that also affect the global community: terrorism, environmental devastation, poverty and disease, and the threat of international tyranny." She moved her gaze to one and then another, drawing them in. "Hass's constantly militant and ham handed overreactions to many issues, such as this Adhan situation, just exacerbate conflict. His spin-meisters hype our fears to justify the PeaceMaker program. We need new tactics with new priorities, all of which require significant reassessment of how our tax resources are allocated."

Lonnie Ames, the environmentalist, said, "Environmental devastation is also *related* to all our problems. We're boiling and trashing ourselves out of house and home."

Max said, "This pointy-head, Jared Diamond, wrote a book quite a while back. *Collapse*. He says ignoring environmental disasters is a thing all failed civilizations had in common. So by Diamond's standards…"

He beamed. "My approaches to waste and plastic disposal qualify me as damn heroic!"

Claire liked this man from the Bronx. "I agree, Max. That's why we want you on board."

Pryce leaned back and smoothed his van Dyke, smiling his approval. Joss winked.

Claire continued quickly. "We must deal with the environment. But we must also avoid the national security disasters I see inherent in the PeaceMaker program, and the financial disasters looming because of economically wasteful military projects of which it is a prime example."

J.D. fixed his blue eyes on her. "I don't follow you."

Claire discussed with them her approach to security, global warming, the deficit, and then concluded, "Some people say I'm too revolutionary. Some say I'm a wild-eyed progressive, or a big-government liberal. Or worst of all, God forbid, a socialist. I consider myself to be a realist who is deeply concerned with both national security and quality of life. My administration would not rely primarily on government programs to bring about needed change, but on motivating the private sector. A competitive private sector, with appropriate regulations, must be the real engine of lasting change. Government should facilitate, and one of my first priorities will be to cancel wasteful military programs or destabilizing ones and apply the funds to other problems. A high priority needs to go to accelerate all efforts to blunt global warming and put a bigger fire under the efforts for alternative energy production, education reform, and infrastructure fixes."

Randall shook his head. "Can't be done. For example, others have tried to kill PeaceMaker. They couldn't. I'm tired of backing smiling pols who make promises but care only about getting elected."

Claire's hands were clammy. "That's exactly how I'm different. I relate to your disillusionment, Randall. It's why I'm running. I can and I will tackle our difficult demons. And with help of men like you, and the support of the people who know me and I believe will support me in great numbers, I can succeed."

J.D. leaned forward, scowling. "Your proposal suggests that it always comes down to money. Is that what you believe, Claire?"

"Our problem, J.D., isn't lack of money, especially if we work with our allies. We've spent approaching three trillion dollars on Iraq alone. Our problem is an abysmal lack of visionary leadership. And yes, it will cost us to win the two-headed war on terrorism and planetary overheating. But what we're doing now simply isn't smart investing."

"I like your proposal, Claire," Lonnie Ames said softly. "I'm just not certain, not convinced, that anyone with the kind of change agenda you represent can get elected. And first you have to get the nomination."

His profound doubt rattled her. A silence fell over them, and no one was more silent than Leo Lombardi, who'd said nothing at all. If she could not convince these men whose aspirations were compatible with hers, how could she hope to convince the country?

Max said, breaking the tension, "Your proposal says, and I know that's true, that we spend one lousy percent of the annual budget on foreign aid. I also know the war budget sucks up more than forty-five percent of our taxes. But my big concern is terrorism, and I like specifics. The proposal was short on specifics."

"Max, we could significantly undermine a major condition that feeds the rage of terrorist foot soldiers if we cancel unnecessary weapons programs and fund projects to reduce global poverty instead. Speaking very generally, who pins their hopes on fanatics? Mainly poor people or people treated unfairly. Desperate people. Who ignores fanatics? Comfortable people. People with positive hopes. We absolutely must change tactics."

Randall thrust his finger toward her to make his point, "That I agree with."

Claire smiled. "So does your brainy Harvard daughter!" It was Randall's daughter who'd helped with the concert. "Each million we lop off the Pentagon's budget represents someone's pork barrel, though, and a fight to the death to keep it. Only strong leaders with powerful backing of voters can fight them. I believe I have that backing."

"Fights that cancel people's jobs," J.D. said. Max and Randall nodded.

"Clearly we have to provide employment," she said, "but why unnecessary military jobs? Why not put people to work on jobs repairing our rusting bridges? On projects to capture and store carbon dioxide? Expanding the use of all of our alternative sources of energy. Even actually establishing bases on the Moon and on Mars? We need to offer challenges like that to excite our young people and to spur innovation. I believe people are hungry for this kind of vision. And if we don't get on the stick it will be Russia or China who establish Moon and Mars bases first. And the historical rule has been that the first settlers determine the rules of a place."

Randall said, "I'll grant that you have credibility with your millions of fans. With everyone, really. But the question becomes believability in the office of the Presidency. Can you deliver?"

They sat quietly, every one with an intent look of concentration, Lombardi frowning. "Look, Claire," he finally said. "I read *Creating the Future,* and I agree with your conclusions. But I have to question whether it's realistic for you to run for President. You've never run for office or run any level of government."

Pryce reddened and was about to cut in but J.D. beat him to it. "The thing is, you're essentially a TV personality. A celebrity. A business-woman. A philanthropist, to be sure. But aside from negotiation, which is admittedly your specialty, a novice in realpolitik."

"Pryce," Claire said, attempting to control the head of steam she could see him building, "has an interesting etymology for *politics.*" She smiled conspiratorially at Pryce.

He relaxed, grinned and said, "Poli- meaning *many,* plus ticks, mean-ing blood-sucking parasites—" He waited for the chuckles to die down. "Reagan and Schwarzenegger started out as movie personalities. Then we have a TV President. The public is used to the idea."

Joss, a life-long Democrat, choked. "I'd rather be denied food perma-nently than mention Claire's name in the same sentence as Arnold's or Ronnie's."

The men in the circle all chuckled.

Randall got them back on track. "If you should somehow manage to win the Democratic nomination, right from the start your candidacy would need the strength of a heavy hitter Vice Presidential candidate to fill out the ticket. Not in public, of course. But I'd need to know who if I were to back you."

"I agree," said Max. "Your VP *must* be a man."

"We haven't decided on anyone yet, of course." They were watch-ing her intently. She was going to lose them unless she said something that would persuasively reassure them. She made a decision. "I'd look at someone like Adam Forsythe."

"Actually, a good choice," Ames said. Max nodded. "A moderate Republican could bring in a lot of people, including Republicans, who are sick of Hass."

J.D. said, "I don't know. He hasn't been the same since his wife died. And Republican insiders are not pleased with him."

The meeting was now twenty minutes beyond the scheduled one hour. Joss, who had slipped quietly away, returned. "Lunch is waiting when you're ready," she announced.

"Look, Claire," Lonnie said. "Here's my honest assessment. Right now, I'm not willing to support, with influence or funds, unless I'm sure your candidacy has a real chance. I've already done some heavy bundling for Mason Crane because I'd given up on trying to stop PeaceMaker and I dislike him less than Hass. But you're starting late and weak. You'll get slammed right off in Nevada and Florida. But you might get something going for the Iowa Caucus and even win in New Hampshire. If you do that, if you win in New Hampshire, I'll switch. Privately. You're going to need a miracle to get through Super Tuesday. Sorry, but I'm skeptical. No matter how much I'd like you to, I don't think you can win against Crane, let alone Hass in November."

Randall uncrossed his arms. "I agree, Claire. If you take New Hampshire, I'll come in. And if Super Tuesday, I'll go public."

J. D. sighed. "Yeah. I can go along with that."

"I'm for eating," Max boomed out.

Pryce stood. "If any of you want to meet with me or with Claire later, set a time with Joss."

Claire stood, her cheeks burning. No enthusiastic, "This is great, Claire." No, "You'll have my check in the mail tomorrow, Claire." Three had said she must win New Hampshire. Randall was focused on Super Tuesday. Max Zell had preferred to have lunch. Leo Lombardi had remained ominously silent.

As she stepped out the door onto the flagstone walk, Max took her arm as though escorting her, and said, "I like your style, Claire. Loved 'Cooking for Lovers.' Yuh sure learned to take the heat in that kitchen a yours. I came to this thinkin', no way am I backing this lightweight woman in what is still a man's world, but you won me over."

He chuckled and she laughed.

"Here's the deal," he continued. "I chip in a little seed money. You take New Hampshire, I provide some solid support. You win Super Tuesday, I come in with all I got. Howzat sound?"

"I thank you, Max. It's fair."

"That it is. I'm also gonna send you my own recipe for an all-day lasagna." He patted her elbow and went ahead into the dining room.

At the door, Joss took her arm. "Lombardi wants to see you after lunch."

They Will Crucify Her, Leo

Claire watched Leo Lombardi as he arrived at the agreed-on bench and sat, facing Star Lake. Walking toward him, Claire understood the flash of recognition she'd felt earlier. His dark hair and youthful, confident stance evoked Savik on the day Claire had met him.

In the few seconds it took to reach Leo, Claire returned in memory to Monkey Lake all those years ago and could almost smell the cotton candy and hear the carousel of the rinky-dink carnival beside it. Savik had been a cocky nineteen then, planning to join the Green Berets, and she twenty-one, a college graduate, and engaged to David.

Savik had knelt beside a little girl in yellow who was crying, and held her hand a brief but sweet moment before the three-year-old's frantic mother retrieved her child. When Savik stood, his gaze had met Claire's.

He'd smiled. Even now the memory made her feel warm. He'd strolled up and asked her and the friend she was with to ride the Ferris wheel. Claire agreed, and then they'd fired rifles at rows of gray wooden rabbits. In a flash, Claire remembered the ribbon she hadn't thought of in years. She'd won nothing. Savik's ribbon said "Sharp Shooter," and he'd given it to her. It still lay in an old jewelry box in a bottom drawer.

The memory disintegrated as Leo Lombardi rose and greeted her with an enthusiastic hand-shake, clasping her hand in both of his as his urbane bearing dispelled the similarities to Savik, the outdoorsman. Apparently the only one of the five men who'd read *Creating the Future*, Leo had endeared himself to her. Maybe he wanted to contribute, but only in extreme privacy.

"I don't want to take a lot of your time, Claire." He gestured to the bench.

As they sat, Claire said, "I'm delighted to give you whatever time you need."

"I'll be frank. I'm reluctant to make any commitment now. But I do wish to tell you, personally, that I profoundly admire what you stand for. Were the money mine, I'd donate generously at once."

But the money apparently isn't yours. She nodded.

He gazed across the lake again. "The Liu Foundation is conservative in its giving. I will take your petition back with me, so my *no* isn't a final *no*."

"May I inquire whether Julia Castellioni might be involved in the decision?"

He swiveled sharply back to her. "Oh, no. My Aunt is now sixty-eight years old and leaves all business matters in the hands of others."

"I find her fascinating!" Claire was as curious as the rest of the world about this wealthy Italian recluse. "Do you…communicate with her often?"

His smile seemed slightly annoyed. "I'm sorry. I'm not free to speak about her…beyond saying that I admire her and am happy to respect her privacy."

Inside, Claire flinched. He was too polite to say, Please, mind your own business. "I appreciate your coming today," she said.

"I shall be off promptly." He stood and offered his hand. "I wish you well."

She shook it, and Lombardi nodded, turned, and headed back to his bungalow.

Joss, always quick, sped toward Claire from her own bungalow. "I'm trying to be cheerful," Joss said. "But you know what? I'm bummed."

"I'm fighting it myself."

Joss rarely showed her emotions. She straightened a bit and grinning said, "After that meeting I actually think I'm really working for an Independent who will run on the Democratic ticket."

"An Independent still can't win. I'd only be a spoiler, which is pointless. Democrats may reject me. But I don't think so."

Joss sighed and then leaned over to hug Claire at an awkward angle— she always seemed to need the reassurance from Claire, a touch or hug—and then left to finalize arrangements with Serena for the kick-off retreat for Alden campaign volunteer leaders.

Pryce took Joss's place on the bench and said immediately, "We have almost half a million e-mails begging to help financially with the campaign. That should be easily over five million bucks. You have roughly ten million you can liquidate tomorrow if necessary with another ten available. That's a lot to build on. We sacrifice Nevada and Florida to focus on Iowa and New Hampshire, and we can do that without any Big Fish."

Claire hugged herself, a gesture of self-protection. "We need, what, a minimum of eighteen million for the New Hampshire primary alone? And if we don't win New Hampshire, that's it. All that money down the drain for a gesture. I'd not only disappoint all the people working to end war, but my failed candidacy would embarrass them. Maybe even 'legitimize' a commitment to PeaceMaker." She shook her head. "We've gotta win."

. . . . .

Leo Lombardi placed a transatlantic call. The sound of Julia Castellioni's voice was as clear as though she sat in the bungalow's adjacent room instead of across an ocean in her villa outside Rome. Aunt Julia was a night owl. She did not own a cell phone.

"Tell me how it went?" she said, her tone suggesting sincere but only casual interest. "What do you think of her?"

"Well, she's even more dynamic in person than on TV. I think she's genuine."

"Did she say anything I haven't read in her book?"

"Not really."

"I do admire the woman. Did she ask for money?"

"Naturally, yes."

"What's your intent?"

"I will take her proposal to the foundation's board. At the minimum, if she can win some of the early primaries, I'd recommend that the Foundation find ways to feed in support, but I ask you to consider giving beyond what I'm allowed."

"Really!" Julia sounded genuinely surprised.

Through his private and secret agreement with Julia, he could never disburse sums beyond a million dollars without her consent. He'd lied to Claire Alden when he said Julia would not be involved. After listening to Claire, he was hoping that Julia would be so enthusiastic that she would use her offshore holding companies to funnel even greater sums to Claire's candidacy. Given that his aunt's personal philosophy was remarkably in sync with Claire's, her hesitation surprised him.

"I didn't encourage her. But I am excited, really excited, Aunt Julia."

"You were right not to encourage her. I'd advise your board not to invest in her. She doesn't have a prayer of a chance to win. It would be money better spent on another hospital."

"Shouldn't we at least encourage her to fight for the changes we agree are so essential?"

"That will be your choice, and that of the Liu board. But as for me providing money over and above, I've learned not to waste money on rainbow chasers."

Speechless, he felt as if she'd canceled his fare on an all-expense paid, first-class, eighty-day around-the-world trip. Apparently sensing his confusion, Julia added, "They will crucify her, Leo. And my gut instinct is that she doesn't know how to fight dirty. She would refuse to fight dirty. And that's what it's going to take."

That was his Aunt speaking all right. Julia was a strange mix, in his mind, of visionary and skeptic. There would be no resources from the Castellioni billions spent on wishful thinking. She had said more than once that he was too idealistic.

Still, there was something about Claire that made him want to fight for her. "I wouldn't exclude the possibility that she might actually do something extraordinary." He explained about the other backers promising to kick in seriously if she won New Hampshire.

"I hope they aren't throwing their money into a bottomless abyss."

"You know, Aunt Julia, without a global transformation of the kind she represents you can build all the hospitals you want, but in my view, you can't build them fast enough to make any lasting dent in humanity's pain and suffering."

She was silent, and so was he. He'd really amazed himself. He'd never spoken so forcefully to Julia. He and his children were her only heirs related by blood, but she'd been extremely cautious about giving Leo power in the Liu Foundation.

The sound of a warm chuckle reached him from across space. "Okay, Leo. I love to hear you all heated up. You keep me posted on your Claire Alden."

A Yellow Rose And An Old Ribbon

At EClaire, Claire, Pryce, Joss and a new campaign team hammered out rudimentary policy positions and started filling the campaign trail calendar with Jake Shifrin, the new campaign manager. Talking heads praised Claire's smart move in hiring Jake since he'd crossed Party lines to back candidates he believed in, and a Newsweek article described him as part of an elite brain trust whose brilliant political strategies had elected many key architects of American policy.

In the early afternoon, Bobby drove her back to The Retreat. She did some personal business. John failed again to respond to any attempts to reach him. Humvee had been moved to a convalescent home. Claire finalized and signed a college trust fund for each of his three kids, since it was still uncertain whether he'd ever work again.

She closed the campaign website and turned the computer off. Alex grew excited at the sound of the exit melody and duplicated it. She took a call from Jake and agreed to a satellite TV interview with American Samoa, of all places, wooing their early February voters who were enti-tled to nine delegates at the Nominating Convention. This had to be her eight-hundredth political decision of the day. Eight hundred and one decisions she would not make.

Looming only three days away was the interview on Rachel Maddow in which she'd declare her candidacy. She eyed the stack of policy files that included national and international profiles, legislation, and his-tories. She must be well prepared and calm, or, God forbid, she could blow it in front of well over three million viewers.

She bundled up and took a calming walk in the mist along the ice-edged stream, said hello to Braveheart, scattered crumbs for the geese and ducks, and mentally planned a light supper for herself and Desi. She'd fix a robust butternut squash soup, a hot, crusty, mixed-grain sourdough loaf, salad loaded with walnuts, chevre cheese and tart apple slices, and for dessert, a few glazed pecans over little scoops of rum rai-sin ice cream. Oh, yeah.

And after dinner she'd sip a cognac by the fire, re-read *Battle Ready*, Tom Clancy's collaboration with retired Marine Major General Anthony Zini about the general's life and brilliant vision for a practi-cal and enlightened military. Adam had set up meetings with several retired but outspoken generals, and Claire was cramming for that too.

Life seemed well back under control when she returned from the walk. Alex squawked and flew to her, crying, "Rise up! Rise up!" He alighted onto her shoulder and nibbled her earlobe.

Outside a car door slammed, and Claire strolled to the window.

At the sight of the florist delivery truck, her stomach did a little excited butterfly number. Today's green-overalled young woman hurried through the heavy mist carrying a single, partially-opened yellow rose in a simple vase, glowing like a tiny sun on this cold day. Light against the grayness.

Claire thanked her, carried the rose into the dining room, set it on the table, and inhaled a strong, cinnamon-y scent. She opened the card.

"Yellow roses warm the heart like an embrace.'" –The Language of Roses.

And below that, the personal note, printed to maintain its anonymity. "I hope this rose, 'Golden Persistence,' conveys my determined admiration."

Surely she couldn't have more than one stalker, and that ricin-wielding lunatic was in jail. Surely a rose couldn't be from anyone crazy. No, the roses had to be from someone she knew. And she knew who it was, didn't she?

Her fear now wasn't about a nutcase but that the roses were binding her into a spell, one that could lead her into a different sort of disaster. A disaster of silliness. A reckless, out-of-control, jeopardize-whatever-you-worked-for kind of disaster. She'd been there once before and decided, *never again.*

She dropped into a dining chair. Alex landed on the table as a satiny petal dropped onto the polished walnut surface. He waddled to the petal, snatched it up, and flew off.

She reread the card. This was a strong message. He admired her, felt unsure of her feelings, and yet wasn't going to go away. Somehow this message disarmed her more than his others had. Memories drew her up the stairs to the guest bedroom.

She opened her cedar hope chest and removed keepsakes, albums and mementos, piled like a layer cake, each a reminder of a period of her life, some layers rich and thick, some bittersweet. At the very bottom lay a light brown, velvet-covered jewelry box.

As she opened it, she heard again the carnival sounds and music playing at the shooting gallery. And oldie. "Don't Worry, Be Happy." In an open pavilion they'd danced late into the night to old and new favorites they shared.

There it lay, fake satin still bright blue. "Sharp Shooter." Hurling himself into manhood, breathless over the charms of her as a young woman of twenty-one. Savik had been, and still was…unforgettable.

She sat quietly holding the ribbon a few moments and then returned it to the chest that stored her past, shutting the drawer firmly. She focused her thoughts on the present. Her life was more than full. The generals, the Tuna Kahunas, and Rachel Maddow were the people in her future.

Never Give Up

Savik stared at the three-week-old copy of *Inquiring Citizen* that he'd swiped from a pile at his barber's. The lead picture featured Claire looking exhausted but still beautiful in an elegant gown, leaning against a lamppost after arguing with Senator Mason Crane.

He gazed out of the condo's ceiling-to-floor window at the Manhattan nightlights. Despite the absurd speculation that she might actually try a run at the presidency, and despite her turning him down for a date— a door she *had* left open— despite their profound differences in philosophy he'd wanted to step into that photo and shield her from the paparazzi.

He tossed the paper onto the coffee table. The thing that had never let him down with women was never giving up. The flowers, the whispered lines of poetry, the romantic dinners were fine. What won out every time, though, was perseverance. Savik had perfected the art.

He rarely dated women who threw themselves at him. They were just too needy. But let a desirable woman elude him, and he had to know why. Lynda had accused him of only wanting the chase. "Capture bores you," she'd goaded. Yet the hunt-chase issue didn't feel like the real problem. Not really. He simply wanted someone who could both draw and keep his interest. Was that too much to ask?

He called from his cell phone, fingers tapping through four rings before she answered.

"Well, hi, Savik," Claire said. She obviously had caller I.D. "Just a minute."

The background of what sounded like many voices—a restaurant or some other crowded place—died abruptly. When she spoke again, the noise had become distant.

"I've caught you at a bad time again," Savik said.

"It's okay. I need a breather. I'm pleased to hear your voice."

"Where are you?"

"Ground floor of the Steinmetz building. We just leased office space."

"Wow. Great central location."

The background roar flared again. Apparently somebody had opened a door.

"Sorry, Savik, could you hold for just a sec?"

Savik waited. Steinmetz, huh? Powerful guy. What the hell was he doing leasing space to an activist like Claire?

"I'm back," she said.

They chatted a moment about work and he finally got out the reason for the call. "I wanted to see about getting together."

A long pause followed, during which someone yelled, "Claire, they're here!"

Maybe she was distracted. Or maybe she was thinking she didn't want to see him.

A cheer sounded and applause.

"Oh, Savik—" she finally said, her voice raised. "I'm sorry. I must go. My calendar is jammed right now, but could I get back to you?"

Damn. "I'll look forward to hearing from you at a more convenient time."

"Great. Bye." Click.

Great, she'd said.

He didn't especially like women calling him, and he downright hated it when he had to wait for the call. Drove him nuts.

If you want something bad enough, though, you never give up.

The Secret

"Hi, Serena," Claire wrote in her email. "I'm a bit desperate." She deleted "desperate" and replaced it with "confused." Of course, Serena would take one look at the time the email posted, 3:41 A.M., and know that if Claire were writing at such an hour to request a meeting, she was, in fact, desperate. "I'm now at the Manhattan apartment I've rented for the duration of the campaign. Joss is sharing it with me, and she's going to visit with her brother, just out of prison. So, I'm taking a break too. I'll return to The Retreat late this afternoon. Any chance you could join me at, say 5:30? The usual place?"

At mid-morning Serena confirmed their date. By that afternoon, Claire had met with Janice Kirkorian, the head of A Bright Future.org, lunched with two Democratic senators, and teleconferenced with volunteer campaign managers in the states of sixteen of the thirty-five primaries in January and February who were organizing petitions to have her name placed on ballots.

By 4:30, Bobby was battling traffic in the Lincoln Tunnel, having successfully ditched a determined paparazzi. Nestled warmly in her ankle-length wool coat, Claire leaned her head against the seat's back and closed tired, burning eyes. She must try again to reach John when they emerged from under the Hudson River.

She awoke to nightfall, however, a bit groggy, in front of the Upper Saddle River Inn, the call to John still not made. Spotlights shined on the inn's ancient gables and dormer windows and on birch clusters, dramatically barren of leaves. She and Bobby walked across a stone bridge over a brook that, judging by its quiet burble, hadn't entirely frozen over. She and Serena often met here because the owners made certain they weren't disturbed.

Serena hugged her in the warmth of the lobby, looking fabulous, all her clothing winter white: boots, long sheath, and hooded cloak. Bobby settled into a booth near the fireplace where he could see the entrance, keep a discreet distance from Serena and Claire, yet could reach them before any intruder could. Claire loved the comfort of the thick red leather padding of the booths and high backs that assured they could not be overheard.

She was going to need a bit more of a kick than wine could deliver and ordered a Belvedere martini, "light on the vermouth with extra olives."

Serena said, "Make it two," and then gave Claire the look that said, let's get down to it.

Claire laced her fingers together on the white tablecloth. "I'm going to tell you something you must promise to tell no one."

"Have I ever talked out of turn?"

"Of course not. It's just that I've lived with this secret for what feels like forever. I made a bargain with David to keep it, but…it almost seems to have a life of its own, and it's stalking me." She felt the flush of embarrassment. "Remember the affair I had so long ago?"

Serena nodded. The firelight shone through wisps of tresses around Serena's face as drinks arrived. "To a successful campaign." Serena raised her glass. "And to finding the right path."

Claire touched Serena's glass and then took a good long swallow, enjoying the cool jolt, the instant flush. "I'm so scared of losing my son, Serena. What he thinks he most needs from me is knowledge of…of something that will take him away from me utterly and completely. I've always thought if I can just tough it out, when he gets himself settled, when he's more mellowed, the knowledge wouldn't have such power."

Serena leaned forward, an impish gleam in her eyes. "And the both of you would live happily ever after. What a lovely story."

Claire bit an olive in half and looked away. Serena's gaze was like truth rays that could penetrate all self-delusion. "The idea has always seemed reasonable to me, but…the man I had the affair with has popped back into my life."

"Ah." Serena sipped thoughtfully. "Let's see. The affair happened before John was born. You said you were twenty-one when you married. John was born right before you turned twenty-two. So the reason your fears about John are linked to the reappearance of the mystery man is that this man may be…John's real father."

Claire's breath caught. *John's real father!* She sipped her drink as Serena waited. "Well, his biological father," she finally said. And then words she'd locked away for years, words she'd rigidly guarded against slips of the tongue and around which she'd embroidered evasions gushed out. "I knew early on that David could not have children. I told myself I didn't mind because I had such ambition and wouldn't have time for kids, and we were soon engaged. Then two months before the wedding, David left for Portland to do his first major building. I was alone and getting pre-commitment jitters. And I met Savik Kodaly."

"Savik Kodaly?" Serena blurted in a hushed whisper, eyes wide. "Isn't he that womanizing, gorgeous hunk of adventurer who came to your mother's service?"

Claire couldn't hold back a chagrined smile. "Yes, and a woman running for President shouldn't have anything to do with such a man."

"I saw him in the columns when he was dating the granddaughter of one of my Questers, a true doyenne of the social pages. I am, I admit, astounded. Not at all that you did it but that it was Savik Kodaly."

"At first, in desperation, I thought about an abortion, but then I talked with Maman." Claire's pulse raced, but she plunged on. "She's the only person, other than David, who ever knew. And I never told her Savik's name. She wanted desperately for me to have the baby, her chance to have a grandchild. And being Catholic, she couldn't stand the idea of abortion. She convinced me to at least talk to David. I did. He blew up and walked out."

Serena waited.

"I was terrified I'd ruined any chance to marry David. I cried hopelessly, thinking he'd either leave me or want me to end the pregnancy, and I already knew I couldn't do that. And I did want a child, passionately, but I also loved David.

"He came back the next day and asked me how I felt about him. I told him I loved him and him only. He asked me what the father looked like. I told him, and he told me not to do anything and went camping for a few days to think."

Claire took another long, bracing sip. "When David came back, he asked, 'Do you want to marry me?' and of course I did. He said he loved me, and that he could accept the child. But then he said, 'only if my name goes on the birth certificate, and no one, not the child's father, not even the child will ever know anything different.' I was delirious with joy. I loved him more than ever."

"What about Savik Kodaly? You didn't think he deserved to know?"

Claire shook her head. "He was nineteen, dropped out of college, getting ready to go off and join the Green Berets. Believe me, he didn't want to know. The affair, or whatever you want to call it, lasted less than five days. And up until David died, he and John and I lived a damn near ideal life." A tear slipped out. She quickly dabbed it away.

"We both have drivers," Serena said, patting Claire's hand. "How about another 'tini?" She waved the waitress over.

Claire excused herself, and after Bobby checked out the women's room, dabbed her face with the wintry cold water. When she returned, her drink was waiting.

"So, my dear," Serena said. "Apparently neither your son nor Savik knows what you have been hiding."

Claire nodded, amazed by an enormous sense of relief. The worst was out. Still, to give really good advice, Serena must know the whole truth. "When David's leukemia required marrow transplants, it was the worst time of my life. And then the nightmare darkened. John insisted on being tested as the most logical donor. I told him he was too young, but that was patently silly and of course the hospital tactfully agreed with John.

"I couldn't think of any reason to not let him be tested—the boy was as healthy as a race horse—so I gave permission and prayed that John would match, or that the hospital would say nothing as to why he didn't. They said only that John's marrow wouldn't work, but John had to see for himself. He knew from high school biology that he was a type B, and when he sneaked a look at the tests, he saw that David and I were both type O. He instantly realized that David couldn't be his biological father.

"He didn't say anything to me then. We were all in such grief, watching helplessly, praying to a deaf god for a transplant donor that never materialized. But after the funeral, John demanded to know who his father was. In my mind, I wasn't ready to break my promise to David."

"When we're young," Serena said, "we so easily get ourselves into trouble. I know I did. Some secrets are good. Yours and David's worked for a while. But secrets do always leave us vulnerable to fate. And fate, it seems, has barged in."

"Yeah. Kicked the doors down. I begged John to be patient. I told him I'd tell him when I could. This just made him more furious. And the truth is, his anger wasn't just about David not being his dad or that I wouldn't tell him who his father was. John and I were already starting to have the usual power issues that teens have. He felt I was too controlling—."

Serena chuckled. "You? Controlling? Never."

Claire felt herself stiffen at the criticism. "I am not that bad, Serena."

Her friend just smiled. Claire let it slide. "John was, he is, unreasonable. It's just all gotten so muddled together. He blamed me for being trashy and disloyal," she winced at the memory almost as painful now as when John had said it and steeled herself to admit the rest, "a slut who had created him from a lesser man than David. My boy disappeared into the mountains where he and David used to camp, and when he came out, he asked if he could live with Maman. He refused to come home. He's never been close to me since. For a while, whenever I tried to talk to him, he'd yell, 'Who's my father?' But then he changed. When I approached him, he'd walk away, saying that he didn't care and really didn't want to talk about it. The thing is, he still doesn't know that David couldn't have children"

Serena shook her head. "Young people can really wallow in victimization."

Claire sighed. "But what's bothering me, Serena, is that Savik says he wants to see me."

Serena nodded. "Why do you think that John's understanding more about his origin would change him? Take him further from you than he already is? That's what this is all about, isn't it? Why you've not already told him. They both deserve to know. Right now."

"Out of the question."

"Is it?"

Claire felt a surge of anger and a flush rising to her cheeks. Serena seemed to be siding against her. "John hasn't talked to me for months. I'm just slowly regaining a connection to him since Maman's death. I'm about to tell him I'm a candidate, which means putting him at risk in many ways. I hope to convince him and his girlfriend to come for Thanksgiving. The right time will come. But not now. And Savik, well, what I need to decide now, why I needed to talk to you, is to figure out if I should see Savik or not."

"Are you really asking me?"

"I'm sorry I'm so tense. This has me tied in such knots. Yes. I am truly asking."

"Does Savik interest you?"

"Yes. He's brilliant, amusing, charming, dashing, successful…."

"Then why the hesitation?"

How best to explain? "John isn't at all like David. And as it turns out, he isn't much like me. He is so very much like Savik. Playboy tendencies. Lust for adventure, like taking off for a whole year at eighteen to just travel on his grandmother's money. I told you when he went backpacking, through the Darian Gap between Columbia and Panama. I was terrified the whole time."

"Ah. It's coming clearer. Your feeling is that if he knew Savik was his father and the two of them got together, that you'd lose John to Savik. Right?"

"Yes. Yes! It could happen. I could see John absolutely rushing off to assume Savik's wild lifestyle. Even flaunting it in my face. Severing all connections to me."

"Some things are beyond your control, Claire. You can't really know what would happen if they met, can you?"

"The very idea of their meeting scares the hell out of me."

They fell into silence.

Serena picked up her last olive and took a nibble. "Here's my thought. One thing at a time. I'll accept that this isn't a good time to talk to John about his real father. But why not take this opportunity to discover, up close and personal, who his father is? Or more specifically, who Savik has really become."

"That's what my heart wants, but good lord, Serena, I'm beginning a run for the Presidency. Is it not insane to even consider seeing Savik? Complicating my personal life?"

"A single male candidate wouldn't deny himself on the campaign trail, right? Surely you could spare some time for friends and a few dates? With discretion, it might even turn into a steady relationship that would enhance your image."

Claire squeezed Serena's hand, realizing her friend had just told her what she wanted to hear all along. The very thought of seeing Savik made Claire feel a burden lift and her heart lighten. "I know how to be extremely discreet," she said.

. . . . .

By 8:30 that evening, Claire sat at the kitchen table in The Retreat, sipping herb tea.

Maman was right. The Catholics were really onto something with the confession bit. What she'd needed from Serena was not so much help with deciding about Savik, but confession. She felt like she'd done eighteen loads of laundry and things were clean, folded, and put away.

She would see Savik, but not call him back until after Rachel Maddow, to allow her time to clear a spot in her calendar. She picked up her cell phone and speed-dialed her son.

Four rings. Then that odious recorded message. "Hey, it's John Alden Trask, the nationally ranked tennis bum! Leave a message. Maybe I'll get back to you."

"John, it's Mom." Claire's hands grew clammy. "I've made a decision that will affect you profoundly. I so wanted to talk to you about it…but since you don't return my calls this will have to do. I don't want you to learn it through the media. In two days, on Rachel Maddow, I'm going to declare my intention to become a candidate for President. Of the United States."

She paused, struggling with confused feelings and thoughts. "I hope you'll support me. But if you can't go that far, I understand. I honestly feel that I may be…Pryce thinks I am…the only person who can stop this administration. So many things are being done that are so wrong for America. Were I elected, I could steer a better course. I must try, no matter what. I know I'm endangering both of us in some ways, but I've become convinced that I must attempt this." She couldn't think what else to say. "I love you, John."

She Just Said What!!

Savik thought maybe Claire had called while he was in the shower. He checked for a cell phone message again. It had been two days and still nothing from her.

Still nothing! He took the cell phone with him into the kitchen so as not to miss any calls and returned to chili-making. She'd said she'd contact him, but that didn't necessarily preclude him from calling back. Right? But he might get the same oh-so-busy run-around if he did. Damn.

He'd left the door to the condo unlocked, and Winn let himself in. "You gotta put in more chili powder," Winn called. "You never use enough, buddy."

"You just got here, Winn. How do you know I didn't put in enough?" They'd had this exchange maybe a million times. "My chili doesn't injure nasal membranes like yours does."

"Yeah. Right." Grinning, Winn set down two six-packs and opened two bottles of sometimes hard to find Double White Ale from the Southampton Brewing Company.

"Winn! You came through! Amazing!" Savik tapped Winn's bottle with his own and took a long swig of the crisp Belgian beer with the bumped up alcohol. "Ahhhh." Tonight would switch his mind off Claire nicely.

Winn guzzled half a bottle, then licked his lips. "Man, the PeaceMaker publicity put CET on the map. We have doubled orders in practically all departments. I need a trip to look forward to. To decompress."

After a dinner of chili, hot dogs, and beer, Savik and Winn would start some preliminary web-research on a trip to either Sumatra or New Guinea. "Fallon is interviewing Levar Jackson," Savik said. He and Winn agreed Jackson was one of the greatest quarterbacks ever. "Want to watch?"

"Sure." Winn switched on the small TV.

Savik heard Claire's voice and looked up.

Winn said, "Hey, it looks like your hot friend is on the Rachel Maddow show."

Savik said, "I'm thinking of asking her out." If she would return his call. A quick and remarkably unsettling thought hit him that maybe she wouldn't. Winn, listening to Claire, didn't respond.

Claire said, "That's why I'm doing it on your show, Rachel. I am officially, tonight, declaring that I am a candidate for the Presidency of the United States."

Savik felt his jaw drop. *WHAT???*

"Wow," Rachel Maddow said, her eyebrows lifting. "That's going to make the Democratic Primary as spicy as some of your famous cooking."

Claire laughed.

"Christ!" Winn said. "She's out of her mind."

Savik shook his head and sighed. The Steinmetz Building. *Duh.* A perfect campaign HQ. It should have been obvious what she was up to. "I'd heard the buzz, but I never thought Claire would actually…This is insane!"

Savik hadn't heard Maddow's question, but Claire was answering. "I'm convinced that with sufficient will, we can, within two generations, or even much less, actually make changes that will make war between nations and within nations obsolete as a means of resolving major social conflicts. The global community is ready for, is yearning for, and for many many reasons desperately needs, a global peace treaty that works."

"Oh my God," Winn hooted. "She's shot herself in the foot right off the bat. Why the hell is she doing this? It makes her look like a total airhead."

Savik flinched at the dripping contempt in Winn's voice, but in principle he agreed with Winn. Abolishing war? What the devil was Claire thinking? He laughed. "I wouldn't want to make war with her. I'd want a toss in bed."

"Oh, yeah? Speaking of …what's with Adrienne? Still after you?"

"She doesn't call often enough now to be a pest. She's smarter than that. But the woman spooks me. Talk about determined. And I don't know what she wants more, to nail me or to get hands on additional dirt through what she suspects are my inside connections."

They continued to watch as Maddow asked Claire why she'd decided to run. Blah blah blah. Then Maddow leaned toward Claire, all sincere and intent. "So I have to ask you, what is this insistence you have about working with women?"

"Woo hoo!" Winn hooted again. "Maybe that's why she doesn't get married. You do always see her with that Asian babe."

Again Savik bristled. He knew Claire's heart to be genuine, and maybe even some part of him wished that her peaceful vision could be real. He didn't like anyone, including Winn, laughing at her or simply dismissing her with Winn's idea of slander. "Don't imagine for an instant that Claire Alden's lesbian."

"So how would you know?"

"She was married to a guy she was crazy about, for chrissake."

"Isn't it time we tried something different, Rachel—?" Claire was asking on the screen.

Winn took another swig of Double White. "Doesn't mean she's not lesbo."

Savik had missed much of Claire's response and leaned forward to catch it, hoping Winn would take the clue and shut up a minute.

"…Most men would like to end war. Many have made earnest attempts. The League of Nations. The United Nations. But there's this sneaky biological urge—in general more pronounced in men than women—to gain status, to rise in dominance, and it eventually sabotages efforts at peacemaking. Women, though, as a group, are biologically primed to ward off war. Anything that could endanger their children. That's why I work so hard to empower women. My current staff is roughly fifty-fifty. That would also be true of my administration."

Winn crossed his arms and leaned against the bar stool's back. "If my dad was watching he'd be laughing his head off. Or maybe be upchucking. You know how Alden and her touchy-feely feminazis blow his blood pressure so high you think his eyeballs are gonna pop out of their sockets. Shall I switch to Jackson on Colbert?"

"No. Hang a bit."

Maddow had asked about Claire's son, John, noting that John hadn't been seen on the tennis circuit recently. "John took his grandmother's death very hard. I did too. I was very close to my mother."

That was it about her son. She was off on her mother. Savik had thought she looked unsure when asked about the boy. Claire rarely looked unsure.

"You know," Winn said softly, "she's a gorgeous woman. Love those big…eyes."

"Right." Savik gave Winn the expected smile. "Big eyes. One helluva woman. Go ahead and switch to Fallon."

He turned his cell phone off, took down two oversized chili bowls, and used a cup to scoop up dinner. Claire wouldn't be calling him, and he would not be calling her.

What A Farce This Will Be

"Tomorrow," Rachel Maddow said, "we'll have Senator Mason Crane with us, the man most likely to be the Democratic candidate for President. You won't want to miss that."

John was seething but thought he was doing a great job of hiding it from Fance. He punched the remote and the TV shut down. Fance disentangled herself from his arms, stretched, and stood up. She wore jeans and the softest pink cashmere sweater he had been able to find, an early Christmas present.

"Well, what do you think?" she said. "I'm even more blown away than when I heard her on the phone the other night! This is amazing!"

He eyed the braless curves that pushed the sweater out just right. "No, you're amazing. My mother is ridiculous."

"John! She is not. I read *Creating the Future*. I think she could win. And man, would that ever make a difference in your life." She looked away from him. "Probably no more Fance."

He pulled her back down against him and held a handful of hair. "What my mom does will never affect what's between you and me."

"Hope so." She smiled. "But your mom…President. Jesus, John, that would turn your world, my world, maybe the whole world, upside down."

"Actually, you have a similar effect on me, but in reverse." He glanced downward. "What's usually down tends to be up when you're around." Which it in fact was, even as they spoke. But she needed to go to work, so he didn't follow through. She smiled, stood, and headed for the bedroom to get her coat—she was due at Whispers at 10:30. She called back, "You going to study?" She was always encouraging him.

He glared at the *LSAT for Dummies* on the coffee table, its pages already looking depressingly dog-eared. "Yeah. I'll give it another couple of hours." He rose and went to pour another glass of iced tea. Fance kept a pitcher ready to help ease him off beer. Now that he wasn't practicing regularly or playing tournaments, he'd started to put on weight.

The plan was to take the LSAT next spring. And if by some miracle he passed, he'd apply to George Washington, USC, and Harvard Law for the fall. Like the condo, law school was something else Grandmere had made possible.

He slammed the refrigerator door thinking how ironic it was to be doing what his mother had nagged him to do for years. But law school wouldn't be for her. It was for Fance and Grandmere. And for his father.

John had been thinking about how disappointed his father would be in a son who had no serious goals and no worthy means of employment. His father's architectural career had been brilliant. The familiar sense of awe gave way, as usual, to a momentary sense of hopelessness. How could he ever measure up to this man he had loved?

Maybe he didn't have the right stuff since he didn't share the same blood. Maybe that explained the difference. This was the fear that sat on his shoulders and weighed him down.

In high school, though, he'd won a debate championship in his junior year, before his dad died. The debate teacher said he had an amazing gift of equanimity and of seeing both sides of an issue, empathizing, and yet staying objective. Everyone always said he had all this potential. His flaw seemed to be that he just couldn't figure out a way to give a shit. Until Fance.

She was making a difference. Caring for her made him care about other things. So, he would give the lawyer thing a shot. Maybe entertainment law. He knew lots of sports stars and, for that matter, movie stars and models.

His path crossed with Fance on her way to the door. He pulled her close, slid his hand to the back of her neck, and kissed her. Soft. Warm. Just a hint of mint toothpaste. That long, blonde and rainbow-pastel hair, rippling like softest silk on the back of his hand. He parted her lips with his tongue, and she stood on tip-toes to press against him, arousing him again instantly.

"Mmmm," she murmured, fingers sliding through his hair.

He opened her coat and felt the curves under her sweater. She moved backward, pulling him several steps with her until she stopped at the wall. She slid her hands under his sweatshirt, pulled it up over his head and threw it onto the floor.

"Don't you have to go to work?"

She slipped off her pink spiked heels and threw off her coat. "Right here, hon" she said, "against the wall. Right now. Hard, fast and deep."

. . . . .

When Fance finally closed the door to the condo behind her, John felt like the light in the room dimmed. Fance. She looked like a Barbie

Doll. Stripper Barbie. Yet there was so much more to her. She had what Grandmere called substance.

He never would have guessed that a stripper, not the wealthy girls he'd gone to school with, not the models, not the tennis groupies, would give him so much pleasure. And not just the physical. She was never in competition with him or kept a hidden agenda. He couldn't even say what it was that made her different. But Jesus….

He threw himself onto the sofa and thought about forcing himself to reach for *LSAT for Dummies* when his land line rang. He checked the number. His mother. Wonderful. He wasn't the least surprised, and this time, by God, he'd talk to her.

He picked up. "I just saw you on Rachel Maddow." The words seemed to bust out of him.

"I'm really glad."

"I was pretty much hoping you were kidding."

She didn't say anything.

"I wonder if you have any idea how much I've had to put up with all these years having a celebrity as a mother. And now you go do this loony thing."

"It's not loony, John." She sounded sad.

"The hell it isn't! It's goddamn embarrassing."

"A lot of people think I could set good forces in motion."

"Right. You *are* good at managing things your way. President should be just your thing. You'd get to control the whole U.S. of A. Hell. Maybe the world."

"It's not about—"

"I listened to your phone message. You want me to support you."

"I didn't ask for—"

"You're worried I'll embarrass you. That's what this call is all about. But I'm the one that's going to be embarrassed. And if by some freak of nature you'd win, can you imagine the loss of privacy and the security guards and all the shit that would fall my way?"

Again she was silent. He waited her out. Finally she said, "It might, instead, be wonderful. Did you consider that?"

"What you really care about, what you're calling about, is to make sure I'll do my part as the dutiful son in this latest drama, right? Be the perfect prop for the latest show."

"I can't even breathe. I'm stunned. You've never talked to me like this before. Not ever. Have I really been so bad a mother?" Her voice cracked.

He knew for sure she was crying. Shit!

"Do you hate me? Is that it?"

His pulse was pounding at his temple. God no, he didn't hate her. "Sorry."

"I want to heal this anger. Maybe it's too late. But I want to. I don't want it like this between us. I tried to call you. To include you. I've tried to help you."

He took a deep breath. "I don't need your help." He said it slowly, emphasizing each word, punching them into her. She went quiet again. "Look, Mother. I don't hate you. We just—I'm just blown away by this. I'll get over it. I always do. And you'll do what you want—what you think you need—to do. I won't…I don't have any more interest in publicly embarrassing you." Damn, he was tired. "I—I have to get up early tomorrow. I gotta go."

He hung up, leaned back, let his head crash onto the cushion of the sofa.

"Shit." A presidential campaign. What a farce this was going to be.

She Wanted To Kiss Him

Tomorrow was Thanksgiving. Adrienne Grantham would spend it alone. Still no Mr. Right captured even though her ideal life's agenda listed her as married by now. As she stepped out of her gym on 58th Street, feeling buff and fresh, her cell rang. Winn Hughes sounded very up.

He told her what she wanted to know and then said, "So, now you owe me. We're on for dinner this next Wednesday, right?"

"I'm looking forward to it," she assured him before they disconnected.

Winn wasn't Savik Kodaly. She wasn't ready to give up on Savik yet. But Winn clearly wanted her, and he wasn't a bad catch. Having dinner with him might even make Savik jealous.

She hailed a cab and climbed in. On her last date with Savik ten days ago he'd said, as usual, that he was swamped with work. One quick drink and he was gone.

Their conversations, most of them on the phone, concerned his own latest international investment work for some company or Lana Boswells' rapid decline. Nothing personal.

They hadn't had an evening together, let alone bed time, in a long while. Still, Savik turned her on like few men ever had. She wanted him. And she was accustomed to getting what she wanted. She paid the cabbie and hurried up her brownstone's steps. She'd have just enough time to change into something more appropriate before heading upstate.

. . . . .

Bobby drove Claire's black Cadillac south from The Retreat on Route 90 through mainly barren deciduous woods flecked with blue-green spruce. To the west across the Hudson, the pinkish-gray walls of West Point came into view in the distance. Her meeting place with Savik couldn't be much more than five minutes away. She set aside her speech notes. A glow of anticipation warmed her. Savik had sent her another anonymous rose right after the Rachel Maddow interview, a red American Beauty. "Red for the passion in who you are and all you do," the note said.

Bobby hadn't liked it and insisted on following procedures more strictly. Joss had been there, grinning like she might know who it was from, and asked if Claire knew who "cared enough" to send roses. When Claire said only, "Maybe," Joss had pouted a little.

That evening Claire called Savik. He had sounded utterly surprised, and the conversation felt awkward at first. For a few moments, Claire thought she'd misread Savik's intention with the rose and that he wasn't interested in a date. She made an offhand comment about always finding room in her schedule for friends, and Savik finally asked her to meet him. Since then, she'd endured fourteen long days, bouncing from Iowa to New Hampshire with a side trip to Illinois in an attempt to close the eight point gap in the polls there, even though the Illinois primary was not until primary Super Tuesday. Since this meeting with Savik was to be one simple, exploratory meeting, not likely to be repeated, she had told no one except Bobby.

Savik had suggested they meet at his cabin. Claire nixed that idea, fearing it would be potentially too intimate too soon, but on boring plane trips she wondered what Savik's place might be like and how it would be to spend time there with him.

Bobby turned east onto a gently curving road that passed fancy mailboxes, one a miniature castle. The distance between homes among the frozen woods suggested land parcels of ten acres or more. Savik's choice of meeting place, his country club, The Grand Mohegan, pleased her. Originally a millhouse built along a stream from rough gray stones, as the club expanded, the building's modernization had retained its sturdy grace. At one o'clock, they drove through the open gate and around to the back. Bobby opened the door for her.

"I have to be at the fundraiser by 6:30, Bobby. I doubt I'll be longer than two hours here."

Tucking her black coat's soft collar under her chin against the chill, she walked swiftly with Bobby at her side, enjoying the hearty smell of what must be a cedar fire in the club's fireplace. She turned a corner and caught sight of Savik a hundred feet away in the parking lot. Every time she saw him, the same rush of anticipation hit viscerally and shot warmth upward to her cheeks.

He slammed the door of a black Jeep Wrangler. He wore a tan sheepskin jacket with a fleece collar, jeans, black western boots and hat, probably a Stetson. She, on the other hand, wore a citified coat over a royal purple sheath, much-worn for swarms of fund-raising dinners.

He turned and saw her. His face lit up and he raised his hand in a quick wave and headed toward her with long, confident strides. They met at the side of the building, no onlookers in any direction. For a long moment they simply stood quietly, watching each other, as if cocooned in a silent bond, just as she'd imagined many times.

She wanted to kiss him. She wanted him to kiss her, even with Bobby watching. Savik's eyes, those penetrating dark eyes, seemed to be absorbing her, maybe the tiniest bit amused at his effect on her.

He cocked his head, reached out and took her bare hand out of her pocket and then held it in both of his. He grinned. "Good to see you."

She chuckled lightly, but his gaze didn't shift. If anything, it intensified. And he didn't let go of her hand. She felt a shock, not merely from physical contact—that wasn't so rare. It was that she didn't really want him to let go. Sneaky little hormones seemed to be attempting a *coup d'etat* against her brain. So. She was still vulnerable to this man. Duly noted.

She introduced Bobby, and smiled as Bobby's subtle body language, a straightening of the shoulders that pulled his coat tight, emphasized his brawn as a warning.

"Good man," Savik said, then to Claire, "Are you absolutely sure that you want to have lunch here? My place is only ten minutes away, and I have the best chili in the world on my range. And cornbread, just waiting to be warmed up."

She'd accepted the country club location because of its propriety. At the time, that seemed sensible. But she and Savik would be observed in public. They would guard their words and actions. The whole point of this meeting was to learn who Savik had become. How he thought. How could she get any true glimpse of him in the country club? At Savik's she would have privacy, and Bobby along as a buffer to anything too personal.

"You know, I think you're right. I think I'd love chili."

"Super. Fantastic. I can show you my horses." He gestured toward his Jeep.

"Yes. I'd really like that. Bobby and I will follow you."

Savik looked at Bobby and then at Claire and nodded acceptance of her terms.

Bobby helped her into the back seat, and soon they were following Savik's Jeep further east along the road into the countryside. In only a few minutes she'd be more or less alone with Savik at the place he'd created for himself in the country.

Not more than twenty minutes ago Claire had been eager. That was nothing to how she felt at this moment. Her heart raced. Adam Forsythe often held her hand a bit longer than necessary, and Claire always managed to wriggle free because such touch, though a simple thing, was not welcome. Other men, even Pryce, occasionally touched Claire's hands or arm or shoulders—never boldly as Savik had done. Joss said that most men fell under Claire's spell and fell a little in love with her. Come to think of it, Joss always touched more than Claire was comfortable with, but that was because Claire was basically Joss's family. Still it was a marvel to think that this man's touch could do what no one else's could.

BlueSky Montana Cowboy

"I've been meaning to ask you," Claire said to Bobby in an attempt to quiet her jitters, "where will you spend Thanksgiving?"

"Got a big family, most of them in Queens. My mom will cook for maybe twenty."

"That's wonderful."

"Yeah. I like family. You'll be at the Retreat?"

Claire winced, reminded that she wouldn't be with her mother or her son…or have a loving mate by her side. No. "I'll spend the day with Serena and her three daughters, grandkids, and sons-in-law. John and his girlfriend are visiting her family."

"I hear Humvee is doing real well and might be coming back to work for you."

"I hope so, Bobby. Maybe by Christmas. That would be the best Christmas present I can imagine. I'd like to keep you on, but it would have to be night duty."

He looked at her in the mirror, gave her a grin. "Night duty is fine with me."

Up ahead, Savik turned off the highway and through a gate with "Blue Skies" branded into its massive wooden arch. The name triggered a sharp memory. During their five magic days, he'd proudly declared that he was, and always would be, a blue skies Montana cowboy.

They pulled up to a sturdy rustic cabin. "Looks a lot like your place," Bobby said.

In spirit and appearance Savik's cabin could have been a twin, or at least a sibling, of The Retreat. Apparently Savik hadn't fixed his place up much, but it was so uncannily familiar. How would he feel when—if—he saw The Retreat. Would he feel the same recognition?

After they both parked, Savik said to Bobby, "Go on in and help yourself to anything in the kitchen or refrigerator. There's chili on the range. I want to show Claire the horses."

"I'll just be around," Bobby said. He looked at Claire, clearly not eager to leave her alone with Savik, or anyone, and implying random spot checks.

Savik linked his arm under Claire's. "My favorite horse is Ramrod. He's actually been with me on a couple of trips abroad where the quarantine problems weren't too big an obstacle." He steered them toward a barn and corral with four horses.

"I like your place," she said.

"That's him. The chestnut quarter horse with the white socks," Savik said. "The black mare is also a quarter horse. The other two are Arabian mares. Been thinking of breeding them."

Claire couldn't resist adding it up. Ranch, country club, expensive horses; she knew he owned a condo in Manhattan; adrenalin-pumping trips all over the world. Quite a lifestyle.

Savik added, "My sister—you may remember I mentioned her—well, she has a son and daughter and they love to come over and ride."

"So. Savik is an uncle." This image she found less threatening. But this meant that John had cousins, and Claire was even more unjustified in hiding John's other family.

"Yep. I like the kids. The boy is turning twenty, and the girl is eighteen. When I'm with them, I enjoy my only real family time. Sometimes wonder what I might be missing."

The words stoked secret hopes, making them seem tantalizingly possible. The stability of a mate and family to provide shelter from the turmoil that would always be around her if she won this struggle for the Presidency was a vision so lovely she dared not think of it. "So do you have someone special? Or do you just date?"

. . . . .

Savik paused to give Claire's question a once-over. That kind of question, from a woman, tended to be loaded. It was a good sign, though, that she was interested in his love life. "No one special. And I don't date much either."

"I lost track of you for years, but with your unusual name and accomplishments, I see you mentioned in the columns. I think I first learned about you again during your divorce."

Savik flinched at the unpleasant reminder. "A tough four years of marriage and an even tougher separation."

Ramrod crept up on them and shoved Savik's shoulder, demanding a treat. Claire laughed. Her laugh had the power to make him smile, no matter what. They'd laughed a lot. And kissed a lot. And twice he'd had her. He'd gone out of his mind for her. All the greater the crash when he left almost at once for duty, and then again when he'd written only to learn she'd married.

"Sorry, fella" he said, stroking the warm, velvet nose. "No apple this time."

Claire patted Ramrod's neck. Savik took her hand and pulled her close. He would let her go at once if she resisted. She didn't. In fact, her eyes were saying, "Kiss me."

So he did. A long, sensual, contact. She smelled of scented soap. Had she bathed with him in mind? The slight breeze brushed strands of her hair against his cheek. The tip of his tongue moved against her lips, and she opened for him. Just a bit. Just enough for him to enter for a moment. And then his own arousal made him draw back. *Too soon, you idiot. She'll bolt.*

She also pulled away. Had she noticed? She was smiling. She slipped her arm through his. "Let's have chili. And I want to see your house."

They turned toward the house. He said, "I'm not sure I can imagine what your last two weeks have been like."

"Very exciting. But very exhausting."

"I actually feel a little odd. Lunch with the potential U.S. President."

Again she laughed. He felt a twinge of guilt over the line about being President. Sadly, she was in for a tremendous letdown. *But sooner rather than later.* He didn't like to think of her being hurt. "You know that running for a political office at any level can be pretty nasty. But this is the big one, Claire. Things will happen that will amaze you. Hurt you."

"I know that. I have thick skin. I'm prepared."

He didn't think so. He didn't think she had any idea what she was in for.

. . . . .

On Savik's porch Claire set one of the four old rockers to rocking. "I bet it's beautiful here in the summer."

"Hey, it's beautiful any time. I like to bundle up in snow gear and sit here and drink hot wine when the ground is three feet deep in snow and the moon makes the whole thing sparkle."

Impossible visions of the two of them enjoying the seasons together popped into Claire's head like sweet dreams. He opened the door and followed her inside. She could smell chili from the kitchen. Bobby, nowhere in sight, seemed to have made himself at home.

Claire let Savik remove her coat and hang it on one of the pegs by the door, his sheepskin jacket beside it, the Stetson over another peg. How cozy and domestic the pieces of clothing looked together.

"Want to see a bit of the place?" he asked.

Since Savik's practice was international corporate investing, she'd wondered if his taste might be sleek and modern, even though he'd said "cabin." But the spirit here was Western, all suede, leather and wood. Huge throw rugs warmed dark plank floors. The place was spare, however. No nick-knacks. Two bronze statuettes, Remingtons. One on a table beside the massive fireplace and the other in a built-in, ceiling-to-floor, fully loaded bookcase. No mounted deer heads or elephant-foot umbrella stands, thank god.

The hallway gallery included photos, mostly of horses and men against stunning backgrounds—snow-covered peaks, rolling hills of pink and mauve desert sand, white-capped waves crashing against black lava cliffs. Each photo feeling more inspiring than the previous one. A few of two healthy kids at varying ages, doubtless the cousins related to John. Savik looked heroic in a Green Beret uniform in several shots.

She remembered he'd stopped one afternoon to help a man with three kids change a flat tire. That heroic streak still attracted her, assuming he hadn't lost it.

They passed two Western-style bedrooms, and her heart rate rose slightly at a stairway apparently leading upstairs to his. She was grateful to pass it by and find Bobby seated at a table in the kitchen. When they entered, he took his empty bowl and a plate to the sink.

"Just leave them," Savik said. Bobby looked to Claire for an okay to leave, and when she nodded, he complied. He picked up a paperback book and headed for the living room.

Savik hustled up two big bowls and two plates, sat them in his oven to warm beside something covered in foil. She took the top off the low-simmering pot of chili, and the escaping aroma made her instantly hungry.

"Cornbread's in the oven too," Savik said. "I left it warming in case you agreed to come."

When they sat down, Savik had added two glasses of ale from a micro-brewery to the feast. Claire sipped. "Mmmm. Dry and hoppy." She dipped her spoon into the chili, ate, and then tasted the cornbread. Savik seemed to be waiting for something. Ah. How many times had she waited, breath held, to see what someone would think of her dishes?

"The chili *is* delicious." And it was.

"I won a chili cook-off once," he boasted.

"I could start you a cooking show. 'Cooking for Corporate Cowboys.'"

He grinned. An awkward silence followed.

"So," he said finally, "how is your son taking to the idea of you running for President?"

She choked on her second bite of cornbread.

Crane Doesn't Know How To Take Us There

"John?" Claire's thoughts scattered at the question. "Well, my son isn't all that pleased."

Savik shook his head. "You can't blame him. He's used to you being famous, but it's probably never affected him as directly as it would if he had Secret Service on his tail all the time. I know how I'd have felt at his age." Savik took a long swig of the ale.

She sure didn't want to talk about John with Savik—sometime, yes, but not yet—and didn't know what tack to take, so she concentrated on cutting another piece of cornbread, which, unlike the savory chili, smacked of commercial origins.

"I've read about him in the papers. Is he still playing tennis?"

Cornered again. "I'm hoping he'll become serious about law school. But he seems drawn to excitement. The tennis. Surfing. He hiked the Darien Gap three years ago."

"I'm impressed. The Darian is not for wusses. My friend Wi—. . ." Savik hesitated, as though he were trying to decide whether to tell her his friend's name. "Well, my friend and I have started planning our next big trek. Three weeks in Sumatra, hiking through dense jungle, seeing some of the most beautiful scenery and wildlife the planet has to offer."

"You'll love it. I stayed there with a Minang family, and we have a school in Nadang. I was close to the jungle there. These gorgeous birds fly out from the trees along the river, and I'd slip away into the thick of it. You get this sense of thriving life. I love the earthy smell, especially after a rain. Love the orchids."

"John might find this trip a blast. My nephew might be coming."

Father, son, and cousin. She pictured them together, all scruffy with half-grown beards, grinning for a photo like the ones in Savik's hall. And strangely she felt herself warming with pleasure at the thought. Not at all alarmed. "How soon will you go?"

"It usually takes us a year to pull it all together. I'd be pleased to meet a young guy who hiked the Darian. But maybe he'll be in school by then and too tied down."

She swallowed her last sip of ale. Savik said, "How about some pear schnapps in front of a crackling fire?"

"Ooh…" She was in the presence of a smooth operator with years of practice. She checked her watch. There was still time. "Lovely."

He disappeared into a pantry and emerged with glasses and an ornate bottle and headed into the living room. Bobby rose from a leather armchair in one corner.

"We're going to make a fire," Savik said.

"I'll just…." *The Big Sleep* in hand, Bobby returned to the kitchen.

She enjoyed watching Savik crossing logs and kindling expertly and admired the curve of the back beneath that flannel shirt. He lit the kindling, returned to her side, slid his arm around her shoulders, drawing her to him. Warmth from his hand soaked right through the silk of her dress as they watched the fire catch.

"Been wanting to ask," he said, "why you're going to beat yourself up against a wall like Mason Crane? Or even worse, Hass? I sort of hate to see you do it."

"That implies that the contest to reach the Presidency would be hopeless. I don't think it is."

"Hell, Claire, even if you get past Crane, Hass has a massive party apparatus behind him."

"He has opposition, and not just from me. I believe he can be brought down."

Savik let her go. He moved to the schnapps bottle and poured them both a glass.

"Good thing I'm not driving," she said, hoping to switch the topic from politics. Her gut told her that danger lurked in that direction.

"Why not let Mason Crane be the one to bring him down? You want a more peaceful world. Crane does, too."

"Ah, but Crane doesn't know how to take us there."

Savik dropped onto the sofa and pulled her down beside him. She let him so close that their hips, legs, and arms touched. She curled against him. "Your fire is looking really good."

"But why you? Politics is brutal, Claire. You have a wonderful life. Why give that up for the sacrifices of political life?"

He wanted to talk politics. Fine. "Because I believe there is a good chance, or at least some chance, that I can beat Mason Crane and then beat Hass. If I don't beat Crane, then he will certainly be the party's nominee, and his foreign policy isn't sufficiently different from Hass's. Take the PeaceMaker program. This last test alone cost ninety million dollars. For the whole program, we're at one hundred and ninety billion and counting.

If Hass wins, he'll give the program a green light with more billions to deploy it. And I know from Crane himself that he approves of it and would also okay it if elected."

Savik stiffened, and then scooted away to the schnapps bottle and while the wood in the fire crackled cheerily, he poured a bit more into his still half-full glass. He said, not looking at her, "The PeaceMaker program is our best hope for defending ourselves."

She absolutely hated hearing praise for the hated program from Savik. She noted that he didn't scoot all the way back to her, and felt the emptiness of that little space between them as though it were from here to the moon.

. . . . .

Savik studied Claire's face, the earnest frown between her eyes, the full, luscious mouth, all the while thinking that the damnedest nonsense was coming out of those beautiful lips.

"The weapon isn't just for defense, Savik. It can be used for a preemptive strike any—."

"We are under attack by zealous fanatics." It was pointless to try to change her views at this late date, but he felt some crazy urge to save her from herself. "Would you have us sit around and wait for them to hit us again? Another 9/11 or Houston Astrodome?"

"Of course not. But—"

"I admire you and what you work for. But I'm a realist, and there's no way to deal with these fanatics but by being stronger than they are." Damn, how could she not understand that?

"True strength comes from assessing our real threats and how best to spend—"

"This is a war, Claire. And we have to win it."

He simply could not sit still and listen to her talking about "true strength." He stood and stepped to the fireplace. Attempting to relax, he stretched his arm casually along the mantle, but realized that with the other hand he was gripping his glass so hard he might crack it.

. . . . .

Claire sipped slowly, thinking that she—that they—should cool down. Savik's eyes were snapping as hot as the logs, he was probably fighting with himself to keep from exploding. Besides, he wasn't really listening. He'd interrupted her at least three times. She also felt shaky because an intense electricity buzzed between them.

Keeping her voice even she said, "If either Party really thought some flea-sized nation would lob a nuclear-tipped missile at Seattle or Boston at the risk of our incinerating them in return, don't you think that the administration might have raised our taxes to take drastic measures to stop it? If they really thought someone would come across our border and explode a dirty, nuclear, suitcase-bomb in Dallas, wouldn't they perhaps ration chocolate and wine, if necessary, to actually secure those borders? But they don't. Using the excuse of security, the PeaceMaker is a means to fatten corporate profits and potentially a way to dominate the whole damn world! "

He leaned toward her, his lips thin, his gaze smoldering.

A loud knocking on the front door caused her to jump.

Savik jolted upright. The hammering came again. "Someone at the door," he said. "Probably for the best." He set his glass on the mantle, and she followed along several steps behind as he strode to the door and opened it.

"Hi Savik," said a beautiful brunette wearing a stunning, ankle-length red wool coat.

Gold Earrings!

"Adrienne!" Savik blurted, clearly surprised.

And, Claire thought, quickly stepping backward before she could be seen, *maybe not at all happy to have a woman show up in the middle of his time with someone else.* In any case, Claire must not be seen here with Savik. This was so very awkward.

"Uh. I'm pretty surprised to see you," she heard Savik say.

Oh, I'll just bet you are, Claire thought. *No one special. Don't date much.* How very embarrassing to have his words come back and bite him. The brunette—Adrienne—stepped inside; Claire heard the click of high heels on wood. She couldn't resist listening.

"But you said you weren't seeing anyone. I was up here for a deposition," Adrienne said.

"And you just decided to stop by?" The sting in Savik's question couldn't be missed, but he'd obviously given Adrienne the same line about not dating anyone. *Men! Aaaugh!*

Adrienne went on, "…and I've been missing a pair of gold earrings. As I was driving up, it occurred to me that I might have left them here. In the bedroom."

"If I'd found earrings, Adrienne, I'd have returned them. And I don't appreciate—"

Claire had had all she could stomach. She hated sneaking. Hated herself for caring enough to eavesdrop. She stepped quietly into the kitchen. Bobby looked up. "Time to go," she said.

. . . . .

It didn't take Savik four minutes to get Adrienne out of the house. He'd said some pretty strong things to her about busting in on him. Strong enough that she understood he wouldn't welcome any more calls.

He leaned with both hands against the mantle, staring at the fire, now starting to die down. Claire had left a note—"It was time for me to get back to town. I thought I'd just duck out. It's not okay politically for us to be seen in any but a public place. Loved the chili. Best, Claire."

Hell. Well, there was one plus. No more calls from Adrienne. As for Claire. It would never work for him with Claire. She was as set in her views as he was in his, those views were worlds apart, and they weren't small matters that might be ignored while emphasizing values they shared. He and Claire were Venus and Mars in spades. It would be a long time, if ever, before he called Claire again. More like *never*. *A real damn shame*. He wanted her every bit as much as he had at age nineteen. Seeing her again brought up feelings he'd thought he'd lost forever.

. . . . .

Claire huddled in the Cadillac's back seat, her worst suspicions confirmed. First, that Savik still caused her to ease her grip on sanity. And second, that everything about Savik would seduce her son in the worst possible way. She was stunned, horrified, that she'd actually contemplated letting John go off with the man on a male-bonding, macho trip.

Her son connecting with PeaceMaker-admiring, politically shortsighted, womanizing, playboy Savik…She shivered. "The insanity stops now."

"What was that?" Bobby asked.

She shook her head. "Just talking to myself." Of one thing she was certain. John and Savik would hit it off famously if they ever teamed up. *I'm sorry, Maman. I tried, but I was right all along.*

We Hit A Cow

Another jarring bump. Curses erupted from her fellow passengers. Claire continued to rest her burning eyes a moment from the long hours in the bus's desiccating heat. The chartered campaign bus had been traveling a picturesque route called "The Currier and Ives Trail." Unseasonable freezing rain blurred the view of snow-covered farms and quaint townships, now restored since the famous lithographers over a century ago enchanted Americans with their prints of New England sights.

The bus engine's drone and the low rumble of chatter of twenty-five staffers on this New Hampshire campaign push created white noise that would make sleep possible if only she had time. In five minutes, though, the journalist who was traveling with them was scheduled to interview her.

Claire's back ached. Since Thanksgiving she'd slept irregularly, a few hours in the very early mornings and the occasional catnap. The last three months had been a blur of campaign preparations, back-and-forthing between fourteen states, dinners, speeches, interviews, photo ops, handshaking. An old-fashioned, real-life, hands-on campaign, not like the 2020 digital nightmare.

At least the frantic activity kept her from obsessing over John's excuses to avoid the holidays with her, and kept her from kicking herself over her disaster with Savik. She hadn't received a single rose since that evening.

Humvee's return to work comforted her in ways she'd never anticipated. His attentiveness and mocking humor was good for everyone's morale, though he was probably bored. Only a few hate letters had come in and one incoherent death threat. The only thing that really threatened her here was political defeat and wasted money. Lots of it.

The bus slowed and turned onto a bumpy side road. She opened her eyes and motioned to the Keene Courier reporter, a pink-cheeked, bespectacled young man named Ben. Next stop was a critical luncheon at West Henniker with a Democratic women's coalition for peace. Their members proposed to spearhead a "Democrats for Claire" campaign to help convince skeptical party members that it was she, not Crane, who could beat President Ernest Hass, who most certainly would be the Republican nominee. But they wanted one-on-one with Claire before committing.

"Your strong showing in the Iowa Caucus surprised many, yet you were far from a win," Ben said. "In national polls you still trail President

Hass by nearly six points and he's barely campaigning. And you trail Senator Crane by an average of 4 points. It appears that the Democratic Party isn't taking your chances seriously while Crane is hogging the media attention. What's your plan to—?"

The bus tossed its passengers as the wheels passed over a pot hole that had to be a bomb crater. The rain was unrelenting.

Someone said, "I hate this goddamn detour!"

Humvee said, "Sign back there said, 'Cantoofuck River Bridge under repair."

Laughter preceded a correction. "Yeah, the *Contoocook* River. It's probably flooded."

"You didn't hear any of that, right?" Claire asked the reporter.

Ben's smile was a tiny bit prissy. The bus skidded, throwing everyone sideways, and Ben's glasses fell off. He snatched them up. Someone wailed, "These slushy roads are a pisser."

Taking a bus on wintery back roads and byways was risky, but the driver said he could do it, and Pryce and their New England PR consultant insisted this was exactly the kind of image-boosting Claire needed. She actually had relatives in the little town of Warner, and had attended a Society of Friends meeting there.

Ben had snapped a photo of her hugging a distant cousin in front of an old miller's waterwheel. Her poll numbers had jumped the next morning, higher, Pryce said, than when she'd spoken at the typical political events that had her zigging and zagging across the state. Last week's Iowa Caucuses, however, had felt like a disaster—nineteen million dollars spent in the state had reaped only a third of Iowa primary delegates.

Today Ben had rejoined her to cover her during a critical appearance on "Inside Politics" and CNN's "Hotseat"—both held at the Merrimack Diner in Concord. Claire said to Ben, "To get back to your question about a plan, our volunteer base is so strong, we've raised formidable sums—"

The bus abruptly swerved. For a second she was airborne. Then Bang! Claire hit hard against the wall. They skidded, fish-tailed and thudded into something. Several women screamed. The bus teetered, still skidding, and finally came to a slightly slanted stop.

Heart pounding, Claire checked the interior then called out, "Are we all okay?"

The driver stood, snow white pale. "I'm awful sorry." He gestured out through the windows, shaking his head, trying to say something. "I…'m… sorry."

Claire rose. "Jimmy, it's okay. We seem all fine." She moved toward the front. All eyes were on her now.

"I hit a cow," he said.

This set off wails, and then people seemed to speak at once.

"What's a cow doing on a road?"

"Is it dead?"

"We're stuck," Jimmy said.

From behind the bus came the mooing sound of cows. The vital luncheon with the Democrats started in twenty minutes.

"Let's have a look," Claire said, donning her hooded raincoat.

Humvee rushed out ahead of her. The driver stepped outside and offered her his hand. In two-inch heel boots, Claire stepped down, slipped before she reached his hand, bumped the steps, hit the ground, and slid into a puddle of slush.

She sat in the puddle, stunned and gasping with cold and heard the click of Ben's camera as Humvee helped her up. She forced herself to smile, posed with her arm raised in a "Ta-dah!" gesture, looking over her shoulder as the clicking camera focused on her muddy backside.

The cow lay still and bloody in the road.

Claire and the others surrounded the poor lifeless thing. Jimmy's face was contorted in misery. Claire put her arm around him as a man in a green plastic raincoat and black rubber rain boots slogged toward them.

"You've killed my Ethel," he said forlornly.

. . . .

The next morning, a Saturday, periodic rainfall had turned back to snowfall. Joss brought newspapers in as the Manchester Suites room service delivered breakfast. Claire luxuriated in warm fleece sweats and Ugg Boots.

"We're up two and a half points in the polls," Joss said as she helped herself from the tray laden with biscuits, golden-brown home fried potatoes, scrambled eggs, and coffee. "The pollsters say viewers loved it that you showed up with mud all over the back of your dress, looked fine from the front, and carried on like nothing was wrong."

Claire chuckled. Joss had of course brought a change of clothing, but Pryce told her to keep quiet about it. The farmer towed the stuck bus out of the muddy area with his tractor, bless him. Thanks to him Claire had made it to her luncheon, the CNN interview, and the town meeting. The whole story made national television.

"Talk about unintended consequences," Claire said, slathering butter inside the steaming biscuit. She took a huge bite.

"'Claire Alden, Muddy, but Unbowed'," Joss read. "Bloggers were all over it, Claire, so it's in the papers, on TV, and gone viral on FaceBook, Twitter, Instagram, TikTok. Everywhere. Ben actually makes you look heroic the way you pulled everyone together as a team and negotiated with a farmer, and then trooped on to do a great job in all your events."

"Voters still aren't responding to my ideas for change so much as my persona."

Joss opened her notebook. "The Manchester benefit dinner with Adam Forsythe is this evening. His presence should give us another little boost. Maybe we'll get lucky and, to miss a flock of terrified Canada Geese, the bus will swerve and dump us into a snowbank. That should be a great visual for a couple of percentage points."

The New Hampshire primary—one of their make or break turning points—was only three days away. "Well, we're hitting crunch time. After Tuesday we'll be scraping the bottom of the funding barrel. If we don't win New Hampshire, we'll lose the big money folks who believe in me. So, geese, mud wrestling, pies in the face. Whatever it takes. Bring 'em on."

A Bar Fight?!

On West Broadway, near the park, in a corner bar not much bigger than a tennis tour bus, John Alden Trask sat alone, empty stools on both sides. He sipped his second Heineken from a glass mug, going slow to make it last. The place was maybe three-quarters full and election coverage on Fox TV droned on in the background, low enough that it was easy to ignore.

He never used to come to Brewster's before he met Fance, even though the place was only a few blocks from what Grandmere had called her *pied a terre*. In his tennis circuit days, before Grandmere's death, he'd helped support a yuppified sports bar where people knew he was a pro. But Fance liked the bartender here and John liked the anonymity. Customers pretty much left each other alone. It was a good place to think.

Fingers spread, he stroked his hair back. He'd quit spiking it, cut off the bleached ends, and let his black waves grow in. Fance couldn't keep her hands out of it. He'd also abandoned his grunge shave in favor of smooth cheeks that didn't irritate her skin.

The two beer limit he'd promised himself hadn't smoothed hard edges. Besides, he'd earned some reward for busting his brains studying. He smiled at the bartender. "Another Heineken, Corky."

Corky still only knew John as Fance's friend; almost no one recognized John Alden Trask in public anymore since he'd changed his look from irresponsible tennis bum to aspiring law student. Which was perfect. If the blue collar types who stopped off here on their way home from work recognized him, they would give him a hard time, especially tonight with the New Hampshire primary results coming in.

"Why they ever let that broad out of the kitchen beats me," one of them had said during the Iowa Caucus. Others had quickly jumped on the bashing pile. John had wanted to stand up and point out, 'Are you kidding? Look at all she's done!' But another part of him wanted to say, yeah, and she's a sneaky, controlling mother too.

The Iowa Caucus vote had thoroughly scrambled his emotions. He'd thought his mother would lose, and so badly that she'd get laughed out of the race right then. His own relief at her strong showing had surprised him. Now in New Hampshire she was six points behind Crane, although the talking heads claimed the race was too close to call. According to national polls, she was supposedly neck and neck when paired against Hass. Still, she would almost certainly lose New Hampshire and that would be the end of all this craziness.

All his intense soul-searching following Grandmere's funeral had changed him. She had always believed in him. He was sorry she had left his life when he was still so rootless. He intended to change that, and he was well on his way. He should feel happier than he did.

Corky slid an open bottle in front of him. John didn't bother to pour it into the mug this time. He slugged down half before he set the bottle back down.

The guys at the bar stopped talking and someone bawled out, "Shit."

It was the red-nosed guy two bar chairs away, a regular who worked a construction site, John turned to the focus of everyone's attention, the TV. There was a newsbreak in the college basketball coverage on the bar's lone set. The screen showed a shabby, whitewashed two-story building with a loudspeaker on top.

Standing on a tiny, second floor balcony, a Muslim man wearing a *gal-ibaya* and white skull cap was calling out in a way that wasn't quite sing-ing, but was foreign and annoying—the call-to-prayer, a controversy that had the American public in an uproar. The caption said, "Detroit, *adhan* protest."

Guys with boomboxes were driving in front of the house playing loud heavy metal, an old song by Iron Maiden, to drown out the *adhan*. John knew the boombox piece from back in junior high. "Number of the Beast." The crawl across the screen's bottom now read, "Muslims in Detroit community of Greenleaf demand equality, protesting that Christian churches broadcast religious music on the hour." Crowds had gathered, people shouting. Hate signs. Police ordering everyone to disburse.

The worker with the red nose said, "I sure as hell don't want to wake up to that caterwauling every goddamn morning." With this sentiment, John agreed.

On the other side of Red Nose, a trucker, his hair the color of raw liver and with freckles to match, bellowed in a way suggesting too much beer. "Fucking terrorists still streamin' in, trying to cram their damn religion down our throats." This was the same guy who'd mouthed off about John's mother during the Iowa Caucus.

"I don't know," John said, loud enough so that the construction guy and the trucker could hear him. "The creeps with Satans and skulls on their T-shirts look more like terrorists, and they're making a lot more noise."

A half-dozen men turned to look at him. Hell! Why had he popped off? Who cared what these guys thought?

The liver-haired trucker said, "These sneaky foreign little bastards don't dare fight in the open. They gotta get a suicide bomber to do their dirty work."

"Okay, whatever," John said. The spirit here tonight was definitely on the negative side. Happily the game came back on. Things quieted down, and then a gorgeous blonde walked in. Black faux fur jacket, tight black jeans and high heel boots, protection against the February snow. Pale blonde hair fell in a cascade down to her waist. Fance. To a man, eyes turned to her.

"Whoa, babe," said Liver Hair. The men watched her walk up to John and kiss his cheek.

To Fance John said, "You're off work early? I wasn't expecting you for another ten or fifteen minutes."

"Yeah." Her tone said, *obviously*, but those green eyes were sparkling with excitement as she sat in one of the old-fashioned bentwood bar chairs. She opened her jacket, revealing her low-cut blouse of black satin. "I'm dying to see if your mom wins."

John immediately checked the construction guy, the trucker, and the Latino who'd just come in and sat down on his right. Was anyone reacting to her mention of "mom?" The men seemed engrossed in their drinks and the basketball game.

"I've been studying until my brain started to burn," John said. "What would you like?"

"Ginger ale…" She put her hand on his thigh and squeezed. "…and switching stations to catch some election results." She took her jacket off and conversation lulled a moment as bar patrons watched.

John motioned to Corky and ordered. When the drinks came, Fance flashed her gorgeous smile. "Hey, Corky. How 'bout we watch the election returns at the next commercial?" Her voice was intimate. Somehow, even when she was just playing or angry or talking about taking out the trash, Fance's voice was intimate. "That okay?"

The entire bar crowd broke out in sudden wailing and swearing at the basketball ref.

"Next commercial. Will do, Fance," Corky said.

Again John didn't bother pouring the beer into the mug. He drank quickly, hoping he might somehow avoid watching the whole damn election stuff. He felt good to have her by his side. Then Corky gestured to the guys to wait one, and changed to a news station.

"Corky! What the fuck!?" Liver Hair bawled out over other groans of protest.

"Hey, guys!" Fance beamed at the men. "I just need a quick update. A quick couple of minutes should do it."

Liver Hair grinned. "Sure thing, honey," he said. "Be happy to *do* it." He smiled innocently at Fance. "A few minutes. No problem." His way-too-much-to-drink smile became a leer. "But you'll want it a lot longer."

The men enjoying this exchange between their buddy and Fance broke into raucous laughter and whistles. John stood, making the bar-stool screech on the old marble floor.

Fance held her own. "I bet your women wonder why it's *not* a lot longer."

Liver Hair's backup chorus ooohed, egging them both on.

"You'll just have to see for yourself," he said.

"That's it." John was about to go for the guy, but the man held up his hands.

"Hey, sorry. It's a compliment. Gorgeous babe like her—"

Fance was now ignoring the asshole, her attention focused on the TV.

"—makes a man screw around with his…words. I mean, twist words. "

"John!" Fance shrieked. She was bouncing on her bar seat. "She won!"

All eyes in the bar switched to the TV. Talking heads on screen were comparing the numbers. The bar was too noisy to hear comments, but the tallies were there to see. Claire Alden, 65,857. Senator Crane, 63,141. Some other guy, 16,018 votes.

The camera cut to Alden headquarters in Manchester. His mother stepped to a podium to speak. TV cameras loved, had always loved, his mother. The glow coming through the TV tonight reminded him of when he was young, and she held him close beside her as she told him stories back before he came to resent the attraction his mother's looks and personality compelled in all those people vying for her time and attention.

A flood of boos swamped the tiny bar.

"Go back to the kitchen!" This from one of Liver Hair's equally drunk buddies.

"No fucking chitchats with bloody terrorists!" Liver Hair shouted.

"Hey!" Fance yelled. "I wanta hear this, so kindly shut the hell up."

Corky dashed over from the other end of the bar and flipped the station back to college basketball.

"We're going," John said.

"Good idea." Fance put her jacket on, unfortunately thrusting her chest forward a bit in the process.

Liver Hair stood, approached Fance, and said, "You know, you've got something in common with the Claire broad. Two things actually." He held both his open palms very close to Fance's chest.

A lightning bolt had been gathering in John's fist, which suddenly struck Liver Hair's jaw. Fance screamed. Somebody shoved her out of the way, but she fell. John dodged a punch and held a hand out to Fance.

Pain exploded in his lower back as somebody kneed him from behind. He fell on top of Fance, quickly rolling off onto his back as she screamed again. He tried to sit up as two guys came at him, one the construction guy. He kicked at both, one foot driving home to the man's gut, while the other connected solidly to somebody's nuts. The guy yelled, "Mother Fucker," and staggered backward.

In a split second, John was up again. Corky yelled, "Stop right now! I called the cops!"

Didn't stop Liver Hair from charging, head down. John grabbed his Heineken bottle from the bar, holding it by the neck like a club, dodged the charge and got off a glancing blow to the back of the guy's head but inadvertently smashed the bottle against the bar's edge.

Liver Hair went onto his knees, but the construction guy had caught his breath. He and another guy who wanted in on the fun grabbed John's elbows. John struggled, but they pinned him.

Liver Hair rose, pulled back his arm, and pounded John hard in the gut. His breath whooshed out. He slumped, his gut in agony, his lungs refusing to inflate. The world was going black at the edges. The two men let go and turned away, but not Liver Hair.

Fance screamed, "John, watch out!"

Still clutching the neck of the jagged-edged beer bottleneck, he used it to deflect the next punch. Liver Hair screamed as glass edges cut into flesh and bone. Blood rose, smeared the man's arm. He grabbed John in a wrestling grip with his other arm, and the two of them went down, rolling.

"POLICE!" a gravely male voice announced. "BREAK IT UP!"

Noise dinned into John's brain a moment. Someone sat him up and he gasped for burning air. He could hear the cops, speaking authoritative

Miranda-type phrases. He was rolled onto his stomach. He could probably see if he opened his eyes, but he kept them shut as he felt the cold steel bracelets lock around his wrists, now secured behind him.

Scare Someone?

Chanting erupted. Claire!Claire!Claire!Claire!

One last time Claire clasped the hand of the New Hampshire campaign chairman and raised it high. Hundreds of supporters redoubled their exuberance, clapping, whistling, waving campaign posters. Her cheeks burned. Elation coursed in waves through her like a volcanic tide.

The grueling campaign here had ended. At 12:30 A.M., all that remained was answering reporters' questions, and then Claire could fall into bed. But not sleep. They'd won New Hampshire!

The campaign chairman hugged Claire and then, taking Claire's arm, guided her to the edge of the stage. Adam stood at the top of the short flight of steps. He had insisted on flying in especially to be with her tonight, partly to encourage speculation he'd be her running mate, and partly for moral support. He hugged her, held her at arm's length, gazing a moment with an intense look in his eyes, and then hugged her again, so hard it pushed the breath out.

"By God, we're going to do this!" Adam crowed. "This is truly the beginning. And you were, of course, magnificent."

Adam's assistant said, "Mr. Ambassador." The assistant looked at Claire. "His breakfast meeting is at 7:30 in the morning. Congratulations, Ms. Alden." As the young man hustled Adam away, Adam turned to her and gave her a thumbs-up.

The New Hampshire Chairman accompanied Claire as they made their way among young and old, all of them smiling, faces glowing—into the Manchester Garden Hotel's conference room. Pryce stood before the reporters, filling them in on Claire's schedule. Joss, waiting to take her upstairs to bed, stood in the back of the room beaming.

As Claire moved to stand beside Pryce, he said, "One question per person, please. And try to keep them short. It's past everyone's bedtime."

The reporters laughed as hands shot up. Pryce would pick those likely to ask softball questions. He pointed to Lucy Gröen from the Manchester Guardian. "Ms. Gröen?"

"How does it feel to have beaten the Senator when only last week you'd lost the Nevada primary and Iowa, and most national polls showed you to be six points behind?"

"Wonderful! Very gratifying," Claire enthused. "I'm certain Senator Crane's advisors are stunned, and I plan many more big surprises for them."

Again the reporters laughed. Pryce pointed to a junior reporter from the New York Times but Phyllis Colson barged in front of the man and shouted at Claire. "You make big promises, like cutting the military budget to restructure for peace, but given that tonight your son was arrested in a bar fight, aren't you misleading voters when you make such claims? Why should voters believe you can deliver any of the grandiose changes you're promising if you can't control your own son?"

For a moment Claire wasn't sure she'd understood what the woman had said. John? Arrested in a bar fight? The room had hushed.

Pryce quickly stepped in. "If what you say is true, you possess information that we've not yet heard. It would be inappropriate for Claire to respond until she learns the facts of the matter."

"Oh, it's true," Colson shot back. "And the public should know just how she can claim to put the public house in order when she hasn't done well with her own."

Claire's mind whirled. Whatever the truth might be, she simply could not let the jab go unanswered. Despite their earlier smiles, reporters would put their worst spin on any avoidance.

"I love my son, as any mother does," Claire said. "But he is his own man now. I can't tell him what to do or fire him if he doesn't do it. When I'm President, my decisions will have much more influence over my staff and cabinet than I have over John. Most importantly, whatever the facts turn out to be, I know John to be a good man."

Pryce quickly called on another reporter. It was an easy question, and while Claire's mouth was talking, her mind was thinking, how and why would John ever get arrested in a bar fight?

At 1:00 A.M., Pryce shut the questioning down. Joss immediately came to Claire's side. With tears in her eyes she hugged Claire. "I am so happy for you and so sorry about John."

Claire let Joss go. "This news Colson bashed me with…I'm really shaken."

"I started calling around the minute she said it. It's true. John was arrested tonight."

"Was he hurt? Was anyone hurt?"

"I don't have details, but they wouldn't lock him up if he was seriously injured."

"I have to fly home tonight. I want to be available if John needs me. While I talk with Pryce, please tell the pilot to have the jet ready to leave within the hour."

Joss left and Pryce came over and took her arm.

Claire said, "Boy, do we ever have to talk.".

"I agree. That bitch Colson is always so damn eager to bring you down. Couldn't let you have one moment of glory if she could prevent it."

"Well, it seems it's true. John was arrested."

"Hell." Pryce drew them into an adjacent, and empty, conference room.

She hurried to add, "He apparently wasn't hurt."

"Fine, but he can hurt the campaign in a thousand ways. This rebellion of his must stop."

"I'm flying back to New York tonight. As soon as I leave you, I'll call one of the EClaire lawyers. She can bail him out first thing tomorrow, and I'll be waiting."

"You know he won't call for help. Probably won't want it."

To this she could only offer silence.

"Look, Claire. How about a sort of bodyguard/nursemaid to shadow the kid? You can tell him since you have Humvee, he should have someone too. Only the someone I have in mind isn't going to ask him nicely to please cut the crap. He's going to insist, if you know what I mean. Scare him a little. At least for the duration of the campaign."

Scare? "What are you saying?"

"I know people."

She felt a ripple of shock. "People who scare people?"

"I've made some…interesting contacts over the years. A certain, let's say, big man married my cousin, and they asked me to do the PR for their humongous wedding. I even met the guy, did some PR for him. No steady contacts, but I think I know where to go for things."

"Pryce! I had no idea. I absolutely do not want you to have any third party lean on John. I promise I'll reach him. I'll talk to him. I will find out about the arrest, and I am just sure, Pryce, that I can convince him how important it is to the campaign….oh, I don't know." She leaned back against the wall and put both hands to her head….So damn tired….

Pryce gently squeezed her arm. "It's okay, Claire. It will be all right. So as long as John doesn't do something totally crazy, the public isn't going to hold you accountable for him. Think of Hass's daughter."

Pryce was trying to reassure her while she was still absorbing the fact that he was willing to have someone scary lean on John. "This is a side of you, Pryce, that I've never seen. It's easy to get seduced that the end—"

". . . justifies the means. Don't worry about me."

"I hadn't." She straightened her shoulders. "Make sure I never have to again."

"Okay, Pryce is wrong. This one time."

She felt a nauseating apprehension about John. His life was a mess, and she was running for President. Phyllis Colson had succeeded in making her feel like she was what John thought she was, a horrible, selfish mother.

· · · · ·

Savik stepped to the door, opened it, and walked out on Claire, slamming the door behind him. Panic welled in her chest. Then the doorbell rang. A surge of relief flooded her. He'd changed his mind. He was coming back. She reached toward the doorknob, and the doorbell rang again. And again. And again.

No. Not doorbell.

Claire pulled herself out of sleep, realizing that it was the phone beside her bed in the apartment that was ringing. She was still exhausted. "Hello?" Her voice had dropped an octave.

"Ms. Alden?" A young, feminine voice.

"Yes. This is Claire Alden."

"Ms. Alden, this is Francine Showalter. Fance. John's girlfriend."

Claire pulled herself upright and swung her feet onto the floor.

"Yes, Fance. I recognize your voice now."

"I'm very sorry to be calling so early. I got this number from one of your calls. I was just gonna leave a voice message. I didn't think I'd reach you."

"I flew back very early this morning. I'm worried sick—"

"I called to tell you that John's been arrested. I didn't want you to read lies in the papers."

"I do know about the arrest, Fance. But I'm grateful you called. It's very thoughtful. Do you know what happened?"

"I sure do. I was there."

"I was told he wasn't hurt. Was anyone else?"

"Not really. He did give the other guy a shiner, and when this idiot attacked John, the guy cut himself on a broken bottle John was holding. The guy ran himself onto it."

"Fance, tell me the truth. Did John actually attack a man with a broken bottle?"

"No, no. The police got it straight right away. The guys in the bar and the bartender saw that the bottle thing was an accident. I suppose some reporters will get it wrong, though."

Claire winced. Pryce was going to have a big task putting out media fires. But thank God that John didn't cause the other man's cut. She didn't want to think, couldn't bear to think, that John was in that much emotional trouble. "Why were they fighting?"

"The guy was drunk. Actually, John also had a couple beers. Anyway, the drunk had been rude to me, and then when he . . . well, he made a dumbass—" There was a little intake of breath. "Sorry. I mean stupid comment about your…breasts and mine, and kinda reached for me, and John just exploded and punched him."

"Our *breasts*?"

Fance's light laugh sounded strained, but the girl had a sweet low voice. "Yes. My god, I can't believe I'm talking to you about this. The guy was totally out of line and said something like big boobs are what you and I have in common."

Claire chuckled and then sighed at life's absurdities. "I called a lawyer early this morning, Fance. John should be out on bail as soon as the court opens."

"I . . . John will really appreciate it."

"I doubt it."

"No, no. I'm sure he will. You know, I wanta tell you how much I admire you, and I'm so glad you won New Hampshire. I just know you can win the Presidency. We need you. The world needs you."

Claire felt a flush of pleasure. "You are kind, Fance."

"I won't take any more of your time. Just wanted you to know that John didn't do anything really bad."

"I know John cares a great deal for you. He's lucky to have someone so thoughtful. Please tell him I love him, and I'm glad he wasn't hurt. Tell him I need to talk to him soon."

They hung up. Claire sighed. A fight. Over boobs. What *was* he thinking?

7:45. Might as well stay up. The Manhattan apartment seemed so bare without Alex. She'd bring him along next time no matter what. She meditated by the window, fending off the Thousand Important Things she would soon be forced to tackle. The images that kept returning weren't the vote tallies on the TV monitors but the odd things that had made such a difference in her life, things over which she had no control. Mud on her coat. Ethel the cow lying dead on the road, the good farmer, her son in a bar fight. She began to mentally repeat the Serenity Prayer, but was interrupted by the phone ringing outside the bedroom/home office of the small apartment.

Joss was up, probably making the coffee she could smell. Humvee had simply crashed on the apartment's one sofa when they'd gotten in at 2:30 that morning. And now the world was calling. Claire showered and dressed quickly. They all hurried to the campaign headquarters in the Steinmetz Building only minutes away where staff and volunteers were gearing up for primary Super Tuesday, only days away. Pryce was video-conferencing one-on-one with the Big Tunas.

Today they'd received many floral arrangements, mostly in red, white and blue, along with bottles of wine and champagne, packages of snacks and candy for the volunteers, and a flood of emails, mostly congratulatory, but a few with messages of hate. By 5:30 P.M., there was still no new word from the Tunas about the financing. A delivery boy from a florist arrived with a distinctive long box for Claire. She knew when she saw it that it would have a rose.

I Can't Live Without You

John stared up at the massive, night-lit inspiration that was the Freedom Tower. Built as part of America's memorial to those who died on 9/11, it rose from a square base to taper into slender triangles and a spire that jabbed the sky.

He held Fance's gloved hand as nickel-sized flakes of falling snow covered sidewalks, lamp posts, parked cars, and buildings. They weren't alone on this snowy evening. Many of the Big Apple's citizens were out on the town and enjoying the shops and theaters in the Memorial Tower complex.

This was their favorite walk, down West Street to the Tower and then through the Reflecting Absence memorial, and back to Grandmere's apartment. The jail experience had freaked him out. Fingerprinting and the photos weren't too bad, but the body cavity search had made it unforgettably clear that he'd joined the ranks of common criminals. The arrest was bad enough. A conviction could prevent him from getting accepted into law school. The screaming and snoring of other residents all night long had been the finishing touch. He'd accepted his mother's help.

"She was really nice, John," Fance said. "And genuinely worried about you."

"I never said she isn't nice."

"She wants to talk with you."

"Probably wants to convince me to stay out of bar brawls while she's trying to become the most powerful person in the world."

"You know, I don't get you."

They turned off the street and into the memorial garden. Snowflakes stuck to the white suede of her jacket. "You are funny, kind, scary smart, and as far as I know, a positive kind of guy. But when it comes to your mom, there is always this bitter, sarcastic edge in your voice."

"Come on, Fance. Let's not talk about my mother."

"Why won't you talk with me about her? I like her. Do you even know who your mom really is or what she actually stands for? Your mom is totally independent."

"Meaning what?"

They arrived at a plunging pool, one of two built on the footprints of the World Trade towers. The pools dipped downward, sort of disappearing, a symbolic reminder of what used to be there but was lost.

He put his arm around her, wishing to God she'd change the subject. Over pizza he'd already covered the whole jail thing, and she was clearly determined to plunge on about his mother.

She shook her head. "I never read a political book in my life before your mom's, but her ideas—they make me feel like it's time to wake up and be part of making a huge historical change for the better. I've read stuff they teach at her Academies—which I bet you haven't. Have you even read *Creating The Future*?"

He felt suddenly embarrassed and let go of Fance's waist. He had not read it. "When did you do all this reading?"

"The day after she was on Rachel Maddow I checked out some stuff at the library."

"*You* went to the library?"

"See? Even a stripper isn't just pussy and nothin' else." She hurled the words stripper and pussy, her voice hot with defiance. "You not only don't know all there is to know about your mom, you don't know all there is to know about me."

"You know you're not just…What the hell difference does it make to us what my mother thinks?"

Fance pulled away and marched toward the second pool.

He followed and caught her hand again. "I'm glad you two talked. I suppose there's no reason for you not to like her."

"You're her son. And I want to understand you. Maybe the two of you aren't so different in the way you see things."

"Our philosophy isn't the problem."

"What does that mean?"

"Forget it."

"I don't want to forget it. What is your problem with her?"

He looked away. Fance pulled her gloved hand from his, and the nearby lamplight cast weird shadows over her angry face. "Okay, fine." Suddenly her eyes glistened with tears. "Don't talk to me. Don't explain. Don't share. But don't expect me to hang around."

He grabbed her elbow. "Oh god, Fance. Don't say that."

She sighed. "John, you still want to shock the world. You want me for shock value. I got a kick out of that too, for a while. Now I want more. I'm going to go back to school. I want to be a writer. A Journalist. I want to write about things I care about. I make good money and can work my way through. So, I think now is the time to…."

He pulled his gloves off, then pulled off hers. Her hand was warm in his. He suddenly could not speak. The thought of Fance disappearing from his life made him feel as lonely as he had when Grandmere died. Going home to the apartment without Fance ever being there again would make it seem as much a prison cell as the one he'd just left.

She didn't speak either. They stood gazing at each other and the tension slowly ebbed; the anger left her eyes.

"I can't live without you, Fance."

"Oh yeah?" She squinted at him. "Set a date."

"Whatever date you want."

Whoa! What had he done? Was that a proposal that had slipped out without hesitation? It was, in fact, what he needed, without a doubt, and...wanted.

Behind her loomed the Freedom Tower. Tiny lights twinkled on snow-covered trees. Her hair, down to her waist, shimmered in lamp-glow. The perfection of the moment raised the hairs on his neck and arms.

A hint of a smile touched her lips.

"I mean it," he whispered. "Pick a date."

"Any date I want?" A dare. She clearly didn't believe he was proposing. "Okay."

"Next January. After the election."

He got down on one knee in the snow. A couple walking by stopped to watch. "Will you marry me, Francine Showalter?"

A slow, dazzling smile lit her face.

Meddling In The Affairs Of Dragons

Just after four in the afternoon Humvee entered the campaign headquarters conference room and handed Claire a large florist's box. Humvee always inspected everything, including this new box, for a potential bomb or nasty substance. He would have read the accompanying card and then reassembled everything carefully. "The florist lady said this admirer like always went outta the way to be anonymous. Places the order using a courier and pays cash. Notes, money, flowers, whatever. Nothin' good comes from weasels who can't own up to their actions."

That was true, Claire decided, in everything except possibly roses and romance. She thanked him, lifted the lid and slid it under the box, which was much too wide and heavy for a single rose.

She opened the green tissue paper. Her breath caught at the loveliness in her arms. She inhaled the sweet fragrance of two dozen roses, their creamy apricot color so soft, the petals so sensuously smooth they suggested naked flesh. Eagerly, she opened the note.

"The very names of hybrids allow roses to speak to the heart." This was the quotation from the rose book. The personal note said, "These roses, 'Perfect Day,' drew me…as I am drawn to you. Congratulations on your perfect day in New Hampshire."

Claire smiled. The win in New Hampshire was certainly worth the marvelous bouquet. If Savik was willing to send roses, he wasn't taking their last date, however disastrous, as a final ending. Well, well, well. Damned, if that didn't please her.

"So, what do you think?" Humvee asked. "No name. They spook me."

"I'm pretty sure I know who's sending the roses, Humvee. It's not a problem." Savik might be feeling guilty for the way things had gone and was trying to make it up to her without risking anything. Of course his timing was awful. In fact, she still shouldn't take his calls, if he called.

Humvee still frowned. "Pretty sure? Until we know for certain, I'm gonna be nervous enough for us both." He left her alone.

Jake Shifrin, the campaign manager, joined her, anxious to hear her idea for a change in tomorrow's speech for the Commonwealth Club. He wasn't going to like what she had in mind. Joss strode in and, inspecting the box said, "Gorgeous roses, huh? What did the note say?"

Claire merely shook her head, and Joss looked a bit crestfallen. It was almost like she had sent them and wanted to see Claire be delighted.

Connie arrived. They were getting down to business when Pryce walked into the room, grinning. "Nice flowers," he said, pointing with his thumb backward toward the common area. He looked sleek—dark brown wool slacks and a gray-brown silk shirt. He'd just returned from his latest meeting with backers. "Every one of them, Claire! The Tuna Kahunas! Max Zell reached me first, but then it was Leo Lombardi. Ames, Blaine, and Gaylord weren't far behind. They're pumped and they'll provide solid financial backing. And they weren't the only ones. I've been taking calls all day."

"Given that it only put us ahead by three more primary convention votes than Crane," Claire said of the delegates assigned in proportion to the vote for New Hampshire, "for all the effort and expense it's amazing how much New Hampshire helps symbolically."

"Let me worry about the voter numbers," Jake said. "That's what you're paying me for. What I wanta know is, will your 'Tuna Kahunas' go public with their support? Crane is going to kick our butts in South Carolina next week." A very visible bunch of endorsements would boost Claire's credibility through the upcoming losses. "We gotta win it big."

"Many are still in the wings," Pryce said. "I've warned everyone she might fall behind at first. Be patient."

"Oh, god, it's witchy woman," Joss said, boosting the volume on the conversation of a round table of talking heads. Joss checked CNN regularly on the conference room TV.

Phyllis Colson was blathering. "She's an atheist! What is a Christian man like Adam Forsythe thinking by appearing with her on so many campaign stops? He's obviously giving the message that he'll be her running mate."

"Joss, give us a break!" Pryce said, irritated at Joss who seemed to be ignoring him.

The bow-tied TV host said, "Forsythe, of course, isn't an official candidate at this stage, and it's my understanding that Claire Alden is a Quaker, not an atheist."

Colson said, "New Hampshire was a fluke. Hass is still way ahead. Alden's a joke."

"I doubt her millions of fans consider her run a joke," said the host, "but it sure must have taken some of the glow off her victory to have her son arrested."

Joss mercifully clicked the sound off, revealing sounds outside the room in the common area. People were screaming. A man was yelling. Whatever could be—?

The door spring open and Humvee burst in and loudly demanded, "Everybody out through the service entrance in the back. NOW! Head for the roof!"

. . . . .

Since it was nearly 6:00 P.M., much of the building had already emptied, and most of the volunteers had left for the day as well. But not all. "I think it's a gas," Claire heard Humvee say into his cell phone. "Send a Haz-Mat team and ERVs immediately." He told 9-1-1 he had smelled fumes escaping from a champagne bottle.

Evidently one of the many bottles popped its own cork. Claire smelled something like Juicy Fruit gum mixed with eucalyptus. Eyes were tearing, noses running. Panic in the air. Since the ricin incident, Humvee had used his convalescent time to study up on chemical and biological terrorism. He said he thought it was an organophosphate and the heavy molecules would flow downward.

Sirens. Flashing lights. Along with several hundred others, Team Claire climbed stairs to the higher levels of a rear parking structure. The fresh air of the parking structure, though freezing, offered the safest spot for now.

Men in space suits. Paramedics. Cops. FBI. All dealing with chaos.

. . . . .

Claire finished answering questions from detectives and the FBI, honing a new hard edge inside. She'd worked through tragedy at the loss of her husband years ago, anger over the stoning in Bangladesh and over the ricin attack, rage at the loss of her mother. Maybe she was at the point Safa Mufti had described. She had no fear left. She would persist.

"They might kill me," she said to Pryce, Joss, Jake, Connie and Humvee, "but they will not make me quit. So anyone working closely with me would be wise to feel the same way. If you don't, I think now is the time to walk. Any walkers? I'd completely understand."

They all looked surprised, but all shook their heads.

Claire nodded. "Thank you. Every one of you. Jake, you're going to have to give this same message to your volunteer coordinators to pass on to the workers."

"I predict you'll have double the number of volunteers by this time next week," he said. "This is going to backfire like shit on whoever is behind this. Pardon my language."

"Okay, then," Claire said, sympathetic to Jake's tendency to use raunchy expletives when emotionally overheated. We still have work to do. Take-out Chinese at my apartment."

Thirty minutes later, they were eating with chopsticks around the apartment's small dining table. Jake said, "Does anyone else wonder who's sending anonymous roses?"

Pryce smiled. "I wonder, too, Claire. Who do you think sends them?"

"They were very beautiful," Connie added. Joss chimed in. "Surely you can guess."

"Look everyone," Claire offered, lifting more noodles onto her plate, "we've got more important things to think about than two dozen roses."

"Twenty-five, weren't there actually?" Joss asked. "Twenty-five means congratulations."

Claire considered Joss a moment. "How do you know that?"

Pryce, staring at Joss, wiped his mouth with his napkin. "You a rose expert?"

Joss hotly pointed out all the roses she'd ordered and sent in Claire's name. The interest in the roses felt slightly off kilter. Maybe, like Maman, they were worried that her admirer intended her harm. Of course, Savik didn't intend any such thing—and he was surely the sender. The simplest explanations were virtually always best, but her relationship with Savak was personal, none of their business. Anyway, it was all moot because she was dropping Savik entirely, roses or no roses.

"One thing is certain…" Pryce with his chopsticks reached for a coconut-crusted prawn. "There are too many violent shortsighted idiots out there, and they're breeding. Sometimes I think what the world needs is a really good plague."

"Christ!" Jake said. "The opposition would spin us all to fuckin' hell if that one got out."

"Really?" Pryce asked with mock incredulity.

"My ex-boyfriend thinks we need wars to control population growth," Connie said, "but he'd never be the one to volunteer to be cannon fodder, or offer his family as victims."

Claire said, "You all know very well there is a better way to get social change than by using violence. The suffragists did it. Gandhi did it. King did it. Nonviolent change gets better results over the long haul.

Now can we please go over the speech Connie and I have been working on?"

As everyone enjoyed a last cup of jasmine tea, Claire leaned forward. "Polls show that Americans agree that the Hass administration is unwilling to cut any cherished military pork-barrels, and they believe I will. And they like that. But we haven't been clear yet with the people on the really big plan."

Pryce jerked his teacup from his lips. "Good god, Claire. Don't tell me you propose to put the Department of Peace idea on the table."

Jake echoed. "If you announce this now, way too many people on both sides will see nothing but a mound of money to be spent on a *big government* boondogle. In Illinois and Pennsylvania, the poll numbers are too close. You'll lose 'em. Get nominated first. Then you can reveal what that department will take on. But not now."

Claire looked at Humvee. "What do you think? Should I tell everyone right now exactly how I intend to shift our defense budget substantially?"

Humvee grinned. "Yeah. If you say it like that. Straight shooters are the best."

Jake waved his chopsticks back and forth as if slicing the air into tiny pieces. "We're still working with your political analysts on the complex strategies involved. We need to package it so it'll win people on its own merits. Win their hearts and then their confidence. It's too soon to be that up front when the logistics aren't fully in place. You'd be fatally vulnerable to ridicule. Your new backers would all have coronaries. He glared at her. "And Humvee will be your new campaign manager."

Claire looked at Pryce and Joss. "If I'm elected, what I propose to do will turn many things in this country upside down. It will be, as a few are already saying, revolution. I'll need the people's trust. I'll only have it if I'm totally honest with them. So I am going to do this. If it sinks the candidacy, better now than later."

No one spoke. Jake blotted his brow. Joss frowned at Claire. Connie looked at her plate. Pryce stood and paced. Humvee decided to go check the hallway.

Finally Jake said, "You hired me to come up with numbers. Demographics. Spin. Image. That's what campaign managers deal with. Issues are down there at the bottom of what really counts in getting the win. Rational debate can't touch a good slogan." He smoothed his thinning hair back. "Look, it's refreshing that you're not a politician and that you have new ideas. Great ideas. But you make this speech tomorrow and you're dead in the water."

Anger tightened Claire throat, but she spoke evenly. "My campaign will be one of dignity, honesty, substance, and issues."

They all just stared at her.

Joss finally said, "What happened to mud wrestling and geese and cows named Ethel?"

Claire sighed. Another long silent pause followed. Then, "Yes, yes. Okay. I suppose I don't have to do it at the Commonwealth Club. Maybe after I get the nomination." *If I get the nomination.*

Joss, in an apparent attempt to change the subject and lighten the mood, pretended to read her fortune cookie message. "Confucius say, 'War not determine who is right. War determine who is left.'"

Pryce, grinning, narrowed his eyes. "'Confucius say, 'Do not meddle in the affairs of dragons. For you are crunchy and taste good dipped in chocolate.' And creating a cabinet level Department of Peace is for certain a dragon."

Everyone laughed. Claire pretended to read her fortune. "Mine says, 'Must get butts in gear big time for Super Tuesday.' And," she added, "meddling in the affairs of dragons is at the top of my list of things to do."

Super Tuesday

Feeling expansive after a pleasant drive from New York down to Washington, Savik piled ham, salami, and cheese slices onto a cut hero loaf and buried them with onions, peppers, tomato slices, mayo and mustard before finding a spot in front of the giant TV screen in Ronald Hughes's home. It was the first evening in May.

Ronnie, along with Winn, Cliff Stanhope, Quentin Frobisher, Duane Drummond, a politician or two, and several prominent backers and wives balanced plates as they stood or sat talking, occasionally watching voting tallies on Fox News. All were expecting Hass to secure enough votes to win the Republican nomination, maybe this very evening. And all were eager to celebrate when Claire Alden was tonight eliminated by Mason Crane. Hughes currently held court near the bar set-up.

Savik along with everyone else was pleased that during the January run up to Super Tuesday, Mason Crane, after taking Florida, had earned 158 convention delegates to Claire's puny 15. Everyone in the room was more afraid of a Democratic Alden candidacy than a Crane candidacy.

"Listen to that! Listen to that! I can't stand it!" Winn was talking to those behind him who were probably having a hard time hearing the broadcast. "That idiot talking head reporter is repeating one of Alden's attacks on PeaceMaker. If she got elected she'd dismantle the Department of Defense or some other craziness."

Duane's wife, Sylvie, a woman with assaultive red hair, said, "Her son's a playboy and a jailbird dating a stripper. Why do her supporters keep insisting she's a Christian?"

Duane belted out, "There's a 'Muslim's for Claire' movement. She could be one of them."

"Her only demographics are young women, college kids, and pacifists," a middle-aged backer Savik didn't know said. "Their damn 'We Need Clarity' bumper-stickers and T-shirts and baseball caps are fucking everywhere!"

New figures for the Democratic candidates in various states were posting. Claire was now holding the lead. "Son of a bitch!" Winn yelped. "Alden is winning!" *Winn*, Savik thought, *has had way too much beer.*

"Relax, Winn," Quentin said. "It's early."

Winn glared at Quentin. *For sure*, Savik thought, *Winn is totally blitzed."*

The crawl along the bottom of the screen kept reminding viewers of the total delegate votes at stake and already cast to win each party's nomination. Jack, a former aerospace lobbyist turned RNC official jumped in. "Actually, each state party draws up its own voting rules. Like, sometimes primary votes aren't bound. Like in New York. Or in California."

"Not bound?" Sylvie said, frowning.

Jack sort of puffed up. He clearly considered himself an expert on voting and was pumped by the chance to show off to Hughes's inner circle. "The people vote. They indicate how they would *like* their state delegates to vote at the nominating convention. But in many states, the delegates don't have to follow the will of the people. They aren't 'bound.' Oh, a few states' rules say they are bound on the first ballot, but on subsequent ballots, the delegates can vote for whoever they want, no matter how the public voted."

"Of course people get a little testy," Quentin said, "if we blatantly ignore public input."

Cliff added, "The way they did in Maine in 2000. At the nominating convention the delegates voted for Bush instead of McCain, who had actually won the most primary votes. That sure pissed off a lot of Maine Republicans."

Jack agreed. "But the public soon forgot. They have extremely short memories. The rules now for Dems is that delegates in all states are bound. They have to cast votes in the same proportion as the people in their state voted. But there is a loophole. The people vote, right, but they have so-called Super Delegates. Party insiders who can vote for whoever they want at the nominating convention. Not bound. Their votes add up to somewhere around fifteen percent of the total Dem votes. So they can sway a close Democratic contest."

Jack looked at Savik as though expecting a response. This man who was so often around Hughes' gatherings was probably full of shit. Winn once called him Jack the Hack. Savik was about to ask Jack exactly what he did for the party when a communal groan erupted.

Winn yelled, "Now Massachusetts is going for the bitch." He turned around and grinned at Savik. "Sorry. I know you know her and like her, but hell, her politics are so screwed up."

"No offense, taken, Winn."

"Some of the early states are a bit liberal-heavy," the party man said, "but today will be her last hurrah, I guarantee. When all the states have voted, Crane will win."

"*Her* wins so far *are* by narrow margins," Savik pointed out, reassured by that positive thought.

"If the damn Wyoming guy and that ex-evangelist senator would just drop out, we'd be home free," Winn said. "They keep sucking away votes that should go to Crane."

The returns continued to pour in, strong for Hass on the Republican side, and slightly but consistently favoring Claire added up across the many Super Tuesday states. As Savik watched, a sickening feeling slowly took hold. Many mid-western states were choosing the Wyoming governor. Most southern states went to the ex-evangelist, as did a serious chunk of the Texas vote. Crane officially won Texas, but only with 92 delegates since the Texas Democratic primary was proportional. Claire had taken 88 of the 222 primary delegate votes available. 88 delegates! In Texas! Many more than Nash, the Democratic Wyoming governor.

The TV talking heads seemed stunned. Demographics experts explained that women made up 54 percent of the voters and were voting heavily for Claire. So were young people. Savik was getting a civics lesson he hadn't planned on. The projected tally if the trend held up could be Crane 559 delegates to Claire's 723.

This was crazy! He had been so sure she had no chance. Even the pundits were surprised. He felt his pulse thumping at the base of his throat. He knew, just somehow knew, that if Claire ran against Hass she could very possibly beat him. Women were not fond of Ernest.

By midnight, most of the guests had left, pleased that their guy Hass was solidly ahead in delegates against his sole competitor. Savik felt he should get back to the hotel, but his brain teemed with horrible scenarios. Claire was coming on strong tonight. Scarily strong. If in July she actually won the democratic nomination…. If then in November she actually beat Hass? PeaceMaker? Probably dead. To say nothing of fabulous CET profits. Should he do something? Could he do something?

On his way out, Jack announced reassuringly, "Crane will win Virginia next week. That's 64 winner-take-all delegates. And then he'll take Michigan."

Savik slumped down beside Winn in front of the television, watching jubilant scenes of Claire supporters, wild-eyed with Claire's strong showing. "Jack sure is a pain," Winn said.

"Why does your dad always have him around?"

"I finally figured out he's Jack the Knife. He and his staff dug up the dirt on Senator Boswell's husband."

By 12:30, Claire's and Crane's tallies, from Savik's perspective, were disastrous. Gov. Nash from Wyoming had garnered an astonishing 258 delegates in total and the evangelist, 143. Voters just weren't getting behind Crane, and this division favored Claire, could launch Claire. The fear in his gut grew.

"Listen, Winn," Savik said, "I need to talk in private to your dad and maybe Cliff Stanhope."

"T'night?" Winn asked.

"Yeah. Tonight. I hate to say it, to think it even, but Claire is going to be a potential goddamn disaster. If things go on like this, our man is in big trouble. Alden shouldn't have gotten a hundred votes let alone 723."

Winn squinted, trying to focus as he stared at Savik. "Okay. I'll get 'em."

Winn left Savik gazing out the bay window into the wintry night. Lights were out in the expensive homes in this section of Bethesda, but quaint streetlights caused the falling snow to glitter. Despite what Jack had said about Democratic popular votes not counting all that much since in a close call party insiders, the Super Delegates, could ultimately decide who would get the most votes and hence the nomination, and that they would surely pick their party man Crane. But Savik's intuition told him that the ground he and Winn were standing on was very possibly in fact a melting glacier.

He had killed for his country and he'd seduced for his country, and he could damn well do it again. Claire had to be stopped. And, thank God, he was actually in a position to make a difference, maybe the critical difference.

. . . . .

Ronald Hughes sat by the fire with Cliff Stanhope and Savik Kodaly, loving Savik's plan to do everything in his power to get on the inside and sabotage the Alden campaign.

"You make the perfect *undercover* man," Hughes said, grinning at his own wit. He opened the lamptable drawer beside him, tore off a sheet of notepaper with a scripture printed at the top, quickly wrote out contact information, and handed Savik the slip. "I believe you already know Jack, whose specialty is finding mud to sling. The other contact you will only know as 'Hyjinx.' He's a bit more physical. Memorize this and burn it." Hughes considered telling Savik that Hyjinx had set up the little simulated nerve gas scare in Alden's headquarters, but decided the less Savik knew, the better.

"You have a top security clearance," Cliff said to Savik. "That will be a big help right up front. It will put her people at ease. No digging around in your private life. And you've worked with military intelligence in the past so you know what we want, the usual sort of thing as well as anything the least bit unusual—anything about her and the people around her, her lifestyle, her health."

Hughes thought Savik looked awfully grim. "We already have people going over her speeches, books, history," he said. "But you may be able to find a key piece of information that brings it all together. You'll be an unsung hero."

Hughes bid the two men good night and they left him alone, feeling good, at 1:30 A.M. Tonight had been productive. And Savik getting inside the Alden campaign....brilliant! He'd also paired Jack with Quentin in starting the Truth in Government Committee to discredit Claire at every turn. He booted his laptop and inserted the new flash drive Hyjinx had given him. Shots of Claire filled the screen, captured through both telephoto lenses and hidden cameras. Hughes smiled at the surprising intimacy of some of them.

Extracurricular Activities

Two days after Super Tuesday, Claire rested her head on the back of her chair, still chilled as she waited for Joss to bring coffee before the speech at The Economic Club of Chicago. An hour ago a rally at the Daley Center Plaza had ended late, her Illinois win drawing huge crowds despite the freezing wind-tunnel effect of the Plaza.

Jake had worked wonders bringing in celebs, and Claire had announced her intent to establish the new cabinet level position focused on promoting national security through formation of a global people's movement for a global peace treaty. The treaty would have sufficient enforcement power to facilitate the ultimate goal of ending war, a project no less grand than John F. Kennedy's challenge for America to land a man on the moon and return him safely to the earth. The announcement triggered a media explosion. Hass's commentator had called her "a woman who wants to spend *your* money her way into the distant future."

Her cell phone rang. Pryce. "Jake's a little worried," he said. "There are only twenty more primaries and/or state conventions left. Ohio is coming up, and that will boost Crane by 91 votes. "

Ohio was Crane's home state. "Right."

"Some are projecting another 220 delegates or so to Crane's 450 give or take. Our polls agree. That would put him in the win. So Virginia's going to be big. And we gotta woo voters in states like Kentucky and Tennessee where we won't win but can pick up delegates in the proportional tally. That means the first schedule change is Louisiana on the eleventh."

He outlined hectic schedule changes and she ended the call, needing to focus on tonight.

It was 5:10. She'd be on in twenty minutes. If she could wow this economically-minded crowd, skepticism about her proposed new cabinet post would be significantly blunted. Economists of impeccable credentials would be at her side: a former member of the President's Economic Policy Advisory Board, the chairwoman of the Congressional Committee of Deficit Review, and think-tank people who'd helped frame the whole endeavor.

Another phone buzz. Savik's number. Again.

With sudden rejuvenation, she sat up, the image of twenty-five pastel apricot roses springing to mind. She longed to hear him. She had not returned either of his two messages since their disastrous date, but now her fingers hit the green *answer* before she could stop herself.

"It's Claire," she said.

"Well, all the gods be praised. I've reached you. You must be horribly busy."

"Horribly. But I'm glad you called, Savik. I do want to thank you for the exquisite roses after New Hampshire." It was time to get things out in the open. "You could sign the cards, you know."

The line fell silent a moment, then Savik said, "So you received the roses? I wasn't sure. That nerve gas scare and all. You liked them?"

Oddly, his tacit confirmation threw her. Had she down deep doubted that they had been from him? And at the same time believed he'd sent them simply because she'd wanted to believe? "Ah...Yes. I loved that luscious soft apricot...."

"A great color on you."

"I appreciate the note of...congratulations."

"I've been thinking about you, Claire. I'd jump through all sorts of hoops for a chance—in person—to explain that little mix-up at my cabin."

She laughed. "Our afternoon did end rather badly."

"When can I see you?" His voice softened. "I...I'd love to see you."

Yes, she did want to see him. Despite everything. She stood and started pacing. "The Louisiana primary is in four days..." Her mind raced. The campaign was supposed to slow a bit after Super Tuesday, but Pryce had just changed all that. She could, however, fly down to New Orleans early Sunday morning instead of Saturday night. "Thinking out loud here. I'm coming to Manhattan on Saturday for staff meetings in the morning and then I'll go home."

"I'll make myself available any time that day."

They agreed that he'd come to The Retreat at 4:00 in the afternoon Saturday, and she'd show him around and make dinner. She hung up, smiling, just as Joss walked in.

"There is standing room only this evening," Joss said, "Was that Pryce?"

Claire shook her head, a little breathless and light-headed. "You remember the man who tried to help me save Maman?"

"Of course." Joss's shoulders drooped. "Big hunk. Kodaly the lawyer?"

"I'm going to have him for dinner on Saturday."

Joss frowned. "Why? That's in two days!"

"I like him. And he seems to like me. So please reschedule the D.C. flight."

Still frowning, Joss thrust the covered coffee cup to her. "You don't have time for extra-curricular activities."

. . . . .

Another heavy snowfall had delayed air traffic. Claire's jet landed two hours behind schedule. Early that morning Savik had called to say he'd bring her a surprise, and that she should be prepared to dress warmly for the outdoors. She'd settled on black jeans, a cranberry cashmere turtleneck and black boots. She took her parka from the front closet and laid it out.

She could hardly wait to see and hear him and allowed the rush of images of what it could be like if they merged their lives. Presidential candidates could still crave intimacy. She glanced at the ticking grandfather clock against the entryway wall. Four minutes after four.

"Love you," Alex called from his cage in the living room, followed by a screech.

She strolled to him, handed him a peanut and sighed. "I'm tired of loneliness."

Clutching it with his claw, he quickly ripped away the hull with his razor sharp bill.

"So, I'm going to give him one more chance, Alex. Am I crazy?"

"AAWWWRRK!"

"Right."

A tinkling sound intruded. Bells. She cocked her head, listening. Yes. Definitely bells, and the sound came from outside. She stepped into the enclosed porch. Humvee was staring as a black horse bedecked with bells trotted toward them on the snow-covered riding trail beside the drive, pulling a sleigh.

Claire's breath curled up in a little white cloud as she exhaled in surprise. The sleigh's black-coated driver wore a red top hat and a green scarf wrapped around his neck, just like a picture on a Christmas card, and Savik sat in the passenger seat wearing his fawn-colored sheepskin jacket. His face was tanned, even now in the middle of winter, probably from skiing.

Claire grinned, feeling like a child. A sleigh! Savik had always surprised her. Being able to catch her off-guard was one of the ways he'd been very different from David. David was solid, reliable, and always on her wavelength. Savik was surprising, exciting, a fascinating opposite. The cold bit into her skin. She stepped back inside the door, grabbed the parka, slipped into it, and hurried to join Savik.

No Matter Who Gets Hurt

Savik stepped down from the sleigh. Claire looked radiant; his surprise pleased her. It would be easy to forget, to just enjoy. He'd have to keep reminding himself that he was here to find out what she needed in the way of help and then show her—convince her—that he could fill that need.

"This is perfect and amazing," she said, stepping through a gap in the snow bank.

He helped her climb aboard. "I tried to think what might do you the most good right now."

He covered her with a red woolen blanket and slid closer to share the warmth and a hint of pleasure under the covers. He wanted to kiss her, despite her guard's discreet presence in an SUV behind them, and then pangs of guilt stopped him. He intended to sabotage Claire and the thing she probably wanted most in the world. This fine strategy of his was going to be a lot tougher than he'd imagined. Maybe he couldn't do it.

"Tapia Park," he said to the driver.

To the jingling of bells, they glided down the snow-covered road over a quarter of a mile to the state park where the late afternoon sun sparkled on fresh, smooth whiteness. They stopped on the bridge that crossed Tapia Lake to take in the forest of stately old firs and white pine among the barren gray branches of hardwood trees.

He loved the way she breathed in the outdoors and pointed out small things like the old woman in a red coat chucking bread to a flock of Canada Geese that no longer fled their upstate New York home in the winter. At a hill, someone had left a hubcap-like bowl sled. She jumped out of the sleigh and insisted they slide down tandem on their keesters. This led to a snowball fight at the bottom of the hill. She got him a good one on the forehead.

On their return trip, and over the bodyguard's objection to being left to get home without them, they took an of-road back way through a wildlife preserve. Their sleigh driver unlatched a wire gate, and they entered her property, stopping at her animal rescue center. He and Claire climbed out of the sleigh. Her guard showed up in the SUV. In the office a burly African-American Claire introduced as Desmond Pruett, or Desi, was splinting the broken wing of a Red-tailed Hawk.

Pruett pointed to a local paper on his desk. "I saved this for you, Claire. You should take Mr. Kodaly to see Braveheart. He's a famous fox, now. There's an article about the rescue center, and they used that photo of you and him. Caption says he's your favorite patient."

Savik held her arm and they trudged to an enclosure along the narrow, ice-edged creek.

She explained about how the fox got his name and added, "He's still too lame to be released."

Savik understood the love in Claire's voice for the fox, beautiful in a thick winter coat. He said, "I once felt a similarly strong affection for a wolf that visited our campsite in Alaska."

Claire looked at him thoughtfully, and he went a little soft inside. Hell. If he let himself go, they could really connect on so many levels. At the house she formally introduced him to another bodyguard, a massive Samoan named Humvee who was taking over, and then they hurried inside. She invited the guard in also. The Samoan declined. "Another cuppa hot coffee would be great when you get a chance."

Savik hung his jacket up on the enclosed porch and entered the living room. The famous Alex was perched, preening, in a brass cage a man could almost fit into. Alex gave them both a sharp-eyed look. "You bandido!"

"I hope not," Savik replied, and laughed, though the bird had come damn close to the truth. As Claire lowered a long covering over the cage she said, "Good night, Alex."

"Night!" the bird said, and Savik chuckled.

Claire led him into the kitchen. A plump Asian woman Claire introduced as Florence said, "I'm going to take coffee to Humvee and leave. Anything else you need before I go, Ms. Claire?"

"No. We're fine. You have a nice evening." The woman left. Claire pulled a sheet of chicken breasts partway out of the oven, filling the room with the smell of garlic and ginger. She ladled a sauce over the chicken. He wanted to put his arms around her. He'd say, "Alone at last," But it was too soon.

Claire poured him a glass of a sparkling wine. He took a seat on a bar stool at a counter. She sat a pretty little plate of prosciutto-wrapped shrimp in front of him. "I have to put the salad together. Would you like to take a look around the house?"

Eager to do exactly that, he downed a shrimp and then wandered, glass in hand, into the living room and then into a lighted room that was evidently her office. The walls were covered with pictures—handsome son at many ages, men, women and kids everywhere in the world, all looking ecstatic to be with The Claire. At her desk he scanned the stacks of papers.

Something banged in the kitchen. Quickly, he riffled through the top items on each pile and found an advance copy of her schedule. That could be useful. He used his cell phone camera to photograph it.

Other piles dealt with her EClaire business and AFWW. Nothing unusual. Shelves on one wall were jammed with books. Filing cabinets fit beneath a wide counter. More stacks of paper. He scanned quickly and the word "*Adhan*" caught his eye.

"*Adhan* and Human Rights Violations," with her handwritten, *OK, C. A.* in the upper corner. Six pages, probably a speech. He hadn't paid much attention to her ideas before Super Tuesday, but had started research since. She hadn't released any comment yet on this *Adhan* call-to-prayer thing—an increasingly divisive mess. Ronnie's tricksters might find dynamite here.

"Are you okay?" Claire called out.

The hair at the back of his neck stood. He moved quickly out into the living room and then called back, "Fine." He'd have to find another opportunity to copy the speech. Again in the kitchen, he stood opposite the central cutting block, watching her arrange lettuce in a fancy pattern. She turned a shining copper mold upside down and out popped a tomato red aspic.

"You've gone to a lot of trouble," he said.

She smiled and captured his gaze with those deep brown-amber eyes of hers, eyes he loved looking into. "It gives me great pleasure to cook for good friends."

"Are we to be just good friends?"

"You have many good friends, Savik. As I learned on our last afternoon together?"

"I was breaking it off with Adrienne before I invited you to the cabin. Her showing up was a total surprise. A damned unpleasant one because it upset you."

Claire handed him the two salad plates. "Why don't you put these on the table? The chicken and artichoke pasta are already there. I'll bring the asparagus."

He laughed. "I'd never deserve you, Claire. I'm a simple meat and potatoes man."

She smiled, as if to say, that's what you may think—at first. She waved him toward the dining room where a chilled bottle of *Santa Margherita* pinot grigio was beaded with condensation. How the heck was he going to get back into the den to photograph the speech?

She poured. "Our sleigh ride was so perfect. I get so tired of politics. Let's talk about your work. Or one of your adventures."

Uh-oh. He needed to know details in order to insinuate himself into her campaign. "Your life right now is far more interesting. I know you're big on women in your employ and in government." He tried to sound casual. "What about on your campaign staff?" A bite of the chicken melted on his tongue. "Damn good. What is this?"

"I call it Chinese-Italian Philandering." She smiled flirtatiously. "Some bruschetta spread, herb paste, garlic, onions, ginger and soy sauce. It's all in the balance—just as with my staff."

"They're philanderers?" He asked with mock innocence.

"My, my, where *is* your mind, Savik? I was referring to balance in life and governing, of course. I'd say my staff is about fifty-fifty women to men."

"Why?" Savik's tone had a sharp edge. He softened. "I mean, why not simply the best person for the job?"

She smiled. "I'm asked this all the time. I usually say that when women make up at least half my work force, their innate prospicience kicks in—with big pay-offs."

"Prospicience….Looking to the future?"

"Right. And planning for it."

"Men can plan ahead." He still sounded more defensive than he intended. *Be cool!* "It's a fact that men are the best chess players."

"That's spatial and immediate. Handy, but men tend to focus on the task of the moment, on winning the immediate goal…." She gave him a sideways look. "…but they may not be so good at anticipating the full outcome of something that will occur, say, nine months later."

No comeback for that one. He grinned and took a bite of pasta. Damn, he enjoyed their banter. He genuinely liked Claire. And he didn't like duplicity, but she still had to be stopped. It was cut-to-chase time. "If I wanted to help you, what good would I be?"

Her eyes widened. "You want to help me?"

He started to put his hand on hers, but instead clenched his fist back. She hadn't cuddled with him in the sleigh, or made her hand available for holding. She'd included him in with the "friends" she loved to cook for. Touching her could be a strategic mistake "Yes, Claire. I do."

"Well, then…" Her tone lightened. "I count on men to offer a fighting spirit and dogged determination to win. Sometimes, regrettably, it's at any cost, no matter who gets hurt. I'd guess that you have that same trench-warfare determination. I often need that sort of grit. I'm not exactly sure what you'd do, but I'd bet my life you're a fighter."

He smiled. "No matter who gets hurt?"

"To win any cause involving great power a leader has to know going in that someone is going to get hurt. Maybe even get killed. Maybe even the leader himself. Or herself. But they have to be willing to enter the struggle anyway."

He raised the wine glass. "Then I am in this struggle for the Presidency." He paused and then added, looking directly into her eyes, "And I am willing to do whatever is necessary, no matter who gets hurt."

She raised her glass in response. "There are limits, of course."

They stared at each other and drank, and he felt better. At least in some small way, he'd warned her. Claire's was a loving heart, but it made her an unrealistic idealist, and she had to be blocked, even if it hurt her…or him.

· · · · ·

After dinner Claire hummed as she put water into the kettle, then took a plate of food to Humvee. Savik was clearing the dining table. When she returned, she said, "I only need a couple of minutes here. You want to put another log on the fire?"

Savik left the kitchen. She was wine-mellow as she stood spooning layers of a light chocolate mousse, cherries soaked in *amaretto*, and a dollop of whipped cream into a single parfait glass, all the while wanting Savik to come up behind her, wrap his arms around her and kiss the back of her neck. But he didn't return.

A few minutes later she carried a tray of coffee and the parfait to the living room to find Savik only beginning to lay a fresh log on the fire. "Had to use your powder room," he said.

Odd that he felt he needed to explain.

They ate the parfait in warm silence. He had been so reasonable during dinner. It had been easy to forget his wild reputation with women and his right-wing politics. She'd loved the conversation with such an intelligent, exciting, and extremely attentive man. He'd really listened and actually wanted to help her.

How many times had she imagined intimacy like this and then told herself, NO WAY! Won't happen. Recently, she'd had a dream of trying to close a door to keep a fire from entering her room, only to have the fire keep blasting the door open. When she woke wanting to scream, she knew the fire was the attraction to Savik that seemed just as powerful as when they were young. She was a mature woman, however, and well beyond impetuousness. She could manage her actions just fine. She did not act on dreams. She would not make the same mistakes with Savik again.

Parfait finished, she threw a couple of large pillows onto the wool rug before the fire. Savik lounged back against the pillow beside hers, studying the flames. The urge to touch his hair was so strong that she held her breath a moment, as some instinct held her back.

He turned and caught her staring at him. He grinned. "I've been thinking about how I could help you."

Thank God. She could breathe again. Safe ground.

"Has your campaign retained counsel yet?" he asked.

"So far I've used people from EClaire."

"I'd be happy to serve as a legal coordinator. Advisor. Whatever."

"Wow." She had a queasy sense of things being too good to be true. "They're working on policy papers now, checking for loopholes, overlaps and inconsistencies."

"I'd be especially good at accommodating international laws, but I could work with federal laws as well. And of course any number of things having to do with the economy."

"But why?" She sipped her coffee. "You don't agree with me politically."

Savik poked the fire as he said, "Well, I think you are truly phenomenal. I want to…understand you better. Maybe it's time the country considered some…changes."

She could not suppress a smile of wonder. He looked intense and sincere. This was exactly the kind of support she craved. With Savik at her side, fiercely determined, competent, caring, companionable…loving as he seemed right now—this campaign would be so much easier to endure. He'd be a balancing influence that would be so good for her.

She scooted off her pillow so she now sat closer, shoulder to shoulder, thigh to thigh. She wanted to kiss him. He didn't move away, but he also made no move to touch her. Something wasn't quite right. This was too sudden….wasn't it?

"Claire? I don't mean to be pushy, I just—"

"No, I'm thrilled. I was just… I mean, you must have…ideological reservations."

"Well, yes. I know men. We can be cruel when we have to—sometimes even when we don't. And I know war. Given the nature of *men*, is ending war a realistic possibility? I've seen men die. I've seen women and kids die. But wanting an end to war doesn't make it actually possible."

"I'm horrified at the thought of John having to go kill people. What would that do to his spirit? His soul? What if he were killed?"

She detailed a few ideas about empowering women in a movement that might achieve global stability and he listened. Really seemed to listen. It was critical that he understood what was motivating her. Power? Glory? Praise? He surely didn't think revenge, but you never knew.

"I know plenty of seriously aggressive women, so I'm not sure you're right about them, but I do know men, and I still say we're stuck with war. But that doesn't mean we shouldn't still try everything in our power to make sure there are fewer of them. That's why I want to work on your campaign."

"That's wonderful, Savik." A tide of emotion welled up, a rush of hope that it just might work. Without thinking, she laid her hand on his leg. "Thank you."

The shock of touching him set her pulse pounding. She drew her hand back. Savik took hold of it, held it in both of his. For a long moment, neither of them moved, neither spoke. She tugged, intending to free her hand. Instead he twisted to face her, bent forward and kissed her. A soft kiss, but intense and lingering.

She didn't pull away. He shifted so that he loomed over her. He eased her down flat onto the rug. The kiss that followed explored her lips at first, and then inside her mouth. She let him in, kissed him back fiercely. She felt his hand move over her breast and felt fire in that place low in her body that for years had felt no such heat. She hugged him close, felt the well-toned muscles of his back. Warmth from his palm seeped through the cashmere sweater.

He kissed her forehead. "You're so damn beautiful."

Warm breath on her cheeks. He smelled of a wood-scented aftershave, smoke, the outdoors and his own musk. She stroked his hair, fingers finding his scalp, and her kiss fired an urge to meld her whole body with Savik's. His moves grew more purposeful, lifting her, sliding his hand under her sweater, slowly raising it, hands and mouth on her bare skin.

The sound of her own moaning broke the spell. Too much. Too fast.

Breathing hard she said, "We need to stop." Her words didn't sound convincing, even to her own ears.

He kissed her again, but his hand slid down and rested on her belly. She knew his next move and blocked it, her hand over her zipper. "We have to stop," she said again.

"I don't want to stop."

"I know. I really don't want to either, but we should."

He kissed her again, a kiss as determined as the kisses before had been.

"Savik."

He drew in a deep breath, then traced the line of her chin with one finger. "Are you sure?"

She felt like crying. "Yes. We have to."

"If I call you again tomorrow, will you answer the phone?"

She smiled. "Yes. I want to see you again. As soon as we can make our schedules mesh."

He leaned back, smiling. "I'm counting on it. Especially the meshing part."

. . . . .

At ten o'clock, Savik gave the Uber driver his cabin's address, a twenty-five minute drive. He settled back. They drove out of the gate to The Retreat, and he palmed his cell phone. First he emailed the photos to Jack, then he dialed Ronnie."

"Hughes here," came the quick, brusque answer.

"I just sent your guy an itinerary and a speech by the lady in question." That's what they were calling Claire. "Possibly something hot. On the Muslim call to prayer. She's going to support a Muslim kid who was arrested and taken only God and the FBI knows where."

"She would do something stupid like that. Does she seem receptive to incorporating you into the team?"

"Yeah."

"Excellent."

Ronnie hung up on Savik. No sympathy for doing the cruel and nasty work of betraying a perfectly…wonderful woman. Winn's father could be a real bastard. But he did care about his country.

Savik closed his eyes, letting his mind review the feel of Claire's lips and body, the sound of that moan that had clearly said she wanted him. Hell.

He felt . . . like a total shit. He'd wanted her before this whole mess, before her unworkable ideas seduced this country out of 723 party primary delegates.

Honey, you're terrific, but we're a total mismatch.

We Have A Leak!

Another death threat was received, this one very knowledgeable about the EClaire private Gulfstream Jet. Extra security checks at the Louisville hangar found nothing but now Claire was two hours behind schedule. The team remained determined to make the flight. Last night Rachel had flown into Louisville to join her, freed up by some university holiday. As the engines warmed, Humvee lifted Rachel from her wheelchair as though she were a feather pillow and set her in one of the tan leather chairs in the main cabin.

Pryce and Jake stopped behind Joss who was stowing her purse. "Let's go, go, go. Hurry. Make some phone calls, will ya?" Pryce prodded Joss. "Tell the co-coordinator—"

"Duh!" Joss glared at him and then flopped into her seat and checked her watch. To Claire she said, "You're supposed to be speaking in five minutes. This really sucks. I can't make calls 'til the captain okays it. Might as well roast and salt me. I'm quietly going nuts."

Pryce and Jake joined a dozen aides in the rear cabin for some private plotting.

"So we're headed to Richmond for a luncheon with…who is it again?" Rachel asked.

"The Coalition of NGOs for International Human Rights," Claire said. I'm speaking on the U.N. initiative R2P."

Which is…?"

"Sorry. It stands for Responsibility to Protect. It's an anti-atrocity measure intended to hold governments responsible for gross human rights abuses within their borders. If they fail to prevent atrocities, the U.N. member nations can and are required to intercede. I'll mention our own human rights issues, including the *adhan* controversy."

"Changing subjects a bit, love," Rachel said, "I'd love to be a fly on the wall at the RNC. They must be hemorrhaging. How'd you win in states like Illinois and Pennsylvania?"

"Jake's savvy campaign committees. We used targeted video conferences and—"

Joss interrupted. "We're all learning the iffy-ness of primary election arithmetic. Claire could lose a big chunk of elected delegates, but we're in deep trouble if we can't get more of the Super Delegates on board."

Snacks were served, including two bear claws for Joss. They lifted off with a jack-rabbit jump into turbulent, blustery late February skies. When the seatbelt sign turned off Joss punched numbers on her cell phone and disappeared into it.

Rachel said, "The time is right for your metanoia. You'll get the nomination."

"The Party keeps a tight lock on things. I can only trust Jake's brilliance to either win enough elected delegates outright or win over enough Super Delegates."

Joss was now pacing in the aisle. "I'm on hold," she huffed.

To Rachel Claire said, "I'm working on countering this notion that I'm a pacifist." She handed Rachel her speech notes. "See what you think of this addition."

"A good idea. This very morning I heard a TV talking head claim you're too kind, too much of a pacifist to guard the security of the most powerful country in a very dangerous world."

"What a load of shit!" Joss said, then, "Oh, no!" She began apologizing into the cell phone.

Rachel added, "Even Gandhi believed in defending the defenseless with a weapon, right?"

"True," Claire said. "He just said not to plan your security based on force. On cooperation, not force."

"Sweetie…" Rachel looked puzzled. "In Bangladesh you hired armed guards!"

"The government wouldn't have let me come without them. And I used a weapon to save Aminah's life. But I didn't come armed."

Rachel frowned. "I don't know, love.

When Rachel finished reading the speech she said, "This is good stuff, hon."

At the sound of pounding feet Claire twisted around in her seat. Pryce, his face red, lips drawn thin, stomped toward her and stopped, Jake behind him. Pryce glowered at her. "God damn it, we've got a leak or someone has a big mouth."

She took his hand. "Calm down, Pryce."

He pulled away. "We have a traitor! You have not yet delivered the speech about the Muslim kid the President hauled off to some outsourced torture chamber, and CNN is reporting that you said in a speech you believe they have arrested the wrong guy. If we were on time, you would have given the speech. But we're late. You haven't. So someone leaked it."

Pryce glared at Joss, then Rachel. Jake looked almost as mad as Pryce. He stood, his head bent, one hand holding his forehead as though he had a bad headache.

"What's he talking about?" Rachel asked.

"It's the *adhan* controversy," Claire said, still staring at Pryce. "A few weeks ago a young man was arrested, suspected of having info on the Tears of Allah. They used the Patriot Act for justification." Claire looked at Jake. "Safa Mufti knows his family and knows the boy personally. He did attend an *adhan* rally, but Safa assured me this is a case of mistaken identity. My view will prove legit. It's the administration that will have egg on its face." She frowned. "But the leak *is* a concern."

Jake checked his watch. "Concern?" He then stared hard at Claire. "How did someone, anyone, outside our inner circle know that was your position, and that you would be expressing it in this speech in Richmond…? Actually what should have been forty-five minutes ago."

Joss said, "There is absolutely no way Connie blabbered."

Claire explained to Rachel. "Connie is my best speech writer." She turned back to Pryce. "Loyal for fifteen years."

"Okay, then who? Florence? Des? Humvee?"

"Be serious!' She thought a second. "There is our new guy on the night shift. And I did clear the speech with Adam. Maybe someone in his office or a janitor at headquarters…."

"How about Savik Kodaly?" Pryce crossed his arms. "You've brought him onto the legal team. I gather you've been talking to him pretty often. Could he have had access to the speech?"

For a microsecond, Claire's camera of the mind saw Savik at her fireplace and saying, "I had to use your powder room." She snapped the lens closed on what was a preposterous thought. "That's ridiculous."

Jake said, "I gotta go with Pryce, Claire. Maybe this leak, this slip-up, about the Muslim boy isn't a big deal. Probably isn't. But I hafta tell ya, my gut twitched. Warning system went off. You've got the patriarchy running scared as hell. They want to stop you, any way they can. We gotta have a watertight ship, Claire."

Pryce jammed his hands into his pocket. "They're already spinning this. 'Claire isn't responsible enough with her facts to govern.' And the goddamn speech isn't even out of your mouth."

"Well, folks," Jake finally said, "this means we have to watch what we say and to whom. But paranoia is poison, so let's keep our cool."

. . . . .

Alex watched Claire from the top of the refrigerator as she finished the salad. The Virginia primary was a heartbreaking all-or-nothing loss, alongside the big loss in Ohio. Claire really needed this one-day breather at The Retreat. In the upcoming primaries, Crane would probably pull ahead. Seeing Savik would re-energize her like nothing else.

With her Bluetooth clipped over her ear, she spoke to Savik while shaping a meatloaf pie. "You said you are a meat and potatoes guy, right? Now that I have a chance to cook for you again, I want to show you what I can do with he-man essentials."

"I'll like anything you cook. Sorry I'm late. I'll be at your door in ten minutes."

"Humvee will let you in."

When she heard the front door open, Alex snatched up a green onion in the middle of its stalk and took to the air, heading for the newcomer. Savik walked in, carrying his onion gift. "Such a prize," he said. He also carried her book, Jeffrey Sachs's *The End of Poverty*, in his other hand. He set the onion and the book on the counter, glided up behind her, and slid his arms around her waist. "An interesting read, but I think Sachs suffers from too much idealism. We'll talk later about this, though. Right now…" He moved her hair aside and kissed her cheek. "All I can think of is you."

She wrapped her arms over his. Being intimate this way felt as natural and familiar as a favorite song. "You know, I appreciate the legal advice, Savik, but I *love* our phone talks."

"I wish we could meet more often."

She turned in his arms and kissed him. Her intention was a sweet kiss. Savik turned it into one of passion, lingering, pulling her tightly against his body. When she could finally catch her breath, she said, "We have an entire night ahead of us."

A loud thump came from the front porch followed by Humvee bellowing, "There's a fire!" He charged into the kitchen. "I just called 9-1-1. It's the Rescue Center."

"Oh my God," Claire said. "Desi!"

Following Humvee, Savik behind her, she ran onto the porch and into the yard. She splashed through yesterday rain puddles toward the

Rescue Center. In four places, flames slashed upward like angry torches in the mid-April twilight.

"What about Desi?" Savik called out.

"He lives at the center," she answered.

Humvee yelled, "Stay behind me, Claire! Way back!"

Everyone Would Understand

She wasn't about to slow up. With Humvee and Savik, Claire streaked past Braveheart's enclosure. The burning barn was still fifty yards away and three separate fires were merging into one. She suddenly couldn't remember if she'd closed the door to the house. She grabbed Savik's arm. "Please, go back. Make sure the door to the porch is closed. Alex could get out."

Humvee looked back and yelled to Savik. "This could be a diversion. Stay with the house and make sure no one gets in."

Savik turned immediately.

Claire could not believe how fast the inferno was growing. Her heart pounding, she now felt heat on her face. A lick of red tongue flashed out of Desi's window.

"Desi!" she screamed. She pushed herself harder. The heat became a wall. "Desi!" she screamed again as she felt Humvee's arms clamp around her, pulling her backward.

"You can't go in there, Ms. Claire."

"Good God help us!"

Still gripping her with one arm, Humvee spoke into a cell phone. "This is charlie foxtrot delta-one requesting additional security. ASAP! ASAP! Possible attack. Claire Alden."

Soon in the distance fire engines and maybe police cars and ERVs wailed. With Humvee's arm still wrapped around her, Claire listened as the sirens grew louder. The flames roared and snapped. White-hot cinders and red sparks shot upward into dark sky.

Savik ran up beside them. "House is secure. Alex inside. I locked up."

A horrifying image in her mind of Desi fighting flames caused her knees to buckle. She sagged against Humvee and then a running movement to her right caused them both to turn. Desi came loping out from behind the southern side of the burning barn.

"Oh, Desi!" She tore herself away from Humvee and hugged Desi. "I was so afraid."

He held her shoulders. "The fuckers called me." His lips were white against his dark skin, the lines on his face hard. He let go of her. "They actually gave me five minutes to clear out."

"Called you?"

"Had my cell phone number."

With Desi safe, her thoughts grew clearer. The fire was no accident.
"Damn!" Humvee said. "I'd hoped I was just being paranoid."
"The animals?"
"Got most of them out," Desi explained. "Into the rear yard."
Their sirens blaring, two bright yellow fire engines with spinning red
lights on top roared up her road and stopped in front of the three foot-
high wooden fence that ran around the rescue center. She ran to the first
truck. The driver leaned out to her. "We need to get closer. Have to run
down your fence, okay?"
"Yes, yes. Of course."
The driver gunned his motor and easily drove over the fence. The second truck followed. In a flurry of activity, a dozen firemen unloaded two
hoses and hooked them to the water main at the entrance to the property. White cascades soon drenched the barn.
Savik put his arm around her as she, Savik, Humvee and Desi watched
flames devour the rescue center. Since no one needed treatment, the
ERV left. The four policemen looked bored but continued to watch the
firemen, who were about to gain the upper hand.
Desi said, "I couldn't save the coyote, but I took all the caged birds
and the two deer out. And the raccoon."
"It's okay, Desi. It's wonderful that you saved any of them. Your per-
sonal things?"
"Gone. But I didn't have much. Rather save the animals." He looked
at Claire with sorrow in his eyes. "I feel real bad that I couldn't find
Braveheart."
A twisting sense of dread settled in Claire's stomach.
Savik asked, "What exactly did the caller say?"
"It was a male voice. No particular accent. He just said, 'Your barn is
going up in flames in three minutes."
Humvee snorted. "Cops'll try to trace the call, but it won't do no good.
Those lice probably used some throw-away cell phone."
Desi said, "The fuckers think they'll scare you off, but they don't know
you like I do."
Claire felt drained. Nauseated. Desi could have been killed.
Billowy smoke clouds rose from smoldering, damp piles. Most of the
barn still stood but it was gutted. The harsh smell of ashes would linger
for days. With the three men, Claire walked around the south corner.
Part of the fence still stood. Something like a big cat hung on it next to
the gate.

Recognition hit her and an icy shiver slid along her skin as she ran toward the body of Braveheart, hanging by his neck. She stopped short, unable to bring herself to touch him. His throat had been cut and blood covered his belly. A nametag like ones worn at conventions hung around his neck with a message. Pasted from large letters cut from newspaper print, the message said, "Get out of the race or worse will happen."

Claire fell to her knees and fat, warm tears washed down her sooty cheeks. Humvee pulled a knife from a sheath under his pant leg and cut the body free. He laid the fox gently in front of Claire on its side. She touched the soft fur, blinking at Braveheart through tears. Despair crashed over her in waves. *Not Braveheart....*

Savik knelt and put his arm around her. She could not stop the flow of tears and wrapped her arms around herself, bit her lip, bowed her head.

. . . . .

They had carried the birds and raccoon to the garage. Desi tied up loose ends with the firemen, and Humvee took on the assignment of talking to the police. Savik walked her upstairs to her bedroom. More exhausted than she could ever remember feeling, Claire slumped onto her bed and called Pryce with her cellphone. Savik stood at the window frowning at the rescue center's smoldering ruins. He was clearly still deeply agitated.

She explained to Pryce, somewhat incoherently she thought, what had happened. "It's late, but please cancel tomorrow's entire schedule. Call Joss and Jake for me. I'm too tired to talk to anyone else."

"I'll cancel everything but the evening speech at the Wilmington with Adam."

"No. Cancel everything."

"Listen to me, Claire. You have to give that speech. Delaware is our only possible win for the next month. Tomorrow morning this bloody attack is going to be on the news, sea to shining sea. You cannot appear to be a woman who goes into a faint when things get tough."

"Maybe I'm not all that tough after all."

"What the...what do you mean? Just last month you weren't going to let them stop you."

"I'm tired. I'm...discouraged."

"Of course. I'll come up right away."

"No, that's not necessary. Savik is here."

"Savik? You called him instead of me?"

"No, Pryce. He was here for dinner."

For a long moment, Pryce was silent. Then, "I don't like him. I don't trust him."

She sagged still further. "Oh please, Pryce. Not tonight."

"I'm so sorry about the rescue center, Claire. But the speech tomorrow is vital."

She wanted to tell him to drop dead. "All right."

"Fine. I'll call Jake and Joss and start working on the media angles right now."

They ended the call and she looked at Savik. "This country could lead the entire globe in such a wonderful, positive direction. Instead we have people who are willing to kill to win at any cost. What happened tonight may not be the worst. They want me gone."

He took the chair next to the window. "Sadly, it's true. I'm worried for you."

"I thought if I accomplished nothing else but stopping the PeaceMaker program, this effort would be worth it. But my God, where will all this end?"

He stood, crossed the room. "You need sleep." He knelt at her feet and pulled off her boots and socks. "I have to say…." He massaged her feet. "I…I don't want you to get hurt. Politics is such a dirty game." He sat on the side of the bed next to her.

She sighed. "I've seen such terrible things, Savik. A stoning in Bangladesh. The bombing and Maman's death. The attack that nearly killed Humvee. The constant threats and hate mail. All because of my message."

An expression of deep pain came over Savik. "I've seen atrocities too." He squeezed his eyes shut. "Best not to think of these things now, though." He opened his eyes and looked hard at her, as if willing his emotions back into hiding places, and then fetched a washcloth from the bathroom. He knelt and wiped soot from her face.

"But I am thinking of them," Claire said as the warmth of the cloth soothed her. "When I was eight, my father was an attaché at the Sudanese embassy. A mob attacked it. I watched everything on TV, terrified by the angry faces and shouting, the hatred in their eyes. My parents were both inside. All I could do was watch helplessly from my grandparents' small set. I was so scared. I could only see the dust and sweat and blood, but it was as if I could smell it."

He set the washcloth aside. "How did your parents get out?"

"Basic negotiation. Afterward, my father was promoted to Ambassador. He said that underneath their fear, people are essentially good. He always helped both sides find common ground and recognize the legitimate needs of their opponent." Strangely, it eased her a bit to share this memory with him.

Savik looked agitated again. "I see how…this had a huge influence on you."

He turned away from her.

She asked, "How have the things you've seen changed you?"

"Oh…" He seemed to be considering how much to share. "During Shining Sword, we were in a Syrian town covertly right after the F117 Stealth Fighter strike. They hit an air raid shelter, thinking it was a Syrian communications center. Hundreds were dead. Over two thousand civilians killed in the overall raid. I saw a little boy beside his severed arm and…."

He pursed his lips, jaw muscles working. "God, Claire…you can't believe how good it felt later to take down some chickenshit regulars hiding among civilians, launching the grenades that drew the strike. PeaceMaker could prevent all this…"

She started to protest that solutions weren't that simple, but he turned back to look at her and put his finger to her lips. "This isn't what you need to be talking about now. I'd love to think of you as never having to deal with stuff like this, just keep doing the good work that you do. That note said if you stay in the race, they'll do something worse. What if they get to John? Your own bravery is one thing, but it's quite another to risk losing a son."

Savik continued without lingering on John, and she relaxed. "I know you didn't intend this, but you're arousing the opposite of peace in people. Everyone would understand if you opted to spare the country lots of turmoil."

She slumped back against the pillows. "Maybe this isn't the right time for a president with my message. Maybe I *am* just too divisive." Part of her felt relieved at this line of thought. She and Savik could just be normal people together. It sounded lovely.

Yet she also resented what he was saying. And every muscle in her body ached.

"Stand up." He rose and pulled her to her feet. "I'm going to put you to bed."

He took off her sweater, unzipped her pants, and after sitting her back down on the bed, pulled off her jeans. *God, he is so tender.* She wanted the world to go away and ached to have her old life back, except with Savik in it. He tucked her in, kissed her forehead, and left.

She lay staring at the ceiling, a screen for her mental projector. Images tortured her: the burning barn, the blood on Braveheart's lifeless body; and then worst of all, the image of John shot and bleeding. In the horrors of her mind, someone had gotten to him.

This was simply too awful. She threw back the covers and stomped into the bathroom.

In the piercing sharp light she stared into the mirror as rage boiled in her chest. Those vile images said more than words ever could about the nature of her opposition. Violent. Bloody. Unscrupulous. She ran cold water, splashed her face again, and dried it.

"Bastards!"

They miscalculated tonight. The only way they could force her out now was over her dead body. And even that…she gazed at her reflection. Even death might not stop the changes she stood for.

Screaming Fanatics

With a glass of cold orange juice in one hand, cell phone in the other, Claire took the incoming call in a chair by the window that looked out toward her meditation gazebo and away from the still-smoldering animal shelter.

"Well, boss," Joss said, "I guess you're awake. I left messages." She was pissed.

"I'm sorry. I'm still stressed. I haven't picked up my messages yet."

"Pryce called. Obviously you weren't so stressed you couldn't call him. And Savik."

"I am sorry if you're angry, Joss. Savik was here. I didn't have to call him."

"He's moving right in, isn't he?"

It struck Claire that Joss might be jealous. "He's good for me, Joss. He was very thoughtful."

"I'll just bet he was. Still, you could have called me. I feel like I'm the last to know."

"I asked Pryce to call you. I was just …wiped out. They killed Braveheart, you know."

Joss gasped. "Oh, man, Claire! Pryce only told me about the shelter. Now I'm the really sorry one." Joss had switched from angry into the sympathetic friend Claire had counted on for years.

Claire quickly explained about the threatening note. Contritely, Joss gave Claire the time they should meet at the airport to fly the next day to Delaware for the wind farm rally.

They hung up. How bitter Joss sounded about Savik. Pryce didn't like him either. Pryce would say it was because he didn't trust Savik, but maybe the root cause for him was also jealousy. Savik was moving into her life and to some extent, crowding them both. But things never stay the same. With time, both friends would surely adjust. They'd just have to.

. . . . .

By the time Adam Forsythe, his two aides, and his U.N. security agent joined Claire and her entourage aboard the EClaire jet, the fire and Braveheart's death were still headlines. Several firefighters had given out details, and Braveheart's story had been taken from earlier articles on the shelter. The press screamed for interviews, but Pryce stalled them.

Buckling his seat belt, Jake said, "Crane's people will spin this by saying that Claire's been attacked by yet another nut because she is so divisive."

Joss said, "Screw them? We tell people it's only made her more determined to fight!"

Adam said, "It's a no-win situation. If she shows grief, why then she's someone who caves under pressure. If she doesn't, then she's cold."

"What I want to talk about," Claire said, "is the progress on this exciting offshore wind farm, but I guess I can't avoid saying *something* about the fire."

They landed at the Civil Air Terminal of Dover Air Force Base at 4:45 and hustled into three waiting limos for the half-hour ride south to Rehoboth Beach and then into the Cape Henlopen State Park. The limos passed hundreds of parked cars and people entering the picnic grounds carrying signs for Claire saying "Claire Has The Vision" and "Metanoia" and wearing "We Need Clare-ity" T-shirts. An angry animal rights group had gathered as well. They waved homemade signs that read, "Who Killed Braveheart?" and "Braveheart's Killer Wants Your Vote!" They cheered as the limos passed.

Jake frowned. "They're *not* here to support wind power. And they're furious!"

Humvee said, "I wish we had more security."

"Many signs imply that Crane did the deed," Adam said, shaking his head.

Jake said, "I'm not so sure. Crane's people may be getting nervous enough to want her out of the race. But setting a building on fire and killing an animal?"

Joss said through tightened lips, "There are plenty of just plain nuts out there."

They entered a cordoned off parking area. Parking staff and a few ropes were all that held back the throng of supporters. Two news choppers landed, blades slowing as they disgorged news crews that ran toward the limos. Claire and the others stepped out. She and Adam both waved.

Shielded by the wind-power organizers and her own people, Claire entered the pavilion that provided seating for three hundred folks who'd paid a hundred bucks or more a plate. A band played as supporters cheered Claire and held up white spinning pinwheels into the steady breeze off the Atlantic. Several miles offshore, the real windmills looked like toothpicks.

Demonstrators poured in from the sides of the tent. They'd waded down into the ocean and were still coming up from behind Claire, chanting, "We need Clare-ity!" The press was vidly filming it all. Some demonstrators still chanted, "Who Killed Braveheart?" The closer they got to Claire, the more they shouted questions. Humvee moved close beside Claire. Adam's UN security man and the team who supervised the parking rushed in, directing people to return to the parking area, but a frenzy had set in.

The press moved closer as demonstrators scrambled to be seen waving their signs with Claire in the picture. Humvee planted himself directly in front of Claire. Adam, sitting to her left, jumped up, grabbed the nearest sign by its stick and screamed over the din at the young woman carrying it, "God dammit! Get CONTROL of yourself! You're acting like an idiot!"

Humvee grabbed Claire around the waist and half carried her as she ran with him to the security of her limo. *What a total fiasco. And what in the world was Adam thinking, swearing at people?*

That night, in the New York apartment, Claire dropped down onto the sofa beside Joss to watch the late evening news. On the jet, Adam had been upset with his profane outburst. Claire knew he had seen and experienced worse mobs. What had made him snap? The news reports thankfully showed none of Adam's anger, and the pundits hadn't yet spun the demonstration. They wouldn't have to. News clips alone portrayed Claire's supporters as screaming fanatics.

It's Been Nice, But I'm Out!

Savik handed the keys of his shiny, dark-blood-red Firebird to the parking attendant, feeling the relief a man feels when he's back in control of his life. He had thought, after the burning of her place, that Claire would cave. She didn't and this had, perversely, made him proud of her. But the primaries were over and Mason Crane held some seventeen more delegates than Claire. Crane's lead depended on the fact that all but 23 of the 714 Super Delegates were on record as committed to him, the Democratic party's long-time stalwart. There was no reason to think that they would change their minds at the convention. Mercifully, Claire's race for the nomination was fundamentally over.

Savik knew what he was going to say to Ronnie and thereby extricate himself from the insanity of the last few weeks. Afterward, he and Winn would play racquetball and Savik would bask in a sense of unfettered freedom. He entered the Cork and Bull just behind the Hugheses, father and son. As they walked to Ronnie's table, Ronnie was humming a vaguely familiar church hymn.

The menu offered fare unlikely to be a part of Claire's choices. Feeling a weird need to revert to food type, Savik chose the least Claire-like things on it: chicken-fried steak with hash browns. "And toast. No, *French* toast, coffee, and a Harvey Wallbanger." Ah, that felt good.

"Coronary on a platter," Winn said. Then to the waiter, "I'll have what he's having."

To Ronnie the waiter said, "Your usual?" Ronnie nodded. Ronnie said to Savik, "So, the Alden policy papers you've been hammering on—anything there we can use?"

To ease his conscience a little, Savik had given Claire his best work on the documents. "Aside from her unrealistic ideas on women and opposition to war, I like Alden. In fact, she's put some brilliant thought into the position papers. But she's lost the race, so the point is moot."

Ronnie leaned in. "Don't think for a minute that Crane has this contest sewn up."

"Dad," Winn said, grinning, "haven't you tuned in? The primary is over. Crane won."

Ronnie said, "It rests on Super Delegates."

Hit with a twinge of unease, Savik thought, What is wrong with him? "Every last state convention is over. There are no more votes to be had. Even the talking heads are saying Crane has the Democratic nomination."

Ronnie tilted his head back as though contemplating the coat of arms above the fireplace. "Nominating conventions can be quirky things. Ernest can beat Mason Crane in a Presidential matchup, and probably by a lot. But if Ernest is pitted against Claire Alden, the numbers grow very close. She has an enormous following."

Their drinks arrived. Savik raised his glass. "To Mason Crane's eventual defeat and the Presidency of Ernst Hass." The men clinked rims. Savik took a deep breath and then continued. "My tour of duty with Claire is over. I've done all I'm willing to do. I've already broken a date for breakfast with her." There. He eyed Ronnie directly, a look that said, *this is final.*

Ronnie grinned. "Sounds like a guilty conscience. Which only means one thing: you've fallen for Alden, the Ballbreaker. No. Queen of the ballbreakers."

Winn's jaw dropped. "Buddy! Say it isn't so!" He tilted his head to scan Savik's face. "You aren't laughing, good buddy. So it's true. Flippin' Jesus!"

Ronnie scowled at Winn. "Watch that mouth."

"Listen," Savik said, "Claire is a fine woman. I did something I hated to help defeat her. There's nothing more I can or need to do. And I want to forget this. I haven't officially ended it with her, but I'm going to." He slugged down the last of his drink.

"Good." Winn downed his also. "Now we can go back to working on the Sumatra trip."

Ronnie shook his head at Winn. "Think, boy. CET has way too much to lose if Claire Alden should win the Presidency."

The food arrived. Hearty, man food. Savik happily dug in, still baffled that Ronnie was fixated on Claire. Half into his sandwich, Ronnie said, "You've worked hard to get inside their campaign, Savik. It's imperative you stay on the inside, at least through the nominating convention, and right up to the election if she should, by some fluke, win the nomination."

Savik held a bite of his chicken fried steak mid-air on his fork, staring at Ronnie.

"Excuse me," Winn said. He rose and headed toward the restrooms.

Savik said, softly but firmly, "I told you. I've done my bit. I'm breaking it off. And she is no longer a problem."

Ronnie counterattacked. "First, "the Dem's nomination isn't in the bag until the balloons start dropping. We have to cover every contingency, even far out ones. You should know that. Second, Crane accepts PeaceMaker. He's no threat. It's Alden that is the threat. Third, we can't let Claire's faction take over the Democratic party. We can't even risk their gaining ground. That movement needs to be cut down. Fourth, this battle isn't over until it's over. We make *no* assumptions. And fifth…" He grinned. "…I outrank any commanding officer you ever had." The smile vanished. "This is a direct order."

They glared at each other. Finally Ronnie began finishing off the other half of the Reuben. Savik felt suddenly full. "I can't trust your people. They're incompetent. In the rush to smear Claire, they screwed things up for me. Jake and Pryce, all of them, knew there was a leak before she gave the speech about that Muslim kid. So everything is tight in her camp. Nothing left in piles on desks. Passwords on every computer file."

Winn was returning from the restroom. Savik leaned forward, his gaze skewering Ronnie's. "I don't want to hear of anything like Claire's property being burned or anyone close to her having an unfortunate accident and have to wonder if anything I said or did caused it."

Ronnie cocked his head. "Oh, so it's the fire and fox thing that's bothering you. You're suggesting that I'd order Hyjinx to do something like that?" Ronnie took another bite and spoke while sandwich bulged out his cheek. "Your copying her speech on the Muslim kid, that's the kind of thing we're after. I don't engage in barn burning and fox killing. That would be reprehensible. I don't operate that way, and I'm damn disappointed that you'd suggest I would."

Ronnie spoke with compelling sincerity and logic. He always did. The intended effect was to make Savik feel like he'd insulted Ronnie by even questioning him. It wasn't working.

Later, outside on the restaurant's patio, he speed-dialed Claire, hoping to leave a message to explain why he'd cancelled on their planned breakfast together and failed to call for three days. When she said hello she sounded light-hearted, but there was an edge that wasn't fully masked. "Well, the illusive Savik Kodaly is calling."

He'd hurt her with his inattention, and breaking off seeing her tonight would hurt her still more, and staying with her would make everything much worse. *Damned rock, and a damned fucking hard place.* "I'm so sorry about the election, Claire, and sorry I—"

"Don't explain, Savik. Just tell me if you're in or out. It's grim. But this thing isn't over yet. I don't give a concession speech until Mason Crane is declared the winner."

"Well, I…I'm *in*…of course. And I've missed you." He could hear what he recognized as the drone of her jet and people talking. "Where are you?"

"Approaching New York. I'm about to meet with Adam Forsythe…."

She spoke as if that weren't the end of the sentence, that the actual end of the sentence would be to confirm that she would then meet Savik afterward, as they had agreed, at his condo in Tribecca.

How should he respond? Was he "in," as Ronnie wanted, or "out" as his conscience was yelling? He said, "I have to go to court in the morning, and I need the evening to prepare…"

"So, I'm devastated over primary results that I've effectively lost the nomination and you're breaking another date? You know what, your schedule sure can't be any more hectic than mine, Savik, and I arranged mine around accommodating our evening together. And dozens of other people's schedules depend on my schedule. These last-minute cancellations can't work for me. I have to say that I'm out. It's been nice, but—"

"Whoa! Wait. Hold on. I had no idea this date would be a deal-breaker. I'll risk a poor showing in court if not seeing you tonight means I'll lose you."

A long silence.

"Savik," she said finally, "I appreciate your companionship. This chaos is, sadly, almost over. Jake tells me it's not over until the convention is over, that I have to "hang in there," but mathematically, I can't win. In a while we can see each other again, but until—"

"No! Don't say any more." Shit. "I know you need a personal life that supports you and doesn't add more hassle. I can be there for you." He forced himself to add, "And I agree with Jake. I refuse to believe your campaign is over. I've just been neglecting my own business so I've had to play catch-up, but—"

"Oh, Savik…" Her voice thickened with what he knew was the effort of holding back guilt-induced emotion. "…what am I thinking? You have been wonderful. Of course I won't keep you from your work."

In his most intimate voice he said, "Thank you for understanding. You name the next free time you have, and we'll do something special."

"I'll miss not seeing you this evening."

He agreed, then they said goodbye. He hung up with enormous relief that despite feeling with his head that he should have severed their relationship, his heart felt only happiness that he hadn't. He was happy. And Ronnie would be happy too.

A Mr. Lincoln Rose

It was Humvee and not one of the new Secret Service people who opened the door of the rented limo. Officially, since two days ago on July sixth, 120 days before the Presidential election, Humvee and Bobby were no longer her official bodyguards. Ironically, even though she'd technically lost the primary race, a detail of three men and one woman hovered constantly and would do so until the nominating convention in August made her loss official.

She had wanted to keep Humvee with her, and he'd loyally chosen to stay. He wasn't doing anything much differently, but she knew he felt demoted. Now he and one of the Secret Service men would stay with her car—presumably with the air conditioning on. New York was blazing hot and all the guards wore suits—now including Humvee.

Adam, with his own security men, waited near the southern entrance to Fort Tryon Park in upper Manhattan. He waved as she walked toward him. She waved back, resolved to keep her disappointment over the primaries to herself.

Heat had thinned the Sunday picnickers, banished joggers, and allowed only lazy strolls in the filtered shade of elms along the promenade. She wore dark glasses with her hair tucked up into her reliable wide-brimmed straw hat that had shielded her from sun of four continents.

Adam had asked for this meeting, but she dreaded having to talk about the race. Jake insisted that she still held a chance of winning the nomination on the convention floor if they could flip only eighteen Super Delegates. Only eighteen! It might as well be one hundred and eighteen. She no longer trusted his pep talk chatter.

Adam embraced her. His white Panama hat bumped her hat.

She pulled away and smiled. "Good to see you, Adam. Sorry to say, I'm…well, could we just amble along and not talk about anything serious for awhile?"

"My dear, I knew we'd both need a quiet walk in the park."

Together they meandered alongside low stone walls that defined the pathways, security details discreetly fore and aft. She focused on the Heather Garden's many heather varieties blooming in pinks and purples among lilies and roses. Finally he asked, "How's John? Do you feel up to talking about him?"

"I ran into him…" She started to say *with Savik*, but didn't want to explain her lover to Adam. "…at a restaurant a couple of weeks ago. He'd studied hard and taken the LSAT. I forced myself not to gush. John had to act for me like it was not a big deal, but his girlfriend was practically hopping with excitement."

"The stripper?"

"Exotic dancer." Claire grinned. "Actually she's quit that job. She makes him happy. He's still angry with me, though." Nearby, a family of six was chattering in Spanish. "English-speakers seem to be in the minority here. Maybe that's why no one's recognized us yet?"

"Possibly. That couple holding hands by the pond is flirting in Russian." He smiled in his overly attentive way.

The trail skirted steep chasms up the rocky palisade that overlooked the Hudson River. At a lookout point with a stone gazebo the wide panorama opened up. A fresh breeze wafted up from the river. She and Adam sat on a bench to let the breeze cool them. She turned to him. "I'm so sorry the numbers aren't looking better. I fear I've failed so many. I am grateful, so deeply grateful for your part, Adam."

"I promise you that Hass's people are plenty worried about the polls showing he can't beat Mason Crane while you might. All it takes is for Crane to make one more unpopular statement or some other unpredictable gaff between now and the nominating convention and eighteen delegates you are trailing by could have a change of heart."

"Adam, you know as well as I that Super Delegates are all party insiders. They owe Crane. He's been their man for years. I don't see, realistically, how any would change now in my favor."

"Jake is a pit bull and he insists it's doable."

"So he keeps telling me."

"Let's head on up to the Cloisters," Adam said.

They were heading into the more crowded section. Rocky trails gave way to walkways, lawns and gardens. The afternoon shadows lengthened. The Cloisters rose above the trees, the late day sun shining on a wall of the tower like a beacon. The medieval architecture gave Claire the momentary feeling she'd dropped into fifteenth century Europe.

"Claire! Eet ees Claire!" a female voice was shouting.

Immediately, the Secret Service trio zoomed in close, spreading their arms to create a human shield against the cluster of people that materialized around her.

A woman in a "Claire-ity" T-shirt said, "I'm writing your name on my ballot if I have to!"

"We love you, Claire!" a young woman carrying a baby said.

Adam linked his arm through hers. "They love you, Claire."

She spoke with that group and then another, all the while being slowly guided, Claire knew not toward what end. They'd reached a kiosk selling cut flowers at the juncture of the walkway and a park road that led to a charming stone building, the New Leaf Restaurant. Adam disappeared for a few moments but quickly returned, one arm behind his back. He nodded at the building.

"Can I interest you in an early dinner?"

She smiled. "I'd love to share dinner with you."

"Excellent." Adam's eyes twinkled, and he brought out a red rose he'd been holding behind his back. "It's one they grow here and most apropos. A *Mr. Lincoln.*"

A rose with a meaning. And that expression on Adam's face…Was it possible she'd been wrong? "Have you been sending me roses, Adam?"

"I regret to say nothing since the bouquet at your talk." He was sweating again. "The lady at the booth over there said, 'a *Mr. Lincoln* is perfect for Claire. She will be a president just as famous.'"

Claire waved at the woman, who was beaming. This was all quite innocent. Claire's suspicions were way off. Of course Adam hadn't sent the roses. Silly to think he would do anything so secretive. There was a tragically romantic streak in his soul, however.

"The lady's right," Adam said. "You will be President."

They entered the restaurant, walked through its quaint interior and chose a table under an umbrella on the terrace. "I didn't really think you'd be free for dinner," Adam said. "My sources tell me you're seeing someone."

Claire smiled. "Sources. That innocuous word. Yes, I am. Savik Kodaly. We are keeping it very discreet, or at least I thought so."

Adam frowned.

Was he angry? Hoping she'd deny attraction to Savik? "Adam?"

He reached into the pocket of his slacks, pulled out a bottle, and took a pill. "Prescription painkillers," he said. "I'm sorry, Claire, I must call my driver to fetch me. A migraine is setting in." He rubbed his head, wincing. "I don't have them very often. Nothing to worry about, but they are rather severe unless I lie down in the dark right away. I'm sorry."

"No need to apologize. Our chat has been a morale booster. And once again, thank you. You and Jake are right." She raised the *Mr. Lincoln* rose. "I'm not giving up."

She watched him leave. A waiter arrived. She apologized, rose, and walked with the Secret Service agent toward the waiting SUV wondering, *would he have stayed and let the pill take effect if I had denied caring for Savik?*

The *Adhan* Riot

In the early evening of August first, Claire joined her extended staff in front of the television at the New York campaign headquarters to watch fires started the night before burning out of control in four suburbs and a central section of Detroit. Riots, Claire thought. Like Paris in 2005 and Chicago last year.

"Do they know yet what started it?" she asked.

"No," Pryce said. "At this point it's all rumor and panic."

President Hass, who was vacationing in Florida, had ordered in the National Guard. "I have instituted Martial Law in Detroit and ordered a nation-wide red alert," he was saying now, "and I advise people in cities with large Muslim communities to remain in their homes if possible. We will not tolerate acts of violence."

Muslims, apparently affiliated with TOA, the Tears of Allah movement, were being gunned down by vigilantes in the streets of Detroit suburbs. So far, eight bodies had been removed from a secured area. Some TV channels were showing politicians praising the decision and commending the President for his quick action.

Mason Crane, the likely Presidential candidate for the Democrats, said the actual guard numbers were inadequate due to Guard mismanagement. So far no one from any media, major or minor, had bothered to contact her for her opinion on the riot and Hass's handling of it. Given that it appeared that Crane had the Democratic nomination sewed up, the media had decided she was irrelevant.

On TV, a young man with a Polish surname could barely speak because of his rage, but he told how his brother had been killed the previous night by a TOA bomb when he got into his car. Claire, experiencing one of many flashbacks to Tabor Towers, understood his helpless fury. Yet the skulls on the young man's T-shirt were disconcerting.

The name of a neighborhood sounded familiar. "Isn't that where they had that protest last winter? Over public broadcasting of the call to prayer?" she asked.

"Yeah," Jake said, "I remember it."

A drone camera was following a group of people who in appearance and dress seemed to be Middle Eastern as they hurried between burning buildings. Shots were fired. Someone fell, a teenage girl. Dodging and ducking, a man returned to scoop her up. Another burst of fire and both went down. Laughter could be heard off screen. The camera's eye moved toward the sound. No one was there, but someone could be heard yelling, "Got 'im."

"Oh, my god!" Joss said.

"Jesus!" Pryce stared at the screen wide-eyed.

Jake shook his head in dismay. "What the hell's going on?"

Claire's stomach knotted tight.

A news commentator said over the live coverage that police were moving in only slowly and the National Guard would likely be unable to reach the area before midmorning tomorrow. Crude bedsheet banners hung on apartment buildings saying, "We beg you mercy!" and "Justice!" On old brick and stucco walls, fresh-looking graffiti said, "*Allah u akbar.* Allah is great," and "Death to infidels." Elsewhere, bright orange placards with white skull and crossbones proclaimed, "Death to TOA fuckers!" A burst of automatic machine gun fire marked the end of the segment.

Joss started pacing. "This is ghastly."

The scene turned to parts of Detroit where lines had formed outside gun shops. Interviewed gun-buyers all said they wanted to be ready to fight the TOA if they came into their neighborhood.

Another interview was with a high-cheekboned Slavic-looking man who knew the boy killed in the car explosion. "TOA wants ta ram their religion down our throats or slit 'em if we don't take kindly to Mohammed and his wailing cowards. They want to start blowing up cars and buses and bridges and buildings here. Well, we're not gonna take it!"

"This is a major vigilante thing," Pryce said during a station break.

"I agree," Jake said. "This could turn into a massive blood bath."

Claire said. "Maybe…a grand gesture could stop it…"

Everyone in the room turned toward her. Joss said, "She has that look in her eyes. Heaven help us."

Claire beckoned to key staff people.

Jake frowned. "What?"

Pryce looked bewildered. "What're you…?"

Claire held them at bay with a raised index finger, and then said to Connie, "Get me copies of our position papers on the *adhan* situation, TOA, and the one on riots." To Humvee, she said, "Gather as many Kevlar vests as you can find. We bought a couple hundred for the

AFWW concert, and EClaire Security has some, I think. My Secret Service team might spare a few. We're going to Detroit."

Jake said, "You aren't going to try to…"

"Yeah, she is," Joss said.

"My former boss will loan us some vests," Humvee said.

"Good, and we'll need white helmets. At least a hundred. Two hundred if possible. And fire extinguishers." To another aide, brought over from AFWW, she said, "Get together some boxes of AFWW T-shirts. White only." She pointed at one of Pryce's assistants. "Please tell my pilots to fire up the jet. And Pryce, I want a small fleet of camera people ready in Detroit. A satellite van on the ground if possible. Loudspeakers. And Joss, you contact the AFWW people throughout greater Detroit, and also in Flint, Lansing and Ann Arbor." She itemized logistics.

Pryce said, "What about the National Guard?"

"And them," Jake said, pointing to the Secret Service team.

Claire said, "We're going to do everything we can, however far that takes us."

. . . . .

Once airborne, Claire continued to follow news reports. A local Arab spokesman, Umar Awad, was interviewed. "Mr. Awad," the solemn newswoman asked, "do you have any idea what started this riot?"

"I do. A member of an ad-hoc group calling themselves TOA Bashers of America shot a muezzin during the midday call to prayer, the *adhan*."

"You're saying a sniper started this?"

"Yes. Some have claimed the man was actually trying to shoot the mosque's loudspeaker, but the muezzin moved in front of it as the man fired. The muezzin fell. Broke his back."

"The police are withholding comment. Were they brought in?"

"Of course, but they didn't move quickly to apprehend the sniper. Our people were terrified that the harassment was growing more aggressive. So last night, TOA members took revenge by bombing the car of one of the young men who had been threatening the faithful as they came to prayer. TOA Bashers retaliated by firing on worshippers at the afternoon prayer. This started a stampede and subsequent rioting. Everyone is in a state of panic."

"So you don't believe the terrorists started this riot?"

"Listen to me carefully. The Islamic community in Michigan overwhelmingly disapproves of Tears of Allah, if these are the terrorists you speak of. Terrorists *are* involved. But the TOA Bashers are terrorists as well. And we are outraged that none of the men killed by the police are the TOA Bashers. The police kill only our people. So members of the Muslim community who were originally moderate are now turning to TOA for protection. This whole incident is a nightmare of stupidity."

The television screen showed more scenes of burning buildings, a grenade explosion and gunfire. Glass shattering. People running, turning cars over. Screaming, wailing, swearing.

Claire thought of Savik and John. *I should probably tell them what I'm doing.* But she didn't want any arguments or judgments and put off calling.

Joss approached from the back of the plane. "Okay, we have two dozen women ready to start email and phone chains the minute we let them know where and when to meet. The Westin at Detroit Metro airport has had numerous cancellations so we have suites of rooms booked for tonight and the Lindbergh Ballroom for tomorrow morning at 9:00."

"Good work, Joss. Do you have any sense of how many warm bodies will show?"

"On such short notice, between 150 and 250 is about the best we can expect, I think."

"Okay. We can do a lot with that. Good. But we could use more. Keep pushing. And that ex-colonel in the Reserves who joined AFWW after her sister was killed in Iraq—doesn't she come from Michigan? Colonel Flagstad?"

"Yeah, maybe."

"Grand Rapids membership I think. We need her for ground logistics in Detroit neighborhoods. Get her down to Detroit somehow. And find somebody to work on a detailed city map of what's going on where."

Joss saluted. "On it, boss." She headed back to the rear, to the hum of busy conversations, computer noises, a printer spewing sheets, three television screens on different channels, the engines' drone.

For the remainder of the flight, Claire poured over her position papers with Jake, Pryce and Connie and worked on a speech to rally the peacekeepers in the morning and possibly touch the hearts of the nation as well. Just as they began the descent for landing, Claire said, "It's horribly clear that this riot could have been prevented."

Seat belt lights came on. Looking out the window, Jake said, "You can see the fuckin' fires. From up here it looks sorta like red coals in barbecue pits."

· · · · ·

The airport was crowded, apparently with people leaving town as quickly as possible. By the time Claire's new mini-headquarters was set up inside one conference room in the Westin Hotel, CNN reported that the body count of rioting Muslims totaled nineteen, but a police commander said, "We claim responsibility for only twelve of that number. There may be another faction involved." Muslim leaders in other cities were furious and calling for public demonstrations to protest excessive violence against Muslims.

"We have your Colonel Flagstad," Joss said. "She was a Civil Affairs Specialist who handled convoy security details."

"Perfect. She's coming?"

"A jet's already on its way to fetch her."

Claire worked straight through the night. AFWW members responding to the call began reporting in to help at about 5:30 A.M. A woman named Hannah, a well known local AFWW member, asked to see Claire privately about strategy. After the Secret Service checked Hannah, Claire met with her in a small conference room.

"My brother is a cop," Hannah said. "An unusual guy. He's made contributions to AFWW, and he works in Hamtranck. He's furious about what's happening, especially the way the National Guard aren't working with the police—who could really help out. The Guard is finally moving in and he thinks the Guardsmen are being lured, that they're working their way into an ambush, but he can't get through to the Guard chain of command to tell anyone. If Guard boys are killed..."

"...we're looking at major backlash," Claire said. "Hysteria. Rioting out of control, possibly spreading to other cities. It could seem like the ultimate *jihad* has arrived. And that alone could make it so. "And you are here because...?

"My brother thinks we can help. But you can't use his name. And he'll be wearing a helmet with a reflective visor to avoid recognition. He's ready to go in alone to try to personally reach the National Guard commander on the ground if necessary. But he thinks, so do I, people with white flags might be far more effective. I'm going to back him up no matter what. Even if it's just us two."

"If AFWW volunteers go in with you, I want to bring in our ex-Colonel who's handling field co-ordination?"

"Oh, please. Yes! My brother thinks if we have even a hundred people willing to risk arrest and the danger, we could make a difference. He thinks that instead of the bridge on the southeast perimeter where,

I gather, your marchers are planning to try to push through to the riot zone, he knows a way through an abandoned drainage tunnel with about a four-foot diameter. It can put us into position near the potential ambush area right in the middle of this. He's checking the tunnel out, making sure it's secure, right now."

"So we'd be gambling that TOA, in the heart of their stronghold, and the Bashers, and, of course, the Guard, won't attack a group made up primarily of women in white?"

"Yes, ma'am."

Once again, images of all the people killed at the Tabor Towers bomb flashed through Claire's mind. The feeling of Maman in Claire's arms. Hannah's plan was along the lines of Claire's original idea only more so. Way more so. The TOA stronghold. The heart of the beast. She could be urging people to serious injury. If AFWW women were hurt, or God forbid killed, there might be no stopping an open warfare with and among Muslim communities all over the country. But just possibly a nonviolent response now could also prevent such chaos. She took a deep breath and stiffened against fear and doubt.

Hannah said, "We have to move in before the Guard can reach that area. 9:00 A.M. will be too late. And Claire…" the young woman was gravely serious. "If you try to go in, you'd be too tempting a target. So you'd have to leave it to us."

"My Secret Service wouldn't let me go in that far anyway. I had to assure them I wasn't personally going to be anywhere near the riot area. Could you be my inside contact?"

A knock sounded at the door. Joss burst into the room. "Claire, you gotta see what's on CNN! And, AND, there's probably four or five hundred people in the ballroom awaiting your instruction, and it's not even six A.M.!"

She and Hannah hurried to the room with the televisions. The Arab world was obviously incensed over what they saw as the unjustified killing of Muslims in America. There were protests in the streets from Cairo, where it was already afternoon, to Pakistan, burning President Hass in effigy. European Muslims in London, Paris and Rome also crowded around the American embassies in protest. Claire thought of her parents. *Dad would be furious at the way this was handled, wouldn't he Maman?*

"Okay," Claire said, "we go with what we have right now before Americans wake up, turn on the news, and panic."

A Well-mediated Chat

At 8:45 A.M. East Coast time, Savik strode into the condo's kitchen fully dressed for the office, turned on the news for an update on the Detroit riot, and poured a glass of orange juice. He popped an egg pastry into the microwave, frowning at the strange images on FOX News.

The Detroit mess required a firm hand. He was as shocked and saddened as any American over the rioting. But. This catastrophe would clearly demonstrate why Claire, with her ideas of appeasement—that's all it was—shouldn't be put in charge of anything more critical than charity. Any doubts about Hass would vanish in the stampede of support for his quick and decisive deployment of the National Guard. And when Claire recovered from the letdown of losing, well…maybe she'd still want to explore what might be between the two of them.

The puzzling image on his screen was an aerial drone shot of people, mostly women carrying posters, white flags, fire extinguishers. A woman with a bullhorn repeatedly yelled "What do we want?" and the crowd roared, "Peace!" All races and ages. But overwhelmingly women. And those at the vanguard wore white helmets, and the newscaster said many of the demonstrators wore Kevlar vests under white AFWW T-shirts.

Whoa! Claire's gang. From the south, according to a voice-over, the AFWW members were marching right into the area that the National Guard was approaching from the north, and so far, all sounds of gunfire had stopped. The President's speech, he said, would be delayed.

The toaster pinged and Savik extracted the egg pastry thinking how damned lucky the women were. "You may escape with just getting your butts kicked hard," he said to the TV.

Last night Claire hadn't returned Savik's call. Why was now evident. At any moment he expected to see her face on the screen. He shucked his suit jacket, loosened his tie, tossed them both on the chair, and then rang his secretary. "I'm going to work from home for a while. Call if anything critical comes up."

By 9:30, the number of AFWW demonstrators had reached over a thousand, and it was obvious that bloodshed had been avoided. Tempers were cooling. A newscaster said, "Claire Alden's foundation, AFWW, working with community leaders, a former US Colonel Roberta

Flagstad, and a host of other volunteers, mostly women, seems to have effected a truce."

Claire's face appeared on the screen. She stood on a blocked-off bridge in front of a bank of microphones and was speaking to a large crowd. Savik poured a third cup of coffee. On the screen, sweat ran down people's faces in Detroit's humidity and overcast skies.

"This riot should not have happened," Claire said. "We all tolerate noise we don't like: boomboxes, leaf blowers, jet planes. I personally am not comfortable with the sound of the Muslim *adhan*. Certainly not at high volume. But the solution doesn't involve becoming hysterical over whether they're trying to convert America or whether it's louder than local church bells. The solution doesn't involve indulging in hate.

"It certainly does not involve shooting a gun off at the offending noise-maker resulting in his death. Violence stirs more violence. People have paid for this folly with their lives. And what is really sad is that most people on both sides do NOT want violence."

Claire's audience applauded, but as usual, Savik thought, she was missing the point.

She continued. "Fear of Islamic radicals wasn't the inciting incident. This was about applying city ordinances on decibel levels and treating all religions with an even hand. That's it. That grievance was the point where nonviolent conflict resolution would have prevented disaster. Yes, a *dialogue*. Not torture. Not high tech spying devices. Not sophisticated weapons. And not shooting guns at each other. A well-mediated chat."

The camera zoomed in on her face. She looked tired.

"We have religious freedom." She paused. The TV camera swept over the faces in a hushed crowd as Claire's voice continued in the background. "That must not change. As the world grows more interconnected, cultures are going to clash. The job of civilized governments is to minimize that clash. To find the middle way."

The camera went back to Claire, up close, and Savik thought how even when she was clearly exhausted, the camera loved her. She looked radiant, burning from the inside with passion. He felt a wave of sadness mixed with guilt.

"The courageous marchers here today have bought us time. Now, may we end in a moment of silence for the injured and those who have lost their lives."

The camera lingered again on the faces in the crowd, praying. Claire sure had lucked out. She was right about the decibel issue being something that could and should have been negotiated. But the point was, she was dealing with Americans in an American context. Naturally they wouldn't fire on a bunch of women dressed in white. But this truce was a lucky fluke and nothing more. Such theatrics could not be the foundation of foreign policy. Foreign terrorists would happily have wiped out the whole lot of AFWW.

He had to admit, though, that it made great TV. He felt a sudden gut-twist followed by a horrible thought. Just how might the electorate at large view what had just happened?

. . . . .

At 11:45 P.M. 0n August sixteenth, Savik walked from his apartment through the lobby of The Piedmont into the balmy night air, and over to the curb where a black limo pulled up at that exact moment. Savik entered quickly. The car sped off. The only other passenger was Ronald Bramfeld Hughes. He opened this strange meeting by saying, "I flew to New York just to see you, Savik."

Yesterday 'Jack the Knife' had summoned Savik to tonight's curbside appointment. "Why the meeting?" Savik asked.

"Have you somehow missed the fact that the President's poll numbers are at his all-time low? The man is being hanged in effigy all over the world, and the Muslims in this country are making a huge stink. The public won't hear until tomorrow that more of our troops are being sent in to protect embassies in four countries. And Crane's people are making hay with that thing about Hass speaking loudly but carrying a small stick." He massaged his forehead.

"The Muslim community suffered a rather high body count, Ronnie, including a nine-year-old boy. That doesn't make the National Guard or our man look good."

"The nominating convention is only two weeks away. Why in holy hell didn't you tell us what Claire was up to with the Detroit fiasco?"

"I'm not her keeper. I called her the night before, but she didn't return my call."

"Does she suspect you?"

"No."

"Is she losing interest in you?"

Savik immediately thought of how he'd almost lost her simply because of his unwillingness to get close while at the same time betraying her. "I'm keeping her interested."

"Not enough." Ronnie glared. "If we'd known about her plan for the mock heroics, we could have sabotaged her. This Detroit nonviolence theatric could cost us severely."

Savik blew his breath out. "I find that hard to believe." He'd been ignoring the news lately.

Ronnie was having none of this. "With the media blathering about how only a few Super Delegates separate Alden from a win, this is urgently a problem."

Savik could not stop himself from an equally heated reply. "The Supers are party insiders. They'll vote Crane."

Ronnie, clearly calculating carefully, lowered the heat in his voice. "We're counting on that. But the poll numbers are nightmarish close, and that gets through to people. We have to keep pressure on Claire. Just in case. No assumptions."

"It has been hell being around her people. I'm the only one not dancing around like a Hip-Hopper. They're all smug about Claire's role in stopping the riots. I have a hard time faking it."

"Maybe you've decided it would be okay if Alden's people run this country?"

Savik felt a rush of warm blood at his throat. "Don't *you* question my understanding of what's at stake. There are some things I can't do. I can't paint. I can't perform surgery. And I can't act like an idiotic liberal about the defense of the country. It's driving me crazy."

"Tough! Your country needs you, Savik."

They rode in silence, circling back to the Piedmont. When the limo stopped Ronnie said, "You could tell them you're playing the role of devil's advocate when you don't wax enthusiastic. But at night, be around her with backrubs, hell, I don't know. Just stay close to her and get us something. I'm not taking..." Ronnie made his face and voice into that of a whining child. "...'*I can't*' for an answer." His features hardened. "Get us something."

Could Anything Possibly Get Any Weirder

For two weeks Savik had given Claire nothing but "upbeat" support, telling her to hang in there. He'd even tried being friendlier with the staff, but it hadn't worked. They were polite to him but not confidential. Daily he received annoying calls from 'Jack the Knife.' Savik had nothing to report other than Claire's schedule and tidbits of speech changes.

Still faking optimism, he now sat in the enemy camp in the sitting room of a hotel suite Jake had reserved for them, across the street from the Liberty Concourse Convention Center in Philly. The suite had three TV screens: two on network stations and one tuned to CSPAN, all showing continuous live coverage. Claire was seated on a sofa, her attention focused inward. She sat quietly watching TV or following social media on her phone. She clearly didn't want to talk.

He'd endured two days of head-splitting hoopla. Bands, hats, speeches, booze. He needed to get away. He rose and said to Claire, "I'm hungry, and I need some air. I'll be back in a while."

"Okay," she said, without even looking up.

He headed for the pool area. A good place for people watching. He was eating a soul-satisfying hamburger when "Hyjinx" slumped down onto the lounge chair next to him. The thug always wore a black T-shirt with an expensive Italian cut gray suit, as if trying to look like a "made" man. Watery blue eyes looked at the world from under thick, lashless eyelids. Meaty nose and cheeks. Bulgy "prison" muscles.

The man Savik knew only as Hyjinx smiled pleasantly, but his attitude was menacing, as if he was toying with Savik. He said with a sarcastic twist in his tone, "So glad to see you again."

"Have we met?" Savik spoke loud enough anyone nearby could hear. Then in a near whisper, "Get lost!"

"We need something nowww—" The man sounded like a bobcat growling. "—dirt on Alden to spread like manure."

"Get the hell out of here!"

Hijinx grinned. "Get something!" he repeated. He stood, turned, and strode away.

. . . . .

Back in the room with team Claire, Savik mixed a second Bloody Mary and paced as the first balloting of the nominating convention began. Eventually the Florida delegate arrived at his nomination point. "...the great state of Florida therefore casts seventy-three votes for Claire Alden..." he paused for effect and then shouted out, "...and one hundred and forty one for Senator Mason Crane!" Wild Cheering from many, most especially the Florida delegation.

"So strike up the band," Joss said facetiously from the floor where she sat cross-legged. Of all Claire's aides, Savik especially disliked Joss. She was cloyingly attached to Claire.

They watched. Voting went exactly as predicted. Great, Savik thought. Things were going to be fine. Then came the state of Kansas. The head delegate was going on and on about a strong *independent* Democratic candidate. Savik frowned. Somehow that didn't sound quite like a description of Crane.

"...and so our party members voiced their concern..." the delegate from Kansas was saying, "...and we've held many impromptu caucuses owing to—"

"Hah! That means panicked back room meetings," Pryce said. "Jesus! They're going to change their vote! They're going to go for Claire."

Savik walked up behind Claire and put his hands on both her shoulders. She was tense as a saluting soldier, but she smiled up at him briefly and gripped his hand. Pryce scowled at him. Pryce was his other least favorite.

"...Kansas casts seventeen votes for Senator Mason Crane and twenty for TV maven and peace warrior Claire Alden—"

"Oh, dear god," Claire said softly.

"Two Super Delegates shifted," Jake said quickly. "We need only sixteen more."

Savik sucked in a deep breath to calm a racing pulse.

For a time, subsequent delegates voted as pledged to do. But then, to the shock and delight of those around him, two Super Delegates from Maine switched to Alden, then three from Michigan, and four from New York. The contest was unbelievably close now—2378 for Crane and 2375 for Claire.

Joss leapt to her feet and flung her hands in the air. "We are sooooo close!"

Pryce approached Claire. "We need to talk. Tawana Thompson from CNN wants to interview you and Governor Nash from Wyoming."

"When?"

"Ten minutes. Nash hates Hass's guts. I don't know why he wants it at this late moment, but I think you should do this interview."

"Pryce, Nash has actually called me a feminist bra-burner. Tell him, no!"

"And, rightly, you've ignored him. But see him. Woo him. Wyoming still hasn't voted. In life there is always a chance. Just a few votes, Claire. Say yes to Tawana."

Savik thought, could anything possibly get any weirder?

Don't Get Your Panties In A Twist

Claire wondered, could a more exquisite form of mental torture ever be devised. Waiting to know. Thinking all was lost. Then you're back in the game. More waiting. Then hopelessness again. What she wouldn't give to be able to wait out this horrible, high stakes uncertainty in her little hut in Sumatra with her adopted Minangkabau family. Those peaceful, healing days now seemed a lifetime away on another planet.

Savik sat beside her. To him she said, "How will I live with loosing? To have come this close. What will it mean to the movement, to all the people, the young ones especially, who worked so hard? And who so fervently believe I can remove a President they fear and loathe." She thought of John. "I need to try calling my son again," she said. She rose and slipped onto the balcony and called his number. Someone picked up.

Fance gushed, "Claire! Oh, Claire! We're following on the TV. It's so close!"

"Thank you, honey. I'm calling to ask you both to come down and be here with me when I make my final speech, however things turn out. May I please talk to John."

"Sure thing." The phone was evidently passed to her son.

"Hello, Mom."

"John, dear. *Please* bring Fance and fly to the convention. There's still time to make it. I would be so happy and grateful to you both to have you here with me tonight. It would make me so proud."

"Actually, I don't even have a suit…."

"Yes you do," Fance said in the background. "I ordered one. Midnight blue."

Dead silence followed, John's hand no doubt covering the phone this time.

And then a miracle.

. . . . .

"John is coming," Claire announced as she stepped back inside the suite. She beamed at Savik. Everyone else acted pleased, but in truth they were all riveted on the TV coverage.

Joss grabbed her arm. "Governor Nash is with Tawana in a room just down the hall."

Within minutes she was sitting with Governor Nash, surrounded by lights and cameras. Nash was bantering with Tawana Thompson.

Popular for his outspoken frankness, Nash was about an inch shorter than Claire and surely weighed less as well. Pundits often referred to him as the cigar-smoking elf.

The Governor moved from chit-chat quickly, to get to what seemed to concern him. Looking at Tawana he said, "Of course, Claire's running too far to the left on this peace thing. But maybe, just maybe, she could dethrone Hass."

Well past caring about diplomacy, Claire leaned forward and said firmly, "My father, Ambassador John Franklin Alden, was a moderate. That's how I was raised. It doesn't mean middle-of-the-road, afraid to commit to things. It means thinking first and not making rash decisions; it means balancing the responsibility of rugged individualism with defending the Bill of Rights, which protects the individual; it also means efficiency in business; it means—"

"Now, Claire," the Governor said, "don't get your panties in a twist, I was—"

She cut him off with a smile, adding, "Governor! You've called me a bra-burner. And now panties? You simply must stop thinking about my underwear and stick to issues!"

The room was filled with an awkward moment of stunned silence. Tawana Thompson looked amused.

Suddenly the Governor burst out laughing. He slapped his thigh. "Damned if she's not right!" He looked into the camera. "I like this gal. Hell, doesn't everybody. She hails from fine Quaker stock and would make a better President than either Cranial Crane or that other fella Americans elected and wish to god they hadn't. And in your heart, America, you know it's true."

Claire could scarcely believe what he'd just said.

"Governor," Tawana said, "Could this mean you're planning to ask your delegates to turn your votes over to Claire?"

"Why, Tawana! That's a grand idea," the Governor said, grinning.

Why Does The Boy Sound So Bitter?

The votes were all in. It was done. Everyone else in the room was on their feet, but Savik remained seated, stunned. How could the impossible have happened?

The sounds around him didn't fully register. Joss and Claire hugging and laughing. Jake and Pryce slapping each other on the back. The collection of a couple dozen close campaign supporters and workers jumping up and down, screaming, and kissing each other. Laughs. Cheers. Grins all around.

He could not just sit here. He shoved himself to his feet, feeling like an elephant was perched on his shoulders. Claire had won. She was now the Democratic nominee for the office of the President of the United States. And the Hass machine would savage her.

Claire turned to Savik, beaming. She had never looked more glowing, more beautiful. She was wearing a red dress. The end tables' lamplight gave her hair a halo of gold. He pulled her into his arms. "Congratulations," he heard himself say.

"Hey, everyone," Pryce Pierce yelled over the din. "Gather your things together. We have to take Claire to the Green Room."

. . . . .

John tossed his suit jacket into the back seat of the rental car as Fance buckled her seatbelt. He pulled into the outbound traffic of the Philadelphia International Airport for the twenty minute drive. It was already after eleven thirty. John switched into the fast lane. "We're going to be too late."

"No we won't." Fance opened the map the rental company had provided. "The delegates are probably still voting. We'll make it in time."

"I'm doing this mostly for you. Maybe a little for Mom. I just want us to survive all the formalities and have the whole thing over, with no hitches." *No lectures.*

Fance studied the map and then said, "Go west on Tinicum Island Road." He turned left and she asked, "Do you think Savik Kodaly will be there? I really like him."

"How the heck can you know you like him? You met him over exactly one dinner."

Fance, her perfume giving off the soft scent of spring flowers, slid her hand along his leg and over the fabric of his new suit to his crotch. "I have very good instincts about men."

His body responded, but he laughed, pulled her hand away, kissed her palm, and then set it on her own leg. She looked stunning in the simple dark blue dress, her incredible, some would say outrageous, hair pulled back at the sides, but still falling freely to her waist instead of the nice braided twist she'd thought would be more apropos. He'd said, "Leave it long." He wouldn't crimp Fance's style for anyone or any reason.

She said, "You know, since the temp position at Meade and Strow ends in three weeks, maybe your mom would ask Mr. Kodaly to find you a temporary job with his law firm."

"Uh…maybe…." Or not, since that would involve talking seriously to his mother.

"And there's something else. We'll be talking to your mom, face-to-face. John, I'm dying to tell her we're engaged." She looked as excited and hopeful as a kid.

"Fine. Since she's not going to be drafted, this crazy race thing will be over, and it won't make any *difference* who I'm engaged to."

"Can we please tell her now? She deserves to know, and it's not like we'd be telling the whole world."

"If the three of us have some privacy and it feels right…"

She kissed him on the cheek and then turned on the radio. "Let me see if I can find news."

". . . But it's clear that this has been a major upset. This is a divided Democratic party. Again, Claire Alden has become the Democratic candidate for the Presidency of the United States. This nomination is totally unexpected, and her race against sitting President Ernest Hass looks to be a brutal one. . . ."

Fance shrieked and then, "Oh, man! John, she did it! Drive faster!"

"No way!" Stunned and confused, he tuned out the voice on the radio. "I don't believe it."

"Well, I believe it. And she's going to beat Hass, too. You'll see."

. . . . .

"Will it actually be a green room?" Fance asked as they stepped out of the convention center elevator into the hallway of the third floor.

Still reeling, unbelieving, he took her hand. "There's virtually never just one room, and I can't remember being in one that was actually green." Wide double-doors opened to a reception table in a large room. Two DNC volunteers, seated behind the tables, gave them badges. They entered a suite of spacious rooms, and contrary to what he'd just told Fance, done in various tones of green.

"Mr. Trask, your mother is with her staff and supporters in the Dolly Madison room, directly ahead." The volunteer gestured toward another room with open buffets piled with food. "And there's food."

"Whoa!" Fance said as she took his hand again and leaned close against him. They wandered among planters of small airy trees and conversational groupings of couches and chairs on thick green and gold carpets. John recognized several Democratic senators, but most of the people were party insiders, no doubt.

The Dolly Madison room vibrated somehow with the rush of sudden power and success. Fance was quiet and suddenly a bit pale. He squeezed her hand. "You're the best person and the most beautiful woman here."

John first spotted Joss Chao, and then, there was his mother, the nominee, off to the right, talking intently with her campaign manager, Jake Shifrin. To his left, Savik, Pryce, and Adam Forsythe were chatting. Savik Kodaly nursed bottled water. His dark hair and deep-set brown eyes made him look just a tad shady. Next to him, dignified Ambassador Forsythe belted down a drink. Pryce's doubtle-breasted, pinn-striped suit and vest would earn him the room's "most dapper" award.

"Who's the guy in the three-piece," Fance asked.

"Pryce Pierce? He's been mom's PR man for years. In a way, this is his show as much as hers."

"The white-haired guy who looks a little out-of-it? He's Ambassador Forsythe? Right?"

"Yeah, he and my grandfather were really good friends. Nice guy."

He and Fance approached the three men, who turned toward them. "Mr. Kodaly," John said, "It's good to see you again." They shook hands. "Pryce Pierce and Ambassador Forsythe, I'd like to introduce you to my . . . girlfriend, Francine Showalter."

. . . . .

Claire spotted John and Fance. Joy smacked her like a kiss at the sight of her handsome son. Claire had already met Fance at the dinner with Savak, but she still marveled at the girl's ethereal beauty. She excused herself from Jake and walked toward her son and his father.

She felt a sudden tightening in her chest. Taken aback, she stopped and drew in a deep breath. They looked so alike. She glanced quickly around, fearing that surely everyone could see the similarity. But no one was gawking. Because of David's dark hair, no one had ever questioned that he was John's father. But David's jaw line had been less pronounced, and his eyes were open and friendly, not brooding like those of both Savik and John.

She hugged her son and slipped her arm around his waist, swamped with feelings of how dear he was, and aching to win him back. "I'm so glad you came. Your father would be thrilled that you're here with me tonight."

Instantly, John's expression changed from the pleasant mask he always wore with her to one of anger. "Who knows what my *father* would think? I sure don't. How could I?"

The sarcasm in John's voice brought conversation in their little circle to a dead stop. Claire released him. How could she possibly have said the wrong thing so quickly? She looked at Savik, who frowned and blinked. Pryce, too, was frowning as was Adam.

Still not satisfied with his lance to her heart, John added, "Do *you* know what he'd think?"

Fance looked daggers at him. "John…"

John blew his breath out and ran his fingers through his hair.

Fance said, "I'm so thrilled for you Ms. Alden, and for the future."

"It's just Claire, Fance. Remember?"

"The future! Damn right," Pryce said. "You should be glad, because we are going to annihilate Hass."

John leaned close to Claire and whispered very softly in her ear. "I am sorry. I hadn't planned on being a pain. The idea of…you know…it just pushed my buttons again."

She smiled. "You're here. I'm happy."

Speaking in his normal voice again, he added, "I am proud of you."

Savik said, "How's it going, John, with your pursuit of the law?"

Fance linked her arm with John's. "He just submitted his law school applications."

"Terrific. What'll you do until you find out where you are accepted?"

"No firm plans yet."

"If you'd be interested," Savik continued, "give me a call at my office sometime. We're always looking for good up-and-comers willing to do scut-work."

John grinned. "That's a generous offer."

Claire warmed from a rush of anticipation. This could be perfect. John and Savik would become acquainted under sensible conditions. "It is very generous."

Savik said, "Of course, I have to see John's packet. But I'd be amazed if anyone objects."

A blue-suited volunteer stepped up to Claire. "They're finally ready for you, Ms. Alden. We have five minutes before your acceptance speech. Follow me, please."

. . . . .

Long after midnight, the convention was finally over. Once in the secured elevator, away from prying eyes, Claire put her arm through Savik's. He felt he'd just viewed a major tragedy.

Senator Crane had spoken by phone to Claire and via TV to the convention. Watching him acting brave while probably wanting to let loose with obscenities was painful. He made no statements about party unity, just focused on hope for the future.

When Claire spoke, many delegates left, but her supporters filled in with frenzied cheering. Savik was pretty well shot as they made their way to her suite, two SS agents with them and one ahead, waiting. Not very romantic.

No one was to know anything about the depth of their relationship. Her egghead strategists had insisted that unless she intended to marry him, any intimate relationship between them had to be strictly hush-hush. He often felt a powerful attraction to her that could easily erupt into passion, a passion they had, of necessity, thwarted. Tonight, at last, might be an exception.

Or maybe not. She had to be even more exhausted than he was. Damn, he had never expected this mess to become this complicated. God only knew what Ronnie would do now.

Claire said, "My hands ache from all the clasping."

"You looked beautiful. You spoke eloquently, like the pro you are."

"This struggle will only go on from here and will become still more intense." She squeezed his arm. "I'm grateful to have your solid strength beside me."

He felt the stab of the all-too-familiar wrenching sense of guilt.

The elevator arrived at her floor and all four of them stepped out. With the two SS guys soon out of earshot but on their tail, Claire said, "Thank you for suggesting you'd hire John."

"We're always looking for good prospects. Although, I did want to ask, why does the boy sound so bitter?"

"He blames me for a lot of things." She hesitated, then held his arm a bit tighter. "When his father, when David, became ill, John wanted to be a bone marrow donor but couldn't. It's complicated. But his unsuitability as a donor made him extremely angry. John's like a lot of young men. He thinks I'm too controlling."

Savik couldn't hold back a chuckle. They were at her door. "You are controlling, Claire."

Savik knocked and a Secret Service agent let them in, and then stepped into the hall, closing the door behind him. Claire turned to face Savik, a blush in her cheeks highlighted by the flaming red of her dress. "I am *not* too controlling."

"I didn't say *too* controlling." He kissed her cheek. "No one becomes the head of something like EClaire, or even A Future Without War, or…" he forced himself to add, "…Democratic nominee for President, unless they are controlling." He pulled her against him and kissed her.

Her body, at first stiff with defensiveness, quickly relaxed.

He pulled back. "I know you're tired, but I want to make love to you. I've wanted to from the moment I saw you that day at the reception after the funeral. I just want you to know it. But after all this, I'd be content just to sleep beside you till morning."

"Actually, it is morning." She took his hand. "And making love with you is not something I can put off even one more minute." She led him toward the suite's bedroom.

To Stop Her We're Going To Have To Hurt Her

Savik sat in a deck chair on the "Bimini Blue Marlin" on a beautiful, clear early September Saturday thinking that if he'd had any sense, he'd have found some good excuse this year to opt out of the fishing trip with the Posse. It was already eleven days since Claire had won the party's nomination, and Ronnie and Cliff just would not shut up about how "fucking disastrous" this was. And what a turncoat Adam Forsythe was for running with her? It clearly would strengthen her chances against Hass.

Sure. Savik agreed in principle. But he choked on the open hatred in Ronnie and Cliff's voices. At least Quentin and Winn looked bored rather than angry.

Savik downed another swig of darkly rich Negra Modela beer.

"Okay," Winn said. "We get it. But it's not the end of the world."

Winn had already caught a whopper of a sailfish and was feeling expansive. He also glowed from a great tan. The contrast between Winn's and Savik's tans and the white skin of Ronnie, Cliff, and Quentin for the first time struck Savik as somehow symbolic. He wasn't quite sure of what. But symbolic.

"Christ, Winn," Cliff said, shaking his head. "You sometimes come off as such a political idiot. How hard have we worked, how many years have we slaved? And now with this crazy, fluky woman, we could lose everything. The polls have it tight. She could beat Ernest."

Savik said, "For chrissake, Cliff, she's not crazy."

Cliff scowled. "You sound pussy-whipped. What happened to your patriotism? Hell, to you're grasp on reality?"

Savik balled his fist and thought of leaping out of his chair and knocking Cliff out of his. Instead he said, "She's just well meaning but fucking wrong. It's our misfortune that she's also charismatic. And she's a far better human being than our sitting President!"

Quietly, and slowly, Ronnie said, "She may be a nice person, but the world needs a strong leader, not a bleeding heart. She must be stopped."

Ronnie had already said "she must be stopped" three times. Savik went forward to the bow to try and think of something else. Damned if Ronnie didn't follow him. Savik said, "Cliff can talk pussy-whipped all he wants, but nobody can say I didn't at least try to derail the train."

Ronnie squinted at him, and then spoke so the others couldn't possibly hear. "I wonder if you ever said anything like that to your commanding officers. 'Sir, I know the enemy broke through and destroyed the town, but at least I tried.'"

"Claire isn't a military target."

"Isn't she? That's exactly how I see her. I think that's why you failed."

Savik rubbed his neck. Maybe Ronnie had, in fact, nailed the problem.

Ronnie leaned in close. "You came to us with this plan to work on the inside, and we relied on you."

Savik looked out at the horizon line. He had never felt this conflicted about anything. Maybe he would never be able to know the right thing to do. Right? Wrong? What the hell! His selfish self wanted to do nothing because he liked Claire. He admired her. But the part of him that loved America and agreed with Ronnie that Claire was too nice to govern in a world of not-nice reality felt that the Presidency was as wrong for her as it was for the country. There just was no easy way out. "All right. There is something that's made me wonder about the relationship with her son and her husband. Something's off center there. You might..." *Good god, where will this lead?* "You might look into that. Something about when the husband, David Trask, was in the hospital."

Winn called out. "Hey! Enough bullshitting. Join the party."

They returned. Ronnie, the "dominant male," spread his legs and leaned far back into his chair, preparing to pontificate. "We have to go to plan B," he said. He gave his son a glare. "Alden as President? Over my dead and rotting corpse. I'll not let it happen."

Savik felt that alarm he'd had once before, at the burning of the animal care center. "You mean you'd do anything, Ronnie?"

"I mean we have to dig in, not give up, not just *try*. For starters, we double our support to Ernest."

Savik had had enough for one day. "I'm going to go take a piss," he said so Ronnie wouldn't follow him. He rose and headed for the main cabin.

. . . . .

Hughes watched Savik stride toward the cabin and a strong twist of envy squeezed at something inside him. If Hughes could have a choice of anyone else's body among all the men he knew, he'd pick Savik's. The man was also a keen lawyer. But when it came to Alden, Savik had lost his edge. Hughes had not. He knew exactly how to treat women.

"Hey, Winn," Hughes said. "Go mix me up a Bloody Mary."

"Fine." Winn stood. "Anyone else want one?"

Cliff and Quentin answered in the affirmative. As soon as Winn was out of earshot, Hughes said, "I think we must agree that we keep Savik and, by extension, Winn, out of the loop from now on when it comes to our most serious work against Alden."

"Hell, yes," Cliff agreed. "Looks like she's bewitched the cowboy."

Quentin frowned. "I don't think we'd need to worry about Savik."

"Wrong, Quentin," Hughes countered. "Savik is unpredictable. Too much of a straight-shooter. If he got his back up he might even, God forbid, go public."

Quentin, always prissy, stroked his thin mustache and then ran his palm back over his hair. The wind had come up. Spray was starting to dampen the men. "So what do you suggest? Are we dropping him?"

"Oh no," Hughes said. "We still need him, and he says he's still in position to deliver whatever he can. Savik is a true patriot, and he still knows Alden would be a tragedy for the country. For the world. The problem with Savik is he isn't willing to hurt her. And to stop her, we're going to have to hurt her. One way or the other."

"We need serious dirt on Alden," Quentin said. "Real or manufac-tured. Something we can pass to Hass's people. Your 'Jack the Knife' hasn't come up with much. The public likes her son and his stripper. Our Truth in Government committee needs a new direction."

"Savik did give us a possibility. Something about the son. But in case we need something a little stronger than dirt, I have a guy who will, without hesitation, fall on his sword for me and for this country. Plausible deniability guaranteed."

Hyjinx was, in fact, at that very moment ready and waiting for new instructions.

Roman Dinner

"A Roman dinner?" Serena asked.

"It needs to be a fun evening." Claire had already invited Savik, Pryce, Joss, Jake, and Adam. "At first I just wanted a thank-you dinner, one to sort of re-group for the coming campaign. We should be ecstatic at the campaign HQ, but Pryce badmouthed Savik again today. There is this terrible, tense undercurrent between Savik, Pryce, and Joss. It's growing deadly to campaign esprit. And given that I'm growing close to Savik, it's not good for any of us. I thought a dinner theme party would help people step out of their usual roles. Anyway, if you come, you can help me to help them have a good evening of food and bonding."

"I'll come, of course."

"You know, this will be a great chance for you to meet Adam. I think you two might hit it off. He's a gem of a man."

"Yes, he is. But my guess is that he's sweet on you."

"He was my father's friend. A good friend and advisor to me. He's just lonely."

. . . . .

The door knocker announced Claire's first guest. Nearly four weeks of frantic campaigning had flown by since the convention, four weeks since she'd spent a wonderful night and all too brief morning with Savik. Florence would let whoever it was in, but excitement that it might be Savik caused Claire to hurry toward the front hallway.

Joss and Serena entered, Serena in white with gold accessories as usual. Joss actually looked great in fire-engine red and silver. Claire exchanged hugs and a European kiss to each cheek with Serena.

Joss grabbed Claire and pulled her into a rather intimate-feeling, bosom-to-bosom embrace. When she let go, she cocked her head to one side and studied Claire's blue silk. "Absolutely exquisite, boss." As they walked toward the living room Joss added, "I just wanted to check with you before we toss work entirely out the window for the evening, if it's okay for me to appoint Brydie McDonald to the campaign committee for college recruitment next week. It's not a lot of work, but Brydie's very interested in recruiting young women volunteers."

"I have to think a bit about it. That committee is already pretty woman-heavy. I was thinking maybe Savik would be good. He could strengthen our outreach to young guys. Savik has a wonderfully strong male image. Let's use Brydie somewhere else."

Joss frowned poisonously.

Claire let Joss's frown go unchallenged and excused herself to make a last-minute check on progress in the kitchen where Magda, the chef, and her team of three were putting finishing touches on a Roman feast. Magda had taken over as if she owned Claire's kitchen. For each of the three traditional Roman course–appetizer, entrée, and dessert–Claire had found original Roman recipes. Puls, a hearty, red-wheat bread, already sat in baskets on the central low table, along with an antipasto-like dish of sweet onions, garlic, and goat cheese.

From the front of the house Claire heard the door knocker again. Savik, with Pryce and Jake on his heels, soon entered the living room and began chatting with Serena and Joss. When Adam, the last arrival, had greeted everyone, Claire invited her guests to see the dining room. She led them into the hallway and paused at the wide entry. They gathered around, all except Adam.

"Wow!" Joss exclaimed. "I just took a Delorean back to the past."

"It's stunning," Serena added.

Claire's decorator had created a Roman dining room, a *triclinium*, where three large couches formed three sides of a square. The decorator had removed the dining set and covered the walls and ceiling with red and black fabric paintings like those in Pompeii's House of Mysteries. A rug that looked like a mosaic hid the wooden floor. Each couch could seat three reclining guests. Three servers in authentic togas would bring dishes to a low table in front of the couches. Alex, in his cage, had been moved into one corner.

"We eat reclining on one side, propped up by a pillow," Claire explained. She directed Pryce, Joss and Jake to one couch and had Savik join her on the center one. "Serena, you and Adam will have the other couch."

They took their places as Adam stepped into the room, looking confused.

"Hail to our next Vice-President!" Joss said raising her wine glass.

Adam apparently didn't hear. "Damn heathen Romans," he said, eying one of the male servers. "Probably designed their togas to make it easier to fornicate and piss!"

Stunned, Claire stared at him. Was he drunk? The others displayed equal surprise at this crude and atypically undignified comment.

"Fornicate and piss!" Alex echoed quite clearly. "Piss! You bandido!"

Joss giggled and Savik chuckled.

Adam sat down as the three servers brought in a drink of wine and honey, followed by lamb meatball soup, called *boleti*. A light Umbrian wine, *Orvieto Classico*, would flow for the entire evening, not watered down, Claire's one deviation from Roman authenticity.

"You should all know," she explained, "that our theme is an idea inspired by Savik. He's quite a Roman history buff."

Pryce gave Savik a sour look.

"I'm really enjoying the chance to feel I'm inside another time and place," Serena said.

Bless you, Serena. The final appetizer replaced their soup: baked mushrooms stuffed with clams, goat cheese, and topped with sweet onions.

"We have five weeks and twelve days left, guys," Joss said. "Five weeks and twelve days until Claire and Adam are the President and Vice-President of the United States."

"Joss, dear," Pryce countered. "No politics at Claire's table. Er, *triclinium.*"

"Tonight is an exception," Claire said, "as long as you pretend that we're having dinner with Plato or Sophocles or Marcus Aurelius, talking philosophy and politics over good food."

"No forks," Adam said, licking his thumb. "I see we're being totally authentic."

"Yeah." Joss downed another stuffed mushroom. "But not much chance of an orgy."

The servers cleared the tables and brought in the main course of three hot dishes: pork, duck with honey sauce, and lamb simmered in milk and wine; and two cold dishes: sea urchin eggs—very like caviar—in a bed of cabbage, and octopus in olive oil.

Adam seemed to have recovered himself. "The tension at the United Nations now is palpable," he said. "Excitement. Hope. There was a general sense of despair when it looked like whoever won, the next U.S. President would support PeaceMaker. But now there's great hope among most of the members that Claire will win and put a stop to it."

Jake said, "The race is all uphill for us."

"Our allies are pulling for Claire," Pryce said, "but the Islamic world, if you can believe what you see from *Al Jazeera* and *Al Arabia,* is having fits of terror over the mere possibility that a woman who so staunchly supports empowering women might win."

Joss said, "I like this eating while reclining."

"So, Savik," Pryce said. He held a bit of olive-oil-dipped *puls* in his hand and gave Savik a direct stare. "What do you think of the Alden plan for a warfare transition?"

"Yeah, Savik," Joss echoed. "We've never really heard your feelings on that one. My guess is you never read it."

"My focus was, naturally, on legal and financial ramifications." Savik downed a bit of honey-glazed duck.

"And he worked hard on that," Claire said quickly.

Adam filled in the suddenly quiet moment. "Well, I, too, am curious, Savik. As a lawyer whose firm is primarily involved with international banking, what do you think of the projected figures for the time required to put together a global peace treaty? After WW II it took only a couple of decades to form the European Union. The global climate agreement took work of about a decade. So, would Claire's estimate of getting the global community to agree to a peace treaty also take no more than a decade? Interstate wars are already on the wane. They are simply bad for business."

Savik shrugged. "'The sinews of war,' as Cicero said, 'are a limitless supply of money.' And Claire certainly intends to snip the sinews. Also like the Romans, Claire has an excellent grasp of planning for what she wants to accomplish."

Certainly intends to snip the sinews. Claire realized she'd been holding a bite of food. She popped it into her mouth. Savik's answer was clever, yet essentially neutral, not the public commitment she craved. He'd probably never even read the intricately detailed strategy she'd put her heart, soul, and precious hours into developing.

"But you do agree," Pryce persisted, "that one key to freeing us from war is to purposely shift our economies?"

"I think, as the ancients warned, there is danger in too much power, and money *is* power. Beyond that, I think that to be a force for good, we can't have weak spots. We live in a global economy, and we become ever more vulnerable. We must have surefire means to protect our country and our financial and other interests."

Joss frowned. "Fancy talk aside, it sounds like you mean we must be able to dominate all other economies. Or do you mean we need to dominate everyone militarily as well?"

"Our biggest threat," Savik countered, "is global terrorism. And the only way to defeat them is to dominate or eliminate them."

Serena, who had quietly been nibbling her food, said, "Of course, we can never defeat terrorism with weapons. A change in ethos. A metanoia. That's what it will take. Killing must become so abhorrent that terrorists are pitied by their fellow citizens and considered foolish, if not infantile."

Savik smiled. "With due respect for a worthy goal, Serena, men make war. Period."

"This food is great," Jake said. "Even the patricians of Rome would have…uh…"

Pryce leaned forward, past Jake, glaring at Savik, and interrupted. "I understand how you might not get it, Savik." Claire felt ill. Her dinner of good food and bonding was spinning off in an unsettling direction. Pryce plunged on. "You might think that Claire is wrong, and we who support her are nuts to think we humans can ever dispense with war. You strike me as a kick-ass, kill-'em-all kind of guy. You may have studied Roman history, but apparently it didn't sink in how their protracted wars led to their downfall."

"Pryce has a minor in history from Princeton," Joss said, her tone rather condescending. "He knows his stuff. He doesn't just play with toy soldiers."

For the first time ever in her experience with Savik, Claire saw him grow red-faced, and his jaw clenched and unclenched. She half expected him to swear at Joss and then leap up and knock Pryce onto the floor.

Instead, Savik finally said, "You have to plan what you want from people. I agree with the Romans that it's necessary to have a plan, and in my view, that plan better include keeping control of the high ground militarily."

"But in the end," Pryce said, wiping one hand on a napkin as though he were dismissing Savik, "the Romans lost their freedom. The Republic devolved into tyranny. So their plan, which relied not only on laws but on force and intimidation to keep others in line, and which excluded the influence of women, wasn't perfect or lasting was it?"

The two men glared at each other.

"Messy, messy, messy," Alex shot into the silence, startling them all. "Piss! You bandido!"

Adam heaved himself to his feet and left the room, saying, "Like many a well-fed Roman, I need to go vomit."

Calamity had struck Claire's party. What in the world could she possibly say now? She stared at her wine glass, feeling a bit like she also needed to go throw up.

The servers arrived with a dessert course, fresh cut pears and grapes, three cheeses, a mouth-watering sticky treat of chopped figs, dates, walnuts, and honey.

"What is up with our ambassador?" Joss asked.

"His behavior tonight is disturbing," Pryce added. "You've been with him for several events, Claire. Had you noticed anything…odd before tonight?"

Having the distraction of Adam to talk about lowered the tension level somewhat. "Not really, except for yelling at a protester. I'm sure he's just . . ." She thought suddenly of his headache medicine and wondered just how strong it was. And exactly what it was. Yet she should probably speak to Adam in private before mentioning the meds. "…a little rattled."

They turned their attention to the dessert, and within a few moments Adam returned. Mercifully Joss didn't ask if he'd succeeded in disgorging his dinner, Roman style. Through the dessert course he behaved with his usual perfect decorum.

Claire had planned for everyone to continue an amicable discussion afterward in the living room, but as soon as they rose from the table, Adam said he felt it was time for him to leave. Jake agreed. Joss and Pryce also seemed eager to depart, so Serena joined the general exodus, leaving Claire alone with Savik.

Claire thanked Magda, her staff, and Florence, and wished them a good night. She gave Alex a final grape before covering him, and then, with Savik, she trudged upstairs, sick at heart.

. . . . .

Savik could tell from Claire's clouded eyes that she was disappointed in the dinner. Thinking to cheer her he said, "I've been wanting to tell you that John is doing extremely well at the law firm. And not just at charming every woman in his vicinity—which seems to be his fate. But doing the small tasks he's given quickly and, so far, flawlessly."

"He's very bright. He should have already finished law school. I am glad and relieved that he seems to be finding himself at last. I think Fance is good for him."

They went into her bedroom, a feminine space. Pale greens and burgundy. Fresh flowers. A big, inviting down comforter on the king-size bed.

She said, "The dinner was a total disaster."

He felt some guilt for that. "I'm sorry that I seem to put both Pryce and Joss on edge."

She leaned against him, and he wrapped his arms around her—where they belonged.

Strange to think this was so since he and Claire were opposed in such important ways. She was an amazing woman. Even their political arguments stimulated him in ways other women never had. He felt comfortable and yet excited with her, fascinated, yet also peacefully at home.

I love her.

And I am betraying her. If she knew what he'd done, she'd hate him, and rightfully so.

"It's not what you do or say, Savik. Although Pryce might try to make it sound that way. They're both upset that I care so much for you. That I'm starting to depend on you. For so long they had me all to themselves."

"I don't know about Joss, but Pryce has a thing for you."

"No, not like you're thinking. He is just fiercely protective." She pulled away and walked toward a wing-back chair as she unhooked her dress.

He moved close. "Well, now, for tonight, I have you to myself." He began kissing her shoulder, revealed where the silk fell away. "And I know that I love you."

There. He'd said it.

She turned, and the pain and disappointment lines in her face transformed before his eyes into a smile of joy. His pulse throbbed in his throat. She let the dress fall to the floor. She stood in a short silky slip of dark blue. The light behind her revealed her silhouette. She obviously wore nothing underneath but panties.

"And I love you."

He pulled her to him and kissed her. She unbuttoned his shirt, pulled it away, and let it drop to the floor. He finished undressing. She turned off the light, laughing, throaty and warm. She took his hand and drew him toward that inviting, king-sized bed. When they reached it, he lifted her, then stretched her out in the center, and lay beside her. They kissed, and Claire was eager.

Tonight, he would make her moan the way she had in front of her fireplace. He slid his hand to her inner thigh and beyond. She murmured as she kissed him, little sounds of pleasure. He let his fingers feel her warmth, her tender readiness. Moonlight revealed the beauty of her face, something unforgettable, even if the magic of this night were their last.

. . . . .

Savik felt Claire's fingers brush his forehead. He opened his eyes to find her smiling at him. Morning sunlight of early fall lay across the foot of her bed and they were covered with only a pale green sheet, warm together despite a morning cooler than yesterday's.

She grinned. "What a night."

"It's rather indecent the way you bloom in the morning after such a...*robust* night. Anyone who sees you would know exactly what you've been up to." He kissed her fingertips, pulled her onto his chest and lingered a kiss on her lips. "By all rights," he said softly, brushing a loose strand of her hair behind her ear, "I should be exhausted."

She drew back a bit, frowning. "Savik, have you read the Alden plan? Tell me the truth. I woke up wondering." She rolled onto her side facing him.

"I'm never going to lie to you, Claire." *Never again.* He meant it. "So no. Not yet. But I promise to read it soon."

"I'll want to know what you think. Honestly think."

"I promise. I'll be honest."

She sighed, stilling frowning. She traced the line of his lips. "I'm worried about Adam."

"Maybe he'd had a few before he arrived."

"Gaffes like that in public, even one, and we'll have a nightmare on our hands."

Savik could easily contact Jack the Knife, alert him to a possible problem with Adam, but he'd done enough damage. No more. No matter how much Ronnie put the squeeze on him. He leaned over her and kissed her throat, wanting to make the time with her last all day.

"Forget Adam!"

You Can't Have Both Of Us

A week after the disastrous Roman Dinner, Claire, Joss and the ever-hovering Secret Service detail entered the backstage area of UCLA's Royce Hall. Her speech, "The Vision Thing: a nonviolence plan for victory over poverty, racism, and war in the 21ˢᵗ Century." For this crowd, this was their century, and having the opportunity to excite future leaders of America always lifted her out of any weariness or discouragement. From the wings, she peeked out at the crowd, now listening to the California Governor, a Republican. Familiar signs papered the walls or flashed from many a T-shirt: "It's The The Vision Thing Stupid," "Democrats for Claire," "Metanoia," and "Men and Women: Partners for a Bright Future."

The Governor, notoriously independent Republican Gloria Mondello, had delivered a national political shocker by throwing her support to the Democratic candidacy of Claire Alden. A global restructuring would demand many crossings of partisan lines, and this was a significant first.

An aide, a kid with beard, ponytail, and starched white shirt, led Claire into the Green Room. Joss, her eyes alight with excitement, grabbed Claire's arm. "Boss, this collegiate push is taking off like the biggest rock star thing you can imagine. Campushottalk.com says..." She read a print-out. "The hippie movement of the sixties zeroed in on peace and love, but great heart and protests were not enough. Where 'flower power' failed, Claire Alden has a plan to deliver the Age of Aquarius."

"Campushottalk.com, huh?"

"Yeah. A mega-website for college students. Dating. Music. Blogs. Some politics. Look! We are going to turn out the youth vote like never before in history. You just have to let me appoint Brydie McDonald to the youth vote board."

"I'm sure she's good. Do find something for her. But Savik is willing to join the youth vote effort. We need a man. Oh, and Joss, please contact the League of Women Voters representative and make clear that I'm with them. Tell the network reps that I'm not interested in fake debates. I will agree to three. But either Hass agrees to the real thing with the League, or nothing. With his ego and hunger to see himself on TV, he'll agree."

"Goddamn it, Claire. What do you have against Brydie McDonald?"

Shocked by Joss's language and acid tone, Claire said, "I have nothing against McDonald..."

"Then why the hell don't you listen to me any more?"

Claire studied Joss. Perhaps she was closer to this Brydie woman than Claire had realized. "But I do listen to you. What is this—?"

The servers and staff were watching and probably listening. Claire drew Joss into a corner. Black eyes snapping with anger, Joss shook off Claire's hand.

"I have worked my butt off for you for years!"

"Joss?"

"And..." Tears filled her eyes. "I have been devoted to you. I have loved you."

Not once had Claire seen Joss cry. Still, this wasn't an issue Claire could or should just concede. "I see Savik as being uniquely qualified to attract young male voters, and I—"

"You have Savik on the brain." Joss's raised voice kept onlookers staring.

"I simply want to keep the youth vote board gender balanced. I have nothing against—"

"Admit it. You're blind in love with the son-of-a-bitch!" A silence stretched between them.

If Claire insisted that Joss quiet down, Joss would only speak louder.

"I don't even have a life apart from yours," Joss wailed. "I'm on call at all hours. I'm the one who deals with all the garbage and shit in your life, so you never have to. But does my opinion count for anything?"

"Joss, of course it does," Claire said quietly.

"Then get that asshole Savik out of this campaign." Joss looked Claire squarely in the eyes. "You can't have both of us. Which will it be?"

"Please listen to me. We're on the last lap of a hundred lap Presidential race. Don't give me this kind of ultimatum."

"Okay then. Fine. I quit." Joss moved to Claire's left, as if to leave.

Claire moved, blocking Joss's exit. "Joss you're upset. Take a deep breath."

"No. You have a fatal blind spot. He's going to ruin everything. I don't trust him. I can't watch what's happening any longer."

Joss moved around Claire. Back straight and without a glance behind, she strode across the Green Room and out the door. Claire could not stop herself from looking into the face of the Secret Service agent nicknamed V-ball because of the volleyball-like roundness of his head. She liked him. The agents kept an emotional distance, but V-ball often seemed amused. He didn't react now though, other than a slight shrug, and then looked away toward an exit.

Blind in love. Could Joss be right? Was Claire only believing what she wanted to believe? Every time she was with Savik, life was so right. The feeling went deep inside her. You can't experience something like that based simply on what you want to believe. She and Savik were good together. And she certainly couldn't ask him to prove his loyalty. Given all that was at stake, she had to be sure though. She put in a call to Margaret, head of the EClaire legal staff.

The student aide approached Claire. "You're on in ten minutes. Please follow me."

Her heartbeat racing, fighting shock, Claire followed. She must convince Joss to . . . to rethink this rash, rash move. How in God's name could she ever replace Joss?

· · · · ·

In her office in the Steinmetz Building, Claire noted the date, October fifteenth. Many weeks now of struggling without Joss. Tomorrow she must face Hass again in their final of three debates. In only three weeks this brutal election would be over, for good or ill, but without one very dear friend. Humvee had picked up much of the personal slack, did general gofer stuff. Between him and Connie and a couple of secretaries from EClaire, she was making do. The staff had lost some of its esprit, however.

"Thank god there is only one debate and three weeks left," she said to Jake and Pryce.

"It's been hellacious, all right," Pryce said, sitting on the edge of her desk.

"The Ambassador is here," Claire's intercom announced.

Claire went out, personally greeted Adam, and brought him back to her office. Pryce and Jake shook his hand. Adam's security man waited outside. No one was smiling. *Hellacious*...the word echoed in Claire's head.

"Is it really that bad?" Adam asked.

"You haven't seen it?" Jake asked.

Claire mouse-clicked over the YouTube video. "Let's all watch it again."

The clip, taken with a cell phone camera, showed the exterior of the United Nations building. Ambassador Adam Forsythe gestured wildly as he yelled at people in suits, identified as State Department aides. The words weren't quite distinguishable, but the tone was furious. A shot zoomed in revealing a reddened face, mouth stretched in a yell—the closing visual.

"Claire, these were Hass's people. Sent to get my goat," Adam protested. "I guess I look like a lunatic, but they—"

"They got to you," Jake countered. "You let them get to you."

"Adam, this just isn't like you," Claire said. "Something's wrong. You need a physical—"

"I know." Adam looked stricken. He sank into one of the two upholstered chairs. "I'm having a series of tests. All set up. In two weeks."

"Two weeks," Pryce repeated flatly. "And in the mean time?"

Adam turned a cold stare to Pryce. "What are you implying? That I'm out of control?"

Silence.

Jake took a seat in the soft chair beside Adam. "Mr. Ambassador, you know how serious this is."

Claire had to say what she had to say. "Adam, we need to put a team of four *escorts* with you…to keep the press and anyone with a cell phone away from you. I'm so sorry."

"Good God, Claire!" He stared at her. "You would really do this to me?"

"You've been…puzzlingly unreliable. If you were me, what would you do, Adam?"

"*I'd* listen to what you have to say! I just need some down time." He let out a deep sigh.

Pryce said. "Until we're sure what we're dealing with, you'll have four new *assistants*."

Adam was no doubt listening to Pryce, but he was staring at Claire. "Incredible," he said. His eyes turned flinty. "This whole campaign process is doing something very harmful to you. Changing you."

"Oh, please..!" Jake said in disgust. "We can't risk another outburst. Will you concede, Mr. Ambassador, that as a temporary measure, this will be helpful?"

"Hhhhmmph." Adam finally took his gaze off Claire and stood. "Fine…Dandy."

She felt a terrible wave of sadness as he left. She was alienating yet another dear friend in this harsh, winner-takes-all battle, and she could see no way to escape it.

One more price to pay, one more cut to the heart.

The Final Debate

Savik handed Winn a big bowl of freshly made chili, they both grabbed a Negra Modelo bottle of beer from the frig, then headed for Savik's den. His latest Roman battlefield, nearly finished, occupied half of the room. The room's other half was reserved for two recliner chairs and two armchairs, all upholstered in dark brown leather, and a 60 inch wall TV. It was already set to FOX and the final Presidential debate had begun.

Winn, who had insisted he wanted to see the last debate, having avoided watching the first two, raised the leg of his recliner, saying, "She looks hot."

"She always looks hot," Savik replied. He also got comfortable, legs elevated. Claire's deep-rich-red pantsuit highlighted her blond hair. Stage lighting always worked for her, even when he knew she was exhausted. Hass, too, made an imposing impression. He'd chosen a dark blue suit and a red and blue striped tie. He was a good six two, in so-so shape as far as Savik could tell, and his full head of blond hair was perfectly cut. He looked younger than his sixty-six years. Savik had to admit, Hass looked very Presidential.

"I'm up for this," Winn said, "but I bet it'll be boring. Weren't the first two?"

"Depends on what you're expecting."

"Most pundits claim they're tied as far as wins. Naturally dad says Hass put her down good. Of course, it makes sense he'd easily whup her in a debate. He's been in politics his whole damn life. For chrissake, she had a TV cooking show!"

Savik was half ignoring Winn, trying to figure out what the current debate topic was, but he still said, "You'd be amazed how they prep her. Jake hires two guys and a team to put on mock debate. James Grogan plays Hass's part."

They both fell silent and listened as the moderator led Claire and Hass through their positions on Supreme Court nominations. In the first two debates they had covered foreign affairs, the economy, immigration, campaign finance reform, and entitlements like social security. Tonight was touted to be about domestic issues like drugs, LGBT rights, reproductive rights, and college affordability.

When Claire and Hass finished slugging it out over how best to deal with problems about legalizing marijuana nationally and how to treat the opioid epidemic, the moderator said there would be a ten- minute break.

"I need a break," Winn said. "Badly. I wonder how many people really sit through all of this."

Savik stood. "Want more chili. Or ice cream. I've got chocolate or rocky road?"

"You know me. Rocky road."

He took his bowl and Winn's to the kitchen and exchanged them for two bowls of rocky road. When he returned to the den Winn was checking out the Roman battlefield. "Which one is this," Winn asked.

"Pharsalus. Caesar decisively defeats Pompey."

The debate had moved to the topic of drugs. Eventually the moderator introduced the debate's final topic, reproductive rights. In Savik's view, this evening Claire and the President had differed almost like night and day on about every subject. He'd found himself agreeing with her surprisingly often. But then, tonight they weren't debating foreign affairs or national security. And he already knew she and Hass would differ totally on abortion.

Hass was a long-time believer in the right to life of even the unborn, embryo or fetus, and the state should decide. Claire was passionate in her belief that a woman should have a right to choose. Or as she had once stressed to him, that she and no one else had the right to control her body. "If you don't control your own body and your reproductive life you are not a free person," she'd said with uncommon heat. As the debate proceeded he heard nothing new from either of them.

Before the moderator could say goodnight to everyone, Winn said, "This must be one of the biggest differences between two presidential candidates that has ever been presented to this country. Tomorrow I don't know who the talking heads will say won. I do know the biggest difference that will stick in voter's minds is the abortion thing. That's like an emotional bomb. Who do you agree with? Her or him?"

"Legal or illegal, if I got pregnant, no one would tell me what to do. Philosophy won't change the hard fact that if you don't have control of your body, you don't control your life."

Winn stood. "That may be true, but your Claire's position on this issue will cost her lots of votes. Maybe an election."

You Want To Replace Me With Savik!?

The day after the debate, on their way to West Point, Claire stared out the window of the black Cadillac SUV hybrid she preferred to a limousine, at passing fields of pumpkins and the orange, red, and yellow display of upstate New York's fall foliage. Even inside the car, she could smell the dry woods.

She and Pryce were alone, no other staff. Jake, Humvee, Connie and several aides shared two other cars in the caravan. Pryce was the only one who didn't seem bothered by Joss's absence. After all their banter, Claire had thought there was a deeper bond between them. Pryce simply stepped in as Claire's gatekeeper and daily companion in addition to his other duties. West Point was only about twenty more minutes away.

The idea she wanted to convey to him was not going to sit well. He seemed to have something heavy weighing on his mind as well. So far she and Price had ridden in guarded silence. Margaret from EClaire legal was supposed to give Claire the report she needed today—she checked her watch—in just a few more minutes, so she stalled a little longer before taking up business with Pryce. "Fall has always been my favorite season at The Retreat," she said. "I love the symbolism of the changing seasons, that dying leaves can create beauty. They remind me that sometimes sacrifice is needed to create something great."

"Did you read those death threats, Claire? You know I forbid you to read them."

Forbid. Pryce was becoming almost territorial. "I didn't read them, although just receiving them reminds me that many people are terrified of the change I represent. Case in point. Not everyone at West Point is happy about me speaking here."

Margaret called as the caravan curved around a bend in the road, offering a glimpse of the pale dusty rose granite towers and buildings of the West Point compound. "Claire, Savik's campaign legal work is impeccable," Margaret said. "Brilliant even."

She cited particulars, and Claire thanked her. Tension melted away. If Savik wanted to sabotage her, he could easily have embedded flaws in the campaign legal work.

"Pryce." She turned from the window to face him. "Jake says our war chest is seriously depleted. He's pulled the TV ads from Oregon, Oklahoma, and Nevada. We now have to go back to our base supporters for a fresh infusion. I know you're heavily burdened filling in for Joss in some areas, so what I'd like to do is have Savik take over as liaison to half of our Big Kahuna's, Lonnie Ames, John Gaylord and Leo Lombardi."

Pryce's whole body stiffened. "You want to replace me with Savik as your connection to the people *I* approached and brought in?"

"Just to take some of the burden off you."

"I don't consider dealing with our biggest financial supporters a burden. Are you unsatisfied with my performance?"

"Of course not. Please, please don't take this wrong. You already accomplish more than ten people could. It isn't fair. And it isn't necessary. Savik's firm deals with big financial clients all the time, and Savik is very sophisticated when it comes to money. I trust him and would like to include him, take advantage of his talents."

"It's more than that, isn't it? Joss was right. You do intend to make your relationship with Savik. . . permanent." Pryce turned away, staring out his own window, shoulders, usually so erect, now slumped.

"This isn't a case of him or you. We can use all the help we can get, Pryce."

They fell into a miserable silence as the caravan's lead car turned onto West Point grounds.

. . . . .

The West Point speech went well. Press coverage was excellent. Pryce was still sulky afterward, but Claire went home to the Retreat, slept in her own bed for a change, and awakened reasonably refreshed.

Now, with Pryce and Jake beside her and Humvee and V-Ball in the third-row back seat, all again in the SUV, they approached the NY campaign headquarters. Claire would meet Connie, greet supporters, give a quick pep-talk, and then fly to Boston for a rally. With only eighteen days until the election, every minute counted. Of the debate, pundits had been saying that the level of the debate was high, that neither side had attempted to slander the other, and that issues held sway, but that Hass had landed several body blows.

She hadn't talked to Savik yesterday, too tired after the debate, so she opened her purse and touched the satiny blue Sharpshooter ribbon. She'd been carrying it ever since their wonderful night after the Roman dinner, a reminder that she had someone behind her whom she loved and who loved her.

The lead car turned into the street housing the campaign headquarters, and Claire's SUV followed. A horde of frantic reporters were gathered in front of the center. She leaned forward to better see out the window. Camera flashes looked like fireworks. Suddenly, she could hear the din of clamoring voices.

"In heaven's name," Claire gasped out, "what is going on?"

Humvee said, "Somethin's really wrong."

The Whole World Will Know
I'm A Bastard

Reporters were baying outside, ringing the vehicle, slapping at windows, banging on fenders and hood. "Is it true, Claire?" "Claire, did you commit adultery?" Camera flashes added to the confusion. "Is it true?" "Is it true, Claire, that…?" "Claire, is it true?"

Connie forced her way through the reporters to reach the SUV. She pulled the left rear door open to climb in. The SS man, the driver, leapt out, pushed back the reporters and closed the door behind her.

Pryce said, "What in the name of all that's holy do they—?"

Connie reached over Pryce and slapped a newspaper folded to reveal Phyllis Colson's column onto Claire's lap. "This is what has their hair on fire."

The headline proclaimed, "**Claire is No Saint.**"

> "It was learned yesterday that former tennis pro John Alden Trask, son of Republican nominee for President, Claire Alden, has a blood type incompatible with that of David Raymond Trask, the man registered as his father on his birth certificate. John Trask was born five days short of eight months after the date on the marriage certificate. There was no process of adoption connected with the birth of Claire's son. A nasty little secret, Claire, dear?"

Blood pounded in her ears, matching the roar outside. She stared at the paper as if an electric voltage within it welded it to her hand. Sweat broke out on her scalp, her lip, her back, under her arms.

> "Is the Alden campaign in serious trouble? Her longtime top aide Jocelyn Chao has quit, citing personal differences. Her running mate, Adam Forsythe, is rumored to have sudden outbursts of anger. And now we find that her playboy, jailbird son is apparently illegitimate. Wonder who daddy is?"

Clutching the paper, Claire climbed over Jake toward the door.

"What are you doing?" Pryce shouted from behind her. "You can't go out there." He lunged to grab her waist. "Wait!"

"We have to prepare a spin strategy," Jake said, grabbing her arm. "I hope to God you're going to tell me it isn't true."

"Don't go out there," Humvee called from the seat in the rear.

A loud thump diverted her. A reporter had jumped onto the SUV's hood, camera aimed at the interior. Claire said, "You're all just going to have to trust me on this."

"No! Hell, your face is red, Claire," Jake said, panic in his eyes.

She shook off the men's restraining grasps. The two SS men in front were watching her closely. She nodded at V-Ball and pointed outside, but he and the other guard frowned at her.

"Make them give me space! *Please!*"

V-ball produced a mini-bullhorn, bounded out of the SUV, and commanded the reporters. "Step back ten feet from the vehicle, quiet down, and Ms. Alden will give you a statement."

"Don't do this, Claire," Pryce said.

She grabbed her cell phone and stepped out into the small circle of space now separating her from the throng. Along with the two SS men from her car, two others quickly joined to guard her. Humvee climbed out and stood close behind her.

She backed up closer to him and whispered, "Thank you."

With her own small digital camera in the phone, she began snapping pictures of the slavering paparazzi. It had a strangely silencing effect on them. She then handed the camera to Humvee who continued taking photos.

"May I?" she asked V-ball, nodding at the bullhorn. She straightened, willed herself into steely calm. "Someone has egregiously violated my privacy, that of my son and of my family. This contemptible act will be investigated. My son's medical history is private. Sperm donation is a private affair. Our private lives are our business. No one else's. No one! So do not make judgments. Others don't know the circumstances and decisions, and never will. And...." She raised the Colson article clutched in her fist. "No matter the parentage and paperwork, how dare anyone suggest another human being's existence is not legitimate?"

"So it's TRUE, then?"

"Who's John's father?"

"Will you state for the record whether you were artificially inseminated? As a bride?"

The horde's frenzy started up again.

"Claire, get IN!" Jake commanded.

She obeyed. Humvee and the SS men climbed in after her and slammed their doors.

"Take me to Savik's law firm," Claire said. "I have to see John immediately."

. . . . .

They rode through Manhattan traffic toward Smithson, Crandall, Kodaly, and Klein. Pryce canceled the staff meeting at campaign headquarters. He and Jake wanted to immediately fly her to Boston and strategize on what further to say about the article's comments about John and on Adam's strange behavior, and decide what if anything she would say at the evening rally. Steel in her voice she said, "All I need, and right now, is to see John."

"Claire," Pryce said coldly, "this is one of those cases where a candidate is asked about skeletons in the closet, and the candidate divulges anything dangerous, and the staff prepares in advance to prevent a catastrophe. Why didn't you tell us? Every Republican and Independent in the country is going to be screaming the same questions."

"Pryce. Weren't you listening?" Claire felt her face heating up all over again. "This is no one's business! And nobody except my two closest friends know anything about it."

"Actually," Jake said, "you scared the shit out of me, but you handled the reporters brilliantly. I predict the public will have a sympathetic reaction. The point is, how did that Colson bitch know to look into John's blood type?"

Yes. How?

Claire had a sickening thought.

"I think we know," Pryce said, tone still cold and hostile. "John's comment in the Green Room at the Convention. Right, Claire? And we know who was listening."

Pryce was so eager to attack Savik. But hadn't she just had the same thought? "There were others besides you, Savik, and Adam. Joss and miscellaneous aides, including Adam's, were within earshot. I wouldn't put it past certain Party operatives to have bugged the whole room."

"You can pretend that others overheard if you want to. Not so. It was you, me, Adam, and Kodaly."

Arrival at the law firm put an end to the uncomfortable talk. She said a little prayer for guidance in the moment of truth that had been forced on her.

. . . . .

Claire waited in a private conference room on the fortieth floor of the Smithson Building, looking out at the skyscrapers of perhaps the most important city in the world. The city would go on without her, no matter what she said or did. The forces that favored the status quo and worked against change, even positive change, could be overwhelming. It would be easy to feel like a gnat, flitting among monolithic boulders, her voice a tiny whining buzz that made no difference. And her efforts at seeking the right moment to share with John the identity of his father, all her attempts at damage control could not have gone worse.

John kept her waiting. On purpose, she thought. At least a half-hour of pacing, staring out the window, and ignoring her cell phone's incoming calls passed. Finally the door opened. John looked more like Savik than ever in his white shirt and gray tie and black slacks. She read the coldness in his eyes. *Oh, god….*

"John, I'm sorry—"

"Of course you are. You had absolutely no idea that Presidential campaigns would get nasty and dig shit up. Gee, who'd have thought anybody would do such a dirty thing to such a nice lady and her hapless son?"

"I never expected—"

"You told them sperm donors are private?" He was close to yelling. "Sperm donors?"

"That did come out fast. I thought I would protect you—"

"Wrong. You thought it would protect *you*. And don't try to tell me it's true. If I'd been a sperm-bank baby, you'd have told me that a long time ago. You've lived your whole life trying to control mess and chaos. Control ugly truths. Inconvenient needs. Betrayal. Dad got cancer from trying to deal with your control."

She gasped. "My god! I deserve your anger, but please don't be cruel. I tried to explain a little when your father, when David died. You ran away and refused to listen."

"Oh, I'm the cruel one. Of course. Anyone who doesn't like being steamrolled by you and then protests with the truth must be cruel."

His face was pale, his lips thin. That fire in his eyes seemed full of not just anger but of hate.

"Your dad made me promise not to tell, to let everyone believe you were his, and when he died you acted like you didn't want to know. I decided to accept—but that was wrong, I should have insisted. But you were, and have been for years, so angry."

"It's always been about you controlling me. I should always have known who my father was, from the beginning. What a hell of a surprise, finding out with that blood test."

"I made him a promise, John."

"So now you're going to blame dad for holding out on me? Enough, Mom! Fance and I are getting married in a few months, but I won't be inviting my parents. My true parents are dead. Dad and Grandmere. If you tell the truth now, the whole world will know I'm a bastard. Isn't that just great. Well, here's the truth from my view. I never want to see you again."

He turned and walked out. Not fast and angry, like his words. Slow and sad.

Devices The Size Of Lemon Seeds

Savik listened on the phone to Claire's tearful voice, heard her choked emotion as she explained what John had said to her.

"Sweetheart, I am so sorry," he said. He'd been appalled when his secretary showed him the tabloid, and as he listened to Claire's pain, he felt a rising nausea. "You don't have to face this alone. John has apparently had blow-ups with you before. He and I are getting along great. He needs time, naturally, to learn that he can trust me, but I'll be working on him from my end. I know he'll come around."

"Those words, coming from you, mean so much to me," she said.

He loathed himself. "Things will work out."

Immediately, he called Ronnie's private number, and got his machine. "It's Savik." He wanted to swear, but reconsidered. "You are one MF son of a bitch. Our friendship is over."

. . . . .

Savik turned off the television. He'd intended to watch the news, but there was Claire, putting up a brave and dignified front. Watching her made him feel even worse.

He stared at the blank screen, alcohol seeping into his brain cells. He never used liquor as any kind of goddamn crutch, yet he reached again for the bottle of J&B on the coffee table, knocking over the Roman *rudus*. *Shit.* He refilled his glass for the…fourth? fifth? time, drained half of it and tried to set the sword into its stand. The landline phone in the den rang and Savik dropped the sword again.

"Fuck."

He lumbered to the ringing phone. "Savik here."

"It's Ronnie. I heard your message." Ronnie said something more, but there was some kind of singing going on in the background. A choir maybe.

"Didn't catch that," Savik mumbled.

The background noise quieted as if Ronnie had shut a door. "Mormon Tabernacle Choir is performing for the President at St. Mark's. What I said was, you're off the hook. And I just wanted to say that I'm proud of what you accomplished. Your country owes you a great debt."

"Uh-huh."

"You drunk, boy?" Ronnie chuckled. "Will you still see her?"

Could he even be in Claire's presence again, let alone "see" her? He said nothing.

"Well, after the election, you'll help her pick up the pieces. Maybe you'll be like Quentin and his liberal wife."

"You're a shit, Ronnie."

Ronnie laughed. Savik hung up.

. . . . .

Hughes left the sanctuary of St. Mark's Episcopal church, ostensibly to use the restroom. His two SS men had cleared the area and were stationed outside. Hughes stood alone at a window that opened onto a balcony. He knew Savik. The guy was hooked on The Claire, all right. He punched another number.

"Yes." One syllable from the deep and recognizable voice of Hyjinx.

"Savik will still see the woman. Bugging him is our next step."

"What would you like? I can bug every item of his clothing with voice-activated devices the size of lemon seeds. I can put them in his shoes, his cell phone, his laptop, his car, up his ass if you want."

"Nanomaterials are miraculous. Let's go for all of the above."

Manage Without Me

Claire's ground floor campaign headquarters office had no windows. She'd spent no money on decorating the space beyond campaign posters and the serviceable office décor already in place. She wouldn't be sorry to see a lot less of this box.

The polls were frighteningly close, two weeks from the election. Twenty more formal speeches to give in six states. She was reviewing current trade policy with China for talking points at the Conference on World Debt in Toronto to be attended by the heads of The World Bank, The International Monetary Fund, and other key players in global finance.

Savik knocked on her door. She motioned him in. He walked over and kissed her on the cheek. "I'm going back to my office," he said. "I'll call you later."

"I thought you had a phone conference set up with Jake and John Gaylord."

Tense, frowning, he stepped away and stood by the door. "Pryce has facts I need. He refuses to share them with me—"

"That's ridiculous! I'll talk to him."

"Claire, I didn't want to put you through a hassle, so I just told Pryce to take over this time. We'll straighten it out later. I do have to go." With that, he left.

She was about to pick up the interoffice phone to summon Pryce, but he barged into her office on Savik's heels carrying a file. Before she could say anything, he slammed it on her desk and leaned over her. "I want you to stop pretending that our leak might be someone other than Savik. It's him. If I give him what he wants, there'll be some scandal on tonight's evening news about illegal campaign contributions."

She gestured for Pryce to take a seat. "Savik wouldn't make up—"

Pryce continued to loom over her. "Number one, we don't want the public to know how low our war chest is. Number two, I've overseen work on our funds to carefully keep them legal, but there are ways to spin things that would look bad in the press, and we'd lose critical time denying charges."

She stood to keep him from dominating her. "I've gone over our finances. He could publish them if he wanted to! We're completely legal."

"If Savik gets hold of a few key items, he would know exactly how to spin things so that we'd have troubles. And he'd do it so fast you'd have another feeding frenzy from the press before the day's out."

"That's ridiculous. It's insulting. It verges on . . . You don't know him like I do."

"You're dead right about that." He snatched the file, opened it, sat it on the desk facing her. "I'm not blinded by his charm and his lies. I know him objectively from his Secret Service file."

"My god, you've been spying on him."

"You don't even know who his best friend is."

"Of course I do. A former college roommate. Winn Hughes, from the Explorer's Club. They go off on horseback riding adventures and all that.'

He leaned over and pointed to a line. "Read!"

She would, but she'd feel terrible doing it. And she didn't want to give Pryce the satisfaction of bullying her. And how could there be anything serious? Pryce's righteous indignation was uncalled for. "I'll look it over."

"Read it now, Claire!"

She glared at him. "Once again, you're overstepping the bounds of our friendship."

"Okay then, I'll tell you. Winn Hughes is the CEO of CET, a laser corporation that played a big part in the success of the PeaceMaker test, a corporation that stands to make tons of money if the program is funded by Congress. Winn Hughes, AKA Winston Bramfeld Hughes is the son of Hass's Secretary of Defense, Ronald Bramfeld Hughes."

Claire felt her insides caving in. She braced her hands on the desk. There had to be some other side to this, some reason Savik had never explained his best friend's connection to PeaceMaker or to the SecDef. Maybe he was afraid she'd refuse to see him—which she would have. Savik loved her. There are things a woman knows. Savik couldn't fake the tenderness and affection he lavished on her in bed. She'd know if his expressions were phony.

"You look pale," Pryce said, "because down deep, you know this is true and Savik is the source of our leaks."

"And you look absolutely gleeful." She glared at him. "I will look the file over, Pryce. I'll give it thorough consideration."

"I just handed you a smoking gun, damn it."

"And I just assured you I'd deal with it."

"Joss was right. You're obsessed with Savik. This is the very reason people fear an emotional sway over a woman in power. Anyone who has what it takes to assume the power of the Oval Office knows what to do with a god damn smoking gun."

Her face felt so hot that her hair could ignite. "Are you saying, Pryce, that I don't have what it takes to assume power?"

"If you don't fire Savik immediately, then…yes, I am. Absolutely. You need my advice more than ever."

"I require trust, Pryce. You clearly don't trust me."

"How can you be so fucking blind about this bastard?"

"Did you not hear me say I'll handle it?" She searched his eyes. "Do you trust me, Pryce?"

"On this issue, no ma'am. I do not."

Is this really happening? A total stranger stood before her. Eighteen years of service and sharing, and he apparently thought she couldn't function unless he called the shots; he believed himself to be the true authority.

"I will decide how to handle this, Pryce, not you."

"Fine. Handle it however you want. Just make sure he's gone by the end of the day."

Resolve turned her voice icy. "We have a serious problem. Your attitude is not acceptable. We cannot work together at this level."

His jaw dropped, but he regained composure and looked as if he were about to argue. Then he turned, walked to the door, turned again and said, "Then manage without me." He slammed the door behind him.

I Didn't Send The Rose

After the blowup with Pryce, Claire hadn't been able to eat for the rest of the day. Her speech at the Conference on World Debt had been rote. Now she gazed out the window of the jet into the blackness of night. They were returning from a speech in Milwaukee.

When she allowed the possibility that it might be true that Savik had betrayed her, she thanked Providence again that she'd never told John about him.

Braveheart! She'd assumed that the newspaper article on the animal shelter had inspired one of the crazies like the man who almost killed Humvee. But could it have been through Savik that her enemies had known how to hurt her so effectively?

Memories of what he'd said and done tortured her. Had she been duped? Why had Savik hidden Winn's connections? That was the big question. The unavoidable huge one. She realized that Savik had virtually never talked about his best friend. But was that intentional? In the chaos of the election madness, she'd never noticed it, and in fact, it could have been inadvertent since she and Savik had so little private time together.

After all, Savik had come back into her life before she'd even considered running for President. That spoke in his favor. But not enough to dismiss the Secret Service dossier and his silence about Winn. All she really had was the truth in her heart of his affection. And she couldn't just accuse him of the leaks. A denial would prove nothing.

Joss gone. Pryce gone. His power-behind-the-throne attitude made their rift final, regardless of Savik's loyalty or betrayal. Adam's public appearances had to be so carefully orchestrated, and today he'd experienced another of his headaches and missed a key ceremony. And her boy…John was gone too. *And Savik…my god.*

Jake contacted the head of a PR firm he often worked with to take over Pryce's responsibilities. As she had done with Joss, Claire decided to send Pryce a letter saying that if certain specific things changed, perhaps working relationships could return to normal. She half hoped this would be the case, but what was vital was that she keep their loyalty. If they chose to, either one could derail the campaign. She'd given Joss a generous severance package and a suggestion to take a well-deserved vacation. She'd do the same with Pryce. And that was the story Jake was feeding the press: exhausted aides needed a vacation.

During the midnight SUV ride back to the Manhattan apartment, she continued to struggle over what to do about Savik. She went to bed with the miserable dilemma unresolved.

Apparently, though, she'd set the right brain cogs fitting into the turning machinery of her mind. When the alarm went off at 5:00 A.M., she awakened with a memory of a mistake in statistics she'd made once in a speech, and the memory of Savik speaking aloud a list of finance figures from what had to be a nearly eidetic memory. A plan fell quickly into place. She started making calls. One to EClaire's top computer geek, and one to the west coast, startling the woman who ran ABrightFuture.orgs's website. Claire apologized profusely for the pre-dawn call. The woman assured Claire that she was happy to help.

By 10:15 at campaign headquarters everything was in place when Savik arrived at her private office. His smile was every bit as affectionate as ever, making Claire feel as if her worry was for nothing—which was one reason she'd enlisted Connie's help. She had to see this through.

Before Savik could initiate their customary morning embrace, Connie knocked on the door, entered without waiting, and said, "Sorry to interrupt, Claire, but this is a potential disaster."

"How could anything else possibly go wrong?" Claire asked Savik, smiling and trying to sound as if nothing really bothered her.

Savik took a seat in an office chair, attentive, concerned-looking.

Connie continued. "I received an email from someone who dug up a quote of yours from a speech you made two years ago at the Joan Kroc Institute of Peace and Justice. It's archived on the Bright Future website."

"And what did I say that is such potential dynamite?"

"I'll pull it up on your computer."

Claire moved aside, and Connie spoke the website URL aloud slowly as she entered it. "abf.org/archive/alden2." She scrolled down. "Here! Let me read it. 'If I were in charge of the world's most powerful country, I'd cut military spending by 75% and thereby feed, clothe, house, educate, and heal everyone on the planet.'"

Savik looked horrified. "You said that?"

"Well, if I did, I was just, you know, exaggerating for effect. Or maybe it's a typo.

Connie said, "They're going to spin this to say you showed your true colors back then and would gut the Defense Department."

"I agree," Savik said.

Of course he did. And that was exactly what the opposition would do. To Connie, Claire said, "See if you can persuade them to pull the speech from their web archives. I'll talk to them if necessary."

Connie said, "I just hope it's not too late." She left and Claire resumed her seat.

Another knock on her door, this one unexpected.

It was Humvee, carrying a single rose in a vase and a notecard. Frowning, Humvee said, "Let me know if there's anything I should do about this."

She looked at Savik, who checked his watch. The rose had to be from him. "I have to be going, I really do," he said. "Client from hell."

The knife inside Claire stabbed new thrust of fear. "Why? We need to talk about the investors…" The words spilled out before she knew what she was doing: her heart wanted to keep him from rushing out and making a phone call that would unleash disaster. "Stay a minute."

She sniffed the rose. White, petals edged in crimson. Lovely. She read the quotation silently. "Purity upended, dipped in a spill of heart's blood, this rose of regret." The personal note said, "Sorry, Claire."

Tears blurred her vision; this was his way of confessing that he'd betrayed her. She looked at Savik, waiting for words of apology.

He stood and moved next to her. "What does it say?"

What does it say? She forced herself to focus. "You can come clean now. What exactly does this one mean?"

He frowned. "This one? I didn't send it."

Why would he deny it if it was his way to confess and apologize? "I'm confused. What about the beautiful peach roses? All the others…"

He winced. "Oh, man. I feel bad that I let you think I sent those roses. It was obvious you didn't know who they were from, and I wanted to see you, and you were so pleased by them and seemed to think I'd sent them. I just let you think I did. I'm sorry. But honestly, I haven't sent any roses."

Of course he had been sending the roses. If not Savik, then who? "You didn't send me any roses? No single roses like this one?"

"No. So you've gotten roses? Unsigned?" He did look totally baffled.

His denial seemed so convincing. "They've come in different colors, and each meant something different, with quotations and mysterious personal notes. Maman thought that someone romantically obsessed with me was or is stalking me. The peach roses were the last before this."

"Ah. I see why you think I sent them. But I didn't. I hate to leave, but I have to. We will talk again soon about these roses. I agree with your mother that it's weird. I'm sorry I lied about the roses." He put his arms around her, pulled her so close his body heat warmed her through his jacket. He kissed her lightly. "You have to believe me when I tell you, I love you."

He kissed her again, intensely. It felt like a kiss given by someone who was going away. A final kiss with an edge of regret.

"I love you," he said again. "But I do have to go."

At the door he hesitated and then turned. "Remember, I love you."

In her heart, she knew, and feared, what was about to happen.

Savik Is Our Leak

Twenty-five minutes after Savik left, Connie knocked and entered Claire's office. "The Bright Future site just had a hit. By a well-defended system."

Claire stared at Connie's pale face.

Connie added, "They're working on finding the source of the hit. It may take an hour or so. Maybe more, depending. I'm so sorry, Claire."

OmigodOmigodOmigod...Omigod... please, no...NO....

She needed air....

"Claire, can I...?"

As if hours had passed, Connie's voice jarred Claire. "Ice water," Claire said.

Connie left. Claire stared at her wristwatch. Twenty-five brief minutes. That was all. Savik had walked out of her office and reported his news promptly. Quite enough time to get a copy of the faked speech from the web.

The crimson-edged white rose taunted her, so beautiful in its vase on her desk. "You liar. You did send it, you god damn bastard." Claire stood, drew the rose from the vase and threw his pitiful gesture of apology into the trash. He'd sent a mere rose to assuage his massive guilt.

She paced and then dug in her purse to retrieve the Sharpshooter ribbon. Often during the last six weeks, when she was stressed by the campaign, she'd held it a moment for comfort and strength. Now she tossed it into the trash after the rose. She wanted to rip the office apart.

She felt dizzy. She returned to her chair and dropped into it. If no one were nearby, she'd scream. She didn't know how long she'd been sitting when the dizziness receded and she was again in contact with the world. *Everything I planned is coming out wrong.*

Connie brought the water. Claire calmly thanked her and sipped. By god, if she won this cursed election, Savik would have turned himself into a Judas for nothing. She was still strong in the polls. She would fight with no letup, with focus and energy and every ounce of brain matter.

After what had felt like a plunge into scalding water, she reached a cooler shore, backing off from her emotions into the safety and control of reality and logic. A new scenario occurred to her. She retrieved the ribbon from the trash, returned it to its place in her purse for later, and called Humvee into her office.

"Savik was our leak," she said to him, amazed at how calm she sounded. "Tell him whatever you need to persuade him to come with you to meet me at the airport this afternoon before our flight to Denver. Do not mention the leaks. Treat him as though everything is completely normal."

. . . . .

At 4:45 P.M., waiting inside the jet for the flight to Denver, Claire descended the steps and crossed the tarmac toward the Cadillac SUV that had just pulled into a parking slot in the VIP parking area of Kennedy International Airport. V-ball trailed her. The shrieking of nearby jets seemed to match the cacophony inside Claire's mind.

Humvee stepped out of the SUV and stepped close to her to be heard over the noise. "I'm dying to break some of this guy's bones." He looked at her, an eager question in his eyes. She shook her head, smiling at her own temptation.

Humvee held the SUV's driver's side rear door open, and she stepped in, sitting well away from Savik instead of close beside him. Humvee closed the door, leaving them alone, and the SUV's excellent insulation instantly muted the jet noise.

"What's wrong?" Savik moved toward her.

"Stop." She took a deep, steadying breath. He smelled, as he often did, like mountain air and sun-dried laundry. "Your most recent betrayal is already on Phyllis Colson's blog."

"Betrayal? What—"

She raised her hand. "Spare me the innocent protest. Maybe the only good thing is that that harpy, Colson, is going to look really stupid when it gets out that the quote about my 'outrageous cutback in defense' isn't on any website and never was."

"You said—"

"And you bought it. Within twenty-five minutes of your leaving my office someone in the Defense Department checked it out."

"Claire—"

"Fast work. But the posting was phony. A beta site. Not on any search engine. A shill. If it drew even one hit, we'd know who our leak was. That hit came so fast it took my breath away."

He was staring at her, a look that seemed to be of incredulous hor-ror. "What are you…? Are you saying you purposely fed me false information?"

"And right after the hit we shut the site down. It seems the false info was swiftly passed along to Colson, however."

Savik slumped and put his head in his hands.

"Please. No bullshit show of remorse. It makes me want to rip your face off. You leaked my speech. My schedules. You're responsible for Braveheart's death and the fire. For John's being dragged into public humiliation. My god, you betrayed your own—" She caught herself.

"I'll say it. It's true. I am guilty—but not to the extent you think."

Savik looked so pale, so stricken, that had she not already fortified herself for over an hour with what she'd say and what she had to do, she might have weakened.

He shook his head, avoiding her gaze. "Things are sinking in for me. Bad things." He jerked suddenly upright, patting his jacket pockets, as if he'd lost or forgotten something. "I didn't think until this moment that I might be responsible for Braveheart and the fire, but now…I might be." He looked at her, hard and intent. "If I did cause that fire or any harm to Braveheart, I certainly never intended it. I am responsible for more than I'd planned.…I thought you were a danger to the country."

"You thought I was a danger to your share of CET!"

"MONEY has nothing to do with this!"

"AND you sent the roses."

He shook his head. "No. My actions have had consequences beyond anything I'd imagined, but they don't include anonymous roses."

Claire opened her purse and took out the bit of blue ribbon with its word in gold—

Sharpshooter. She flicked it at him. It fell onto the leg of his pants. He picked it up. "I'm sure you have no idea what this is, but I have no more use for it. I never want to lay eyes on you or hear your voice again, Savik. In fact, I never want to think of you again."

She knocked on the window, and Humvee, as directed, immediately opened the door. Savik reached across the seat to stop her. He climbed out but Humvee blocked him from Claire. On leaden feet, she marched back toward the plane.

She Has A Stalker Of Sorts

As Savik turned back to the SUV, Humvee locked the doors with one click, glared at Savik, then turned and followed after Claire, effectively stranding Savik at the airport. Given the slightest provocation, the massive, tattooed Samoan looked like he would happily tear Savik apart. Savik moved away from the SUV, looked at the faded blue ribbon with its gold printing in his hand, pocketed it, and took a last look at Claire boarding her jet.

He hurried into the VIP lounge for private jet traffic, entered the men's restroom, and once inside, patted his clothing and fingered everything in his pockets. He felt nothing unexpected, yet the only explanation for what had happened had to be in his clothing. Had to be.

He stripped off his jacket and felt along the bottom hem and cuff edges, ignoring the man in a suit who eyed him suspiciously. Nothing in the hems or lining. He pressed his fingers along the collar at the back of the jacket's neck and felt a small knot. He squeezed it and the knot moved. Like it was slick.

Savik wanted to rip his jacket apart to get at the thing, but instead, folded it over his arm and walked through the lounge where a few corporate types sat waiting for their jets to be fueled and loaded. A group of young rowdies with freaky hairstyles entered carrying cases for musical instruments and settled in one corner. Savik approached the concierge—an elderly gentleman whose job it would be to provide any of these VIPs with just about anything they wanted. Savik offered his ID. "May I borrow a sewing kit?"

The man looked at Savik's card. His Adam's apple bobbed. "Why certainly, Mr. Kodaly." He opened his desk's bottom drawer and handed Savik a zippered leather case.

In the restroom's anteroom, Savik sat in a chair beside a briefcase table and used the tiny scissors from the kit to snip a few threads of the suit he'd had custom made in Hong Kong. The tiny lump he sought had been forced in between the collar's seams. He worked the hard knot out onto the surface of the table. As it hit it sounded like a plastic bead, though a tiny dot-sized microphone was black and fuzzy. The thing looked like a wood tick, just beginning to swell up.

Bugged. Almost literally.

He wanted to stomp on it. But were there more? He picked it and the jacket up and entered one of the enclosed private stalls, hung his jacket on the door's inside hook, and pulled down a mini-shelf designed to keep elegant leather briefcases off of restroom floors. He set the little bug and the sewing kit on the shelf, took his shirt and tie off, and, after more diligent fingering and snipping, discovered one of the infernal things in each item, cold fury building in him with each snip. He put his shirt back on but removed his shoes and pants. More probing and snipping, undoing expensive tailoring. It yielded a bug in his left back pant pocket.

Savik wasn't finished. He found one of the nasty things in the waistband of his underwear. His goddamn underwear. And then he found where a hole had been drilled in the heel of his shoe. It took probing with a steel toothpick on the Swiss Knife he carried in his briefcase to dislodge that one.

There were six in all, lined up on the pull-down shelf. When he returned home he'd have to check all of his clothing and shoes. Hell, he'd have to check every inch of his condo and car. In fact, he'd have to hire a professional to debug everything he owned. He felt as if he'd been infected with plague, infested with maggots.

Ronnie. Hyjinx. Goddamn those fuckers. Goddamn their asses to fucking hell.

He lined the six tiny beasties in a row in the palm of his hand. Keeping his voice low, he said. "Attention, assholes!" He paused for effect. "She outfoxed us all. And if you try and use me again, I'll have a good story for the press." He flushed the toilet, let his enemies listen a second, and then dropped the devices into the whorl.

. . . . .

Seated in heavy traffic in the back of an Uber he'd been obliged to take home, Savik's anger at Ronnie still churned inside him. He pulled out the ribbon. As soon as he'd seen it, he'd known what it was.

Sharpshooter.

Memory transported him to a sunny afternoon at an amusement park where he'd just met the most beautiful woman on Earth. When he first saw her, he could not look away. It was like the time he'd seen the De Beers Millennium Star, a 203 carat flawless diamond, on special exhibit at the Smithsonian. You knew right from the get-go you'd only be given a few fleeting moments, and then some authority would say, "Move on," and the press of the crowd would carry you away forever from a dream of impossible perfection, beauty, and sparkling clarity. You couldn't take it with you.

He'd felt like that when he saw Claire. To hide his embarrassment over his fascination with her, he'd acted like a hotshot, coming on to her with nothing to lose, wooing her with marksmanship and rock songs. And yet, amazingly, apparently she'd seen something in him too.

The day he'd dreaded since he'd proposed his plan to Ronnie, yet had dared to hope he might somehow escape, had arrived in full fury. He'd stupidly imagined that his newfound determination to be truthful and his desire to help John might have the power to undo and atone for the devastation he'd wreaked. That was not to be.

He entered the Piedmont Building, rode the elevator up to his floor. He wandered through the condo, trying to think of something that mattered. His career? What the hell for? His Roman battle models? Joss Chao's sarcastic words came back to him. "Playing with toy soldiers." He saw the framed Roman coin Adrienne had given him. The thought of going back to her bored him intensely—as did the idea of going on a date with someone new.

He was fucked.

And he'd done it to himself. With a little help from his so-called friends. Friends. Jesus. Had Winn known about the bugging?

Savik called him, and Winn claimed to be shocked and denied knowing anything, angry to even be questioned. But how could Savik be sure? When the ends justified the means, who the hell could you trust?

He poured a tall glass of J&B and found his earplugs. A professional could come in later. Now he turned on the most obnoxious acid metal rock station he could find on the radio, and began looking for bugs. Each time he found one, he put it in front of a speaker.

· · · · ·

In his study at home on Wednesday evening, twelve days before the election, Ronald Bramfeld Hughes took a disturbing call on his encrypted cell phone from his agent, Hyjinx. "Savik has gone completely toons."

Hughes listened carefully to Hyjinx's report of the electronic snooping results that morning, heard about the discredited blog, heard how angry Phyllis Colson had been at looking like a liar or a fool publicly, and listened especially carefully as Hyjinx related that Savik had found the bugs and what he'd said and done. Hughes clicked off and thought about it.

Things were seriously out of hand.

Staying encrypted, he called Cliff Stanhope, relayed most of the information. "We've tried to sabotage her, ruin her, discredit her, and she's still ticking."

"Yeah, we gotta stop this queen cunt," Cliff said, making Hughes wince.

"I have some things in place, Cliff, but I need your help. I want to explore another approach. Let's go duck hunting in the morning and work it out."

By 6:15 A.M. the Camo-Cabin was set up on the shore of Hughes's property on the Chester River, camp heater cutting the dawn chill, Winchesters loaded, coffee poured in thermos cups, decoys in place. Dolly, Hughes's Black Labrador Retriever, ran around outside the blind, excited and impatient. Two SS men remained by Hughes's Land Rover back near the cabin.

The ever-present mallards, many mergansers, widgeons, and canvas-backs flew by or swam in the river channel. All were out of season. But then, this wasn't about duck hunting. With gray morning light entering only through the blind's rifle slits, Hughes explained to Cliff where things stood. By 9:00 he and Cliff had no kills, but they'd refined what Cliff called Hughes's "Projecto Clinico." Hughes wasn't too sure the words were correct, but who cared about that?

"This is brilliant," Cliff said. "It will give Ernest the election, but it's possible that she could eventually disprove everything." Cliff looked Hughes squarely in the eyes. "The doctor will have to disappear."

Hughes nodded, a small twinge of conscience bothering him. This was a war, he reminded himself. "Actually...." He checked to make sure the Secret Service men were still out of earshot. "...I'd like her gone too. But that would be risky."

A gust of wind brought a smatter of rain on the Camo-Cabin's water-proof canvas top. Rain pinged the surface of the water. Hughes barely noticed. "Did you catch that bit about Claire getting anonymous roses?"

"Yeah. Little bell went off when you mentioned it. Seems she has her-self a stalker of sorts. Any idea who?"

"No." Hughes looked directly at Cliff, willing him to get the picture. "So, what do you think?"

"Uh huh. We just might be able to use that."

Hughes grinned and nodded.

A pair of gray-brown birds with big bills streaked in just above the surface, splashing as they hit. They righted themselves and bobbed within range.

"What are those?" Cliff asked.

"Eiders, I think. Could be there's a storm at sea. They're legal."

Cliff and Hughes both fired and hit the sitting birds. Dolly yelped and swam in after them, joyous in the fresh kill.

The Abortion Thing

John was shopping with Fance inside Bloomingdale's in Manhattan, the kind of thing he normally would hate only a tad less than facing an execution squad. This trip wasn't too bad though. Fance had made decent money as a stripper and had managed it well, saving for an education, but she'd never owned nice things. Not that John gave a shit about brands or having the best money could buy, but he could understand attraction to quality—in anything.

He watched Fance pick up a delicate crystal wine glass, her face showing not just admiration, but delight and maybe a little awe. He moved closer, lifted her hair back from her ear, and whispered, "Let's take these home."

A kid getting a first bike couldn't look more thrilled. It was the first time John had ever been able to do anything like this for anyone. He felt like a hero, not that Fance needed heroics.

Fance studied several different shaped glasses, comparing their prices.

Sometimes he felt like saying to his dad or Grandmere, who in some strange way he imagined still looked out for him, you mean I get to be this happy? Or is this a cruel trick? Is there some fine print I should read that says once you find a way to fit in on the planet, you get cancer or a bomb goes off? Somebody you care about betrays you? For some dumb reason, loving Fance dredged up all his fears and at the same time demanded whatever courage he had in him, because nothing could make him give her up.

"I was kinda hoping to have a bridal registry," Fance said, shy with embarrassment, as if she thought she was asking for the moon and had no earthly right to.

"Honey, whatever you want."

"Really?" Again, the magic in her eyes. "Then we should tell your mom soon, because her guests would be the main ones interested in the…What's wrong?"

He hadn't told Fance the full extent to which he'd disconnected from his mother. Since Fance didn't know her own father at all, she didn't think it was that big a deal that John didn't know his. He also hadn't told her the thing he'd never told anyone, that his mother had betrayed his dad, that his very existence depended on betrayal. No one could really understand how rotten this made him feel.

"Maybe we don't need so many guests," she said quickly. She looked as if she was used to handling disappointment, not like a martyr who puts a guilt trip on you, but as if disappointment was the natural way of things. "It's okay. I didn't really…."

"Hold on. I want you to have this registry thing and as many guests as you want, but I guess we need to talk."

Abandoning the glasses, they walked to Central Park, holding hands, strolling, talking among the falling leaves, late afternoon sun shining through the golds and reds, shining through Fance's hair. She no longer smoked; she'd given it up for him. She'd softened, but her toughness was never far away. He explained everything. She responded with understanding.

She held him close for a moment. "Thank you for telling me."

"Now let's go buy those glasses."

They headed back, but Fance was quiet. At a stoplight she said, "I love the bridal thing, and I won't beg you to invite your mom, but I can't judge her the way you do. I'll always hope that you'll work things out with her. And I would talk to her. I'd want her to…to be a grandmother to any children we might have someday. Can you live with that?"

Bejeezus. Children.

At least she'd said someday. The light changed and they moved on, Fance still waiting for his answer. She wanted to be a proper bride, and he was holding her back again because of his war with his mother. And Fance was still supporting him, sacrificing, yet holding her own.

He stopped her in the middle of the busy sidewalk and cupped her face in his hands. "You are such a good person. I know I need to be a better man, and I'm going to do my best. I can live with your terms, and I'll try to work something out about the wedding."

"It's Claire's son!" a woman shrieked.

"And that stripper!" another said.

John turned. A crowd of over a dozen people stood at a newsstand. All were staring at him and Fance. All were gaping.

A man called out, "Did you know about all those abortions?"

A woman held up an evening tabloid with Claire's picture and its headlines screaming, "SHE HAD THREE MEXICAN ABORTIONS!"

"BullSHIT!" John thundered without thinking, moving to shield Fance. And then he realized in that split second how instantaneously he'd known the headline was false. Not because of anything his mother had said; she was adamant that a woman had the responsibility and right to decide when she should bring a child into the world. He just knew who his mother was. She would never have used an abortion as birth control. She just wouldn't have done this.

The women with the paper called out. "It was the Truth in Government committee that discovered this."

Fance pulled him away from the staring crowd, hurried them down the nearest subway entry. As they waited she rested her head on his shoulder. "This abortion lie is terrible and vicious and ugly. I wanted her to win, John. Oh, I wanted it so much."

. . . . .

Savik sat in darkness in his condo, a drink in his hand, staring out at but not really seeing the night-lit view of Manhattan. If he were able to hold Claire now, he knew how her breathing beside him would feel. He stopped himself. Three days had passed since she'd cut him out of her life, and dreaming of intimacies with her would only throw him back into a pit of depression.

The bloody little bugs on him had Hyjinx's and Ronnie's fingerprints all over them. Not literally, of course. And now this damning accusation about abortions. A doctor, Rodrigo Beltran, had performed them, according to press reports, his whereabouts unknown. And played over and over on every TV and social media outlet was the snippet from the final debate with Hass of Claire saying, "I would never have an abortion."

If anything could destroy her chances, this seeming outright lie about this flaming hot subject was it. Could Claire have gotten even one abortion? He knew her reverence for life, her belief in personal responsibility. He didn't believe the Beltran abortion garbage. None of it.

A question pierced the emotional, alcohol-induced fog he'd created— cut right through the scotch and the mesmerizing view. Had he lost the great love of his life for a noble reason or not?

Savik had always known that warriors sometimes had to do horrible things and make wrenching compromises to win. War was brutal and its morality murky at best. But with one's country at stake, losing wasn't an option. Ronnie was an unscrupulous man, a Secretary of Defense who propped up Ernest Hass, a man who himself had no obvious moral center. Ronnie's fear of Claire being the most powerful decider in the world, however, had completely corrupted Ronnie's thinking. He had gone off a moral cliff. Willing to win against what he feared, he clearly was willing to do "whatever is necessary." Literally "whatever!" Savik had been living these months with Claire as if constantly fighting a war, telling himself it was his duty to his country. Yet who defined the battlefield? Ronnie?

And Doctor Beltran? Poor guy. Now that he'd been outed, if he wasn't already dead he soon would be. Ronnie could not allow a weak link in this enormous abortion lie to live. Savik finished off the drink and picked up the bottle to pour another. He hesitated and then set it back down. "Enough!"

He rose, turned on the reading lamp beside the sofa. He found Claire's plan on his Kindle reader, the plan he'd promised her he would read and still hadn't. This time he would read the thing, and with an open mind, painfully forced open, but wide open now.

Our Treasure…A Future Without War

At 10:50 A.M. Sunday, nine days before the election, a man at the door of the Angel's View auditorium in the new World Trade Center Tower handed Savik a program for Claire's speech to the Investor's Club. Like a groupie following a rock star, Savik had come simply because he longed to see and hear her.

Most attendees would be Wall Street insiders, but the public was allowed on a limited first-come, first-served basis. Claire sat on the raised dais wearing the red suit Savik liked. The auditorium, with comfortable seating for three hundred, looked almost full. Savik found a seat near the rear.

As he settled in, a stocky man to his left said, "You ever hear her talk before?" His minty, Tic Tac breath blasted Savik.

"Yes, I have, indeed." Savik replied.

"This election is running too damn close to call. Or it was before they found out about the abortions. In any case, most of my clients are in defense. They figure that if she wins, the economy will tank."

"I've started to doubt that. It'll simply shift in another direction."

"Oh yeah. Away from national defense. Riiiight."

The man's open cynicism, the words and tone which Savik had so often heard from Ronnie and Cliff and a host of others, sounded so familiar. He recalled a brain study his secretary had described. When subjects lying in a brain scanner were asked to analyze statements about the weather, they engaged the logical part of their brain. When they analyzed statements about politics or religion, though, the emotional part of the brain took over.

Savik would have sworn under oath before the Supreme Court that emotion had played no part in his thinking about Claire's politics, yet clearly it had. As it did for Mint Breath. Emotion, apparently, was the reason even smart people often could not draw rational conclusions when it came to religion or politics. That and probably money, which meant greed and/or fear of losing money—also emotions.

Savik asked, "Any chance you've read her plan for her administration?"

"Hell, no. Those things are dryer than a Methodist potluck."

Savik smiled. "I actually found it interesting."

The sight of long blonde hair on a statuesque young woman caught Savik's attention. Fance took a single seat still available in the third row. From the dais, Claire smiled at her. After the usual introductions, Claire stepped forward, miked so she wasn't tied to the lectern.

"I'm so pleased to be here near Wall Street, the symbolic heart of America's financial interests, and speaking to hard-nosed realists." She smiled. "I know that many of you, perhaps the majority, remain skeptical about an Alden Presidency."

She always spoke as if she'd somehow gotten to know you and was speaking to you personally. Direct eye contact, the right pause, the sincere tone. Chatty one minute, disarmingly frank the next. *Charisma!*

"I'm here to assure you, and this country, that I, too, am a hard-nosed realist."

She gave parts of the stump speech he'd heard before, pointing out that she didn't propose to institute a process that would bring world peace. "Peace implies tranquility, everyone living in conflict-free, mutual accord. I say as a hard-nose, that will never happen. We humans will always have conflicts. But we can do without wars."

A small group in front applauded, more from politeness than passion. She broached homeland security and immigration. No mention at all about whether she'd had three abortions.

She moved into her financial message. "Our best minds are paid to plan for the next war. That's necessary. But to free ourselves, to build a better future, to achieve enduring national security we must pay an equal number of great minds to plan how we will end war. Then we allocate our assets accordingly. I detest the PeaceMaker program most of all because it diverts billions of tax dollars that could eventually be trillions from programs that could defeat the appeal of terrorism to disempowered people." She leaned forward and smiled as if to share a secret with them. "And by the way, trying to use a massive space laser to fight terrorists is like using an elephant gun to kill cockroaches."

The audience laughed. A scattering of applause broke out. Mint Breath leaned close to Savik. "Well, she definitely has a point there."

Savik fidgeted, uncomfortable at finally comprehending what he should have understood months ago. While he'd read last night, he'd been eager to find holes in Claire's arguments that might affect PeaceMaker, and indirectly his investment in CET, and thereby justify his betrayal.

It hadn't happened that way.

He'd fallen into bed convinced that America's spending *was* totally out of whack. The President had never heard of a new-fangled weapon he didn't love, and loved more than less glamorous, less macho ideas for repairing roads and bridges or funding school lunches let alone anything to support assistance to other countries or efforts to promote democractic, humanitarian values. To Hass, every shadow was an existential threat. And Ronnie's kind of perpetually paranoid thinking was partly also responsible for the President's views. Savik had slept miserably, his mind wrestling with the probability that he had betrayed Claire for a dangerously provocative worldview.

Claire paused, as if thinking what to say next. "A man I know," she finally continued, "who loves this country and who has a deeply historical perspective, recently quoted Cicero who called unlimited money 'the sinews of war.' Cicero knew this two thousand years ago. If the world's economies unthinkingly continue to allocate massive sums for inventing and buying weapons and preparing for war instead of working to end wars, it's obvious what our future will hold."

Savik was stunned. She'd remembered his words and used them. She was thinking of him. A wave of emotion flooded him. She even understood his patriotism. He wished she knew he was here, listening, and that he had, at last, read her plan.

"Our generation can change history." She paused, drawing them in, challenging them, exciting them. He listened for the slightest sound. There was none. "We work, live, and die for what we treasure. Let it be said of our generation that our treasure was a future without war."

Claire took a step back. For a brief, thoughtful moment, the auditorium remained dead silent. Then Fance stood and clapped wholeheartedly. Others rose. More applause followed, at first from the polite ones but then building as others also stood.

Savik rose and clapped. Perhaps feeling social pressure, Mint Breath did too. This audience wasn't wildly enthusiastic compared to Claire's committed followers, but they seemed to be absorbing, and considering, that they might dare to risk putting hope in something extraordinary. Even history-changing. Revolutionary!

He crumpled the program, emotion swelling into a bloody urge to cry. He'd had a chance to be by her side, and he'd blown it.

By god, there had to be something he could do to make things right.

· · · · ·

Outside, Savik waited for Fance. His anger at Ronnie had hardened into resolve. When she saw him, she smiled a lovely, friendly smile, obviously unaware of Savik, the Judas.

"Hi, Mr. Kodaly," she said.

"It's just Savik, Fance. I see you're here without John.

"He's still pissed with his mom."

"I'd like to talk to him. To both of you, really."

"John's meeting me for lunch at Donohue's. It's only four blocks. Join us."

"Perfect."

A scant half-hour later all three were seated at a table in a cozy room with checkered floor, wood paneling, and red table cloths. "I want to confess something," he said. They had already ordered and were sipping iced teas as they waited for sandwiches. "John, I doubt that your mother has told you about what's happened between her and me?"

"I don't really talk to my mom."

"Then here it is. She's thrown me out. And rightly so."

Fance's eyebrows shot up. "Thrown you out?"

He told them about the bugs and Claire's leak of fake information and then the really hard part, about putting Ronnie onto John's possibly not being David's biological son.

John rose, his hands spread on the table, his chair scraping the tile floor. He glared at Savik. "You son of a bitch!"

Fance tugged at his arm. "The man is trying to apologize. Maybe you should listen."

She turned to Savik, her own face tight with anger. "Why would you do such a thing?"

Savik shook his head, searching for words to express his remorse.

"I liked you," John said.

"And I like you," Savik replied. "I have a reason for what I thought I was doing, but you'll find it pathetic."

"No doubt," John shot back as he slowly sat back down.

"I thought she was a danger to the country."

Fance crossed her arms and frowned. "That is pathetic."

John said, "Maybe we agree there. Masses of people are following my mom because she's promising them something she can't deliver. Nobody can end wars. She's not realistic. I love her . . . in my own way. And it's brutal the lies they're telling about her. But promising people to end war is dishonest and cruel. I could see how someone might consider it dangerous."

The waiter interrupted to deliver their food. Until he left there was silence.

Savik broke it. "I think maybe we're all too close to her. I think I only heard what I expected to hear, not what she is actually saying. She doesn't claim she can end war in one Presidential term or even two. But that with sufficient will and a plan, a global peace treaty could be in place much sooner than people can imagine."

"Not me," Fance said. "I've heard her very clearly. She knows exactly what she's doing."

"Fance's right, John. Claire's followers get it. Some only with their hearts, but some, like me, finally, also get it with their heads."

John hadn't touched his sandwich. He continued to glare at Savik. All the media attention had no doubt hurt him badly. If Savik could at least repair some of the horrible damage he'd caused between mother and son....

"I've betrayed your mother. She'll never trust me again. Pryce let her down and Joss has bailed on her, mostly because of me. Rumors are circulating about her running mate being unable to govern in her place. And now this abortion thing with the damn election only nine days off. She loves you, John. I can swear to you that's true. And god knows she needs you."

"That's rich." John made a scoffing sound. "What she needs is to move people around like chess pieces, and when they finally can't take it any more, they bail, like me."

Savik struggled to keep his words calm but failed. "For god's sake, man. Your mother is human. Yes, she has the need to control things. She didn't get where she is because she's lucky. She's flawed, an imperfect human. Can't you forgive whatever wrongs you feel she did you? She's a great leader, and it's going to be our sin if we don't do what we can to support her."

Again, silence.

"Look," Savik said, "I believe I know who's behind this concocted story of three Mexican abortions. That doctor did not cook this up. I don't know how I'm going to do it, but I have to try to undo the damage. And with only nine days left, our backs are to the wall. If I need you, either of you, will you help me?"

I've Been Trained

Savik had left the lunch feeling relieved that first Fance and then, reluctantly, John had agreed to help Savik with anything he needed. After pacing and scheming for two hours, Savik called John's number at 3:20 P.M. John answered.

"I've come up with a way to try to corner the guy who does the dirty work for the person I believe is behind all this. I know him only as Hyjinx. I think through him I can force the hand of these bastards, but I have to know where to find Hyjinx and be ready to follow him anywhere. Can you go to the office ASAP and trace a partial license plate number?"

"Sure," John said. "No problem. I've done similar searches."

"I once saw the son-of-a-bitch with his car. It's a 2018, black BMW, and the first four letters of the D.C. license are BD32."

"You remember the guy's license plate?"

"I've been trained."

"I'm walking out of the condo as we speak. I should be able to nail him down in a couple hours max." John clicked off.

Savik next called a car rental agency and then spent a few minutes locating the phone number for an old girlfriend, Anna, a makeup artist on Broadway who was often on tour with a company production. He prayed she was in town. She answered on the fifth ring.

After a few pleasantries and catch up, Savik said, "I need a huge favor."

"An emergency blow job?"

"I'm serious, Anna. I need you to come right away, right now actually, and fix me up with a disguise. I need to be able to stand right next to you and you wouldn't recognize me."

"Right now? This afternoon? You must be kidding."

"I'm desperate. If you can't come, can you put me onto someone who can?"

She chuckled. "Do I get a toss in the hay as payment?"

"How about knowing that you are doing something to help Claire Alden be elected President?"

"What the hell are you talking about, Savik?"

"Can you come? And make me look nondescript?"

"Now I'm curious. I would like to see your handsome face again. Be there in an hour."

It was raining. He stood in front of his city view remembering Claire's face when she'd left him. Occasional lightning flashes cut ragged, platinum strokes through the dark gray of the sky. If he was wrong, and Hass's people, not Ronnie, were responsible, all of Savik's effort would be a futile waste of time. The alternative, of course, was to do nothing. Not an option at all.

Money. He'd need a lot of it. In the den he opened his hidden floor safe and extracted an envelope holding cash. He counted it—a little over five thousand in one hundred dollar denominations and five hundred in twenties. He set the envelope with its entire contents on his desk. He fetched his digital camera and placed it next to the money. Since he had to be ready to go anywhere, he put his passport in the envelope as well and then closed the safe.

Anna arrived with a massive canvas bag. He hung her raincoat, with its fresh smell of rain, in the entry closet. She grabbed him and kissed him on both cheeks. "I've actually missed you, you bastard."

"I'm extremely grateful, Anna. You're a genius with this stuff."

"Why the rush? And can I at least have a glass of wine?"

"Of course." He went into the kitchen with Anna trailing. She asked for the open Cabernet. He poured. "I don't exactly know what I'm doing or when I will do it. I just have to be ready to act immediately."

She gazed at him a moment. "Claire Alden means something to you personally."

Savik nodded and walked with the wine in one hand, fetched her bag, and brought it back to his small kitchen table.

"Okay, none of my business." Anna pulled stuff out—a big mirror, makeup in various shades, a wig with a man's haircut and gray hair of medium length, a matching upper lip small mustache, several makeup brushes and pencils and miscellaneous containers. "We'll start by changing the shape of your face."

She set up the big mirror, telling him to sit, then opened a square tin box that held wedges of plasticene. She made him stuff four of the things, two uppers and two lowers between the cheeks and the gums. "Feels really weird," he complained.

"You'll get used to it."

She had him frown and scrunch his face, and then she sponged his skin with a liquid makeup a shade or two paler than his own skin and followed with a powder, so that when he relaxed his face, dark "wrinkles" appeared. He looked at least ten years older. She then sprayed his face with something she called "fixier."

With a tiny brow comb, she painted in a little white in his eyebrows and then demonstrated how he should put on the wig and mustache. He studied the change in the mirror. He felt like a chipmunk. His cheeks actually were plumped out in a sort of distinctive manner, but he had to admit, he looked a lot different and even felt himself starting to disappear. He felt the first real rush of confidence that he could pull this off.

"To be really nondescript, clothing can hide you more than anything," she said.

He led her into the bedroom, a bit nervous about that move, but Anna seemed to have accepted that this was not a rerun of old times. She rummaged in his closet. "You haven't explained how I'm helping elect Claire," she said, her hands passing over suits, sport coats and shirts. "I'd like to think it's true, and not just a silly ploy to get me here."

"You heard about the abortions yet?"

"Sure. Makes me very sad."

"Don't believe it. And what you're doing is going to help me prove it isn't true."

She beamed at him. "I knew it. I just knew it wasn't true."

She finally chose the oldest jacket in the closet, a heavy, much-worn tan corduroy, a blue-gray golf shirt, and khakis. She pulled a big pad with straps out of her bag to give him a pot belly to match the chubby cheeks. He tried everything on, and she added a pair of ordinary black-frame glasses with a slight tint to obscure his eyes.

"Done," she said. "Just keep your mouth shut, and your own mother won't know you. You have a very distinctive voice."

They parted with a friendly hug. "You save Claire's reputation and you'll be an even bigger cowboy than I thought," she said as she waved at him from the corridor outside.

His phone rang soon after. John sounded pleased. "The guy's name is Wesley Mott." He gave Savik Hyjinx's street address in Alexandria, Virginia, and also a land line phone number for W. Mott at that address. "I couldn't get a cell number. If you need anything, call. My phone'll be on all the time."

Savik thanked him and from his cell phone with its caller ID blocked, Savik tapped in the number immediately and listened to Hyjinx's message. No pickup. Was the guy not home? Or monitoring calls? Now what? All this makeup for nothing?

It didn't matter. He still had to keep trying. MapQuest gave him a route and driving time to the Alexandria address, a little over four hours. He packed his essentials in a shoulder bag. Now seven in the evening, the rain and lightening were still putting on a show. Savik called again. No answer. He turned on the news. They were saying that the doctor who performed the abortions had done so in a clinic in Tijuana, Mexico, and that John's birth occurred because the doctor talked Claire out of having a fourth abortion. They even showed a picture of the doctor.

Savik snatched up his cell phone, and quickly found another TV station showing the alleged abortion doctor's picture. Savik snapped two quick photos of the doctor and memorized the features of Dr. Rodrigo Beltran, the lying son of a bitch.

He dialed Wesley Mott/Hyjinx every half-hour and at 8:30, smiled grimly when a familiar voice said hello. *Fabulous!*

Savik clicked off, hoping his mark would stay home for the rest of that Sunday night. By nine o'clock he was in the rental car headed for Virginia. He should reach Hyjinx's place by one or so in the morning.

His mind churned as the windshield wipers thumped back and forth. He kept shaking his shoulders to try to keep loose. Doubts crept in. He turned onto the New Jersey Turnpike thinking he was probably an idiot. The good doctor was probably already dead. Or what if Ronnie dispatched Hyjinx on a mission, some unrelated mission, while Savik was driving?

He forced the doubts aside and, despite the rain and potentially very slick road, increased his speed.

Señor Ko-dalee?

The drive seemed to take longer than four hours, but it was approaching one o'clock A.M when Savik reached the outskirts of Virginia. He had outrun the rain. At 1:30 he cruised past a darkened bungalow in Alexandria, actually a suburb of Washington, D.C.

After parking around the corner in a spot that allowed a view of the garage, he lowered the passenger window enough to provide fresh air and used the beer-belly cushion for a pillow. He would close his eyes but remain alert to any sound of the Beamer leaving before he made the call at 6:00 A.M. that would promptly reveal all.

At 5:45 he moved closer to Hyjinx's bungalow, passing scattered cars parked along the empty, quiet street. He waited, the camera in his lap. At five minutes to six he couldn't wait another minute. With his cell number still blocked, he dialed Ronnie's private home phone number.

"Who the hell is this?" Ronnie growled when he picked up on the second ring.

"I know you're behind this damned abortion lie, Ronnie, and for what it's worth, I woke you up good and early to tell you that I know you're not going to get away with it."

Rustling noise on the other end. "What the hell, Savik—"

"I may not be able to prove you're guilty, but I just found out that your Dr. Beltran is offering to sell information to Claire's people. And I wouldn't be surprised if, one way or the other, the shit doesn't eventually land on you."

Savik tapped his cellphone off. He realized he was breathing fast and took several deep breaths. He stared at the bungalow, praying. If Hass's people were the guilty party, Ronnie would simply be puzzled as well as pissed at being awakened, and nothing would happen. If the abortion doctor was already dead, the trail also dead-ended. Again nothing would happen. But if Hyjinx rolled out...well, then, Savik was in business.

Did he imagine it or did he hear the sound of a phone ringing in the bungalow? He was way too far from the house. The sound had to be wishful thinking. He stuffed the fake belly into place against his abdomen and waited. *C'mon, c'mon....*

At 6:26 Hyjinx bolted out of the house carrying an overnight bag. Savik suppressed a rebel yell. It could just be a coincidence, but he didn't think so. Using the camera's telephoto function, he snapped five or six shots of Hyjinx in his gray Italian-cut suit and black T-shirt before the bastard shut his car door and sped off.

Savik's heart kept up a steady pounding as he trailed reasonably far behind the BMW. Any minute Hyjinx might catch on that he was being followed. Within a couple of blocks, however, they entered a freeway and Savik's heart rate settled a bit.

They parked in long-term parking at Dulles. At the American Airlines ticket counter, Savik, sweating under the belly padding, moved behind his quarry. Hyjinx turned around and scanned the crowd. Savik could hardly believe it, but Hyjinx looked right past him. The disguise did its job.

On the way in Savik had snatched up a car rental brochure. He placed two hundred-dollar bills inside, their tips showing slightly. He studied the thin and extremely bored-looking ticket agent.

Hyjinx left. Savik stepped to the counter, subtly placed the brochure and his credit card before the man, and spoke softly. "I want a ticket for the same flight and destination as what the guy before me purchased."

The man subtly eyed the brochure, slipped it into his pant pocket, and said, "So, you want a ticket to Cancun via Miami?"

Savik gave the man a smile. "Sounds about right."

Savik passed through security and entered the public lounge for the flight to Miami to find Hyjinx drinking coffee, eating a donut, and reading a paper. Their flight took off on time at 8:35 A.M.

Cancun. Apparently the good Dr. Beltran had spirited himself off to a resort or somewhere in the surrounds. The man would have to be pried away, kept safe, and leaned on to tell the truth. Five thousand dollars simply wouldn't do all that.

In the forty minutes before their connecting flight from Miami to Cancun, Savik called his broker and instructed the broker to wire a cashier's check made out to Rodrigo Beltran for the total sum of cash Savik had in a money market fund, a little over ten thousand, to be delivered, discreetly, to Savik at the Cancun arrival gate.

Then he managed to reach Leo Lombardi. If he was going to beat any bribe Ronnie had offered Beltran, he would need a lot more money. "You once told me that you know someone in Italy with deep pockets and lots of influence there," he said. "I'm onto a lead to disprove these abortion lies. But I need cash to counter a bribe. Can you help?"

"Let me assure you most strongly," Leo said, "that my Italian contact would find helping to clear Claire a worthy investment. I can personally assure you that you'll have whatever you need—up to one million. Beyond that, you must call me."

One million! The amount surprised him. He laughed. "I think I can achieve what I want at something below a million."

"Fine," Leo said. "Please keep me informed."

Savik's flight arrived in Cancun at 3:45 local time. He removed his jacket in the warm air of the plane's debarking tunnel. Clearly the doctor was alive or Hijinx wouldn't be here. Hyjinx could lead him to the man. By god, there was a fair chance of success. The bad news was that the bloody stuffed pillow was already starting to make his belly itch like crazy. They entered the terminal.

"Señor Ko-daLEE?"

Shit!

Hyjinx, a few paces ahead, looked in the direction of the man who had called out Savik's name. Savik caught the man's attention and nodded slightly to indicate they should move to the side. Apparently the man from the bank hadn't received or hadn't understood the message that discretion was essential. The airport was crowded, however, and the din of voices might have obscured Savik's name. Hyjinx kept going as if he hadn't heard anything. The Mexican man's pronunciation had been bad—maybe unrecognizable.

Savik flashed ID, accepted the cashier's check, and hurried to follow Hyjinx, praying that the courier hadn't blown his cover. He had now lost Hyjinx in the crowd. Suppressing panic, he snagged a taxi and immediately showed the driver Hyjinx's picture on his cellphone camera's small screen. Have you seen him?

"*Bien feo, ese,*" the cabbie offered, shaking his head. *Really ugly, this guy.*

Win Or Die!

"I have bad news, Claire" Jake said as he entered the sitting room of her suite at the Omaha Hilton. "I do hate to dump even one more downer on you."

She glanced at her watch. 4:40. She'd told the investigator she'd hired that she'd call him at 4:45. He had a team working to find out who put the Mexican doctor up to making a false abortion report. At 5:15 the limo would arrive to take her to her next speech venue, the Omaha Civic Auditorium's Mancuso Hall. "I have five to spare. What's up?"

"The guys watching over Adam say there's something severely wrong with him. He's having big mood shifts, from depressed to angry, and a lot of the anger is directed at you. He still holds you responsible for keeping him 'penned up.' To them, his behavior has grown seriously unstable. He's going in for more tests."

Ye gods, what next? Not one workable idea came to mind as to what to do.

Jake continued. "I had them cancel all his public appearances, saying that he's come down with a severe case of the flu. We have to hold out at least until after the election."

"Eight days. That's a pretty long bout of flu."

"But not unreasonable. It won't stop speculation but it'll keep him away from the press."

She glanced at her watch again. "I have to make a call." Jake left, and Claire reached the private investigator.

"Bad news" he said. "His receptionist said the good doctor is on vacation."

"I'll just bet. Using an alias in some remote place."

"No doubt. The nurse who first told us she was sure you had never been to their office has changed her story to say that a woman in a hat and sunglasses could have been you. We're looking into any threats or sudden wealth that may have come her way."

"What about the so-called Committee for Truth in Government being somehow linked to the doctor?"

"All we've come up with is that it's financed from an offshore outfit in the Caymans, Geiga Bank. We're following a few public committee members and looking into their finances as well. Nothing dramatic yet to take to the press, unfortunately."

Nothing to combat the horrible lies. She hung up and immediately Connie entered the sitting room, clearly excited.

"A staffer at ABrightFuture just called to say that they're putting enormous resources into digging into the story. That's her word. Enormous. Since it's good news, Jake thought you needed to hear it right away."

"Call back and thank ABF for me."

"But here's some more possibly good news. Reporters from the Washington Post and New York Times are asking questions all over the place. Like someone has maybe fed them a bone with some meat on it. Maybe they'll expose this abominable lie in time to help us."

Or not. *Win or die.* Savik had once shown her a model battlefield of Julius Caesar fighting Pompeii against ghastly odds and said that Caesar had won mainly because the choice was win or die. She shouldn't think about Savik. Or John....

Claire wouldn't die—in all likelihood—win or lose this election, but if she did not win, things that were dear to her could. All because of ruthless bastards who had concocted this lie. Win-or-die was exactly how she felt.

She checked her watch. Sighed. Stood, and to Connie said, "Time once more to face the public, the independent people of Omaha."

Bet They Used To Make Sacrifices Out Here

Savik rode in the back of a taxi heading north from the Cancun airport, discreetly following Hyjinx's taxi. Unlike the tourist traffic, Hyjinx's cab turned north onto a highway that ran away from the road to the southern end of Cancun's barrier island. There a hundred hotels, many four-and five-stars, enjoyed phenomenal real estate directly facing the Caribbean.

Savik's driver's first name was Salvador—Savior. He'd certainly saved Savik from the instant failure of losing Hyjinx. "I'll pay extra if we don't lose them," Savik had said, "But don't get close."

"El Feo is the fare of my friend Chui, " the cabbie, Salvador, had said. "I can follow easy."

As he also turned north, the cabbie said, "So *El Feo* is no here for pleasure but for beeznis?" He continued to refer to Hyjinx as *El Feo*, the ugly one.

"Yes, business." *The business of killing.* This was going to be tricky, the timing critical. Wringing the truth out of the doctor was the whole point of Savik's chase. Savik needed to let Hyjinx lead him to their mutual target—before Hyjinx could murder him.

They were now speeding past a swampy mangrove preserve. Low dry tropical forests backed buildings and houses, and soon a tract of modest homes widened into suburbs. Traffic intensified as they passed a shopping mall and then a *corrida*, a bull ring.

Hyjinx's cab turned left onto a road numbered 180. Salvador followed. Civilization grew suddenly sparse. After a couple of miles, the cab signaled right, visible from the substantial distance Salvador kept between them. "Only roo-eena this way," he said. "El Meco."

"Roo-eena? El Meco?"

"Like Chichen-Itza? But no so much touristas."

Ah. A ruin. Why would Hyjinx go to a ruin? "Drop back a little more, *por favor.*" Maybe Hyjinx had lured Beltran out here. To avoid witnesses? A green van full of tourists was also headed toward the ruins. "Stay well behind the van, Salvador. It'll hide us."

The road curved east and onto a dusty road. Soon the van parked near a small pyramid. Two other cars were present, but Hyjinx and his cab were nowhere in sight.

Goddamn, had he lost Hyjinx?

"Your man. He gotta be here. Maybe there?" Salvador pointed west toward the main structure. "More parking over there. But we go there, he see us."

Hyjinx was definitely up to something. This was not a culture stop. Savik grabbed his shoulder bag and gave Salvador a hundred dollar bill. "If I'm not back in…say a half hour, you probably should leave. And *muchas gracias*, Salvador. Good driving."

Savik stepped out of the air-conditioned cab into warm, humid air, his wig, mustache, and belly itching maddenly. He approached a some-what rounded pyramid, maybe two stories tall. A black vulture soaked up sun at the top, a perch from which Savik might scan the stone parade ground the jungle was trying to reclaim. But that perch would expose him.

A cluster of people, tiny in the distance, descended the stairs of a grand temple at the other end of the complex. No one nearby. Gray moss hung like curtains in the stand of trees that blocked one side of the small pyramid.

Savik approached the large pyramid circuitously, hiding in the shad-owy greenery. Birds called against the high-pitched drone of cicadas. A howler monkey hooted. Savik's skin crawled, as if someone or even something were watching him.

He squatted to pick up a jagged rock, and his shoulder bag fell, the bag with his money. It and the disguise slowed him. He yanked off some hanging moss from trees, wrapped his shoulder bag, jacket, and fake paunch in it, hid the bundle under a broad-leafed shrub, and darted back into the low forest edging the ancient parade grounds.

Where was Hyjinx?

The great temple, maybe fifty yards away now, rose like a small moun-tain, a complicated tiered structure with crumbling stone doorways and massive carvings. A lone figure ascended on the south side, a man in a black T-shirt and gray pants.

So this must be a rendezvous. Savik's plan was working. The doctor would show up, probably expecting some bonus, and Savik would rush in, stop the assassination, and then wring the truth from the doctor. He sprinted over ancient stone paving, avoiding tree roots and vines.

Sweat bathed his face, back, and stomach as he circled around to the north face of the temple, now dark with long afternoon shadows. Savik gripped his stone, an awfully crude weapon, and scrambled upward to the level having tunnel-like entrances into the temple. What had Hyjinx promised the doctor to lure him to such an isolated place? A man's body could easily be hidden at least for a time in one of these dark shafts.

In moments, Savik reached a stone godhead, hid behind it, and scanned for his quarry. And there the scumbag was, leaning against the temple wall, pushing down on the tops of black gloves to check his watch. Apparently the doctor hadn't yet arrived. Savik lost sight of Hyjinx as Savik climbed up to the next level, hurried along the eastern face, slowed, crouched, and silently eased over to the ledge a few feet above to be in position to defend the doctor.

Hyjinx wasn't there. Which meant—

A figure rushed Savik from behind the godhead at the other corner. With split-second reflexes, Hyjinx dodged the blow Savik aimed at Hyjinx's jaw, instead hitting the thug's ear. Hyjinx's slashed ear spurted red. The two of them fell together. Their momentum allowed Hyjinx to land on top. Savik forced a roll. They toppled off the ledge. Savik dropped the rock, pushed off the wall with both hands to land on his feet. Scrambling for footing, he dodged blows and got in a few.

Then a solid hit in the ribs knocked his breath out. Those gloves on Hyjinx…sap gloves, loaded with steel shot. Another clock to the jaw with the shot-loaded gloves and Savik was down. A strong elbow ground his cheek into the stone. Wire tightened around his neck.

The son-of-a-bitch chuckled as Savik writhed beneath him. "*Hola*, Gray Hair. Losing Claire aged you, huh? Bet they used to make sacrifices out here."

Pain searing a circle around his neck, Savik collected his strength, heaved, and bucked Hyjinx off, loosening the horrible wire cutting off his air. Red sparks flashed. He gasped as blood flooded back into his head. And then a hammer-like thump to the back of his head left only blackness.

I'm Here To Make An Offer

"Señor?"

Savik's head throbbed as he squinted his eyes open. A shadowed figure spoke.

"You okay, *señor?*"

"Unh…" Blackness surrounded him.

"I call *Emergencia?* Maybe the *Federales?*"

Savik put a hand to his head. "Unh-uh…" Savik remembered Hyjinx ambushing him. The temple. The doctor? Probably never even here; the trap had been set for Savik Kodaly.

"*El Feo* got you good."

"Salvador?"

"*Si, señor, a sus ordenes.* I wait twenty minutes and look for you. I have the…binocular. I see *El Feo* attack you. You fight. I run here. He hit you on head. I am no close, but I yell, and he roll you inside *El Meco* and run away."

Savik sat up in the semi-darkness. His eyes had adjusted, and he spit out the plasticine in his cheeks and forced his mind past the throbbing pain at the back of his head and the burning in his neck. He moved his feet, his arms. They still worked. He faced a rectangle of deep blue sky and the entrance to a stone corridor. He snatched the wig and mustache off. Salvador, eyes bulging at the transformation, helped him up, and they worked their way outside and down the pyramid.

"You're a good man, Salvador," Savik said. "Thank you. I'm sure *El Feo* would have killed me if you hadn't come."

The man was pleased to be useful. Savik breathed deeply, regaining his strength as they returned to the cab. "I'll pay you well to find out where your friend Chui took *El Feo.*"

Salvador agreed to try. Savik stopped to pick up his jacket and shoulder bag, and soon sat in the cab listening to the irritating static from the dispatch. Hyjinx had a twenty-minute lead.

"Aay!" Salvador said. "*Lo siento, señor.*"

"What? Did they lose him?"

"No. He going to *Casitas de Ixchel al norte.*" The cab took off as Salvador explained. "Dispatch say *El Feo* make Chui cause *accidentes.* Now road is blocked *al norte.*"

Savik swore.

"I take you to Punta Sam," Salvador said. "Maybe you rent a boat. Pass the traffic."

"*Sí!* Let's go!"

Salvador took local roads and streets, talking as he drove at reckless speeds. Savik, he explained, should go straight north up the coast. "And when you see the *palmas* with the white paint around them and *ramadas* on the playa, you got right place. Tie boat there. I drive up. Meet you later."

"*Gracias, hermano*," Savik said.

The cabbie raised a fist of solidarity. "Chui takes *El Feo* the long way to the *Casitas de Ixchel*. Gives you more minutes."

Ten minutes later Salvador drove to a pier where Savik might rent a boat. The best he could come up with instantly was a jet ski.

Savik thanked Salvador, stowed his shoes and bag in a compartment of a Kawasaki jet ski, roared away from the jetty, and headed north as the sun was setting.

Ocean spray soaked his clothing, chilled him. The land receded as he pounded at top speed across waves, then turned north following the coastline. His destination lay roughly two and a half miles away. The beauty of a reddening sky, the smell of the sea, and the shine of the distant white beaches brought a longing to come to this beautiful place with Claire. *I'm doing this for you, Claire. I owe you this.*

Savik soon approached three little jetties with the *ramadas* on the beach behind them, and the palm tree trunks were painted white, lit by floodlights. Boats and miscellaneous watercraft were docked for the night. Sandy-haired teenagers climbed out of a paddleboat, laughing.

A man stepped out onto the dock from an eighteen-foot motorboat carrying fishing gear and a fish. His hairline receded, white hair. Beltran.

Lucky man, Savik thought. Savik had found him before Hijinx. At thirty feet from the shore, Savik watched the doctor disappear on a path that curved into a jungle of palms and flowering bushes separating the private bungalows. Savik's heart stopped a moment, but then the doctor reappeared, heading for the door of one of the *casitas*.

Savik was closing in on the beach as a shadow near the door sprang from behind a bush, stretching something taut and wrapping it around Beltran's throat. Beltran dropped his fish and gear. Hyjinx dragged the doctor by the neck behind the *casita*.

Savik roared the jet ski up onto the shore and raced after them barefoot. At the corner, Hyjinx saw Savik. He dropped the limp doctor. He side-kicked Savik who deflected the blow. Savik grabbed the opposite leg and lifted, flipping Hyjinx. The man rolled and rose to a crouch. Savik landed a solid punch to his jaw. Hyjinx fell against a glass-topped patio table next to a lighted Jacuzzi. The table tipped backward and crashed, shattering the glass.

As Hyjinx reached for a glass shard, Savik kneed him in a gut as solid and tough as gristle. Using one hand, Hyjinx grabbed Savik by the hair and slammed Savik's jaw with the other hand. Stunning white pain added to earlier pain.

Hyjinx pushed Savik off, picked up a small stone figurine by the Jacuzzi shaped like a fish, and grabbed it like a club. Savik, on his feet again, lowered his head and charged wildly, forcing Hyjinx to miss Savik's head, smashing the stone fish against a terra cotta pot that exploded with a bang.

The man deflected Savik's charge and shoved him, with a mighty splash, into the Jacuzzi. Steam blurred the stone woman that poured water from a jug into the pool beyond. And then his head was forced underwater, Hyjinx straddling his back.

Savik, craving air, squirmed, floundered. One foot found purchase against a step. He shoved upward with all his strength, stood, and gasping, flung Hyjinx against the stone waterfall. A look of shock came over Hyjinx's face, blood gushed from the back of his head into the water. He went limp and slid into the pool on his butt, water up to his neck. He'd hit what Savik realized was a headdress of the moon goddess.

Gasping, Savik heaved himself out of the Jacuzzi. Beltran was not where Hyjinx had dropped him, but the white line of the garrote's cord and handles showed up against the dark grass. Savik grabbed it and returned to Hyjinx. He pulled the slug out of the water, rolled him onto the grass, and used the garrote to tie unconscious Hyjinx's hands behind his back.

Panting, Savik faced the Caribbean where a full moon was rising directly in line with the goddess statue. He rushed back to the *casita*. Through a window he saw the doctor inside throwing things into a suitcase. Savik entered without knocking. Beltran turned and pointed a gun at him.

Savik held up his hands in a *halt* gesture. "Put the gun away, you idiot. I saved your pathetic life, though you sure as hell don't deserve it. I'm here to make you an offer."

A Classic Case Of Moral Gray

By 2:15 in the morning Savik had made it back to New York. He made it to the office at his usual hour. Collar and tie loose to ease the tender red line around his neck, head throbbing despite painkillers, and aching all over as if he'd been beaten with a board, Savik nevertheless felt great. Redeemed.

The scumbag doctor was safely on his way to Rome. He hoped Hijink was securely in the custody of Mexican police, not altogether a sure thing given Ronnie's major Mexican connections. Savik had pried from Jake Shifrin that at 12:30 Claire would have a private lunch with Leo Lombardi. If Savik could join Claire and Leo, Savik figured he could personally give her the good news and at the same time thank Leo for the money and the Italian sanctuary for Beltran.

At 12:25 P.M. he climbed out of a taxi in front of the intimate Chichi's Garden Restaurant. It was Tuesday. One week before Election Day. Possibly too late to save Claire's candidacy. He had, however, done his best.

What he wanted was to tell Claire himself about the doctor's recorded confession, admitting that he had been paid by Hijinx to lie, and see her reaction. Hell, just to see her. Maybe his efforts in Cancun would soften her anger. A Secret Service man and Humvee stood on station outside the restaurant's front door. Humvee held out a hand to block Savik's path. "She said you can't see her, sir."

"Jake told me about the Lombardi lunch. I just need a few minutes with them both."

Humvee didn't move. Savik heard a car door slam and Jake walked up. "What's up, Savik?"

"I have to see Claire. And the head of her Secret Service team."

Jake shook his head and Humvee lowered his arm, obviously figuring Jake outranked him.

Jake said, "You haven't figured out you aren't welcome?"

"Very shortly," Savik countered, "the Secret Service will have in their hands proof that the story about abortions was a lie."

Savik quickly explained about Ronnie, Hyjinx, his own visit to Cancun, the bribe he'd paid, and the doctor's trip to Italy. There he would soon record a message implicating The National Committee for Truth in Government, explaining that he had been paid by Hyjinx.

And further, that Savik knew for certain that Hyjinx did dirty tricks for Ronnie Hughes. Humvee's and Jake's mouths dropped open at the same time. Their eyes had opened wider with every revelation.

"Goddamn it, Savik. I don't know whether to beat the shit out of you or hug you." Jake went inside the restaurant and returned after a few minutes. "We're grateful, Savik. V-ball is passing the information to the head of the Secret Service. You have proof Hughes was involved, or will it just be your word?"

"The doctor's confession plus my testimony is sufficient proof you'll need to prove Hyjinx set the whole thing up. I don't have solid proof that Ronnie ordered it, but I'll testify convincingly that his call ordered Hyjinx to do the job. That part may not stick though."

"And I doubt this Hyjinx will dump on our SecDef. Too bad."

Savik kept his voice even, almost afraid to ask. "What did Claire say?"

"She's relieved to hear about the confession, and thanks you sincerely, but—"

"Are you going to let me in?"

"No. She was quite specific about that. I'm sorry."

It felt like Hyjinx had just slugged him again. If bringing news this good hadn't softened her anger, Savik couldn't think of anything that would. Jake was staring at him, resolute, a rock barrier. Savik turned and stepped to the curb to hail another cab. What a fool he'd been to think Claire would relent.

. . . . .

At a private reception in the stately Andrew Carnegie library, the provost of Carnegie-Mellon University stood beside Claire, introducing her to guests. Claire could smile again without feigning warmth. Though she couldn't allow Savik back in her life, she felt as if a war inside had ended. His remarkable heroics touched her and almost healed the places where she'd kicked herself for caring for him. Miserable poll numbers still hung over her like a funeral pall, but she'd released her fate to the winds, and what followed was a welcome sense of liberation replacing a tight fist that had been pounding her spirit flat.

An ebony-black, nattily-dressed African-American man with a goatee stepped forward with a stunning woman, Dr. Crispus Symes and his wife, Dr. Adella Symes. Both were University benefactors also on the faculty. Behind the two doctors, Jake, Connie, and Humvee stepped into the room. All three were grinning. Connie gave Claire a big thumbs-up sign.

The female Dr. Symes said, "I assume you've heard the good news? My daughter phoned while we were waiting to meet you. She said the bloggers are saying not only that the dreadful abortion thing was a lie, and possibly paid for by some organization that has connections to our Secretary of Defense, who everyone knows is an ally of President Hass. That abortion doctor in Mexico has confessed that he took a twenty-five thousand dollar bribe."

Jake stepped up. "I'm afraid Claire must move on," he said, smiling.

Claire excused herself and headed to the door with Jake and the Secret Service detail running interference. Humvee and Connie joined their parade and Connie hugged Claire.

"We have fabulous news!" Connie said.

"Is it true?" Claire asked Jake. "Hughes has been implicated?"

"I just heard the weasel being interviewed on Fox. I quote, 'Just because I fear what an Alden presidency would do to the national security of this country does not mean I would engage in this low sort of behavior. I deplore the overzealousness of The National Committee for Truth in Government.'"

Connie and Humvee laughed. Connie said, "He can deplore all he wants, but our SecDef is screwed. ABrightFuture came out with it first, that Hughes also has financial ties to PeaceMaker through his son's company, CET. No wonder he fears Claire. The bloggers are onto it now."

Jake said, "The big papers won't be far behind. Hughes may escape prosecution but his career is going to tank. I talked to Janice," Jake continued. "A Bright Future received sudden infusion of money from six sources, especially the Lombardi group. They are using it to place TV and media spots debunking the abortion lie. And just between us, she felt there was something odd about how some of the money came in all at once and without clear attribution, but clearly there is no way to give it back."

Claire felt almost light-hearted. "It seems we have a secret benefactor. One who gives money without any hope of attaching strings. A very rare breed."

Jake spoke as they all piled into a stretch limo. "Janice has gone out on a limb legally to take the money, but she's worried the media won't reflect the moral outrage that could make the critical difference. We should have some polling results by tomorrow."

"So we're still alive?"

"Oh, most definitely. Alive and kicking up our heels."

. . . . .

Speeches, interviews, plane flights, and bad food crammed Claire's final days before the election, all on very little sleep. Poll numbers rose after the doctor's confession, but they still placed Claire and Hass neck and neck. Four days to go and reporters clamored for reports on Adam's "flu." Tabloids printed lurid stories of a secret heart attack that left him in a coma.

At the airport in Richmond, Claire and the team gathered over coffee and muffins. "If Adam had shown his true colors before the Convention," Jake said, "We could have asked Governor Nash to be your running mate. Nash would have delivered the Midwest."

"Adam is one of the main reasons I decided to run," Claire said hotly. "I refuse to believe that he's changed irreversibly. His doctors just aren't running the right tests or something."

"We have to do something," Jake said. "You're going to have to tell him that if you win, you'll be revealing his 'health' problems publicly and announcing a replacement immediately. I vote Nash. In fact, we should contact Nash right away."

"I'm rescheduling Miami," Claire said. "We'll turn the plane around and head back to New York. I'll talk with Adam personally. We'll have our video people film me visiting him in his jammies looking really flu-like, if we have to."

. . . . .

Security and staff all waited in the entry hall to Adam's Manhattan penthouse. Claire was alone with her old friend in his elegant living room surrounded by a lifetime's collection of Asian art and furniture. The white stubble on his jaws aged him, and in his jogging suit he lost his ambassadorial élan. She smelled alcohol on his breath. His eyes were red and watery. He sat silent, staring at her as if battling a smoldering anger. He hurled a stapled report at her. "There's nothing wrong with my heart!" he said. "Read it! Toss it out to the press! Put it on a website!"

Tears came to Claire's eyes just watching this brilliant statesman in such inner torment.

Dear God, if she were elected and anything happened to her, Adam clearly could not function. Her duty was inescapable. If elected, she would replace him at once.

Adam ran his fingers through his unwashed white hair. "Do what you have to do," he said.

"I'm so terribly—"

"Please spare me! Just tell me what you need."

She explained. He wordlessly donned a robe and posed for the video crew Claire brought in, raising an absentee ballot. Bad case of the flu, the press was told again.

. . . . .

Twenty-six hours before the polls would open, Claire lay in bed in a Miami hotel room wide awake with the power of one thought. She didn't want Governor Nash as her co-pilot. She'd already forbidden Jake to contact him. But what exactly should she do if she won? Who did she want? The public would go into a tailspin.

Phyllis Colson and the Republicans would kill her on the issue. They'd say she'd undoubtedly known before the election that Adam was faltering. She'd cheated the public, they'd say, and they'd be right. Here was a classic case of moral gray...of doing what was for the better good. Should she win, she'd face a thousand such choices.

Her cell phone buzzed. It was Humvee. "Adam Forsythe has been missing since 6:30 last night after dinner. Jake has people on it, trying to find him. I am praying that the press does not find out."

A Black Rose

Election Tuesday at last. At quarter to nine in the morning, accompanied by her security detail, Humvee, and Florence, who was carrying Alex in his travel cage, Claire arrived at Tabor Towers. A suite of rooms awaited them, as did the ballroom and a "campaign room" with TV monitors and phone banks.

She'd already voted and her schedule was jam-packed right up until 4:00 P.M. when she would attend a final 'Thank You' party for major supporters. After that, she and Team Claire would watch the returns. Adam should at least be with them, but he still hadn't been found. She realized that she was both terrified or furious.

She checked her watch. Ten minutes to spare before the interview for Polaris Satellite Radio. Florence went up to the suite while Humvee and Claire's security team followed her as she peeked into the ballroom, bedecked with red, white, and blue balloons in overhead nets. In the campaign room the action at the TV monitors and phone banks had a frantic air.

Once upstairs, Humvee knocked on the door to the suite. An SS agent with startling, light-blue eyes, a woman Claire didn't recognize, opened it, saying "It's clear, Ma'am."

Inside, flowers practically upholstered the sitting room, their scent creating spring in November. Gerbera daisies in bright colors, chrysanthemums in fall colors, boatloads of red and white carnations. And roses.

Alex, freed from his cage, landed on Claire's shoulder. Florence set down her copy of EClaire to help with the overcoats Claire and Humvee had worn against the stiff wind that had chilled the city.

Humvee asked, "Where's Connie? I was thinkin' she'd meet us here."

"I decided rather last minute to give everyone at the 'Thank You' party a basket with EClaire products tied with big red bows. Connie is scrambling to organize that. Janice Kirkorian and the Bright Future team will be there. The AFWW New York people. My TARA supporters. They've all been so magnificent."

Claire paused, suddenly sad. "Things feel incomplete without Joss and Pryce, but—" She shrugged. "—they'd probably tell me to drop dead."

Humvee plunked his considerable bulk onto a sofa. "What about Mr. Kodaly? He's damn sorry for what he did."

"Well, Humvee…," She chose the most comfortable spot for the phone interview, a chair looking out the tenth-floor suite's window at a view of Rockefeller Center. A phone sat on a small table beside it. She stroked Alex under his chin. "I guess no one is all bad. What Savik did about the doctor was wonderful. I know he's sorry. But trust is something—"

A knock on the door interrupted. Humvee opened it and exchanged a few words with the Secret Service woman, then brought back a floral box, already untied but re-closed.

"This isn't good," Humvee said. "I wish we could just ignore it."

He lifted off the top of the box and opened the green tissue paper to reveal a black rose as rich as velvet. The inner linings of the petals were deepest purple.

Claire shivered. The rose's beauty couldn't block an ominous blackness. She lifted the card which had already been opened and read by the Secret Service and Humvee. The first message was from *The Language of Roses*:

"The black rose accompanies the journey into what Hamlet called, 'The undiscovered country from whose bourn no traveler returns.'"

The personal message sucked her breath away. "Dear Claire, Today you join the ranks of Gandhi, Martin Luther King, Jr., Lincoln, JFK, and Bobby."

"Oh, dear God!" she murmured, staring at the card in her trembling hand.

Alex flapped off her shoulder, squawking.

Humvee laid the box with the dreadful black rose on the table as Claire continued to stare at the card with sick fascination. "The Secret Service is real upset," he said. "She said for me to tell you that this is why they'll be upping your security."

For a long moment Claire was with Maman again in this very hotel a year and a half ago. *If someone wants to kill badly enough, they'll find a way. Extra security only makes them more devious.*

"Ms. Claire, you should cancel all your public stuff."

Claire barely heard Humvee. Martin Luther King had said the day before he was assassinated, that he'd glimpsed the Promised Land but might never enter it. He'd been always followed by the possibility of assassination.

A sense that she was going to die sank into her bones. The universe was laughing at all her attempts at organizing chaos, mocking her with this rose. Was her role to be a martyr? Was that what fate had in mind for her after all?

Humvee was staring at her, grim-faced.

"I'm not …in control of my fate. But I haven't cowered before and I won't cower now. V-ball and his team are in charge of doing their best to keep me alive. If they succeed, good. I will pray they don't fail. But I have to proceed."

"I'm gonna stick extra close, then," he said, adding a comforting nod. "We all have to choose what we can do. I'm not a smart man, but this will be my part, Ms. Claire. I'm with you, all the way."

She rose and hugged him. Yet his commitment brought an even greater sense of finality. She ached with a sudden need to hug John. A shocking thought struck.

"What am I thinking! My son….I must talk to John. In private." She made the call in the bedroom. His number was ringing before Florence was out of the room. He didn't answer. "John, I've had a terrible scare," she said to his voice mail. "I need to talk to you. It's absolutely…..Oh, John, you must let me tell you about your father. Everything. Today. Please call back the minute you hear this message."

She returned to the sitting room.

Florence's face mixed worry and fear. "Humvee told me…Are you okay, Miss Claire?" Tears formed in her eyes. "You should not go out today."

"I have to, Florence." Again, as if Maman were in the room, her voice came to Claire. "Maman tried so hard to tell me. It's one thing to be in control of yourself, but it's quite another to want to control others— no matter how good your intentions. My poor son. My prodding and maneuvering him was part of what drove him away. And now it may be too late." She rushed to the desk, sat, and found pen, paper and envelopes in the top drawer. She checked the time, her heart racing.

Humvee sighed. "Florence and I were talking. This person, this crazy one, must be someone you know well."

Faces flashed before her. "I can't believe that. I don't want to believe that."

"My dear son," she wrote just as the phone rang. The interview. No time left for thinking or worrying or fixing things. Claire picked up the receiver.

She Has To Follow Her Destiny

With an extravagant bouquet of brightly-colored daisies, mums, and lilies in hand, Savik approached the hotel room where Claire was staying. He hoped Claire would see the flowers' vivid colors as an appreciation of her style. Something bold and bright yet still elegant, he'd told the florist, but definitely not roses. Every time he thought about her secret sender of roses, his skin prickled. Anonymity in this case was right up there with stalking.

He'd been angry and frustrated at her refusal to see him, and yet, what should he have expected? Instant forgiveness?

The Secret Service guard at the door was a woman with sky-blue eyes. Savik showed her his security pass, one he'd had when he was touring with Claire and which had probably been forgotten since Claire hadn't involved the SS. Savik returned the pass to his pocket. "I'm here to see Ms. Alden." He gave her one of his best smiles, guaranteed to make a woman's heart—and suspicions—melt.

The woman with the beautiful blue eyes did not smile back. "Sorry. She's not here."

"Then I'd like to leave the flowers and a note."

After another look at his pass, she said, "I'll need to do a pat down."

He would expect nothing less. "No problem." She patted him thoroughly, including a firm skim right up to the groin, and then, finding nothing ominous, knocked on the door.

Florence opened it. "Hello, Mr. Kodaly," she said, a bit warily.

He stepped into the room and was immediately deflated to find it nearly paved in flowers. Even his bright bouquet would be lost. "I'd like to leave a note," he said to Florence.

She gestured to a desk.

He pulled out paper and pen, and as he wrote Claire's name, Alex landed on his shoulder, a note card in his bill. "Thanks, Alex," Savik said. He took the card and started to toss it on the desk when he saw the words "black rose." He read the full note, his pulse ratcheting up with every syllable. He turned to Florence. "Where did this come from?"

Only shaking her head, Florence pointed to a box on a table beside the window. Savik walked to the box. Inside lay a black rose tinted with purple at its center.

"We tried to make her to stay in today," Florence said. "She would not."

His mind raced. "This has to be from someone who knows her schedule…and has for a long time. An insider." They stood in silence staring at the beautiful, but deadly, black rose.

Finally Florence said, "I am nosy and read many cards. For a time, I thought the pretty words were from you, and I was happy to see Claire happy."

"Were the notes always intimate?"

"Yes, always very personal." Florence scrunched her face into a frown. "I have my own idea. I never liked the way that Miss Joss looked at her. Very…possessive like. It bothered me. And she is a rough one, that one. Bad breeding."

"That's pretty much how I feel about Pryce. Very possessive. And he's damn pissed now." Savik had another quick thought. "For that matter, Adam Forsythe has known her and been close to her for years, and he's been acting downright weird. Angry at her. Shit." If Claire won the election, Adam could instantly become President….Had he really been on Claire's side? What if Ronnie had somehow gotten to him? What if he'd become Ronnie's secret weapon? Hell, who knew how long Ronnie had bugged Savik and what he'd learned? Did he know about the roses?

He clinched his fists. "Does the Secret Service know about this?"

"Oh yes, of course."

No wonder the shakedown. "Didn't they forbid her to go out?"

"Mr. Kodaly, they said they would guard her very carefully, but she said she could not be afraid. That she has to follow her destiny."

"That sounds like her." The Secret Service would most likely protect Claire, but what if Ronnie had somehow gotten to one of them? For the SecDef it wasn't entirely beyond the realm of possibility. "Do you have her schedule, Florence?"

After an agonizingly slow ride down the elevator, he caught a taxi. "Take me to the Kramer Abuse Center, on 54th west," he told the cabbie.

Traffic started backing up six blocks from the Kramer Center's location. If Claire was running on time she should already have been there for about ten minutes. When the cab stopped in total gridlock a mere two blocks from the center, Savik paid the driver, stepped out and sprinted toward the five-story building.

Somebody Means Business

A former run-down and seedy apartment building was now the Kramer Abuse Center. Claire mingled with guests while Humvee hovered close, her SS detail doubled in size. A Kevlar vest added heavy bulk to the red blouse she wore under her white suit.

The building's inner courtyard had been transformed from a trash-littered, brick-enclosed space into a pocket sanctuary the size of a tennis court. Rusty-red stone paved the area and contrasted with a mini-forest of small potted evergreens. Bright chrysanthemums flanked a waterfall that coursed down the wall farthest from the street.

To one side, near a slightly elevated dais, a massive statue—a loving depiction in brown granite of a mother, father, and child—stood angled in a corner. She smelled air scented with cardamom and cedar from small pots of burning oil. Against another wall, tables offered food, drink and the EClaire gift baskets.

Connie, standing near the waterfall, gave Claire the sign that it was time to close. As Claire moved through the standing crowd toward the dais, she patted Fance's shoulder. Fance had joined ABrightFuture and had been working their phone banks. Rachel sat directly in front of the platform so that she, along with four others in wheelchairs, could see.

As Claire passed by, Rachel gave her hand a squeeze. She, Serena, and hopefully John would later join the team to watch election returns. Claire pushed that thought away, banished the image of the black rose, mounted the dais, and faced reporters and a hundred fifty grinning, happy supporters. Humvee stood beside her, two Secret Service men behind, and one in front of her platform, near the statue.

. . . . .

Savik displayed his pass to an SS man and hurried through the entry to the Kramer Center. Signs indicated that the Alden Party was in the courtyard.

Just outside an arched entry, he showed the pass again to a burly Secret Service man who recognized him. The man made Savik stop and submit to a search. V-ball stood, arms crossed and body erect, just inside the entry. He nodded at Savik.

Already searching the crowd, Savik said to him, "This death threat is different. Somebody means business. This person knows her. He, or even she, could be here right now."

V-ball kept his eyes on the crowd. "The only people here are known supporters and people with press passes whose names are on a vetted list. Everyone has been searched."

"This fixation on Claire goes back months. Lots of these people could be prime suspects."

"We know that." V-ball briefly snatched a look at him in a way that said, including you.

"Okay. But think about this: you know I was bugged. That's what ultimately put me onto the guy, Hyjinx who works for Hughes. I can't prove it, but—"

V-ball scowled, his gaze fixed again on the crowd.

How to explain about Ronnie. Man, this was complicated. "Whoever arranged for the abortion lie may know something about the roses. Maybe you're looking for the wrong thing."

V-ball remained silent.

"Do you hear what I'm saying?" Savik asked.

V-ball frowned, nodded, stepped away and spoke quietly, presumably into his earphone.

Savik realized he wouldn't put anything at all past Ronnie, and moved warily along the wall toward Claire on the dais, not knowing exactly what he was looking for.

Claire said, "We've come a long way together, and now we are at the White House doors, waiting to see if the people are going to invite us inside."

Savik wanted to look at Claire, but did not pull his gaze from the crowd. Just as he'd singled out those women at the Tabor Towers bombing, he hoped to find a person or persons who should not be here.

He scanned purses, postures, attitudes, body language. In a few seconds he'd considered ambush positions, trajectories, tactical advantages. Finally he stood by the wall at the front of the courtyard, across from the massive stone statue and almost in line with Claire. He allowed himself a quick glance at the side of her face. Surely she must have noticed him approaching her.

As if reading his mind, Claire looked his way, and what he saw in her eyes was wariness. Did she actually think it might be him? That he was creeping up on her to kill her?

She looked forward again. "When I next lay my head on a pillow—after we know the final results—I'll think of all of you. No matter how this election turns out, we've ignited a fire in people's hearts. And it's because of you that many more people will start demanding change."

Applause and cheering hoots erupted—except for a man seated in the front row in a wheelchair. He didn't applaud, merely stared as though mesmerized. A reporter's badge stood out on his dark wool sport coat, so he was not necessarily an admirer. Something about him bothered Savik. A plaster cast on his right foot extended up underneath the pant leg of his khakis. He wore gray-tinted glasses somewhat obscuring his eyes.

The man's short hair was reddish brown, but the phrase that popped into Savik's head was 'really good wig.' Bony nose, but puffy cheeks. Sweat glistened on the man's forehead.

Savik's pulse surged. His gut said, this was the guy.

Those cheeks….

Chipmunk cheeks! Savik thought of the disguise Anna had rigged.

And then, despite the tinted glasses, Savik knew those eyes!

He lunged, pushing Rachel and her wheelchair aside as he scrambled to reach Claire's former PR man, Pryce Pierce. He grabbed the man by the shoulders, and yanked him up out of the wheelchair yelling, "It's him! It's him! It's him!"

"Fuck off!" Pryce yelled, shoving back. Pryce reached into his pocket and pulled out a PDA that Savik instantly knew was a detonator.

As Savik grabbed at it, Pryce twisted. The leg with the cast slammed into the back of Savik's knee. The two of them fell onto the stone paving. Pryce's hand hit the floor; the detonator slid from his grasp and stopped several feet away. He dragged himself after it.

"Bomb!" Savik shouted. From the corner of his eye he saw Secret Service men on the platform converging on Claire.

Screams. Panic! Savik crawled on his elbows toward the detonator, but Pryce would easily reach it first.

The bomb was either in the cast or in Pryce's wheelchair. Savik went with his instinct. He scrambled to his feet, grabbed the back of the wheelchair and shoved it with every ounce of force his adrenalin-powered muscles could muster toward the small space between the large stone statue and the wall behind it.

Everything happened in freeze-framed moments. The wheel chair rolled away toward the statue some fifteen feet from him, Pryce's outstretched hand reached for the detonator, the wheelchair disappeared behind the statue, and Pryce pressed the detonator button.

The concussion and sound hit Savik simultaneously.

I'm Sorry About Claire

First Savik heard sounds—crying, moaning. Then the distinctive acrid smell of explosive material choked him. Coughing, he opened his eyes to find two Emergency Care guys in white pants and blue shirts cutting his shredded and bloody left pant leg.

His head felt stuffed with plastic popcorn. He wasn't hearing sounds sharply. He shoved up onto one elbow, shook his head, and looked around.

Several bodies lay nearby, some wounded, and some not moving. Emergency care personnel busied themselves. Several fragments of the half demolished statue lay on the cracked pavement. The blast appeared to only have reached the front third of the courtyard, its force checked by the statue.

"You shouldn't move," said the bigger medic, a man with a thick black mustache. "Someone's coming with a stretcher."

"Claire? Ms. Alden?" Savik moved to sit all the way up. The medic pushed him flat.

"We put a tourniquet around the leg. You should keep still."

Savik stretched to look beyond the medic's squatting form to where he last saw Claire. Blood drenched her hair and was smeared over her face and upper body. Two medics eased her onto a stretcher, rose, and rushed away.

To Savik's horror, no one was bending over or even standing by Humvee, and Humvee's green shirt and black slacks were blood-soaked. Another Secret Service agent also lay unattended and appeared to be dead. Savik looked to his left just as two more medics lifted Pryce's body onto a stretcher. The man looked unconscious but was twitching. *May he die a death of slow agony.*

Savik grabbed the medic's arm. "How badly is Claire hurt?"

"I don't know."

A woman dressed in the medics' white and blue laid a stretcher on the floor, and as three of them hoisted Savik onto it, a searing fire lanced up his leg into his groin. Connie rushed to him as he was carried toward the door. He grabbed her hand.

"Claire? How bad?"

"She's barely conscious." Tears streamed down Connie's face. "All that blood…."

They trotted him to a waiting ambulance. Once inside, Savik heard a woman moaning. Fance lay on the other bunk, clutching her side.

Savik gagged. Bands feeling like those of steel around a packing crate tightened around his chest. He held his breath to try to block the worst pain of his life in this worst moment of his life.

The ambulance took off, siren wailing. Absurdly, Savik remembered that he hadn't yet voted. In only minutes the whole country would know that Claire was hurt. Or worse. How would that affect voters in the West? Did he really care? No, but he knew that Claire would—if she knew.

Claire—and the world—betrayed in the end by someone close to her, by a friend. How ironic. How cruel. Not her enemies. Her friend! How can we protect ourselves from those close to us. The horrible thought and her bloodied image kept strobing in his mind. To come so far and then to die.

. . . . .

The ER doctor helped Savik into a wheelchair and handed him prescriptions for pain pills and antibiotics. "Stay off your feet for the next day or two. Elevate the leg as much as you can. You're lucky no major vessel was cut."

To make room for other injured people, orderlies wheeled Savik out into the ER waiting room. Winn stood and bounded over.

"Goddamn," he said to Savik. "You are one tough piece of meat."

Savik felt overwhelmed by a sudden wave of good feelings from just seeing Winn's face. "What d'ya think of the scar this'll make?" Savik nodded at the fifteen inches of white gauze along his thigh. His blood-soaked pant leg had been cut off. Blood had splattered the remaining pant leg as well.

"Looks like great bragging material."

Savik managed a fleeting smile and covered the leg with the hospital blanket.

Winn pushed Savik toward the nearest elevator. "What my dad did to Claire with that abortion doctor? I'll never speak to the SOB again. It made me sick. He crossed way over the line. You have to believe me, man. I had no idea that he'd ever go that far. I swear."

Savik looked up at his friend. Humility and thoughtfulness made Winn seem older. Savik gave his forearm a shake. "Well, I've pretty much done what I can to screw your dad's career, so if you can forgive me, I guess I can believe you."

Winn gripped Savik's shoulder. "I'm sorry about Claire."

Savik's eyes stung on the edge of tears. He distracted himself by looking down the hallway toward the noise in the hospital's main reception area. Print, TV, and digital media packed the space wall to wall.

Winn wheeled him in the opposite direction. "We gotta avoid them. They'd mob you for an interview. The TV had a shot of you in the fracas. They are all over the fact that you've survived two bomb attacks on Claire. Been a big hero stuff. Like you're maybe fated to save her."

"Anything tragic becomes a ghoulish feast for everyone."

"Yep. The attack on Claire is showing more than election coverage is and trending bigger than everything else. The clips show Claire hurt really bad and unmoving. They even showed a split-second shot of Humvee and the Secret Service man leaping in front of her. A forensics expert speculated that if Claire makes it, it will be because of them. And you." They reached an intersection of corridors. "All of her people are waiting upstairs, on eight. Near Critical Care. The whole hoard. We go there, right?"

"Yeah."

Winn rolled him away from the rear exit.

"What time is it? Too early for election results?"

"Almost 8:00. Some results are in. A few polls closed at 6:00."

"So early?"

"Yeah. Kentucky, Florida, Indiana. Some others. A talking head said closing at 6:00 tended to keep working people from the polls. Tends to help Republicans. Not this year, though. Heavy turnout in all districts. Hass has the lead. Of course those were states expected to go for him."

In the elevator Winn hit the button for the eighth floor. "For what it's worth," he continued, "I wouldn't hate it if she won. I hope to God she makes it."

"If she does and wins, you'll lose a lot of money."

"Not all that much. CET is doing fine. Probably still will. I just won't become the decadently wealthy guy of my dreams. But you know, decadence is overrated."

Savik smiled and the door opened onto the living-room-sized waiting area on the eighth floor, packed, as Winn had described, with Secret Service people, Rachel, Serena, Jake, Connie, and Florence. Virtually all of them except the always dour Secret Service detail were talking. He heard Pryce's name a time or two. And then to his great surprise, he saw Joss.

Joss turned and, seeing Savik, approached him. She lifted the blanket and stared at his bandage and the blood all over his clothing. "I understand," she said, "that you're responsible for digging up the dirt on the crooked doctor."

Savik nodded and readjusted the blanket. A tense silence strung itself out between them.

"She's fortunate," Joss said, "to have your support. I …I've let her down. Badly."

Joss had obviously been crying. Before Savik could respond, the elevator dinged, the door opened, and John came out. His hair was wild, T-shirt and levis rumpled. Serena moved to him and asked, "How is Fance?"

Savik and everyone else crowded around him.

"It's serious. A big chunk of rock broke two ribs, and she has a collapsed lung." Red rimmed John's eyelids, and he wiped his eyes with the back of his hand.

The elevator bell dinged again, and this time Adam Forsythe stepped out with his personal assistant at his side. Everyone turned and gawked. From their comments, it became obvious that he'd been missing. Evidently, as Savik had suspected, the "flu" story wasn't true.

Jake stomped across the room and braked in front of the Vice Presidential nominee, fist balled and hitched near his hip. "Where the hell have you been?"

"I'm truly sorry, Jake. I am—I've not been well." He lowered his voice. "I spent the last two days at Columbia Presbyterian. An exploratory biopsy. I wouldn't let Reggie," he gestured toward his assistant, "say anything until we knew the results. There seems to be something wrong… well. . .." He lowered his voice. "I have a brain tumor."

"What the—?"

"I'm on a new and powerful medication now. I'll explain later. How is Claire?"

"Damn good question," Jake answered. "The doctors haven't told us a goddamn thing. And people are still voting in other time zones, or choosing not to vote, not knowing…what a helluva thing. You need to make a statement, Adam."

John gently interrupted. "I asked earlier but they wouldn't let me see my mother. I want to know if anyone has called Humvee's family."

"Hell, John," Jake blurted, frowning. "I don't think so."

Jake spun around. "Did anyone call Humvee's family?"

When no one made a peep, John said, "I'll do it then." He and Connie withdrew to a corner, and Savik watched the boy make this tragic call.

Winn said to Savik, "Handsome guy."

"I've watched him mature at the office. He's brilliant and he's diligent. And, like his mother, he also takes on the hard tasks. I know she'd be very proud of him right now."

A woman in a gray business suit and a nurse in green scrubs entered the waiting room. "I need to speak to John Trask and Savik Kodaly," the businesswoman said.

"Here," Savik and John said simultaneously.

"Would the two of you please accompany me into the hall?"

John wheeled Savik out of earshot of the others.

"Ms. Alden is in extremely serious condition," said the woman in gray. "A stone fragment hit her head and triggered deep bleeding in her brain. She has a skull fracture. Left temporal area…" The woman glanced at her clipboard

"All of which means what?" Savik said, his pulse pounding in his ears.

"The fracture tore the dura mater, the tough membrane that protects the brain. She's bleeding, creating a substantial clot there. It must be surgically evacuated and the bleeding halted. Most serious is the deeper damage."

She looked at Savik, but he couldn't even think what to ask.

Again the woman checked her clipboard. She looked up again. "She is fighting to stay lucid which is positive, but surgery as soon as possible is essential to avoid any permanent neurological decline."

"What do you mean," John interrupted sharply, "by neurological decline?"

"Unless treated quickly, this kind of trauma can be fatal, Mr. Trask. For some reason she is refusing to sign the permission for surgery until she speaks to both of you. Time is critical. So if you will go with this nurse, she'll take you to pre-op immediately. Please urge Ms. Alden to sign quickly."

Savik and John followed the nurse to the elevator and descended to the second floor and to a door that said "No admittance." She walked them inside, and to a bed where Claire lay surrounded by blinking gizmos and the smell of hospital astringent and medicines. Her head had been shaved, and a massive bandage covered the left side of her skull. Both eyes were ringed with purple. The mattress was raised about thirty degrees at the head of the bed. Her neck was in a brace to keep her head from moving. Savik wanted to cry.

"I'm lucky," Claire said. "I'm alive to tell you what I should have told you long ago."

John took his mother's hand.

Savik thought, can I take her other hand? Should I? Why am I here? Has she forgiven me?

. . . . .

The pre-operative sedative she'd been given had taken away Claire's blinding headache. Now was the time for truth.

"You are going to be fine," John said.

The sight of his red-rimmed eyes touched her. "How is Fance?"

"She's hurting, Mom, but she's going to live. Just like you."

Tears slipped down John's cheeks. He brushed them away. She was too weak and groggy to touch his face, but she squeezed his hand a little. She looked at Savik in a wheelchair. He was biting his lower lip. "You both know that David wasn't John's natural father. And now you need to know that you are father and son." It was strange that saying this didn't hurt at all or even frighten her.

Savik took her hand. His felt reassuring, warm and strong. "What are you saying? You're saying…John is my son?"

"Yes. Look at him….look at the two of you." She closed her eyes. Each word was draining her strength. The pre-op relaxant was dragging her down. With great effort she opened her eyes to see them studying each other.

"Why would you keep that a secret from me?" John said, shaking his head.

"Your mother shouldn't tire herself any more before the operation," Savik said.

"No…I need to answer." Blackness crept into the edges of her vision, but she fought to stay awake. "You've always been a rebel. When your father, when David, was alive, I couldn't tell you. I promised. I'd always let you believe you were his. But…you were so angry. I thought when you saw the dashing, successful, playboy—." It was becoming hard to think, to talk. "I'd lose you to him. I love you…so much. Couldn't lose David and you too. My sin. Grandmere warned me so many times. Forgive me."

The nurse, who had left them alone, approached the bed. She carried a clip board. "We really need to move you into surgery. Now. Please sign."

Savik stepped back. Claire nodded. Ready for whatever awaited her, she scrawled her signature with a weak hand.

She looked at each of them. A final glimpse? "Love you both," she whispered, closing eyelids too heavy to hold open. Orderlies were rolling the bed toward the other end of the room. Love you both, she thought, picturing her son and Savik as she gave herself over to the darkness.

. . . . .

Emotions clashed within Savik, a wave of sorrow crashing against a powerful stream of joy. Never before in his life had he felt he had so much to lose, and now that he had something valuable beyond anything else in his life, he didn't know of any way to hold onto it. Despite his having done nothing to deserve any parental claims, this strapping, fine young man was his son. His and Claire's. And Claire was fighting for her life.

John hadn't uttered a sound and kept studying the floor.

"So what do we do?" Savik asked. "I have this crazy urge to hug you."

"I'm still pretty much in shock. I don't think I'm up to hugging….yet."

They turned and John walked beside Savik in silence as they left the pre-op area and entered the elevator. The silence wasn't hostile or empty. They both looked straight ahead, and then, simultaneously, at each other and smiled. Savik's whole world was changing so fast, it was like trying to hang on to the wildest Brahma bull ever to buck a man off its back. They stepped out into the hall and headed toward the eighth floor waiting room.

As they stepped inside the room Savik said to John, "Look, there should be a coffee machine down the hall. We should talk a little. In private. We have a ton of stuff to sort out."

His son nodded. "Fine. Well, maybe a little later. I need to think for awhile first."

Jake Schifrin hurried over. "How is Claire?"

Conversation in the room stopped and heads turned their way.

Savik explained about the operation only.

"America deserves updates," Jake said. "John, I think the first should come from you."

John turned to Savik, a question in his eyes. Savik nodded in an exchange that felt completely natural, like any father encouraging any son. And then, the miracle. Savik would never be able to put into words the strange, strange sensations that swept through him as this extraordinary young man—his son—hugged him.

Pray To Your Higher Power

Savik sat in his wheelchair near the hospital's front entry, watching his son John face reporters. The media swarmed and police battled to keep them from obstructing hospital service. Red and white lights flashed. A crowd clogged the streets. Bullhorn messages ordered people to keep back.

Jake had coached John. "If Claire supporters think she's dead or dying, they might not vote. Everything she's worked for would be lost. That must not happen. You must not give any hint of Claire's true condition."

Cameras zoomed in on John and the clamoring horde stood frozen in a moment of rapt attention. Looks of sympathy softened most faces in the crowd. Looks of self-importance and opportunism betrayed those who expected a young playboy who dated a stripper to say exactly the wrong thing. Savik could only inflate at the pride he felt. His son!

"People of America, I know you share my devastation." John hesitated, clearly grappling with strong emotions. "Your concern is so palpable, I could feel it through the walls of this hospital. I'm grateful for your prayers, as I know the other families of those injured in this deranged attack are as well." He spoke firmly now. Savik saw a boy becoming a man. "I'm also grateful that Mom talked to me before undergoing an operation to remove a blood clot caused by a skull fracture. Her chances are good, and you know that she gives her all for the chance to make our country and the world a better place. She'd want me to ask that you to please vote. I believe—" His voice cracked a little. "—with all my heart that all will be well."

. . . . .

John had faced the press many times on the tennis circuit, but addressing the whole freaking nation was entirely different. He found himself trembling and feeling humble.

He returned with Connie and Savik to the eighth floor private waiting room. Rachel, Serena, Joss, Jake, Winn Hughes and the others told him how well he'd done. Adam Forsythe had gone to the hospital chapel, meditating and praying, before delivering his own statement later to the press.

The TV rebroadcast the clip of John's announcement but John couldn't watch. Jake at his side, he stepped to a window facing the rear parking lot which was now jammed. People sat in their cars or milled about. Folks with RVs had hauled out folding chairs. Life was so strange. Standing in the eye of a deadly hurricane couldn't feel any more disturbing.

He couldn't wait to tell Fance about Savik but she was sedated and sleeping. Fance would live, he kept reminding himself. At least he could count on that. He had to.

Jake said somberly, "We've taken Pennsylvania and Virginia. Claire will be especially pleased. New York looks strong. Along with Michigan and the New England states."

Jake kept talking optimistically as if he were sure his mom would make it. Every time Jake spoke like that, John felt the exact opposite. Most of the women sat with tears on their cheeks. Sniffles. Blowing noses. Savik kept looking at the carpet, pressing his hands against his forehead. Winn sat beside him, steadfast.

John turned again to the window and the dark sky. The day had been a mind-blowing surreal nightmare. And yet….he had a father. After all those years of fearing he'd come from a night in which his mother had acted like a skank with some studly drunk, he had a father he could admire. One who had acted in a very wrong-headed way, betraying his mother for what he thought were the right reasons and creating disaster, but then finally doing the right thing.

A lot like me.

Another rise of tears welled up and stung his eyes. He desperately wanted his mother in his life. Mom…Grandmere…both victims of an insane bomber….

"Why in the hell do some people want my mom dead so much?" he asked Jake.

"That's a good question, kid. What I've decided is that people who crave revenge on others are really pissed at God. Angry at the All Mighty for allowing disasters or hardships or disappointments in their lives. But since you can't get back at God, taking over the divine vengeance job is their next best thing."

"Look!" Joss said. "Texas went for Hass."

The male commentators' tone intensified. John turned to listen.

"…and late voters in Illinois, Ohio and New Jersey, according to exit polls, are overwhelmingly voting for Alden, virtually assuring New Jersey, at least, for the Alden camp. The South is strongly Republican in this race, but projected Electoral votes now put Alden only slightly behind with 138 to 140."

"There are interesting numbers from the western states as well," Tawana Thompson from CNN was saying. "As though people may be flocking to the polls after hearing John Alden's touching speech. Is that fair to say, Jack?"

"It's quite possible, Tawana. California polls are open for three more hours. Based on exit polls, that race is very close there, with Hass taking inland precincts, and coastal areas being pro-Alden. California could prove to be the deciding factor."

· · · · ·

Claire's surgery had lasted two and a half hours so far. Savik ached with frustration, wanting to leap out of the wheelchair and pace, but of course he couldn't. The wound throbbed. John had gone down to talk with the families of others hurt in the blast and then to sit by Fance.

Hass had pulled ahead in Electoral votes, 218 to Claire's 196. Savik needed another round of pills, which weren't to be taken on an empty stomach. He and Winn visited the vending machines, ate a late dinner of dry power bars and chips washed down with bitter coffee.

Savik told Winn about John. Winn pounded him on the back, and in turn confessed that he was seeing a woman he thought was "special." They talked in ways they hadn't since their late night/early morning sessions in college. The clock in the cafeteria said quarter after twelve. Claire had been in surgery for almost four hours. Surely there would be news soon.

They returned to the waiting room to find Jake in the hall pacing and talking on his cell phone. Connie said, "Campaign headquarters is mobbed. Telegrams and emails are flooding in from all over the country. From all over the world."

"Any news from the OR?" Savik asked.

Connie shook her head.

Serena made room for Savik to stretch out on one of the sofas and elevate his leg. Joss flipped TV stations. Each news station showed the front of the hospital while scrolls on the bottom kept updating the vote counts. Cameras, lights, and news vans vied with throngs in the hospital parking lots and nearby streets, many people raising lighted cell phones and flashlights. Hundreds carried lighted candles.

Adam stepped outside and cameras zoomed in as he took a microphone. "Thank you for your love and concern for Claire Alden. When my wife died, I turned to God with a hopeless question. Why? And I ask this question again now because, turn to my maker I must when human catastrophes are unbearable alone. I don't always receive answers, but I find strength somehow, and out of that strength, there is often a positive outcome."

On screen, Jake approached Adam, who held up a hand to the reporters for pardon as he listened to Jake. Adam nodded, expression unchanged. Savik sat up, holding his breath. No one had come out of the OR, so Jake couldn't be reporting to Adam on Claire, could he?

"My fellow Americans, this is a stunning moment," Adam said. "California has gone for Claire Alden. This means our Claire has just been elected to serve as the next President of the United States."

Joss shouted, "Oh my god!" Savik let out his breath slowly. The TV panned the crowd, people keening in joy. Many broke down and wept.

Winn grabbed Savik's arm. "She did it, partner."

Behind him, Savik heard the OR door open. He straightened up so fast he pulled painfully at the stitches. Claire's chief surgeon stepped into the room, blotting his forehead.

All In Good Time

The surgeon paused as John rushed into the waiting room.

Please, Savik prayed. *She has to be okay.*

John asked, "What's up? There's a near-riot outside…?" His face had gone white. He looked at the surgeon, obviously dreading the worst.

"She won," Savik said quickly. "Your mother has won the election, and…." He let his voice trail and looked at the surgeon.

The man took a deep breath and spoke to John. "We've had to induce a coma. We successfully removed the major clot, but we temporarily lost her. Just under five minutes. We're not sure why. She suffered what's called a 'coup and counter-coup' contusion, meaning that there is damage where she was struck, as well as additional damage where her brain bounced against the opposite wall of her skull and deeper inside as well."

John leaned against the wall for support.

"Her chances?" Savik asked, his voice hoarse.

"I can't promise anything. She should survive, but please do not be overly optimistic. There is the possibility of some neurological damage, ranging from minimal to severe. For now we will keep her in a medically induced coma. Until her ICP levels drop and hold stable." He looked directly at John. "I'm sorry, but the best I can say is that we'll not know her status or be able to give you a prognosis until we take her out of the coma."

"Hell," Winn whispered under his breath but loud enough for Savik to hear…and agree.

. . . . .

Savik took a week off from work and, of course, gave John the time off as well. The two of them along with Serena, Rachel, Connie, and Joss alternately sat with Claire or slept beside her round the clock. Five of her Secret Service people, including V-Ball, rotated in a schedule of watching over the President-elect. Pryce Pierce died and no one paid much attention. No one mentioned to the press the anonymous love notes and roses he'd sent Claire. The media focused on the fact that he'd quit Claire's campaign over rivalry for power, and that he'd once been on medication for suicidal depression when his wife left him.

People around the globe held candle-light vigils, prayer meetings, masses, and informal gatherings, focusing on Claire's recovery. Cards piled up at the hospital, at campaign headquarters, at EClaire, and

AFWW. A wall of floral bouquets accumulated at the front of the hospital, to be donated elsewhere every other day.

Music from the CD of the "AFWW Unity Concert" could be heard in passing cars, elevators, on the radio and television. Or they played "Claire de Lune." As one commentator put it, "The extent to which the whole world is focused on a common hope in the heart of humanity offers a very positive glimpse of what might be."

But behind the scenes of all this public hope, Savik wrestled with the horror that Claire might die. Or worse, that when the doctors brought her to consciousness, she might be severely compromised or mindless.

Adam Forsythe underwent a procedure to remove some kind of tumor through a non-invasive method called the "gamma knife." It lasted three hours, and Adam went home, took a nap and was fine. The tumor had caused his headaches and strange behavior and could have affected the fate of the nation, but was rendered almost instantly harmless by a miracle of medical science.

Soon after Claire was placed in the coma her ICP levels began dropping. The drugs keeping her there were stopped, but her other treatment continued, and at 6:47 A.M. on November eleventh, 2020, she moaned softly. Savik was watching her. The purple rings around her eyes had faded to blue and yellow.

"Hi, gorgeous," Savik said softly. He held her hand and squeezed lightly.

She smiled faintly, opened her eyes and looked at him, gaze altering ever so slightly with amusement.

"Hi, Sharpshooter," she said.

In that second, he knew she was herself.

. . . . .

Leo Lombardi was smiling as he held the phone to his ear. He'd never felt greater hope. "She is going to be fine, Aunt Julia."

"Well then, I believe I'll be able to die a happy woman. I only wish I could have lived long enough to witness all the changes she will bring. Metanoia, Leo. At least I had a part in it."

. . . . .

"Kee-ryst!" Hughes said to Cliff Stanhope, thumping the front page of the Washington Post with its huge picture of Claire Alden leaving the hospital and waving at the mindless hordes cheering her on. "That Pryce Pierce was a total screw-up."

Cliff snorted. "Damn shame the nutcase pulled that fucked up attempt before Hyjinx got to her. She's the Prez now. She'll be protected by SS. Virtually untouchable now."

He and Cliff were having coffee and doughnuts in the kitchen of the Hughes home in Bethesda. "The Cork and Bull" had asked him not to come in on Sundays any longer since the security required to keep angry people away from him crowded out room for other customers. Bloggers insisted he was indeed behind the bribery of the Mexican abortion doctor, as the weasel was himself proclaiming from somewhere inside Italy.

"You sure Dr. Frijole has no direct proof you sent Hyjinx to bribe him?" Cliff asked.

"None. They can investigate 'til their dicks fall off. They can't prove anything."

"At least no one has connected you yet with Sphere 9. But Ronnie," Cliff leaned forward, using his superior size to establish some sort of dominance, "...all this attention. I'm worried. I think Justice might somehow make the connection. And if they start looking into Sphere 9 financials we could both be in serious trouble."

Pfhhh! Hughes scoffed. "There is no way that can happen. My connection is untraceable."

"Maybe." Cliff looked doubtful.

Hughes grinned and raised his mug. "Don't worry, Cliff. We're covered, and we still have plenty of time to rescue the country from the clutches of Claire Alden."

Cliff raised his mug as well. "Right! Were covered." His tone said he wasn't all that sure.

. . . . .

On a snowy evening in January 2025, Savik stood in his tux, waiting for the President to take his outstretched hand at the first dance of her Inaugural Ball.

She looked as radiant as Miss America and stately as a queen in a slim red gown bedazzled with thousands of shimmering beads. Her hair, having only a couple of months to grow out, was quite short, but she wore ruby and diamond earrings that compensated nicely.

As soon as she had regained nearly full health, two weeks ago, he'd asked her to marry him. She declined. "I'm too busy, now, to deal with a marriage. And it will take time for me to feel the kind of trust I need to feel in a husband. But if you're willing, I'd like you stick around. You know. Unofficial First Boyfriend."

The music for this first dance was slow. After all, the President wasn't supposed to exercise too much yet. But she could glide as beautifully as ever, and holding her still excited him the way it always had. Impossibly, the world went away during that exclusive moment with her, and he longed to kiss her bare shoulders.

All in good time. He could be patient. He was a master of patience.

At the end of the dance, before he had to release her, he reached into the inside pocket of his tux and retrieved the item he'd saved for this moment. He offered an old blue ribbon that said, "Sharpshooter" to the President of the United States.

She tucked it discreetly into her gown. "Close to my heart," she said. She smiled, and then winked at him.

John danced next with the new President, and then with Fance, who looked to Savik like a goddess in a silver gown that pushed the limits of propriety for affairs of state but didn't exceed them. The two, in as happy a merger as ever there was, would marry next month.

Adam Forsythe was there with Serena. Rachel and Joss were hanging out together. Savik danced with Claire again until Governor Nash cut in. Safa Mufti, Aminah Roy and others from the AFWW schools were there. Savik's sister's family attended; John was especially interested in his new cousins. Winn came with his new fiancée. He no longer spoke to his father, who was now under investigation by the Justice Department for defense contract rigging.

Des and Florence rubbed elbows with billionaire backers Claire still called the Tuna Kahunas, along with the Steinmetzes, Janice Kirkorian and other women from Claire's many organizations. Rhoda Carr, Carly Simon, and other stars from the concert attended along with the new cabinet members that had caused such a stir.

Claire had followed the precedent of the first woman president of Chile, Michelle Bachelet, who in 2006 had formed a "parity government:" Claire's extended cabinet would be composed of ten men and ten women. And of course in attendance there were diplomats, judges, foreign heads of state, and selected Senators and Members of Congress.

"This is the most wonderful party I've ever been to," Claire said to Savik during the last dance of the evening.

There are looks that say more than words ever could, eloquent looks that allow feelings to travel along the line of sight directly into another's eyes and proclaim joy and gratitude, optimism and happiness. They all registered on Claire's face and more, and Savik knew he mirrored all those things back to her. And more.

The words were puny things compared to this look. Still he had to say them. "I love you, Madame President."

And, as Tawana Thompson of CNN put it, "A revolutionary new spirit has come into the White House and has spread throughout the country and across the planet. It's tragic that this victory had its human cost in blood and suffering, and forces resistant to change may bring more violence, but the presidency of Claire Alden launches a bold commitment to change that offers genuine hope. Surely we all wish her, and those who will serve with her, God speed."

ACKNOWLEDGMENTS

Peace Seeker has had at least three earlier versions, and it origins go back many years. A number of talented people generously donated time and expertise to its creation and I want to thank them. First, Barbara Durniak – Vassar Research Librarian, who helped with details about the Vassar library and its holdings. John Negroponte – Former U.S. Ambassador to the United Nations who, when reached by phone somewhat by accident, shared his valuable time to explain details about the offices of our United Nations ambassador.

I am profoundly indebted to members of my writer's groups for their always honest reviews: A. B. Curtis, Donna Erickson, Pete Johnson, and Judith Levine, the Friday team; and Chet Cunningham, Al Kramer, Bev Miller, Tom Utts, and others of the Monday evening faithful. My niece, Annamaria Alfonso, and long-time friend, Linda Wexler, provided the kind of encouragement and enthusiasm for the story that made me unwilling to let it simply die when, at the time before Hillary Clinton made her run, I could find no publisher interested in a book about a woman running for the US Presidency.

My agent, Richard Curtis, since retired, read early and late versions of the story and was as disappointed as was I when told that yet another book about a women running for President wasn't anything their New York houses were interested in. I will always be grateful for his support for my work over a number of years, both my published fiction stories and my first nonfiction work about the biology of the human potential for peace.

And for her enthusiastic encouragement and professional guidance on the design of the cover and text interior, I am indebted to my friend Robbie Adkins.

Finally, I take this opportunity to thank my friend, my book editor, and my writing buddy Peggy Lang for her years and years of love and support. Support not only for the works of fiction I've written, but also for my works of non-fiction. Her editing made all of them so much better. But I especially thank her here for our work together on early versions of Peace Seeker. She might not recognize what I've done with it in these many subsequent years, and might not agree with them, but I feel her wonderful, creative input on so many of its pages.

ABOUT THE AUTHOR

Dr. Hand is a published novelist, writing two Bronze Age epics and several contemporary women's action adventures. This includes the award winning *Voice of the Goddess*, set against the background of Bronze Age Crete.

She is also an evolutionary biologist and peace ethologist. She earned her Ph.D. in biology from UCLA with areas of specialization in animal behavior, communication, social conflict resolution, and gender differences. After a Smithsonian Post-doctoral Fellowship at the National Zoo in Washington, D.C., she returned to UCLA for two years as a research associate and lecturer. Her work on social conflict and war and the place of women with respect to war includes four books, several videos, an extensive website project, AFutureWithoutWar.org, which includes essays and related links, and speaking engagements in the US and abroad.

More information about Dr. Hand can be found on her personal website www.judithhand.net.

Book Titles
  Fiction:
    Voice of the Goddess
    The Amazon and the Warrior
    Code Name: Dove
    Iron Dove
    Captive Dove
    The Good Thief – written with Peggy Lang
  Non-Fiction:
    Women, Power, and the Biology of Peace
    A Future Without War
    Shift: The Beginning of War, The Ending of War
    War and Sex and Human Destiny